FORESIGHT

Book 3 of the Timesplash series

Graham Storrs

First published Pan Macmillan Australia, 2015

This Edition, Copyright © 2018, Graham Storrs

ISBN: 978-0-9945899-9-6

Published by Canta Libre
Cover design by Graham Storrs
Edited by Tara Goedjen and Kate O'Donnell
Interior design by Write Into Print (writeintoprint.com)

This is a work of fiction. Names, characters, places, brands, media, and incidents are either the product of the author's imagination or are used fictitiously. The author acknowledges the trademarked status and trademark owners of various products referenced in this work of fiction, which have been used without permission. The publication/use of these trademarks is not authorised, associated with, or sponsored by the trademark owners.

Dedication

All the Timesplash novels are dedicated to the three brilliant and beautiful women who are at the heart of everything I am and everything I do; my mother, Audrey, my wife, Christine, and my daughter, Katherine.

Chapter 1

The Earth Moved

Ice-cold rain slapped at Jay Kennedy as he juggled bags, coat, and umbrella out of the cab and stepped quickly across the pavement into the foyer of his apartment building. The building greeted him and called the lift. It was after nine on a Tuesday evening and no-one else was about. He entered the lift and confirmed he wanted his own floor. The doors closed and it started rising.

That's when the Earth moved.

The lift shook and rattled but kept going. Jay's first thought was: *Explosion?* He could hear a deep rumbling that went on far too long. *Earthquake?* The lights flickered. He dropped everything he was carrying and moved back against the corner of the carriage. He called up a twenty-four-hour Berlin newsfeed on his commplant. An earthquake in Berlin? He'd lived there more than two years and had not heard of such a thing.

"Whoa, what was that?" the anchor was saying in German. The man looked around, obviously frightened. Out of shot, there was the sound of equipment falling over.

"It feels like an earthquake," his co-anchor said. She put a

1

hand to her ear and added, "We're starting to get reports from elsewhere in the city. It seems to be—" She stopped mid-sentence, staring at something Jay could not see.

"Oh my God," said the anchor.

The lift stopped and the doors opened. Jay grabbed up his belongings and ran out into the hall. For an instant it seemed as if the floor and walls twisted sideways. Jay stood rigid, staring at them, but everything looked square and solid. It could have been a trick of the eye, a moment of paranoia. Yet his heart, already racing, doubled its pace and his stomach knotted. It had looked like something all too familiar. Leaving his stuff in the hall, he went to his apartment and hurried inside, syncing his commplant to the big virtual displays. He pulled up feeds from all the major European networks and then called the office.

For a long time, there was no answer. And that was scary too. Jay ran a section within the Military Intelligence division of the European Defence Force. There was always someone manning the netID he'd just called. Always. Yet tonight the number rang and rang.

Then he noticed the chair—an armchair that usually stood by the window. Now it was at the other side of the room. Only it wasn't. It was still by the window. There were two armchairs. Two identical armchairs.

"Yes, Chief." The voice sounded flustered. The face in the display belonged to a young soldier whose gaze kept flicking sideways, nervously, as if he were keeping an eye on something that had him worried.

"Connect me to Captain Harnois," he said. Jay's office was across town in Unter den Linden. The TV studio was at least two kilometres away in Prenzlauer Berg. Jay's apartment was in Torstrasse. That meant the affected area was at minimum a three-kilometre circle.

While he waited for Harnois, another shock hit his building. Crockery rattled in the kitchen. A painting fell from the wall. He needed to get out of there and into the street. It would be marginally safer outside if… He hardly dared name the terrible possibility.

"Daddy?"

He spun round at the sound. His daughter stood in the kitchen doorway.

"Cara? What are you doing here?" One obvious possibility presented itself. One that would be consistent with… with whatever was happening. Cara's mother must be in trouble. "Is Sandra all right?"

Cara looked shocked. "What?"

"Sandra. Is she here? Is she OK?"

Cara gaped at him. "What are you saying? Mum's…" The words seemed to catch in her throat.

"She's what?" He closed the distance between them. "Where is she? What's happened?"

Cara's face was white. Her lower lip began to tremble. In a small, weak voice, Cara said, "She's… She's dead."

It hit Jay like a blow to the chest. "Dead?" How could she be dead? It wasn't possible. He tried to frame a question, overwhelmed by the enormity of it. "How?" he asked, at last.

Tears began to roll down Cara's cheeks. She looked pleadingly into his eyes. "Daddy, what's wrong?"

"Wrong? You mean this?" He cast his eyes around the room. He noticed an ornament on a shelf that he had never seen before. It reminded him of the danger they were in. "We need to get out of here," he said.

"Harnois here, Chief," a voice from his commplant said.

He seized on it like a lifeline. "Captain, what the hell is

going on? Is it a timesplash?"

If so, it was the strangest one he'd ever seen. Even as he asked, he noticed the newsfeed displays around him. There were fires burning in Rome, a plane crash in London, an earthquake in Japan: disasters everywhere.

"We don't know yet, sir. We're trying to collate reports, but there are so many. It looks as if, whatever it is, it's affecting the whole world. If it's the backwash from a timesplash, sir, it's bigger than anything we ever simulated."

Jay looked away from the display as a deep rumbling shook the floor. Cara was still watching him with a tear-streaked face. "I've got to do something first," he told the captain, "but I'll head for the office as soon as I can." He hung up and took Cara by the shoulders. "We've got to get out of the building. It's not safe here."

She resisted him, twisting her body as if she didn't want him touching her. "Why are you being so weird about Mum?" she asked. "What's the matter with you?"

"Honey, we need to get out of the building. It's some kind of backwash. Something massive. We'll be safer in the street." *Maybe.* The news about Sandra came back to him in a rush and stopped his breath. When he could speak, he said, "I'm sorry to hear about your mum. You know I always…" But there was no time for that. "Come on, we have to go."

Cara shook her head. "No. You go." She began to struggle in his grasp and he released her, shocked.

"What are you doing?" he asked. She backed away from him. "Cara?"

"What's wrong with you? What's going on?" She pointed at him, accusingly. "You didn't even have that suit on when you went out with Laura. Then you come in here talking like you don't know about Mum, acting surprised to see me. I

4

don't know if you're even my real dad."

She was distraught, her voice sounding more frightened with every moment. He stood still, trying not to alarm her. Could her mother's death have unhinged her like this? He didn't know what to do. He needed to get her outside. For a crazy instant he thought about throwing her over his shoulder and carrying her out. His breathing was becoming ragged. Her behaviour scared him. The backwash that was going on around them, the news about Sandra and Cara's growing fear of him were ripping his composure to shreds. He summoned up one more attempt at calmness.

"Cara, I don't understand what you're telling me. I didn't know your mum was dead until you just said so. I didn't know you were here until I saw you. I haven't been out with anyone called Laura. I've just got back from work. Now, look, we can talk about this, sort it all out, but we should do it outside. Do you understand? It isn't safe in here."

Cara started to shake her head again, building up to another outburst but, before the words came, the floor shook and a crack shot up through the outside wall. Plaster exploded into the room, floorboards splintered, and glass erupted from the windows. They both flinched at the sudden violence. It was alarming but the real horror, from Jay's perspective, was the second armchair. It had begun flickering. A pale aura surrounded it and it was moving, sliding across the floor towards the other chair, just a few centimetres, then snapping back to where it started, all in the blink of an eye.

Jay couldn't wait any longer. He grabbed Cara by her upper arm and heaved her into motion. She was a tall girl, but slight, and he had no trouble dragging her across the room and out the door into the hallway. He went straight to the staircase: the lift would be suicide.

In contrast to the carpeted opulence of the public areas, the emergency stairs in his building were plain concrete with a painted metal handrail set into the wall. It was cold in the unheated space, made colder by the white glare of the lighting. Cara was no longer fighting him but he kept hold of her arm as they hurried down the stairs, their steps clattering and echoing.

They went down three floors before Cara suddenly pulled up and grabbed the handrail, almost jerking Jay off his feet. He lost his grip on her arm.

"Come on!" he shouted. The building was shaking constantly now. It might come down on them at any moment.

"No!" Cara glared at him, as if daring him to try moving her. The stubbornness in her face was an expression he'd often seen on her mother's.

"Yes," he insisted. "You must see we're in danger here." He would pick her up and carry her if he had to.

"How could you forget that Mum died? How could you forget I've been living with you for a year? How could you forget Laura? It's not possible. It's not right. Nothing makes sense."

He reached out to take hold of her again. And stopped.

She had a faint aura around her, just like the armchair. His heart thudded. Thudded again. *Not Cara. No, not Cara.*

"Darling," he said, gently. "Please." He held out a hand for her to take. "Please let me get you out of here." As if that would make any difference to what was happening. But it was all he could think of.

She started crying again and shook her head. "I don't understand anything," she wailed. "Are you even my dad at all?"

Jay swallowed hard, fought to keep his voice steady. "Of course I am. I don't understand it any more than you do, honey. Something very strange is happening—and I wish to God it would stop—but I'm still your father, I still love you, and I only want to make you safe." She looked as if she'd heard him, as if she believed him at last. "So, please, let me get you out of here. We'll work it all out, I promise. We'll get to the bottom of it. But, first, we need to get outside."

She studied him through big, wet eyes. He could see her struggling to decide whether to trust him. Then she reached out her hand to his, slowly, half-reluctantly. His heart leapt. He took a shuddering breath. He stretched out his hand a little farther for hers. Their fingers met.

And passed right through each other.

In a blind panic, he rushed to his daughter, clutching at her, but she was already fading. His arms passed through her. He stepped back, stunned. Before his eyes, she vanished like smoke.

He stumbled and fell. On his hands and knees in the concrete stairwell, he gasped for breath, fighting the nausea that threatened to choke him.

Cara was gone.

Chapter 2

K Section

Jay could not tell how long he'd been sitting on the cold concrete steps before he came to himself again. He was shivering and his legs were stiff when he tried to stand. Slowly, he stumbled up the stairs, gradually regaining his mobility as the exercise warmed him. By the time he got back to his apartment, he was running.

He could no longer hear the ominous rumblings. He couldn't be sure but he thought they might have stopped at about the time Cara disappeared. The second armchair was gone. The strange ornament was no longer on his shelf. Apart from the crack in the wall, everything was exactly as it should be.

He dialled Sandra's netID but the service could not connect him. He dialled her local police headquarters in the UK and was put into a queue. Almost snarling with frustration, he hung up and went back out into the hallway. His bags, coat and umbrella were on the floor. He picked them up, kept the coat, and tossed the rest into the apartment. He put the coat on as he rode the lift down to the lobby.

"Good evening, Mr Kennedy," the building said through his commplant. "May I help you with anything?"

Yes, it could, for once. "Get me a cab. Tell them I'm in a hurry."

"I'm sorry. There are no cabs available."

"When can they get one here?"

"I have checked fourteen cab companies so far, and they all say they cannot offer a service at this time."

Jay clenched his teeth and ran out through the doors. He'd have to get to the office on foot. He got as far as the pavement before he stopped and looked around. There were multiple-vehicle collisions in every direction. One was clearly caused by a metre-wide crack that ran across the road. A car had toppled into it and several others had rear-ended it and each other. But other tangles of vehicles had no obvious causes. It seemed as if some had just run off the road into streetlights or the fronts of buildings. One car was burning. People milled around the wreckage, checking for passengers, helping people out. As he watched, two women pulled a man from a bus. He was bleeding from his forehead and they laid him on the road to tend him.

Jay resisted the urge to help. His top priority was to get to his office and start working out what had happened. If this was the result of a timesplash, it was his job to find out who'd done it and stop them before it could happen again. He set off at a jog. Every street had its share of traffic accidents and snarl-ups. He had to make a two-block detour at one point because the street was full of rubble from what seemed to have been a massive explosion in one of the buildings. There were no police, no fire tenders or ambulances yet. It could be a long time before the emergency services got on top of this.

By the time he reached the European Defence Force

Military Intelligence building, he was hot and panting, his coat and jacket under his arm. He gave the façade a quick check as he hurried inside. No obvious signs of damage. That was good. Maybe none of his colleagues had been hurt. As he ran down the corridors to K Section, he tried calling Sandra again. As with the previous dozen attempts, there was no service. It was hardly surprising. If what he was seeing in Berlin had been repeated across the world, every switchboard on the planet would be jammed.

The EDF soldiers at reception waved him through but he stopped and insisted they check his ID. Then he told one of them to grab a couple of first aid kits and get out onto the street to help anyone they could find. "It only takes one of you to watch the desk," he said when they started to quote standing orders at him. "It's an order. There won't be any come-back on you." Although he was a civilian, as head of K Section, Jay had the honorary rank of colonel. The soldiers snapped to it and Jay hurried on.

He found the duty officer in the Operations Room, surrounded by tactical displays. Everyone was head-down busy, flicking through data, talking on the comms. Already people looked frazzled. The tension in the room was palpable. He set his jaw against the urge to call Sandra again. It would have to wait.

"Captain," he greeted Harnois.

The Frenchman looked around at him. "Chief. Glad you made it."

"Are you busy?" The captain opened his mouth, probably to ask Jay what the hell it looked like. Then he grinned. After two years of working together, Harnois was finally beginning to understand his boss's sense of humour. "Come on," Jay said. "Let's get out of this madhouse and you can brief me."

They went through to a small meeting room. Harnois took a seat while Jay poured them each a coffee from a pot on a side table.

Harnois began speaking when Jay brought the mugs over. "We've heard from Interpol, a few national intelligence services. Others we can't reach. It looks as though all of Europe is affected, China, India, Africa. We're not sure yet about the U.S., but definitely Canada and South America. It seems to be worldwide." He took a sip of his coffee and grimaced. "It may be even more widespread that that." Jay raised an eyebrow. "I've got Rochelle trawling the newsfeeds, looking for oddities. She just told me that ESA reported unusual sunspot activity—a near doubling of them—that started when the event began and ended when it stopped."

Jay had no idea what to make of that, but filed it away for future reference. "Any idea what it was?"

Harnois gave his best Gallic shrug. "The backwash from the mother of all timesplashes? What else could it be? Someone went back in time and shot Alexander the Great in his cradle. It was bound to happen, no?"

Jay shook his head. "It didn't feel like a backwash. I mean, there were some slight similarities, but it wasn't right."

Again, Harnois shrugged. "You should know." Within the temporal crimes community, Jay was famous for having survived the world's biggest backwash: the one that had destroyed the Washington Metropolitan Area two years earlier and sparked the revolution that still raged in the United States.

"If it was a timesplash," Jay insisted, reacting to the doubt in the Frenchman's tone, "where's the centre? You've seen the modelling that CERN did on major events. There should be one area of massive destruction with less and less as you move away from ground zero. If they shot baby Alexander the Great, northern Greece would be a molten caldera, the rest of Greece, Bulgaria, Albania would be wiped off the map. Beyond that, southern Europe, Turkey, North Africa would be wrecked, but there'd be survivors. Farther out, the damage would be less and less. The Americas, China, Australia might not even feel it. I get the impression it wasn't like that at all. It's more… evenly spread—and a hell of a lot milder than such a massive event should be. Do we have satellite imagery?"

"We're putting it together now. We may have lost some satellites and we can't reach all the tracking stations we'd like to. You know, it might have been centred on Northern Siberia, or Antarctica."

"It might." If someone had jumped back ten thousand years and shot an elk or a penguin crucial to the history of the world. *"Anything else I should know?"*

"You're off to see the Ice Queen?" By which he meant the Director of Military Intelligence, Dr Barbara Crystal.

"I'm sure she's been asking for me."

Harnois smirked. "There isn't any more to tell you. We've barely begun, really, and comms everywhere are a mess."

Jay nodded. "When I get back, I want Thalman ready to brief me. Is she here?"

"Came in ten minutes before you did."

"Good."

Jay went up to the top floor. He had to pass another checkpoint with human soldiers and then present his credentials to a door guarded by two robot sentries. The director's office, like the rest of the building, was buzzing with activity. Crystal was surrounded by her staff and, from the way she was scowling at them, Jay supposed she was not in a good mood. As soon as she saw him approaching, she waved everyone else away and focused her scowl on him alone.

"There he is," she said. "The man of the hour. Care to explain how the whole world just got clobbered by a timesplash while K Section was taking a quiet nap?"

"I don't think it was a timesplash," Jay said, trying not to let his irritation show. The woman's management style involved metaphorically poking her subordinates with a sharp stick to get them jumping. Normally, Jay didn't let it bother him, but today he was not in the mood.

She regarded him with a curious expression. "Interesting move, Kennedy. Of all the things I thought you might say, that was not one of them. What's your evidence?"

"We're still assembling it. Things are a bit chaotic. This... event... does not have the characteristics of a backwash."

Her expression changed subtly. He saw her swallow. "I saw some strange..." She stopped. There was hurt in her eyes. "I spoke to my father." Jay waited for her to say whatever it was. She swallowed again. "He died eighteen months ago."

"And after you spoke he just faded away, didn't he?"

Her gaze snapped onto his. "I've read the reports. I've heard of these 'echoes'. Is that what it was?"

"No, Ma'am. This is something new. We've only ever seen echoes during the splash itself, never in a backwash, and then only of the bricks, not of random others."

She was still watching him intently. "You saw one too, didn't you?" He nodded. "How can the dead come back to life, Jay? Is it the tempocalypse?"

Tempocalypse was the title of a very popular book that predicted the end of the world coming after repeated

13

timesplashes irrevocably screwed up spacetime until causality was no longer reliable and chaos overcame the Universe. It was the kind of book that used biblical passages as evidence and could justify anything at all by saying "quantum" and "uncertainty principle" often enough.

"I don't normally approve of book burning," Jay said, "but in that case, I'd make an exception. You know it's complete rubbish."

"I did before my dead father dropped by for a chat."

"We'll work it out, whatever it was."

Her moment of vulnerability was over. "Do that. And do it quickly. I'm making a presentation to the Defence Standing Committee tomorrow at zero nine hundred. Make sure I've got something solid to offer them."

Chapter 3

HiQua

Lee Shaozu didn't like being summoned, especially by that prick Waxtead, and especially when he knew exactly what the fool wanted to whine about. He glanced down at his Armani suit and found not a single speck to mar its elegant lines. He entered the lift. Its digital display said it was seven forty-three AM. Lee's Rolex app, running in his commplant, said seven forty-two. *Typical sloppiness,* he thought. *They can't even get the building's clocks set to the right time.* He reached out to select the floor from the touch panel and his manicured finger hesitated briefly over the thirty-six before pushing it firmly. No sense worrying about being on the top floor of the HiQua London headquarters. If last night's disturbance happened again, it probably wouldn't matter where he was. People had died in their cars, in restaurants, out walking the dog. It was luck, that's all. And Lee had always had good luck.

"You're late," Waxtead complained as his PA showed Lee into his office. "I said seven thirty."

Lee ignored him and crossed the broad room to a sideboard on which a buffet breakfast of breads, cheeses and cooked meats had been laid out. He took a piece of melon from the fruit platter and swallowed it.

"Anyway, you're here now, so let's get started."

Oh how Lee despised the man. He poured himself a cup of black coffee and went to sit down. He took a sip and looked for the first time at Waxtead. The HiQua CEO was a pasty-faced Englishman in his late twenties, a few years younger than Lee but already running to flab. Not half the man his father had been. When he took over the company five years earlier on his father's death, the share price had tumbled. Since then, it had slid a little more each year.

"They're saying it's the tempocalypse," Waxtead said.

Lee closed his eyes, trying to control his temper. He'd seen the headlines too. "Tempocalypse Now?" "Boffins Baffled!" The usual rubbish.

"Morons," he said.

Waxtead watched him, clearly plucking up the nerve to say something. "What if it was because—?" he began, but Lee jumped on it, fast.

"It wasn't. Whatever happened last night was nothing to do with that." He looked the CEO in the eye and said, "You'd better stop thinking like that and pull yourself together. Yesterday was a big day for us. Payday. The first of many. HiQua made millions. You, personally, made millions. And so did I. We've got a good thing going here and you are not going to screw it up by listening to tabloid newsfeeds and their doomsday pseudoscience crap."

"I spoke to Hong."

"You did what?" Lee was really angry now. "I run the Special Projects team. You have no business going round me to talk to them directly."

Waxtead bristled. "It's still my company. You have no

right to speak to me like that. I need to know what's going on."

Lee let his lip curl into a sneer. "I tell you what's going on," he said. "Yesterday should have demonstrated what an excellent arrangement we have. Do you think you could have pulled that off yourself?" He gave Waxtead a chance to say "yes" but nothing came. "You will leave the Special Projects team to me. Do you understand? If you screw this up..." He let the threat hang.

"I only asked him what he thought about last night," Waxtead whined.

"And what did Dr Hong tell you?"

"He said he didn't know."

"And you asked him if he thought it was our fault, didn't you?"

Waxtead managed a spark of defiance. "He said it was a worrying coincidence."

Lee clenched his jaw, not trusting himself to speak for a moment. "If he chooses not to proceed, the project goes with him. You understand, don't you? And if he talks to the newsfeeds, can you imagine how much jail time you'll serve? And that's notwithstanding any spurious connection between our work and the so-called tempocalypse." He stood up and put his coffee cup on Waxtead's desk. "Insider trading is one of those crimes where nobody has any sympathy for the perpetrator. The public hates you for ripping off their pension funds and the establishment hates you for getting caught and making us all look bad. Fraud is an ugly word in the mouth of a prosecution QC. You should try and remember that."

He left the room, leaving Waxtead looking dumbstruck behind him. HiQua had been a valuable instrument so far—it had funded the project and bankrolled the investments. And now it was too late to find a new home for his team. Waxtead was weak and stupid, which had of course been a good thing, but now it threatened to become a liability.

"Can I see you for a moment please, Mr Lee?"

Farid Hamiye's stubbled jaw and broad chest were the first things to greet Lee as he left the lift at the fifth floor. He stopped and regarded his Head of Security for a moment. Hamiye was a handsome man, and built like a rhinoceros. As ever, his expression was blank and his eyes inscrutable. But Lee didn't need to ask if this was important: Hamiye knew better than to annoy him with anything less.

He gave a quick nod and led the way to an empty meeting room. "Yes?" he asked when Hamiye closed the door.

"You asked me to keep a scan going for suspicious activities, unusual recruits, staff meeting with government agencies and so on." Lee waited. Hamiye gestured towards a display at one end of the room. A picture appeared of an extraordinarily beautiful woman in her mid thirties. She was walking across the foyer of an office building and, although plainly dressed, she would, Lee imagined, stand out in a crowd anywhere she went. "The analysts flagged this one," Hamiye said. "Sandra Malone. She joined the company three months ago as a low-grade tech in the software-testing division in Oxford. She's over-qualified for the job: has a degree in physics and a masters in temporal engineering."

Lee raised an eyebrow. Definitely interesting.

"It gets better," Hamiye said. "Two years ago, she was in the U.S. when the revolution began. My friends in the Met say she had been kidnapped by Zadrach Polanski, the rebel leader. He's believed to have died in the timesplash that took out Washington, although that's not confirmed. So I dug a little deeper." Lee smiled. Hamiye was unstoppable when he scented trouble. "Sandra Malone is said to have been instrumental in bringing down a brick called Sniper eighteen years ago."

Lee knew that name. "The Big Splash? That Sniper? The one who almost destroyed London?"

"The very same. Press speculation at the time said she was working for MI5."

Lee looked at the woman in the picture and shook his head. "She would have been a child."

"Seventeen. So probably not officially on MI5's payroll, but they used a lot of kids back then to infiltrate the splashteams."

"And you think she's still with Five?" Lee sat down, staring at the woman on the screen. This might be bad. Very bad.

"I don't know. I need more time to follow up and nail down her activities, find out who her associates are."

"You've got it. Use whatever resources you need. From now on, this woman is under twenty-four-hour surveillance. Agreed?"

"I already have a team out there bugging her house, her car, her place of work, her phone, and her person. We'll know everything she does, starting in an hour or so."

"Good. Make this your top priority. I want a report every three hours."

Hamiye nodded and left. Lee remained in the meeting room, alone with his thoughts.

A potential MI5 agent, known to have been involved in at least two of the world's most notorious timesplash incidents, suddenly turns up as a HiQua employee? That couldn't be a coincidence. Could it? HiQua employed three hundred thousand people worldwide, thirty thousand of them in the UK. Even so, why would a woman with qualifications in physics and temporal engineering be working as a software tester? On the other hand, why didn't she lie about her qualifications? Or, if she were still working for MI5, why didn't she invent something less unlikely?

He used his commplant to drive the display, delving into the company structure and employee records. The Oxford office she'd joined made software for factory robots. It was a tiny cog in the HiQua machine. How could it benefit a spy to be located there? He pulled up Sandra Malone's picture again. It seemed incredible that a woman who looked like that was a software tester. Spy, he could believe. Supermodel, definitely. Software tester? Well that just seemed far fetched.

He killed the display and stood up. There was no point in speculating until he had more information. If there was anything going on, Hamiye would find it. Right now, he needed to see Hong.

* * * *

The Special Projects Laboratory was also on the fifth floor of the HiQua headquarters building, but that was just the admin areas and a few show projects to dazzle the press with. The real work took place on an industrial estate in North London, in a long, low building with shuttered windows and a sign outside saying, "Clarke Engineering Ltd". Because of the traffic chaos all over the city, Lee took a company helicopter—the unmarked one. He was met by Hong's assistant at the helipad and escorted inside to the scientist's office.

Hong stood and greeted him. Lee regarded him with

distaste. A shambling man of about sixty, Hong had unkempt grey hair, a paunch, and looked like he bought his clothes from church jumble sales. All of which was ridiculous given how much HiQua paid him. Hong could have afforded gene treatments to keep his hair black and stop his skin sagging, a personal trainer to eradicate the paunch, and, if he had no taste in clothes, could at least have hired a style consultant to dress him. *What on earth does he do with all the money?* Lee wondered. He made a mental note to ask Hamiye to check if Hong had a weakness for gambling, drugs, or women.

"Waxtead called me," the scientist said without preamble. They spoke together in English even though Mandarin was the first language for both of them. It was one of Lee's rules. He wanted Hong to draw as little attention to himself as possible. Speaking excellent English was a part of that.

"I've told you not to speak to him."

"But he called me direct. What was I supposed to do?"

"Use your common sense. What you're not supposed to do is babble to him about how we might have caused last night's catastrophe. You have to remember the man has no sense of perspective. He's practically a child."

"I didn't say that. He kept asking me if we'd caused it. All I said was that it was quite a coincidence." As he spoke, Hong held his right hand in front of him, flicking his fingers as if to emphasise or illustrate what he was saying, but in fact, quite randomly. Lee tried not to watch them. It was another of the man's infuriating personal quirks.

"So, do you think we caused what happened?"

Hong reared back. "No, of course not. How could we possibly? It's just… Well, the coincidence is unsettling."

"But that's all it is?" Lee pressed him.

Hong didn't seem as certain as Lee would have liked. "Yes, yes. What else could it be?"

Neither man had sat down since Lee walked into the room. "Don't talk to him again. Do you understand? If he gets it into his head that we're causing some kind of backwash, there's no telling what he might do. If he calls again, just say everything's fine and that you've left a test-tube boiling or something. Then tell me at once."

Lee studied Hong's face. The old man was blinking his eyes and looking unhappy. "Don't worry," he said, making an effort to sound soothing. "It's nearly over. Yesterday's result was a triumph. You should be very proud. We have one more scheduled for tomorrow and, if your device is ready, the big one two weeks later."

Hong nodded, looking distracted. "Yes, yes, everything is ready. It will be perfect. But you're forgetting the first trial."

Lee frowned. "What do you mean? The first trial was a success. We didn't get any data but it went well. Yesterday's success was proof of that. From what the first trial taught us, the recalibration was spot on." He smiled encouragingly. "It's also made us all rich. What are you talking about?"

Hong looked away, agitated. "I don't know. I don't like coincidences. Something's not right."

Lee had spent enough energy coddling the old fool. It was time to be firm. "I don't like that kind of talk, Doctor. If I hear it again from you or your team between now and the final run, there will be consequences. Just make sure your machine works and keep your staff quiet. I will not tolerate a leak from this facility. Especially now that we are so close." Hong's nervous twitching and pacing was beginning to irritate him. "In fact, I'll be sending a few more security personnel, just to ensure things go smoothly."

"There's no need for that. My team is not a security risk. Most of these people have been with me for over three years now. They are dedicated to the project and they are all eager to see their work rewarded."

"Then keep them in line. I don't want you to lose anybody at this late stage."

"What do you mean? What are you saying?"

"You know what I mean, Doctor. There is a great deal at stake here. People are watching. And a lot of money is riding on your success. Do you understand me?" The scientist stared at Lee, aghast. "Dr Hong, do you understand me?"

Hong nodded. "Yes. But I assure you—"

"Don't assure me. Just do your job." He turned to leave. "And stay away from Waxtead. I'll be back the week after next to watch the final run."

Chapter 4

Laura

Dr Laura Thalman, head of the K Section technical team, was in her workshop the next morning when Jay arrived. She looked up from her work and smiled when she saw him.

"I tried to get hold of you last night," Jay said, "but you were unavailable. I looked for you here—they said you'd gone home."

She got off her stool and took her lab coat off as she spoke. "Sorry about that. Comms were down for my whole neighbourhood. Power too. I came in but I had to go out again and help. There were people... So many..." Her face fell.

Jay nodded. "You don't have to explain."

"Why don't we get out of here and talk over coffee?" she asked, already heading for the door.

"Sure, but let's make it the canteen. I don't have time to go outside." As soon as he spoke, Jay remembered Cara standing in his apartment saying, "You didn't even have that suit on when you went out with Laura." It hadn't even occurred to him until then to connect Cara's Laura with his head teknik.

He fell silent as they walked up the corridor and took the stairs to the next floor, barely noticing his companion's puzzled frown. *Could* Cara's apparition have meant this Laura? In the two years he'd been running K Section, he'd thought several times about asking Thalman out on a date. She was an attractive woman, smart and funny, and they'd always got on well. But she was his colleague—worse still, his subordinate. It wouldn't have been right. Then there was his relationship with Cara and Sandra. Since he'd discovered he had a teenage daughter, just two years back, his emotional life seemed so dauntingly complicated that dating was just too much to face. Yet, if he were going to take any woman out in the evening, Laura Thalman would perhaps be the least unlikely candidate.

"A *pfennig* for your thoughts," Laura said as they entered the cafeteria and headed for an isolated table.

He cleared his throat. "I was just wondering if last night's event might somehow have manifested people's deep subconscious desires."

They sat down and she studied his face. "Are you serious?"

He shook his head, remembering Cara telling him that Sandra was dead. "No, just very confused. Something very strange happened. People saw some disturbing things."

"What did you see?"

"It doesn't matter. Look, Laura, you're one of the world's leading authorities on time travel. You've had more direct experience than most. You study this stuff and work with it all the time and you're one of the cleverest people I know. Is there any way that what happened last night was the backwash from some gigantic timesplash?" She drew a breath to speak but he held up his hand. "Wait. Let me give you two minutes to think about your answer while I fetch us some drinks."

He hurried off to the dispensers and came back with two cups of coffee and a selection of cakes. He arranged them on the table and sat down. As soon as he was settled, Laura took up the conversation where they had left off.

"All the weird physics aside, a timesplash is conceptually simple," she said. "People, or things, are put in a displacement field and lobbed like bricks back into the timestream." Jay didn't really need this, but he was prepared to listen if it meant she was working her way to a helpful conclusion of some sort.

She seemed to remember who she was talking to. "Of course, you know all this, but humour me: maybe we'll see what was the same last night and what was different if we look at what we know from the beginning. So, you're lobbed back," she went on. "And you end up in the past, but you don't belong there. Your very presence creates a temporal anomaly. Yet the past is fixed—it has happened and it can't be changed. So, the Universe resists the anomaly and thrashes about correcting itself. You're an irritant and it reacts with a kind of flare up. That's the timesplash."

She took a sip of her coffee, looking at Jay over the rim of her cup as if to check that he was still listening. "A timesplash shouldn't matter. All the weirdness with spacetime and entropy is just the past putting itself right. In the end, the brick is yanked back to the present and everyone back then has no idea that it even happened—the past returns to exactly the state it was previously in. We've measured this now to within the size of a proton and to tiny fractions of an electron volt."

She leaned back in her seat and smiled. She had a nice

smile, he noticed, the way he'd been noticing her eyes as she spoke. All because of what Cara's ghost had said?

"Of course, despite the Immutability Principle, it does matter what you do in the past because, if you make a big enough splash, the ripples flow downstream to the present. That's the backwash—the thing that levelled Beijing and Mexico City and, lucky you, Washington. And there's another astonishing thing that the new temporal physics has shown us. The present is a real phenomenon. The Universe we know is actually a wavefront propagating through a kind of proto-Universe consisting of a sea of randomness, an unformed possibility of existence, waiting for the present to make its choices."

"Very poetic."

"It's pretty awesome, don't you think? Anyway, it's a barrier beyond which the backwash cannot pass. Those ripples of acausal mayhem from the timesplash hit the present and can't go any farther. They dissipate their force by turning the present to chaos, messing with causality in a kind of low-powered rerun of the original splash. Of course, I don't need to tell you what a backwash looks like."

Jay gave a tight smile. He'd never spoken about his experiences two years earlier in Washington DC, but the whole department seemed to know. They probably knew about his role in the London timesplash too. Maybe even Ommen, back in 2048. It gave him a kind of cachet among his fellow intelligence officers. To them he must seem like an old soldier who'd been on the front line at famous and bloody battles. Sometimes, it even made Jay feel old. Old at thirty-eight!

"OK," he said. "Let's get to the part where last night couldn't possibly be down to a timesplash."

She smirked, as if to say, "I knew you'd get bored." Then she got serious. "Two lines of evidence. One is that the detectors at CERN didn't pick up a lob. As you know, they monitor twenty-four/seven and they're sensitive enough to spot even a ten-megawatt displacement field anywhere in the world. There's a small possibility that they screwed up somehow, but it's highly unlikely. If there was no lob, there was no timesplash, and last night was not a backwash."

Jay pursed his lips. "What if the lob took place away from the Earth?" He was remembering that odd report about sunspot activity. "Would they still spot it?"

Laura's eyebrows went up. "You mean like in space?"

"Sure. If you were going to send a nuke back to take out Augustus at the height of the Roman Empire, you'd do it from space—send an orbiting nuclear missile back and trigger the lob remotely." They'd run simulations and it was frighteningly possible. A nuke in first-century Rome would certainly create a world-enveloping timesplash, but you couldn't easily send one back because when the splash was over, that explosion would be yanked straight back where it started in the present and crammed back into a tiny space. The lob site was ground zero, not just for the sudden re-expansion of the nuclear debris, but also for a backwash that would turn an area the size of Texas to slag.

Laura was sceptical. She'd seen the simulations too. "And where would the perp be while all this went on? On the Moon?"

Jay held up his hands in an I-don't-know gesture. "The point is, could it be detected?"

"Is that what we're looking at?"

"It probably depends on what you say."

She looked uncomfortable. "The only factor that matters

is distance from CERN. I'd have to check, but, obviously, the minimum range is a twelve-thousand-kilometer sphere around Geneva. You know, the diameter of the Earth? Unless your perp was in orbit over Australia, or whatever is opposite Geneva, then they're bound to be spotted." She thought about it for a moment, clearly disturbed that there might be that small window of possibility. "I'll put in a call and find out. Unless you think I should do it now?"

"No, not yet. So what if the perps had found a way to mask themselves from the CERN detectors?"

Laura blew out her cheeks. "You really are clutching at straws, aren't you? That would be very unlikely."

"More unlikely than an orbital nuke?"

"Yes. You'd have to invent some completely new physics that we don't already know about. There's no lab in Europe that could do it."

"What about the Chinese? They'd have the physicists and the resources."

"Well, if anybody was capable of pulling off something like that, it would be the Chinese. But what would be the point?"

Now it was Jay's turn to look incredulous. "If you wanted to attack a foreign power with a timesplash, you wouldn't want the whole world knowing about it. You remember, that's why K Section exists: to stop all the bad guys from going rogue with malicious lobs." She pulled a face at him. *Cute*, he thought. *Seriously cute.*

"All right, what's the second reason last night couldn't be a timesplash?"

She took a drink of coffee and sat back. "It doesn't look like one. I've seen the satellite pictures and there is just no centre to it. When you make a timesplash, the backwash flows through to the present in a particular shape—"

"An eleven-dimensional sphere," he said.

She smiled. "Sorry. I forgot again."

He smiled back but said nothing. The last time he'd considered the geometry of a backwash, he'd been in an armored car careening through Washington, DC, with Sandra beside him and Cara in the back, trying to decide just how long they all had to live.

"So you know it is very localised," she went on. "And it spreads from a single point at a well-known rate. We saw nothing like that last night. It was as if it hit the whole planet, everywhere, at the same moment."

"If it happened in the Earth's core," he said, "or so far out in space that it seemed to…" He trailed off, running out of ideas that sounded even slightly credible. He looked down at the table. Cute she may be but trashing all his ideas was not what Dr Thalman was employed to do. He looked up to find her studying him. "Something caused this, Laura. Something that had at least a passing resemblance to a timesplash. I saw spatial distortions. So did others." As well as people who could not exist. "And it happened on our watch. K Section is supposed to be on top of this. If someone triggered some new kind of backwash, we should have known about it before it happened. That's our job. As Chief Scientist, I expect you to be giving me answers—or, at least, suggestions."

She began, "I can only work with the evid—" but he cut her off, rising as he did so.

"I don't expect miracles, but we need to understand this. We need to make sure it never happens again. Do you know how many people died last night?" The question was unfair and he regretted asking it, only it was there in his mind all the time. If someone had used time-travel technology to cause last night's catastrophe, he had failed in his job. His Section had failed. He was responsible.

"Look," he said, in a placatory tone. "I don't mean to browbeat you, but I need answers, and fast."

She stood too and regarded him for a moment. "Can I call in a consultant?" she asked.

"You can call in the massed pipes and drums of the Scots Guards if it will help."

She stepped around the table and made for the exit. He watched her go. A consultant would mean security clearances and lots of admin, but he didn't suppose anybody would cavil at that under the circumstances.

He checked the time. He needed to brief Crystal in twenty minutes and he had absolutely nothing to give her. He would spend the time calling colleagues in other security services, hoping somebody had something they could share. He would also try reaching Sandra again. And his mother.

Chapter 5

Sandra

After taking much time and trouble making her way to the HiQua offices, Sandra Malone found them closed, with a note on the door saying staff should work from home for the rest of the week. She peered inside but could see nobody there. The parking lot was empty. For a moment she stood by the entrance wondering what to do. She checked her commplant and got the same "emergency services only" message she'd been getting since last night. She really, really wanted to speak to Jay. If anybody knew what was going on, it would be him.

In frustration, she headed back home. She was on foot. While a lot of the minor accidents from last night had already been cleared up, there were still enough obstacles on the road to make driving a problem. Fortunately, she lived only three kilometres from work. She could see the roofs of her housing estate from the HiQua entrance. It was bitterly cold, so she pulled her collar up against the wind and stepped out briskly.

As she passed along the high street, she saw a coach in the parking lot of the local church. A small crowd of people were milling around it, some carrying placards while others tried to squeeze theirs into the coach's luggage compartment. One of the banners said, "Leave Time Alone"; another said, "So are the sons of men snared in an evil TIME when it falleth suddenly upon them". The people in the group looked perfectly normal. She had no idea where they might be going or what exactly their protest was, but it irritated her that, with all the chaos in the streets, they would choose today to make a nuisance of themselves.

She passed the window of Tom's Martial Arts Centre, a shabby little place, crammed between a lawyer's office and a dentist. Four nights a week, Sandra visited Tom's to practice karate. On two of those nights she taught a beginners' course to a roomful of skinny eleven-year-olds. Tom himself was overweight and had a sloppy, careless fighting style. Sandra had beaten him easily in their first few sparring sessions and he had ceased to spar with her after that. He was a terrible example to the students, yet he was the owner and he taught the advanced classes. There were a couple of promising young men, working towards their black belts, and they gladly came in on Tom's nights off to practice with Sandra. They understood, without ever needing to be told, that Tom should not hear about it.

Farther up the street, a middle-aged woman was dragging broken sheets of plasterboard out through the front of a grocery store and piling them with other building rubble in the street. The woman's face was wet with tears. Sandra stopped and offered to help but the woman looked at her with an angry frown, threw down what she was dragging, and turned to face the shop door. Her fists were clenched and she shouted into the dim interior, "I wouldn't be having to clear out all this shit if the stupid bastard I married didn't do every bloody thing half arsed. I told him to get proper builders in and get the job done right for once in his stupid life, but no, he always knows better than everyone else." Without even glancing back at Sandra, the woman marched inside, crunching across the rubbish-strewn floor, still shouting for the benefit of whoever was inside.

Sandra walked on. Her own street, when she came to it, was relatively unscathed. A house a few doors down from hers had a window pane lying in pieces on the front lawn and another near the end of the street had a crack in its brickwork, but her own house was intact, despite all the rumbling and shaking that had gone on. She noticed a van parked up the road bearing the livery of the local electricity company and hoped that wasn't a sign their power was off.

"Cara!" she called, entering the hall and stripping off her coat, scarf, and gloves.

"Mum?" Cara came wandering into the kitchen as Sandra was reaching for the kettle.

"Coffee?" Sandra asked.

"I've just had one. What are you doing home?"

"Office is shut. I'm working at home until further notice."

"Cool." She wandered away again but came back. "The electricity man came. He wanted to check something or other."

Sandra's heart beat faster. "You didn't let him in, did you?"

Cara rolled her eyes. "No, Mum. I told him to come back when you got home."

"Good girl. Don't ever let anybody in. Ever."

Cara sighed and set off again. "Yeah, I know."

"What are you studying today?" Sandra called, before Cara was out of sight.

"Developmental psych."

"Interesting?"

Cara shrugged. "Kinda." She gave Sandra a little smile and headed on to her room.

A degree in psychology was not what Sandra wanted for her eighteen-year-old daughter. She'd wanted Cara to study something more practical and useful—like engineering or medicine—but Cara wanted to be a world-leading criminologist. Which was no doubt Jay's influence. Having a father who used to be a cop must have coloured her thinking. Since he and Cara went to Washington to rescue Sandra, Jay had been his daughter's hero. Neither of them knew what Jay did now, some secret squirrel stuff no doubt. All he would say was he had become a civil servant in the European bureaucracy. To Sandra it meant intelligence work for sure. To Cara, his reticence just piled on the mystery and glamour.

She took her coffee through to the living room, slumped into her favourite armchair and flicked up a display to watch the newsfeeds. She was still cold from her walk and cuddled the hot drink as she watched the scenes of tragedy and loss unfold. The tsunami that had hit countries all over south-east Asia was the worst of it. Thousands had died. Possibly hundreds of thousands. They would not know until rescue teams could reach isolated towns and villages and count the dead. But even the small stuff was serious—the road accidents, the people caught in collapsed buildings, or by fallen power lines, the people who'd died in gas explosions and house fires—a handful of fatalities in every town in every country added up to a major global catastrophe. There were even pundits speculating that the number of suicides over the next few days or weeks might outnumber the accidental deaths. People had seen things. There had been ghosts and demons, poltergeists and angels. For a few minutes, the veil that separates the dead from the living had been torn aside.

Muting the feeds, she tried calling Jay again. This time she got a signal but he didn't pick up. His face appeared and asked her to leave a message.

"Jay, just call me, OK?" she said and hung up.

She called Jay's mother, Dot. It was the sixth call since the previous night's weirdness, but Dot hadn't heard from Jay, either.

"Are you still coping, Dot?" she asked. When Jay had finally found out about his teenage daughter, he had insisted on taking Cara to see his mother. Sandra could hardly object, but she had insisted on going with them to apologise in person for having hidden Dot's granddaughter away from her for sixteen years. It had been difficult at first, but, in the end, Dot had been so pleased to have Cara in the family that it swept away all the resentment and anger. Over the past couple of years they had visited one another quite a few times and got on well, despite Dot's constant harping on the theme of Jay and Sandra getting back together.

"I'm fine, love," Dot said. "I've found a builder who said he can come by in a few days to put a tarp on the roof. He doesn't know when he can actually fix it though, what with everything that needs doing. It's just a few missing tiles. As long as it doesn't rain till he gets here, I'll be fine."

"I could drive over and do it myself," Sandra said. She'd never fixed a roof before but how hard could it be?

"Oh, good grief, no! I'm not having you driving all that way with things the way they are. You just stay where you are and look after Cara. She must be so frightened."

Sandra laughed. "You'd think nothing had happened. I'm beginning to wonder if she even noticed it."

Dot was shocked. "But after what happened to her in America, isn't she terrified?"

Sandra shrugged. "Apparently not. Did you understand Jay when he was that age?"

"I've always been able to read him like a book." She fell silent, then said, "I wish we could reach him."

"Me too. I'm hoping he can tell us what happened last night."

Jay's mother looked anxious. "Was it one of those timesplash things, Sandra? You've seen them. You know what they're like."

Sandra had seen them all right. Twice in her past, they had nearly killed her. "It was nothing like anything I've seen before, Dot."

"The newsfeeds are calling it the tempocalypse," Dot said. "They had a man on talking about it this morning."

A surge of anger rose in her at the irresponsibility of the media channels. They needed real scientists on the feeds right now, reassuring people, not self-appointed gurus spouting quasi-religious rubbish. "That's just nonsense, Dot. Trust me, I know. Jay will tell you the same when you get through to him." Sandra thought for a moment. Apart from Cara, Dot was the closest thing Sandra had to family: she didn't like to think of her alone and anxious at a time like this. "Dot?" she said. "What do you think of the idea of me and Cara coming for a visit? My office is closed for the rest of the week. They said I should work from home but there isn't really anything for me to do." She saw Dot preparing to object, so she talked faster. "It would be great to see you again, and Cara would love it. She always likes to see you. And I bet Jay would be pleased to know we were all together and safe."

A small smile crept across Dot's worried features. "It

would be nice," she said. "I haven't seen you since Christmas."

"That's settled then. I'll get us packed and we'll be there by—" She was going to say "lunchtime" but there was no telling how long the journey might take. "Well, we'll be there as soon as we can."

"You be careful on the roads, love."

Sandra could see how much brighter Dot seemed. Maybe she'd been hoping for a visit. She had certainly acquiesced to the suggestion with very little fuss. She said her goodbyes and went to find Cara to tell her the news and get her moving. But she had gone just a few paces when the doorbell rang. She turned and looked at it.

People did not call on Sandra. She discouraged friendships and she had no relations. Even Cara's friends were kept away. The sign on the gate said, "No salesmen, no charities, no visits without an appointment." She knew how it must look to the neighbours, but she wanted it to be clear. They were not in hiding, exactly, but they did not advertise their presence, either. It had been Sandra's habit since Cara was a baby to live a reclusive, friendless life. She had too many old enemies to risk being noticed. And the fewer people who knew she had a daughter, the better. Despite all of these precautions, her past *had* caught up with her two years ago and it had dragged her and Cara into extreme danger. Jay too.

So she went to the door and turned on the exterior cameras. A display showed several views from around the house. There was just one man there, standing on her doorstep, wearing an overall with the electric company's logo. She studied him for a moment. He was a man of average build, in his forties, no sign of a gun, hands dirty, fingernails short, shoes scuffed: everything about him was consistent with him being what he seemed to be.

"Yes?" she said into the intercom.

"South Star Electric," he said. "Are you the householder?"

"What do you want?"

"We've had a few problems with meters suffering damage in the quake last night," he said.

"Yes?"

"We're checking all the houses in the area. There could be a fire risk. It'll only take two minutes."

"Can I see your credentials, please? The plate's under the intercom." Sandra had no reason to doubt he was a genuine electrician but she had a process.

The man at the door reached out and touched his fingers to the metal plate. His commplant communicated through the electrical field on his skin and his company credentials appeared on the display Sandra was watching.

"Just a moment while I call your office and check," she said.

"Check?"

"I'll just get them to confirm who you are and that you should be here."

"Couldn't you just let me in? We're already well behind on our schedule."

"It won't take a moment," she said.

The man outside seemed agitated. "Look, I'm sorry, missus, I can't hang around here all day," he said. "I'll come back later." He turned and walked quickly away, heading straight for the van she'd seen earlier.

Her heart rate jumped. She swore under her breath then ran to Cara's room. Her daughter was immersed in her studies, stretched out on her bed, her face half-hidden in a full VR mask. Sandra had to grab her by the shoulder and shake to get her attention.

"What's the matter? What's up?" Cara pulled off the mask and sat up, eyes wide.

"Something's going on," Sandra said. "I want you to grab your bag and get out of here. Go to your grandma's—she's expecting us anyway."

"What's going on? Is someone here?" Cara glanced at the bedroom door as if there might be a stranger standing there. "Oh God, is it starting again?"

Sandra saw the fear growing in her daughter's face and felt terrible for frightening her like this, but something odd was happening and she needed to make sure Cara was safe.

"It might be nothing at all," she said. "But I want you to go to your gran's so I know you're well away from here."

Cara blinked. "Right now? This minute?" She looked towards her wardrobe. Inside was a bag she kept packed and ready for emergencies. It contained everything she would need to disappear for a while. Sandra and Cara always lived with the possibility that they might have to make a run for it.

"Just grab your bag and leave the back way. Catch a train to London if they're running, or a bus if they're not. Don't tell Dot anything. Just say I'm doing something for work and I'll be along later."

Cara got off the bed and went to fetch her bag. Sandra felt a surge of relief that her daughter wasn't going to argue. She was a sensible girl. A good girl.

"What about Dad?" Cara asked. "Have you told him?"

"I don't know what it is, honey. It might still turn out to be nothing."

"When will you get to Gran's?"

Cara's bag was a light backpack. She pushed her VR mask into it and slung it over her shoulder.

"You'll need something warmer than that," Sandra said, grabbing a heavy jumper from a drawer. "And take your coat and scarf from the hall. It's freezing out there." Cara took the jumper. "I'll probably be there a couple of hours after you," she added. She went to the window and looked out into the street. The electricity company van was still sitting there. She could imagine the men inside discussing what to do about Sandra's refusal to let them in. Maybe they were calling their boss for instructions. "You need to get going."

Cara nodded and went to the hall to collect her coat. "Is it to do with what happened last night?" Sandra shrugged. It seemed like a reasonable guess. "If you're not there tomorrow, I'm calling Dad," Cara said.

Sandra grabbed her and kissed her. "I'll be fine. Don't worry. We've had false alarms before, remember?"

Cara gave her a long, troubled look and left without another word. Sandra felt her throat choke up. *This is no way to make a child live*, she thought. Yet she could think of no other way. She had made enemies, lots of them, dangerous, ruthless enemies who might at any time reach out to punish her. Obscurity and constant vigilance were the only defences she had.

She waited until Cara was out of the house then went to get her own running-away bag. She set it down by the front door with her coat and went to a window to check the street. The van was still there. The men inside would either come back for her, or they would drive away and try something else. Probably the latter. If they were here to kill or kidnap her, they would have done things differently. They must have wanted access to the house for something else. To plant a bomb? To install bugs? Still there was no movement. What were they waiting for? Then, as she watched, the van pulled away from the curb and began moving up the street. She waited until it turned left at the end of the road and rushed out to the car, grabbing her things on the way.

She threw the car recklessly out of the drive and into the street, racing after the van, determined not to let it get too far ahead of her.

Chapter 6

Hunting

Jay's second meeting with Crystal had not gone well. His boss seemed to think the previous night's event had been his fault. Telling her it wasn't a timesplash didn't seem to appease her at all. Whatever it was, she seemed to believe, K Section should have seen it coming and prevented it.

"It might have nothing to do with time travel," he'd said.

She'd just looked at him as if he were an imbecile. "The Security Standing Committee is in emergency session in about two hours. Do you expect them to believe that?"

He told her about the failure of CERN to detect a displacement field. He explained the satellite evidence showing no centre for the disturbance.

"All negatives, Jay," she'd said. "I can't tell people that all we have is a lack of evidence. I don't want a lack of evidence. The Chairman doesn't want a lack of evidence. Nobody wants me to tell them what we *don't* know."

With a tight jaw, he'd told her he would do what he could.

Now he was in his office staring at the newsfeeds of the mounting global death toll and wondering what to do next. The stock market had plunged. The gold price was through the roof. A war had broken out between neighbouring nuclear-armed fragments of the old Russian Republic. There was concern in Berlin that the "quake" might leave some parts of Europe without the net for days if not weeks.

He checked his messages and there was a missed call from Sandra. He called back immediately.

"Jay?" She accepted the call voice-only. He could hear the sound of a car engine, other traffic, a slight strain in her tone. She was driving. "It's not a good time."

"I just wanted to know you and Cara are all right. I haven't been able to get through."

"I know. We're both fine. What happened last night? Was it...? You know."

"No. Not as far as we can tell. It's something different. Worse in many ways."

There was a brief silence in which he heard her curse under her breath followed by the squeal of tyres. He was going to ask what she was doing when she said, "I spoke to your mum this morning. She's OK. Cara's gone to visit her. I'll go soon too."

Jay felt a rush of relief. Everybody safe. Everybody OK. "Thanks, Sandra. I owe you one."

There was another silence. "No," Sandra said. "I don't think so."

He knew what she meant. For sixteen years she had hidden the fact that they'd had a child. The last time they'd spoken about it, she'd called the deception the biggest mistake of her life. He was inclined to agree but, more than two years on from the shocking discovery, the overwhelming anger that had filled him was beginning to ebb. Maybe it was time they spoke openly about it again.

"Look, Jay, this really isn't a good time. I'm sort of in the middle of something. Can I call you back?" Her regret sounded genuine, but he wondered what on Earth could be so important at that moment.

"Yes. Yes, of course. I'm pretty busy myself or I'd come over." More silence. "Goodbye then."

"Bye, Jay."

The line went dead just as an astonishing news item came up on the feed. He turned up the volume and gaped at the images of St Peter's Square in Rome.

"... this amazing footage of Pope John the Twenty-fourth addressing an awestruck crowd from his balcony." The feed anchor sounded suitably impressed. Pope John the Twenty-fourth had died eighteen months earlier after a freak storm had ripped the tail off the aircraft he was flying in. "Amateur video footage of the ex-Pontiff's speech is being examined by church officials. Some are already calling it a miracle, while others say it is a fraud perpetrated by the Vatican to try to prop up falling church attendance, pointing to several references the late Pope made in last night's speech to events that have happened since his death." The anchor leaned in to the camera, and Jay thought he saw a hint of worry on the man's smooth brow. "Perhaps, of all the things that we've reported on today, this is the strangest—and maybe the most significant."

Jay turned it off. He'd called a meeting of his senior staff and he needed to muster his thoughts. He'd spoken to his opposite numbers at Interpol, MI5, and the Centro Nacional de Inteligencia and none of them had the slightest clue. Or, if they did, they weren't sharing it. Initial reports from his own team amounted to much the same. None of them had any idea. They had received no intel prior to the event or after. Whoever had done this was flying completely under the radar of Europe's intelligence services.

If anyone had done it at all.

He stood up and paced across his office, then returned to his chair and sat down again. He needed to think, but his mind seemed to be operating in a vacuum. There were no clues, no intel, no hypotheses from the technical team, no demands from terrorist groups—nothing! Just a dead Pope murmuring in Latin to a terrified audience, and his daughter, standing there saying, "How could you forget that Mum died?"

* * * *

The electrical van pulled off the A40 into a semi-derelict industrial estate on the outskirts of Oxford. Sandra dropped back but kept the van in sight. She scanned the map of the area, displayed on her car's windscreen. There were just a dozen or so businesses active on the estate: a motorbike repair shop, a decorative tile retailer, a kitchen renovation company—the usual miscellany. Then she saw one that jumped out at her: B & T Security, Limited. It was obvious now where the van was heading.

She pulled over two hundred meters from the shabby brick building and watched as the van pulled into the garage beside it. The big window at the front of the shop was opaque, with the company name stencilled on it. She grabbed a pair of binoculars from the glove box. There was a front door, also with an opaque window, with a "Closed" sign illuminated beside it. There was no other entrance she could see but perhaps there was one from the garage. She zoomed the map on her windscreen and switched to an aerial photo view. Behind the building were a concrete yard and a large shed. Going on the positioning of paths, she judged there was a back entrance.

For a moment, she considered breaking in, surprising the two men, and demanding to know what they were up to, beating it out of them if necessary. The guy who'd come to her door didn't look tough but she'd only seen the other guy in glimpses as he'd driven the van. He didn't seem particularly big and scary either, but size wasn't everything. They might be armed, and there might even be others inside the building. She took a deep breath and fought down her impatience to confront them. Instead, she called Cara.

"Hi, Mum." From the muffled tone, Sandra could tell Cara was sub-vocalising, meaning she was not alone.

"How're you doing?"

"I'm on a train. A very crowded train. It's a limited service as far as Ealing Broadway, then there are supposed to be buses from there to Paddington. It's going to take hours to get there."

"You weren't followed?"

"I don't think so. I did the things Dad showed us, you know, checking reflections in windows, suddenly doubling back, all that spy stuff. I didn't see anybody. Where are you?"

"I'm following the guys who were pretending to be from the electric company. Turns out they work for a security company. My guess is that if we'd let them in our house would be full of bugs right now."

"Are you going to beat them up?"

Sandra tried to sound offended, as if that were the last thing she would ever think of doing. "No. I'm just going to watch them, see what they do next."

"Sounds boring."

"Yeah. Oh, I spoke to your dad. He's fine. I told him

where you were going. I expect he'll call later. He's being Mr Important today, trying to work out what happened last night."

"Doesn't he know?"

"Seems not." A small, grey van with the words "B & T Security" on the side pulled out from the back of the building. There was one driver: the man who had called at the house. He was driving manually—essential with the roads in such a mess and net coverage so patchy. "Gotta go, honey. Talk to you later."

"Mum, be careful."

"You too."

Sandra considered her options. The choice was either watch the building or follow the van. In her opinion, action won out over inaction every time. She slid down in her seat so she couldn't be seen as the van went past, then bobbed back up to watch where it went—back onto the A40 heading for London. It looked as if she had made the right choice. Someone had paid these local guys to bug her house and now it seemed the boss wanted to give them fresh instructions. She started the engine and did a U-turn. She glanced at the battery level. There should be enough juice to get her to London if the grey van didn't take too many detours. She drove slowly, letting the van get a good lead. There was no need to be close behind him until they reached the capital. Then it would get tricky, but for now she could relax.

* * * *

Jay was scowling when he walked into the conference room. He scanned the half-dozen team leaders to check that everyone was there. Laura Thalman nodded to him as his gaze touched her and he nodded back, reflexively.

"All right," he said. "I won't keep you long. I want progress reports. Keep it brief. We'll go round the room. You first, Pierre."

Lieutenant Pierre Fourget was a stocky man in his late twenties, square jawed and intense. Career military, he ran the two special-ops teams assigned to Jay's section. The young lieutenant and his men were the sword in Jay's hand. They also often heard things as they hunted through the sewers of Europe's festering underground political movements. He looked Jay in the eye and said, "*Rien.*"

Jay nodded. "Nothing at all?"

Fourget shook his head. *Well, he kept it brief,* Jay thought. "Keep looking, Pierre—all of you—this is your number-one priority. Donata?"

His head of counter-espionage, Donata Sismondi, was a heavy-set Italian in her fifties. Intelligent and calculating, she seemed to consider every question a potential trap. "You want to know if we have found who made last night's timesplash?" she asked.

"We don't think it was a timesplash," Jay said. "But, whatever it was, yes, I'd like to know who caused it."

She cocked her head and narrowed her eyes. "If it was not a timesplash, why is K Section looking into it?"

After two years of working with this team, he knew Sismondi well enough to know she wasn't challenging him, merely clarifying the parameters of his request. "Our remit is not just to prevent the Union's enemies using temporal displacement technologies against it, but also any other techniques for using time as a weapon."

"So you don't think it was a timesplash, but you think it was to do with time?"

"Until someone can rule it out, we'll treat last night's event as an attack with a new kind of temporal weapon. What do you think, Donata?"

She shrugged. "You are probably right, eh Laura?"

Jay cut in before Laura could reply. "Did your operatives find anything?"

Donata shook her head. "It is early days. These things take time." She smiled. "No pun intended."

"Any leads that look promising?"

Again, the shrug. "We will see."

So damned cagey! Why can't the woman just say "no"? He moved on. The head of Jay's analysis team had the most to say. The analysts had classified and categorized the various phenomena that had occurred during the event. "There were quakes," Kadan Dudding said in his crisp, Oxbridge accent. "At least two hundred of them above magnitude five, spread all over the major fault lines. Only four above magnitude eight, thank goodness. We believe something like one percent of all people saw an apparition—either of someone who should have been somewhere else, or of someone who is dead. Some of these appearances were quite public," he was clearly referring to the ex-Pope's impromptu speech, "and some seemed to involve physical manifestation. In one case we had a wife return from the dead and stab hubby five times with a kitchen knife. Lots of witnesses." He paused for effect. "There were a number of displaced objects—including a half-built housing estate that turned up in a field near Barcelona. Almost everything else that happened last night can be attributed, more or less directly, to one of those three causes—including the many traffic accidents."

"Any pattern to what we're seeing?"

Dudding winced. "We really don't have enough data yet.

Union-wide communications is still a little bit patchy."

"Any *hints* of a pattern?"

Dudding considered for a moment. "Nothing we've heard so far is inconsistent with the hypothesis that these phenomena are completely randomly spread. We're trying to get precise timings, to see if there is a point of origin, but no luck so far."

"What about the sunspots?"

"Sorry, what sunspots?"

"Someone told Captain Harnois there had been a report of extra sunspot activity."

"Really? I'll look into it."

There were a couple more reports before Jay finally turned to Laura. "Do your people have any ideas yet, Laura?"

She shook her head. "No, nothing at all." She smiled sadly. "As things stand, I don't think we can even rule out sunspots. However, remember that consultant I mentioned? She's already airborne. Should be here in an hour or so."

Well, let's hope whoever it is can read tea-leaves, Jay thought, *because solving this looks like it'll take psychic powers.* He thanked Laura, let people ask a few questions and throw out some wild ideas, then sent them all back to doing what they were trained for, gathering intelligence.

And what do I do now? he wondered, watching his staff file out of the room. It wasn't even lunchtime and he already seemed to have exhausted every possible avenue of investigation. He felt his chest tightening, felt the weight of the challenge on him. He had to keep things moving forwards, had to direct everybody's efforts as efficiently as possible, keep the big picture in mind and guide his team towards a solution. But in his mind there was no picture, just the image of Cara turning to mist in his hands.

He went to his office and sat at his desk. All around him he popped up virtual displays. European Defence Force Military Intelligence had countless Petabytes of data it could lay at his fingertips, right there in that room. He knew the answer was out there, somewhere. All he had to do was ask the right questions. He moved his hands into the sensor fields. Tentatively, he began to explore.

* * * *

Farid Hamiye was a big man, long limbed and deep chested. He dressed expensively but casually and enjoyed the knowledge that his handmade Italian shoes cost more than most of the people around him would earn in a month. He sat at a table in a café in the great mall, one arm over the back of his seat, one leg stretched out beside the table, long fingers touching the espresso in front of him. He also enjoyed the way that women stole glances at him as they passed. Unlike the shoes, that was not a gift of his new-found wealth. Even as a boy in Lebanon, the girls had looked at him like that.

His gaze wandered around the brightly-lit space, across the faces of the shoppers, past the doorways and stalls. He was a businessman, perhaps, idling away a few minutes between meetings. He saw nothing suspicious. No-one was watching him. He was in a blind spot for the mall security cameras. He checked the time. Birdman was late. He was about to call him again when he spotted the little weasel making his way through the crowd, scanning for Hamiye. The "security consultant" was out of place among the lunchtime shoppers, shabby and nervous. Hamiye supposed Birdman's business was not doing well. Hardly surprising, when he made himself so conspicuous.

At last, Birdman spotted him and came over. His gaze twitched around the mall as he sat down. "Are we all right to talk here?" he asked in a whisper.

Hamiye ignored him and signalled to the waitress. She, of course, was being unusually attentive. "Another espresso," he said, "and one for my friend." When she left, he turned to Birdman. "You wouldn't think a little shithole like this would serve good coffee, but you will be surprised. Now, tell me how you managed to screw up such a simple job."

Birdman made his hands into angry claws and shook them. "I don't know. Either she's the most paranoid woman I ever met, or she's some kind of red-hot professional and she made me in ten seconds flat. I've never seen anything like it in twenty years doing this job. She must have a lot to hide, that one. Even her daughter wouldn't let me in."

Hamiye cocked an eyebrow. There had been nothing on Ms Malone's employment file about a daughter. Her next of kin was given as Jason Kennedy, a man he had yet to track down. "You really are an incompetent little rodent, aren't you, Birdman?"

The security specialist bristled, but his eyes were shifty and cautious. "I didn't do anything wrong. As soon as she got too nosy, I just made an excuse and cleared off. No harm done."

"Really? So you'd be surprised to hear that Ms Malone is just fifty meters away, pretending to look at bedding?" He shot out a hand and grabbed Birdman's arm as the man's head twitched sideways. "And if you try looking over your shoulder, I will break your neck." He smiled pleasantly as the waitress brought their coffees. She simpered when he thanked her, then moved on.

"All right, Birdman, you can go. Go now. She won't follow you. It's me she came to find."

Birdman stood up. He made a last rally to protect his dignity. "What about my fee?"

Hamiye regarded him with an amused contempt. "You will not be hearing from me again, Birdman, and I will not be hearing from you. Do you understand?"

The smaller man looked as if he had more to say, but he managed to keep his lips pressed shut and left without another word.

Hamiye studied Sandra Malone. For an MI5 spy, she stood out like a sore thumb. Tall, slender and extremely beautiful. Even in casual clothes she looked magnificent, upright and athletic, poised and elegant. He had rarely if ever seen such an attractive woman. Dressed well and wearing makeup, he imagined she would be breathtaking. The idea of her posing as a software engineer in a provincial town was ludicrous. He studied her for so long that, as she assessed him in shop window reflections and with surreptitious glances, it must have become obvious to her that he had seen her. With a look of annoyance, she turned to face him. He smiled back at her and gestured for her to join him.

The briefest of hesitations was all that gave away the fact that she was not completely fearless. She strode over to his table and sat down.

"All right," she said. "What's all this about?"

He found her accent a jarring disappointment. His own was impeccably upper-class English, something he had worked hard to achieve. Hers was really quite commonplace.

"I'm very pleased to meet you, Ms Malone," he said. "I haven't met an MI5 agent before. That is who you work for, isn't it?"

"I work for HiQua. In their software-testing division. Who are you and why are you trying to bug my house?"

"I'm pretty sure you know exactly who I am. Your colleagues back in Vauxhall are probably feeding you my résumé right now—what little they know of it. Or have you already seen it?" He sipped his espresso and waited for her to speak.

"You're quite an arsehole, aren't you? What the hell makes you think I know or care who you are except that you've just had your hired moron try to bug me?"

The woman's attitude was so contemptuous he felt his temper rising despite his customary discipline. "All right, let's stop playing games. I know who you are. You know who I am. What I want to know is why you're spying on HiQua. We have some extremely confidential projects underway and we don't like minor civil servants poking their noses into our business. Do I need to remind you that our CEO, *Sir* Roger Waxtead, is a personal friend of the Prime Minister *and* the Home Secretary?" He waited for a reaction but got none. "So you might want to pull your horns in—and I hope your superiors are listening to this—because there's an awful lot of shit about to roll downhill onto their pointy little heads if you don't. Am I making myself clear?"

Hamiye's irritation grew as he searched for any sign of intimidation or even concern in the woman's face. All he saw was anger and stubbornness. It was bad enough that her ridiculous department thought they could run a covert surveillance operation on a company like HiQua, but it was worse that there were real secrets such an operation might stumble upon. Worse still was the fact that he had to confront the woman openly like this instead of shutting everything down quietly behind the scenes. But worst of all would be if the woman were stupid enough not to back down and let her superiors handle the matter. That could get messy.

When she said, "Let me make something clear to you, Mr Whoever-the-hell-you-are," he groaned inwardly. "I don't know what the hell you're talking about. You must have me mixed up with someone else because I don't work for MI5 and I never have done. I'm not spying on your company—whose major crime, as far as I can tell, is the coffee they provide in my office—and if I find you or your people sneaking around my house again, I'm going to the police."

For a moment he felt a stab of uncertainty. Her act was so convincing he actually began to doubt what was so obviously true. This woman was no software engineer. She'd sussed Birdman in a heartbeat and then trailed him here with no difficulty at all. Not the behaviour of an innocent person but that of a skilled agent who was trying to take him for a fool.

She stood up to go and he let some of his growing anger show. "I will take whatever counter-espionage steps are necessary to protect my employers' intellectual property—even from the government. If it comes to a pissing contest between Europe's third-largest corporation and some jumped-up department and its time-travelling Mata Hari, you will lose. I promise you. Don't say you weren't warned, Ms Malone."

She walked away, but not before leaving him with a parting sneer. He watched her disappear into the crowd then took a long, deep breath. Stupid, stupid woman! He forced his anger to subside, forced himself to relax. She would report back and her superiors would tell her they were closing down the operation. Her cover was blown. What else could they do? Still, it galled him that she had been so completely unafraid of him. It made him want to threaten her more, do something that would really scare her, if only to knock that cocky look off her face. And his own anger also irritated him.

He rarely let anybody get to him like that. He wasn't that man. He let his eyelids fall closed, then opened them again. It had been a stupid, pointless encounter and he would almost certainly never see the woman again.

He called Lee, saying he wanted to come in and report on their spy. Neither of them spoke about anything important on the phone. Lee was still at the Special Projects office—not the one at HiQua head office but he real one. They arranged to meet there and Hamiye turned his mind to how he might spin the morning's bad news to his boss.

Chapter 7

The New Consultant

Sandra studied the map of the mall and its parking lots. There were two exits but they fed into the same road. If she parked in the right spot, every vehicle that left the mall would have to pass by her. She ran to her car and raced to get into position. She assumed that her quarry would head straight for his own car and leave. He didn't seem the type to loiter unnecessarily. While she waited, she called Jay again.

"What do you mean, you need an ID?" Jay asked.

"Why do you always have to ask stupid questions?" She knew he wasn't really that slow, he just liked to stall while he worked out his responses. It was his most infuriating trait.

"What do you mean stupid?"

She clenched her teeth to stop a scream of frustration escaping. "Look, some bloke came to the house today pretending to be from the electric company but he was really there to plant bugs."

"What?"

"Shut up. Cara wouldn't let him in and neither would I. So he buggered off and I followed him. He's from some one-man-and-his-dog security company in Oxford, but he led me to a mall in London where he met someone else."

"You followed him?"

"This other bloke is a player, built like a brick shithouse, looks Arabic, dressed in designer casuals, very sure of himself. I'm following him, now. I want to know why I'm being targeted."

"Targeted?"

"I haven't got much time, Jay. He'll be on the move any minute now. Listen, he seems to work for HiQua. He thinks I'm MI5 and I'm spying on the company. There's obviously something fishy going on."

"Fishy?"

"Jay, he mentioned time travel."

At last, Jay was silent. "You should cut and run," he said. "Get Cara and come to me. Whatever's going on, you can't handle it on your own—and I'm too busy to come and help. I can arrange transport for you both. Just tell me where and when."

"Jay, doesn't it strike you as a bit of a coincidence?" Her chest tightened just thinking about what it might all mean, this big fat scary coincidence. She knew Jay was right and she should get out of there. But what if this guy was really up to something? What if he knew who was behind last night's catastrophe? She couldn't just walk away from that, could she?

She saw a car turning out of the mall onto the road. It was a flashy antique Tesla Roadster, looking like it had just come off the assembly line. "I think I see him. Jay, just get me an ID on those pictures I took of him. That's all I need you to do. Cara's safe at your mum's place. Gotta go."

The Tesla was picking up speed fast. She turned on the engine and ducked down, peering over the window sill.

"Gotcha!" she cried as he shot past. Slamming her foot down on the accelerator, she bounced over a grass verge and a side road and onto the main road, causing a hapless shopper to swerve for her life. She pressed the pedal to the floor and kept it there. Her quarry was the type who would drive hard and fast and her own little runabout was no match for his muscle car. But, if she flogged it to death, and took a lot of crazy risks, maybe, just maybe, she could keep him in sight.

* * * *

Jay stared at his commplant display for a full minute after Sandra had hung up. Of all the times for her to go off looking for trouble, this was the worst. He called his mother. She was expecting both Cara and Sandra and didn't know yet that Sandra had gone chasing villains through the streets of London. He asked her to call him when Cara arrived safely, saying he was worried about her travelling in the aftermath of last night.

"Oh you don't need to worry about that girl," his mother said. "She's the most sensible eighteen-year-old I've ever met. Reminds me of myself at her age. Funny how genes sometimes skip a generation. Anyway, she's with her mother, and we both know Sandra can take care of herself."

After the call, he sat with his thoughts. Cara was probably all right. So was his mum. It was Sandra who was likely to get herself into trouble. He stared through the window at the Berlin skyline, dark against the cold, grey skies. He'd spoken to Sandra about just this scenario. She wasn't supposed to go off tracking down anybody. She was supposed to drop everything and run. Nothing else was safe. The kind of people who might go after her were vicious killers—exbricks, organized crime, terrorist organizations, rogue governments. Any of the old timesplashers, the bricks, even the tekniks, could want her dead for her betrayal of Sniper and others all those years ago. Many of the bricks who had survived from back then had moved from the anarchic mayhem of timesplashing to the more stable pursuits of organized crime and international terrorism. Such occupations were a natural outlet for their talents. And any old criminal organization might just want Sandra for her skills as temporal engineer, a teknik, the way Polanski had when he kidnapped her to help launch his damned revolution with a bloodbath in Washington, DC. And that had been just a couple of years back.

Now it was happening again. Some demon from their past had surfaced. Somebody was stalking Sandra—maybe Cara too. He slammed his hand down on his desk and stood up. They needed to hide. They should be lying low. He, Jay, should be over there helping them, protecting them, not standing around in this bloody office, doing nothing.

With a start, he realized that nothing was exactly what he was doing. He sat down again at his desk and pulled up the pictures Sandra had sent. He saw a handsome, Middle-Eastern man in his early thirties. The man looked smug and arrogant and Jay detested him on sight. He ran a facial recognition program and retrieved the man's file. Farid Hamiye, born 2035 in Lebanon. Not much known until he turned up in Europe four years earlier. Worked as a freelance bodyguard for a short while, then joined HiQua in London. His current position there was Head of Security, Special Projects Division. Clean record.

He sat back in his chair and studied Hamiye's face. It all

seemed pretty straightforward. HiQua was doing something secret at its Special Projects Division. Hamiye had turned up Sandra's name on a routine sweep and, because of a twenty-year-old connection between Sandra and MI5, had jumped to all the wrong conclusions about her. Paranoid about being spied on, he'd tried to find out what she was up to, and ended up on the receiving end of Sandra's own paranoia.

The question was, was Sandra in any danger? How far would Hamiye go to protect his company's secrets?

He called Sandra to tell her what he'd found, but she wasn't taking any calls. So he put his thoughts into a voice message and sent that instead, hoping she'd listen to it before she did anything stupid and dangerous. He was about to call Cara and set her the task of calling her mum every ten minutes to tell her to check her messages, when Laura Thalman knocked and poked her head around his office door.

"Jay? Our new consultant has arrived. I thought I'd just quickly introduce her before she and I get down to work."

Jay waved her in and watched as she ushered a plump woman of about his age into the room. He started to rise to greet her, but stopped in mid-motion.

"Jay!" the woman said, beaming. "My goodness, haven't you done well for yourself? Head honcho of all this! And Sandra didn't say a word about it."

"Olivia!"

Laura looked from one to the other in surprise. "You know each other?"

"Oh, we're old friends," Olivia said. She hurried around the desk and Jay submitted to the usual over-familiar hug. He'd met Dr Olivia Bradley exactly twice before. The first time was when she was working as a teknik for MI5 in 2050.

It had been Olivia who had controlled the lob that sent Sandra and him back to 1902 to save Lenin from assassination. The second was when he brought Sandra and Cara back from America. She had been Sandra's boss at the University of East Anglia where they were running timesplashes for the Direct History Department, observing historical events with purpose-built micro-drones lobbed back through time. As far as Jay knew, she was still at UEA. Olivia had been a good friend to Sandra and his daughter and it seemed that, in Olivia's mind, that friendship naturally transferred itself to Jay.

He gave Laura a quizzical look, wanting an explanation. Olivia Bradley was a world leader in deep time exploration but he didn't see the connection to what had happened last night.

Laura understood. "Dr Bradley was my external PhD supervisor," she explained. "We keep up an on-and-off correspondence about the latest theoretical developments in time travel. It was something Dr Bradley said a few months ago that led me to get in touch about this… conundrum."

"And what was that?"

Before Laura could answer, Olivia jumped in. "Just some wild hypothesis I came across. It's hardly worth mentioning."

"But you've been doing some work on it, haven't you?" Laura asked, suddenly concerned at Olivia's reluctance to talk.

In reply, Olivia turned to Jay. "I've been working with the Ministry of Defence of late, Jay. I still have my chair at UEA. Did Sandra tell you I got the promotion? Anyway, I turn up there and give the odd lecture, but mostly I'm based at Aldermaston. So, anything I could tell you about the work I do there would be rather classified, you understand."

"Aldermaston?" Jay said. He hadn't known about any time-related work going on at the UK's top military research laboratory and, as the man responsible for time-travel counter espionage for the EU's military intelligence directorate, he bloody well should have. He tried to keep the annoyance out of his voice as he said, "The MoD is running timesplashes at Aldermaston?"

Olivia blinked at him. "Oh dear. Have I said too much? I just meant that I'd have to check your clearance before I talked about what I'm doing. When Laura asked me to come out here, I thought we'd just be talking about ordinary time-travel stuff. I didn't know she'd be interested in… anything else. I suppose I should have guessed though."

"Ordinary time-travel stuff? Look, my clearance is as high as it goes, Olivia. Higher than anybody you know at Aldermaston, that's for sure. What's this 'anything else' you think I can't be told about?" He saw the distressed look on Olivia's face and backed off. He held up a hand. "All right. Don't answer that. I'll make a few calls and then I'll come and talk to you. Meanwhile, please do not leave the building. Laura, Dr Bradley is in your care until I've sorted this out."

Olivia bit her lip. "Jay, you're not going to get me into trouble, are you? I only came here as a favour to Laura."

He shook his head. "Don't worry. Somebody's in trouble, but it's not you. Look, I need to make those calls right now but, before you go, can I just ask you to tell me one thing? Are there any applications of this classified work you're doing that could possibly have led to what we saw last night?"

"I—I really don't see how. Even if… No, I really shouldn't say any more. I'm sorry, Jay."

* * * *

Sandra had lost him again. She'd lost him several times in the past hour but this time it seemed to be for good. She was in a dingy suburb in North London, somewhere she had never visited before and never wanted to visit again. It was mostly half-derelict residential buildings, abandoned and full of squatters. It was hard to tell if last night's event had hit the area badly or whether it always looked like that. It seemed unlikely that this was her target's destination but she drove around the streets anyway, hoping to spot his fancy car. If that didn't work, she had no other option but to give up.

Young men sat in groups around fires, watching her with sullen eyes as she passed. The recession in Europe ground on and on, with three poor harvests in a row. More global-warming-legacy crap. Likely to last another hundred years, they said, and likely to get worse before it got better.

Jay had told her that the EU had pinned its hopes on cheap American grain starting to flow again, but that was two years back, before the new American revolution flared up. The one she had unwillingly helped to get started. Now the EU was giving arms to the revolutionaries and filling Canada with fighter drones and laser batteries to dissuade the Chinese from joining the fray, further draining the economy.

It had seemed like a good thing to Sandra when the job at HiQua came up, testing software for robots. A lot of the machines she worked on were farmbots and, on a good day, she felt like she was contributing to the common good. On a bad day, she felt like just another cog in the gears of a faceless mega-corporation, profiteering from the distress of a continent that could barely feed itself.

She would give up the search soon. She had listened to Jay's message once she lost sight of the Tesla and could slow down. The majority of her pursuit had been so crazy fast that she daren't answer his call, however curious she was. She didn't want to think about the number of speeding fines she'd picked up. The chances were good she'd have her license suspended for this morning's work, if she wasn't disqualified from driving for life. Well, Cara would just have to ferry her around like she'd ferried Cara around to dance classes, and horse riding, and rock concerts. It might be quite nice.

She drove out of the rat's nest of private houses and up an approach road for the North Circular Road. There were warehouses and wholesalers, small factories and engineering works to left and right. This was hopeless. What would a man like Farid Hamiye be doing in a place like this? She needed to find somewhere to stop so she could check the map for places farther on that might be more promising. She also needed to get to a fast-charge station so she could top up her batteries. She'd been running on empty for the last quarter hour.

The main road was in view and the decision was made. She stopped studying the passing buildings and their parking lots and put her foot down. And immediately slammed on the brake. Thirty meters ahead was a familiar sign: the world-famous interlocking H and Q on a blue background that she had seen every morning above her place of work for the past three months. It was a small sign, attached to a gatepost and, as she edged her car up to it, she could see beneath the logo the words "Goods Entrance". There was nothing else. The wire mesh gates were closed and from them a white concrete drive led to a low, unexceptional building. A large painted board above the main entrance said, "Clarke Engineering, Ltd". A helicopter was parked on a tarmacked area nearby—it had no logo on it but it was painted in HiQua's distinctive blue. There was no sign of Hamiye's muscle car but Sandra didn't care. This was the place. It had to be.

Chapter 8

Foresight

Lee Shaozu was not used to being let down by his employees, least of all Hamiye.

"We just need to neutralise the Malone woman," Hamiye was saying. "If Waxtead were to make a call to the Prime Minister asking what the hell MI5 was up to, I'm sure that would shut down the whole investigation."

Lee studied Hamiye in silence. The man was waiting, hands behind his back, feet apart, gaze fixed on a point somewhere above Lee's head. *Like a soldier, standing at ease,* Lee thought, perhaps something Hamiye had picked up in his years fighting endless, pointless wars in the Middle East and North Africa. It was a stance that signified deference, putting Lee in the role of superior officer, but it didn't appease Lee at all. He disliked the implication that Hamiye was just a soldier carrying out orders. Soldiers didn't take enough ownership of their superiors' problems for Lee's liking. If things went wrong with a mission, a soldier could just shrug it off and wait for new orders, pushing the problem back onto his officer's shoulders.

Yet, of course, Hamiye was right. The way to sort this out

was for Lee to tell Waxtead to call Number 10. "But that doesn't really help us much, does it, Farid?"

"I... er..."

"It doesn't tell us why MI5 is snooping around. It doesn't tell us what they know or what they're looking for. You see, it could have been something completely unrelated to Special Projects. It could have been just about anything. Only now we'll never know. Five might well get off our backs but we won't get the chance to ask them any questions. Do you see?" Hamiye gave a reluctant nod. Lee let a little more anger show in his voice. "Worse still, the woman saw you. If she had any presence of mind, she would have captured your image through her commplant and will have passed it to Five for identification. So they now know that Special Projects was involved in trying to bug her, making it look as if we have something to hide, not just at HiQua, but here, right here, in my division. So, even if they didn't have any suspicions before about what we're doing here, they certainly do now."

"Sometimes," Hamiye said, "on an operation, things go wrong."

Lee could hear his security chief beginning to push back, beginning to resent being lectured. *Good*, he thought, *if I can't evoke guilt in the man, at least I can humiliate him.* "I don't want to hear your excuses, Farid. You need to lift your game. There is a lot at stake. You know how close we are."

"I do, but—"

Lee raised a hand. "No buts. Get back to London. I'll see you there later."

Hamiye looked ready to explode but all he did was nod curtly and leave. Lee took a few moments to reflect on what had happened. He would have to get Waxtead onto this straight away. He told the personal assistant in his commplant to set up an appointment with the CEO for late afternoon. No doubt his "boss" would be terrified to hear that MI5 was involved. No doubt he would want to whine and complain about it. No doubt Lee would need to slap him down and put him in his place again. It was becoming too frequent a necessity.

As for Hamiye, he was right. Sometimes these things went wrong. There was no need to doubt the competence of the man. In fact, it was extremely rare that Farid ever misstepped. The Malone woman must indeed be an exceptionally good agent.

* * * *

Sandra tensed her muscles against the cold. She'd waited just half an hour in the car, watching the Clarke Engineering building, but already the chill was seeping into her bones. Her breath hung in grey curls in the frigid air and the windscreen was a fog of condensation apart from the tiny rectangle she rubbed at from time to time with aching fingers. Yet she dare not turn on the heater for fear of running her battery flat. She needed to save enough juice at least to get her to the nearest garage, which, her commplant told her, was two kilometres away.

When the cold had first reached her toes, she had started asking herself whether she wasn't just wasting her time. Jay's view was that it was a matter of commercial sensitivity, that HiQua had jumped to all the wrong conclusions, and so things would probably sort themselves out if she just left it alone for a few days. She asked herself again whether maybe she could have misread the situation as she pushed her hands under her legs to try to warm them up. But Jay was always too relaxed about these things. He talked about the probabilities, as if it were all some big game of strategy. But Sandra thought about the consequences of someone from her past coming after her and Cara. Polanski had found her two years earlier and she and Cara had almost died. The probabilities didn't matter. No risk was worth taking.

And it kept bugging her that Hamiye had actually mentioned her association with time travel. It wasn't a surprise that he knew. If he knew that she had once worked with MI5, he would know what she had been mixed up in. But it was her MI5 connection that should have been preying on his mind, not the fact that she had travelled in time. She could see that this was a very nebulous excuse for following someone halfway across the country. But even the barest mention of time travel had set alarm bells ringing. What if this was nothing to do with HiQua? What if Hamiye wasn't worried about commercial secrets? What if it was all about time travel? What if they were hyper-sensitive to her presence on the payroll because there was a timesplash being planned—or could Hamiye even have plans to involve her?

Even so, she told herself, it was no reason to freeze to death in her car. She should just pass what she knew on to Jay and let him deal with it, let him tell the local police, or whatever the protocol was. The idea of turning the engine on and feeling warm air around her filled her with relief as she gave the command to switch on the car. Next time she went off chasing suspicious characters, she'd take a heavy coat with her, and some gloves, and a woolly hat, and a flask of—

She killed the engine and dropped down in her seat. Hamiye's car was pulling out of the main gate. It turned away from her and accelerated hard up the street towards the North Circular Road.

Now what? Follow him?

She dismissed the idea. She knew where to find Hamiye if she needed to. But Clarke Engineering, Ltd., on the other hand, was a mystery. Why would Hamiye drive straight there after she outed his little plot to bug her? Why was there a helicopter parked outside a crummy little engineering works? Who was in there and what were they doing? She hesitated, thinking again about warmth and comfort. "Bugger," she said and got out of the car.

$$* * * *$$

Olivia Bradley put down the phone and looked sheepishly at Jay. "Well, that seems to have settled that," she said.

Jay smiled. "The General explained that you can tell me anything at all about your work?"

"Oh, no question about it. He was most emphatic."

"Good." He turned to Laura. "Why don't you start by explaining why you thought bringing Olivia out here would be a good idea? Then Olivia can tell us if you were right."

They were in Laura's lab, in a small conference room off the main workshop area. The chairs were uncomfortable and the flask of filtered coffee Laura had set in the centre of the table contained a brew unfit for human consumption. He made a mental note to improve the conditions down there as soon as the current crisis was over.

"Well," Laura began, obviously wondering quite where to start. She guided a wave of hair off her face with the middle finger of her right hand and Jay noticed what a delicate gesture it was. "You know there has been a lot of academic work on time travel over the past couple of decades? Most of it has been trying to retrofit the work of Faber and Dickson into what we all thought we knew about physics." He knew about Faber and Dickson, a couple of unemployed doctoral students who, at the height of the global depression now called The Adjustment, had quite literally built the first lob site in their kitchen. Dickson had died of a drug overdose two years later and Faber was killed not long after in an accident at a splashparty when a lighting rig collapsed.

"It hasn't been a successful venture, so far," Olivia said.

Laura explained. "Before the new time formulae were worked out, we were struggling to unify relativity with quantum theory. Now we have a completely new understanding of time that fits with neither." Olivia wanted to jump in with something but Laura kept going. "Which is where Olivia comes in. I heard her ask a question at a conference recently that implied there had been some progress in fitting metatemporal pseudo-space with quantum theory—a many-worlds interpretation of the timefront."

Jay held up his hands. "I know you're dumbing it down for me, but you need to get a lot dumber than that before I can grasp what you're trying to tell me."

Laura eyed him sceptically, as if she thought he might be joking. "It sounded to me," she said, "as if Olivia had a handle on how the future arises from the present."

Jay caught his breath. "What?" He turned to Olivia. "Is she saying you've found a way to travel into the future? And you're working on that at Aldermaston?" It was a wild surmise but his imagination was on a hair trigger.

Olivia was shocked. "Good God, no! I mean..." She was flustered and for a moment looked from Jay to Laura and back without seeming to know what to say. "It's what the military wants, of course. They'd love us to build a FORESIGHT machine but we're miles away from that.

Honestly, we're still fiddling about with the basic theory. It'll be years before we know if a future shot is even possible."

Jay sat back, open mouthed. "But the future isn't made yet," he said. "Everybody knows that. The Universe we know stops at the present. The future is just a jumble. Chaos. It doesn't take form until…" His grasp on physics was tenuous at best. "Isn't the present like some kind of wave that moves into this future mish-mash and organizes it into the next moment, and then the next? How can you go forward in time if there's nothing there?" *And what would it mean?* he asked himself. *What could criminals and terrorists do if they could jump forward in time?* "Holy crap. Tell me this isn't true."

Olivia shook her head. "Well, it's not. It isn't true. It's just some scraps of theory and a lot of military wishful thinking."

"Foresight," Jay said, his voice weak with apprehension. "They've got a project up already to build it, haven't they?"

"All they've got is an acronym," Olivia said. "Future Observation and Reconnaissance Equipment for somethingorother Intelligence Gathering… Strategic, I think. No idea what the H stands for but the T is probably 'Time'. They want to be able to look ahead to see what the enemy is doing and then use that information to outsmart them. They see it as a sort of machine that can take spies into the future and bring them back again."

"The FORESIGHT machine," Jay said.

Olivia screwed up her face. "They might as well call it the TARDIS for all its resemblance to reality."

"Holy crap," he said again.

"You see why I asked Olivia to come?" Laura said.

"So Aldermaston caused last night's event?" Jay asked.

Olivia shook her head. "No way. I tell you, it's all airware at the moment, people sitting around with whiteboards drawing Hong diagrams."

"Hong diagrams?" Laura asked.

Olivia spoke quickly, apparently mostly focused on convincing Jay there was nothing to worry about. "It's a kind of vector that describes unfolding future possibilities at a quantum level. Derived from the Schrödinger equation. Very clever, actually. A sort of many-worlds Feynman diagram."

Jay and Laura watched her in silence until Jay said, in a flat voice, "Who's Hong?"

Olivia blinked at what she obviously saw as an irrelevant turn in the conversation. "He's a Chinese physicist. Was, I should say. He died in a fire or something, about three years ago. Pity, 'cause we could really have used someone like that in our lab."

Jay looked at Laura and she looked back at him, clearly thinking the same thing. He got up and walked across the room, feeling the urge to kick the furniture around, but holding it in. If the Chinese had developed a new time-travel technology... If they could see the future... None of his thoughts would resolve themselves. But it was all someone else's problem, anyway, not his. Espionage was another department. He tried to re-focus.

"You haven't run any experiments? Sent a mouse forwards or whatever?"

"Good God, no. I keep telling you. It's all a military wet dream at the moment."

"What about the Chinese?"

"The Chinese?"

"Could they be running experiments?"

The physicist bristled. "I hardly think so."

Jay ignored her wounded professional pride. "But they could, couldn't they? If they have a three-year head start? If

Hong isn't as dead as they say he is?"

"What? Now look, Jay, I know you're in intelligence and everything but that's no reason to be completely paranoid." Jay continued to stare at her, willing her to consider the possibility. She grew more irritable but said, "Even with Hong, we'd be ten years away from doing the kind of experiment you're talking about. Twenty, for all I know. It may be completely impossible. And, anyway…" She looked Jay in the eye and he could see she was about to deliver the *coup de grace*. "Even if FORESIGHT was working. Even if you could get inside it and visit the future, it wouldn't matter. The timestream only flows one way. There would be no backwash. It's a physical impossibility." She said it again with extra emphasis. "A physical impossibility, Jay. Whatever caused last night's weirdness was nothing to do with travelling to the future."

Chapter 9

Surprise

Sandra made her way through an adjoining property—a place selling carpets and floor tiles, closed up and abandoned for the duration—and climbed a fence at the back of Clarke Engineering. She was at a spot where there were few windows and piles of palettes. An abandoned forklift truck gave her some cover from any cameras that might be watching. The fence was strong and new and topped with razorwire. She had to hunt out a rubbish skip and retrieve a strip of discarded carpet to throw across the top of the fence before she dared attempt it. Her hands were almost numb with cold and she tumbled dangerously into the engineering-works yard when her grip on the fence failed. For a minute, she crouched behind the forklift, shivering, waiting to be sure no-one had seen her and raised the alarm.

All remained silent. She cut across to the wall of the building and peered in through a barred and dusty window. It was an empty room—some kind of storage area with electrical components in bins, reels of cable—nothing interesting. She moved on to the next window, then the next. It was the same. All the windows were barred and inside was nothing worth seeing.

She rounded a corner and moved along the back of the building. The wall ran unbroken for twenty meters, was punctuated by a door, then ran on again for maybe another twenty. The only windows were high and narrow, also barred. There was a large wooden reel lying in the yard on which heavy cable must once have been coiled. It comprised two wooden discs, with a fat, wooden axle connecting them. It was a meter across with a two meter diameter. Perfect. She heaved it onto its edge and rolled it over to one of the high windows. Then she pulled it onto its side again, cursing the weight of it, and climbed on top. By standing on tiptoes, she could get her nose over the windowsill and look inside.

She saw a large room with a bare concrete floor. Half a dozen people in white overalls moved about, tending equipment. Every one of them was Asian. The walls were lined with banks of grey electronics cabinets. The ones with glass fronts she could see were packed with circuit boards. Others had high voltage warning signs on them. She felt her stomach knot. Was she looking at supercapacitor arrays? She scanned the room quickly, searching for the chest-freezer-sized boxes she feared she would find. And there they were, stacked four high, filling the far corner: focus fusion reactors, enough to deliver hundreds of megawatts to the capacitor banks. And from there it would go to…

She had to strain her neck to follow the thick cables snaking away from the electronics to the low platform in the space below her window. For a temporal displacement rig, it was odd. The platform was circular and six tall columns rose up around it in a perfect hexagon. They curved towards one another, well above her eye level. Within this giant birdcage, at the dead centre of the platform, sat a black sphere, two meters in diameter. About the height of the tallest teknik tending the machines.

She had a sudden flashback to another room on another continent and another sphere, this one made of clear plastic. "Because it has to be done and no-one else can do it," a dead man's voice said in her memory.

Her heart was racing. Whatever fancy refinements they'd made, those stupid bastards at HiQua had built a lob site. What possible commercial benefit a lob into the past could give anybody, Sandra could not imagine—unless they planned to run it as some kind of fairground ride. There was always talk about so-called chronotourism. Entrepreneurs with more money than brain cells were always trying to get a scheme up and running, but no government would ever license them. The risks were far too great. She'd read speculation about sending microbots back in time to grab cells from extinct animals—gorillas, polar bears, even dodos—sequence their genes, and bring back the knowledge of how to remake them. Fine if you were a palaeontologist but unless you were raising the dead on a Jurassic Park scale, she still couldn't see what was in it for HiQua.

"Seen enough?"

She jumped so hard the reel she was on rattled. In a flash, she dropped to a crouch, turning to face whoever it was.

Farid Hamiye was standing well away from her, pointing a stunner at her chest. Her sudden reaction made his grin fade for a moment, but it was soon back in place. She had no cover except the reel she was standing on and the distance between them was too great for a surprise attack. Her heart was hammering, but she forced herself to remain calm. As casually as she could, she jumped down off the reel and stood facing him.

"I thought you'd gone," she said, cursing herself for letting him creep up on her.

"Well, that makes two of us. Lucky I spotted your car parked in the road as I drove away. If I hadn't come back to investigate, I might never have had the chance to meet you again." She smiled and took a step towards him, needing to close the distance. He took a step back. "Don't," he said, "or I will shoot you."

She stopped and raised her hands, still smiling. "I suppose you're wondering what I'm doing here."

He smiled back. He had a great smile. "I suppose you're going to give me a load of rubbish about getting lost or some—"

She dived right, hearing the whine of the stunner's discharge as she hit the concrete and rolled, then up onto her feet and into a headlong charge straight for him. He'd missed and that meant she still had a chance to reach him and disarm him. But he was cool, and fast. His second shot hit her in the shoulder and her body convulsed as fifty thousand volts streaked through her nervous system, clenching every muscle, blasting her thoughts to fragments. The last thing she felt was skidding across the ground to fetch up at his beautiful shoes.

* * * *

"No, you're not listening to me." Cara tried to keep the tears out of her voice. Why wouldn't the stupid man just listen?

"I'm sure she's all right, darling," Jay said. "She's just a bit late, that's all."

"No. Someone came to the house. She went after them. Now she hasn't even called for more than two hours. She's in trouble, Dad." *And I'm stuck at Gran's,* she thought, *and you're over there in Berlin.* "You have to do something. You have to come here and find her. It's happening all over again."

"I can't, Cara. You know I can't. I've got a whole section to run and there's a crisis on. Your mum's a very resourceful woman, she'll—"

Cara shouted over him. "If you tell me that one more time I'm going to scream!" She took a breath. "Look, you know what it means if someone's stalking Mum again. You of all people know what kind of danger she's in if one of your old enemies gets his hands on her. Why won't you do something? And after last night too! Do you think it's just a coincidence that the whole world turns to shit and the next day people turn up looking for Mum? Do you?"

Jay was beginning to look exasperated. "Yes," he said. "Yes I do think it's a coincidence. What happened last night wasn't a timesplash. Maybe it has nothing to do with time travel at all." He paused for a moment and Cara thought he looked a bit shifty, as if he didn't really believe what he was saying. When he spoke again, he was on a fresh tack. "Your mum's been in touch with me during the day. It all sounds like some kind of mix-up. It's something to do with that company she works for. They've dug into her past and made the MI5 connection and now they think she's some kind of spy. That's why they sent someone to bug the house. It's all just a misunderstanding, honey. Yes, she thinks there's a time-travel connection but you know your mum: she sees ghosts from her past behind every tree."

None of which convinced Cara. "So you're just going to abandon her?"

"No! Of course I'm not. I'll do something, all right? I'll sort something out."

"What?"

"Something." He looked irritated. "I don't know, but it's a storm in a teacup, you'll see."

Cara could see she wasn't going to get any farther. "It better be nothing, for your sake."

"For my sake?"

"If I tell Mum you just left her alone to die, she'll come over there and kick your arse. And you know she can."

Her father's face was a scowl. "No-one's going to die, all right? Least of all your mother." Again he had that shifty look.

"So you're going to do something?"

"I said I would." Cara humphed, letting her displeasure show. "Look, I've got to go," Jay said. "You haven't been worrying your gran with all this nonsense, have you?"

"Of course not! And it's not nonsense!"

Jay gave a non-committal smile. "I really have to go, love. Say hello to Gran—and to Sandra when she gets home."

He'd hung up before she had time to remonstrate. *Bloody man!* How could her own father be such an idiot? She should get on a plane and go over there, bang on his office door and demand that he do something.

Or…

She put in another call. "Dom?"

A young man with ginger hair and a long face stared at her in surprise. "Cara? I mean… Hi! How's it going? Wow! What about last night, eh?"

"Shut up, Dom, and listen. You're, like, a genius hacker, right?"

Caught between the scent of trouble and the opportunity to show off to the beautiful Cara, the young man hesitated. "Well…"

"I need a favour," she said. "I'd owe you big time." Cara

was used to boys doing her favours. But Dom was wavering still. What was wrong with the boy?

"Please, Dom," she said, wheedling.

"I'd like to," he said, still uncertain. "What is it you want?"

She smiled at him. "Oh, thank you. I just need you to hack someone's commplant."

"What? Whose?"

She took that as an admission that he could do it. "My mother's. She's in trouble and I need to find her. I want you to look at her commplant and tell me where she is."

"Your mother's gone missing? Have you called the police? Was she caught in the quake?"

Cara shook her head. "It's not like that. And I don't want the police involved. Look, I can't really explain, but I have to find her. Will you do it?"

He looked pained. "Well, I suppose I could reach in and extract her Galileo coordinates. It would be pretty easy if you could get me a couple of numbers off her installation documentation."

"No problem." She had full access to the household files. "When can you start?"

"As soon as I get the details from you."

Cara was already searching through the documents. She'd have to make up some story for her gran but that wouldn't be too hard. She'd probably need a car too. She set an agent hunting through local hire companies for the cheapest deal. She started thinking about what she needed to take with her.

As she worked, memories started to slide into her mind unbidden. Waking up a prisoner in Duvalle's house in Washington; her mother face down on the floor of Polanski's lob site; a dead FBI agent lying on top of her as machine-gun rounds zipped past like angry wasps. A shudder went through her and she gritted her teeth. It wouldn't be like that. Not this time. She'd just go and get her mum and it would all be over. She fought the clenching of her stomach, the tightening of her throat. She had to go get her mum, no matter what. If it had been the other way round, her mum would take on any odds to save her. She knew that for a fact because she'd seen it. Now it was her turn.

She wished she were just a bit more like her mother—fearless and strong and capable. "Well I'm not," she said aloud, angrily. "I'm just me and that'll have to do."

"Cara?" Dominic was looking at her anxiously. "Is someone else with you?"

"What? Never mind. I've got the documents. What do you need?"

* * * *

Jay stared at the wall for a long time after the call with Cara. His relationship with his eighteen-year-old daughter was complicated. He still felt a vague guilt about having missed the first sixteen years of her life even though it had been Sandra who had kept their daughter's existence a secret all that time. Which meant that along with the vague guilt was a very focused anger. He had been furious with Sandra.

Yet, for Cara's sake, he and Sandra had maintained what little relationship they had and even built on it over the past two years as Jay tried to spend as much time as possible with his daughter. He still felt the anger. It still came between them. But, truth be told, sometimes he needed to deliberately fan the flames these days. Now he had to fight the urge to forgive and forget, to let go of his feelings of betrayal, the grief for a loss he had not even known he'd suffered. His therapist—and without that support he felt he might have gone mad these past two years—told him to let go of his anger and move on with his life.

Jay looked down at his hands, clenched into fists on the desktop. What his therapist didn't seem to understand was that, without this anger he knew he would forgive Sandra anything—even keeping Cara from him—and go running to her like a doting puppy. His love for Sandra was a weakness, a mental aberration. It had blighted his life, and he would not give in to it like an addict begging for another fix.

For his own peace of mind, he sometimes wished he might never see Sandra again—but there was always Cara. She wasn't a child any more, yet he still felt she needed him, needed both of them, and needed them to be friends. That dreadful time in Washington had set their relationship on a strange and, he thought, precarious footing. She thought of him as a hero, the man who had flown halfway across the world to rescue her mother and who had succeeded in getting them both out of an insanely dangerous situation. But Jay knew he was no hero. He was no braver than the next man and his rescue of Sandra and Cara from Washington had been simple good luck. It could so easily have gone the other way.

So he'd been at pains to disabuse Cara of the notion, to emphasise the dullness and routine of his life, his own ordinariness. And now, maybe, she might believe him at last, now that he'd refused to come to her aid, refused to take her concerns seriously, acted like the craven bureaucrat he wanted her to believe he was. The last thing in the world he wanted was for Cara to see his world as glamorous. He wanted her future to be safe and stable and very, very dull. That way she might live to a comfortable old age.

He should be feeling good about it, he supposed, and yet

he felt awful. He felt as if he'd stabbed himself in the heart. The idea that his lovely Cara might stop seeing him as her white knight was surprisingly painful.

He pulled up the file on Farid Hamiye again. His search agents had added more information about the man's past. It seemed he had fought in several of the internecine wars that plagued his native Lebanon but had moved beyond that to become a mercenary for hire across the Middle East. When he moved to Europe a few years ago, he had been a genuine refugee, with a price on his head offered by at least three Islamic militias—one of which had since formed a government in part of the old Saudi Arabia. He sounded like a dangerous and ruthless man. He looked it too.

Jay got up and went to the lift, taking it down to the first basement level where Lieutenant Pierre Fourget and his team had their office-cum-gym-cum-firing range. Fourget was there, sitting at a virtual display, moving his hands through the sensor field. There was almost no-one else around in the large, open space. On seeing Jay, the Frenchman raised his eyebrows and grunted a greeting.

"Pierre." Jay pulled up a chair and sat facing him. "I need you to do me a favour."

Fourget settled back and regarded Jay with his steady blue eyes. It used to unnerve Jay that the lieutenant spoke so little, but he had gradually come to appreciate the man as a calm and peaceful soul. He needed no pleasantries, offered no gossip, stuck to the point and said only what he knew to be true. In their way, the two men had become friends. Others in the office thought it was odd. Fourget was stocky and solid where Jay was tall and slender. The younger man was taciturn to the point of rudeness, while Jay was friendly and polite to the point of deference. Fourget was a soldier, a trained and effective killing machine. Jay was the contemplative, almost intellectual type. Then there was the French and English thing. It was hard for people to see what the two men had in common. But Jay saw it and so did Fourget. On the day they met, Fourget had said, "You look like an academic, but I have read your file, Monsieur. Welcome to K Section." Jay had shaken the proffered hand and the two had never looked back.

"I want you to find a friend of mine and make sure she's all right," Jay said.

A small frown creased Fourget's broad brow.

"It's not entirely personal," said Jay, "but it's nothing to do with the current crisis. I'd have trouble explaining this to Crystal, but my friend believes she has stumbled onto someone in London who may have something to do with timesplashing. Now she's gone missing and I can't raise her by phone. So I want you to check that she is all right. You don't have to go yourself, but send someone good."

Fourget's blue eyes did not flicker. "Your friend, she is Sandra Malone, *oui?*"

Jay took a breath. This would look bad if Sandra was just being paranoid and Crystal ever did hear about it. He reminded himself that he'd promised Cara he'd do something. The poor girl was probably sitting at home trusting that he had things in hand. "Yes, it's Sandra."

Fourget nodded. "Then I will go myself."

Jay had a sudden attack of conscience. "I don't want to jeopardise your work here. This has to be our top priority."

"My teams do all the work. I merely coordinate. I can coordinate from London just as well. Besides, we are not finding anything." His shrug was eloquent. He might as well be out there doing something useful.

"Thank you, Pierre. I'll send you everything I have. When can you start?"

Fourget stood up and grinned. "I just did."

Chapter 10

Precipice

The voices were not loud but, even with her eyes closed, Sandra could tell a lot about the three speakers. One was an older man with a Chinese accent. He was anxious, frightened even, and very unhappy about what was going on. The second was younger, more confident, angry. He also had a hint of Chinese in his accent. This one is the boss, she told herself. The third was also a man, young, vigorous and larger than the others. His cultured tones were also confident but she could hear the irritation behind the overblown English politeness. She knew their names too, having listened to them for a couple of minutes, pretending to be unconscious still. The old one was called Hong, Dr Hong, the boss was Lee, Mr Lee to the others, and the young man was her old friend Farid Hamiye.

"No," Hong was saying. "You *can't* keep her here." He'd said the same thing in various ways several times now. "This is a research establishment, not a prison. Mr Lee, you must understand. My staff are already jumpy. They think... Well, you know what they think. How do you suppose it affects them to see..." he hesitated "... this person carrying an unconscious woman through the building?"

"What was I supposed to do with her, Doctor? Throw her in the recycling bin?"

"I do not care what you do with her! Mr Lee, you must see that this is intolerable."

There was a silence as they waited for Lee's pronouncement. Eventually, he asked, "Whatever made her come snooping around here? Does it make sense to you, Farid?"

She could hear the smile in the big man's voice. "Why don't we ask her? She's been conscious for at least the past two minutes."

It sounded as if Hong swore in Chinese while Lee gave an exasperated tut. Sandra opened her eyes and gave Hamiye a baleful glare. She could see now what she had only felt so far, that she was duct-taped to an office chair. She turned her gaze to Lee, a tall, good-looking man, impeccably dressed, who regarded her with an expression of distaste. "Would you mind telling me," she asked, "what the hell you think you're doing?" Her eyes flicked towards Hamiye. "Your pet monkey drew a stunner on me and shot me without provocation. Now it seems I have been kidnapped and tied to a chair. I insist you release me this minute or I will call the police."

Lee looked across at Hamiye, who said, "It's OK, this facility is shielded. No-one can call in or out except through the comms gateway. I set it up so we could keep an eye on the staff."

Lee nodded, satisfied. He turned back to Sandra. "Why are you spying on us, Ms Malone?"

"You should call me Sandra. I think it's really creepy when the evil gang bosses get all formal like that. Besides which, it was your bad boy here who started it. He sent some clowns round to my house to bug it."

"We know you work for MI5, Sandra," Lee said.

"You don't know shit, fancy pants, and your pal Farid just brought down a ton of trouble on all your heads. Hong?" She turned to the scruffy physicist. "Do you have any idea how illegal it is to build a displacement rig? Since what happened to Washington, the new laws would put you and your fellow conspirators away for life. And quite rightly too. Are you all insane?"

Hong put his head in his hands and sat down heavily on the edge of his desk. He said something plaintive in Chinese and Lee snapped back at him in the same language. Then Lee turned to Hamiye. "Hong's right, she knows too much. You need to take care of this."

Hamiye's face was very still as he asked, "What did you have in mind?"

Hong was on his feet again in a hurry. "No, no! You cannot kill her. I won't have that. There will be no killing."

Sandra didn't like the way this conversation was going. She should have called Cara before she came in—or Jay. Now she wouldn't get a chance. She heaved at the tape binding her but it didn't give at all.

"Don't worry, Hong," Lee said. "We could not kill her now if we wanted to."

"Why not?" Sandra and Hamiye asked at the same time.

"Because half an hour before you brought her in, I called Waxtead and told him the woman's name. I made him call his friend, the Minister of State at the Home Office, and complain about how MI5 had sent her to spy on us. I imagine that, by now, the head of MI5 will have the name Sandra Malone ringing in his ears. If she turns up dead, there will be a chain of suspicion pointing right back to me, personally. If she merely disappears, there will also be suspicion, but at least there will be no body and I won't be under arrest." He said this last part with a meaningful look at Hamiye.

Hamiye's face remained blank.

Lee went on. "But that is all right. We have two more trips planned. One for tomorrow and one in two weeks. Tomorrow's trip will go ahead as planned. The final trip will be brought forward. Can you do it two days after the next one, Doctor?"

Hong blustered and shook his head. "Absolutely not! We need to recalibrate after tomorrow's shot. There may be re-engineering. Reprogramming… I would need a week at least!"

"Three days," Lee said.

"No, it can't be done so soon. It would mean—"

"Dr Hong!" It was the first time Lee had raised his voice and it shut the doctor up at once. Sandra studied the dapper executive more carefully, trying to see what it was about him that could scare the old man so much. "Could you do it in three days if your life depended on it?"

Without speaking, Hong nodded.

"Farid," Lee said. "You will keep the woman locked up somewhere—here if you like—until after the second trip. Four days, that's all. Hong will set aside a secure room for you. Do you think you can do that without screwing up?"

Hamiye was clearly offended by Lee's tone but he directed his anger at Sandra. "Yes," he said, glaring at her. "Of course."

"Good. After the second shot, this whole operation is over. There will be a fire at this facility that will destroy all evidence of our involvement. You understand? Not that it matters, because we will all have left the country by then. You can do what you like with the woman once I'm gone."

* * * *

Dominic's grinning face appeared in the display. Cara grinned back, guessing he had good news. "Well?" she asked.

"Your mum's commplant is off the grid."

"What?"

"Either she shut it down, or she's somewhere with no signal at all."

"That isn't possible." There was nowhere in the whole of Europe that didn't have net coverage. It was a well-known fact. But then, the infrastructure had taken a beating the night before and there might still be places with no signal. No— she'd just seen a newsfeed item about the government launching thousands of comms balloons and drones to make sure every inch of the UK was covered during the reconstruction.

"It's as if she's left the country, or is being jammed," Dominic said. He was still grinning and it was starting to annoy Cara.

"So?"

"So I hacked into her location log. Every commplant keeps a record of where you've been for the past forty-eight hours. It's required by the 2053 Detection of Crimes Act."

"So you traced her movements?"

"Yes, to a place called Clarke Engineering in Enfield. That's where the signal stopped."

Cara was already pulling up a map of the area. Enfield was a suburb in North London, just inside the M25 motorway. If she had a car she could be there in an hour or so. She looked at Dominic, who was still grinning, waiting for his pat on the head. "Where do you live?" she asked, but she got his profile up quicker than he could answer. He was miles away in Preston, Lancashire. "That's no good. OK, thanks Dom." She cut the call just as his grin began to waver.

She checked the time. Early evening. Was there such a thing as a twenty-four-hour car-hire service around where her gran lived? She queried her search agent. If she couldn't find anything, she'd call a taxi. She'd use the emergency credit line her mum had set up for this kind of situation and hang the expense. It could be life or death.

It was only as she started to call the car-hire company that she had her first misgivings. If her mother was a prisoner at this Clarke Engineering place, they must have guns, or plenty of hired muscle, or something. She'd seen Sandra fight and no-one could have taken her without a major struggle. So how was she going to get her out of there?

In her running-away bag she had a stunner and a hunting knife. It would have been enough for her mum to storm an enemy stronghold but not Cara. Sandra had tried making her take karate lessons with that old fraud Tom in the high street but that kind of thing had never interested her. "I'm the brains of the family," she'd said. "I'll leave the rough stuff to you." She'd stuck with the firearms training long enough to learn how to use a handgun and to hit the target most of the time but, again, it had not held her interest.

Truth be told, the violence Cara had seen in Washington still filled her with fear, still haunted her dreams. It had been shocking, stomach turning, and she had a dread of it ever happening again. She'd seen a man beaten to death, two men shot, her own mother beaten senseless…

Fighting was something she wanted no part of. Learning to fight seemed like inviting the violence back into her life.

And yet, here she was again, with her mother missing, probably in danger, needing to do something about it, and being hopelessly feeble and helpless. She felt her stomach clench and tasted bile in her throat. "Oh no," she said aloud. "No, no, no. You're not going to pieces while Mum needs you."

She finished the call and ordered the car. It would take almost an hour to drive itself to her because so many London roads were designated non-automatic until the worst of the debris had been cleared away and damaged roadside beacons had been repaired. Cara didn't mind. She had lots to do. She needed to study this Clarke Engineering place and find out what she could about it. She should maybe call her father again and try again to persuade him to help. Then she had to talk to her gran and either explain everything or make up a really good lie.

* * * *

They waited in the hotel bar while Olivia went up to her room "to freshen up" as she put it. Jay looked around at the luxurious furnishings and fittings, the brass and chrome, the deep carpets. "I hate hotels," he said.

Laura smiled. "They are all about mitigation," she said. She seemed cheerful, in contrast to Jay's mood. "The people who run this place know you don't want to be here. So they try to make it as painless as possible by giving you as little as possible to complain about. I suppose you are trying to say that you have travelled too much and stayed in too many places like this." She sipped her drink and smiled again.

"You'd never think there's a global crisis going on beyond these walls." It seemed immoral somehow that there was muzak playing and he was sitting there, warm and comfortable, sharing a drink with a charming woman.

"Do you ever relax, Jay?" She was being playful, teasing him, as if they were on a date or something. And the idea rekindled the memory of the night before and all the implications of what Cara's doppelgänger had said. It was as if he'd walked into a parallel universe in which Sandra was dead and he was finally free to enjoy the company of another love. He looked at Laura looking quizzically back at him. She was attractive, intelligent. Again he wondered what it would be like to spend his days with a woman like her.

"Tell me how you got on with Olivia this afternoon," he said, pushing the idea aside. "Did you make any progress?"

Her mouth opened in surprise, then a hint of mischief appeared about her eyes. "We had a long chat about Sandra Malone," she said, watching him. "She sounds like an extraordinary woman. Tell me about her."

"She… er… What?" He frowned, irritated with himself for being so easily thrown off-balance. "Well, there's nothing to tell. She's just someone I knew a long time ago."

"Someone who was in Washington with you when AR2 started."

AR2 was what the media had taken to calling the long-running war in the U.S.. "Olivia talks too much."

"And you barely talk at all—except about work. Olivia says you rushed over to the States to save the fair Sandra like a knight of old rescuing a beautiful princess."

"It wasn't like that. Can we get back to why we're here?"

Jay felt hypocritical saying it. When Laura had told him she was having dinner with Olivia at her hotel and asked if he'd like to join them, he'd said yes straight away. He was exhausted after a sleepless night and a stressful day and he'd thought only about how pleasant it would be to have dinner with Laura. And now he was playing the grumpy, work-obsessed boss, trying to shut down the conversation.

"I don't want to talk about Sandra," he said. At least that was honest.

She eyed him speculatively. "I don't really want to talk about her either. I really just wanted you to open up. We've worked together for a long time now but I don't actually know anything about you. Would it not be nicer if we were friends? I sometimes look at you and think you need a friend. Someone close."

Jay opened his mouth to speak but had no idea what to say. The moment was a precipice. Say one thing and he might step over into the dizzy, thrilling tumble of a relationship with this woman. Say another and he could step back onto the safe, level ground of his lonely life. He drew a breath, not yet knowing which way the world would turn.

"Hello, you two. I hope I didn't keep you waiting too long."

Jay looked up at Olivia as she bustled about taking a seat and let out his breath, leaning back in his chair. Laura too, he noticed, leaned back.

"We were just chatting," he said. "Laura was about to fill me in on what you two came up with to explain last night."

"Ha!" Olivia exclaimed. "That won't take long." She started off on a rambling excursion through the improbable scenarios they had explored and the scant evidence they had collected.

Jay turned as casually as he could to look at Laura and found her studying him, deep in thought.

Chapter 11

Convergence

Jay had told him not to worry about costs, that he'd sign off on anything he felt he needed. So Fourget took one of the department's private planes and hired a fast car when he reached Heathrow. On the way, he had the techs trace Sandra Malone's commplant and spent some time studying her file and re-reading Jay's. Of course, Jay's file was restricted but that had never stopped him in the past. He had learned early in his career that the more you knew about what you were up against and who you were working with, the longer you survived.

At twenty-eight, the lieutenant had seen plenty of action, at first as an infantryman in the EDF's endless border wars with the Middle East and the former Russian Republic, and later as a commando in special operations farther afield. He had distinguished himself in every role he'd been given and EDF MI had rewarded him with his current job in K Section—Temporal Counter-Terrorism. He was military to the core and hated the EDF MI practice of using civilian management in some of its more sensitive sections, but Jay Kennedy was all right. Jay was ex-MI5 and had seen plenty of action in Europol's Temporal Crimes Unit. He'd also been instrumental in saving Berlin and London from devastating timesplashes and, in Washington, had shown the kind of courage under fire that only someone who had been in similar situations himself could appreciate.

If Jay Kennedy had been in the military, he would have had a chest full of medals by now.

The London streets were more of a mess than those he had left behind in Berlin. The English didn't have the same efficiency and pride in their work as their German cousins. Many streets were still designated non-auto and he had to drive himself or endure major detours. Fortunately the M25 had been cleared and, once he reached that, he could let the car drive itself and get back to his studies.

Sandra Malone was an interesting character. Despite what Jay had said about her having potentially useful information, Fourget had suspected this mission was based on purely personal motives. The photos and video of her in the file added to his cynicism. The woman looked and moved like a supermodel. She was outrageously beautiful. It would be easy to imagine a quiet, socially awkward man like Jay Kennedy being hopelessly, idiotically infatuated with such a woman. However, now that he'd learned more, he wasn't so sure.

Malone was way more than just a pretty face. She had degrees in physics and temporal engineering and had worked as a teknik, building long-range displacement rigs for a British university—until some crazy in the U.S. had kidnapped her to help build the rig that destroyed Washington. Since then she'd had a few menial jobs—either lying low or establishing a cover, he guessed. She'd saved Jay's life once in Berlin, and had been on the timesplash with him that had saved London. Orphaned early, a splashparty girl from the age of fourteen, she had been the bitch of one, if not two, of Europe's leading bricks back in the day.

So, intelligent, beautiful, and with a taste for psychopathic men. She also had a black belt, eighth dan, in Shotokan karate. Used to compete for her university karate club. He would never have guessed it to look at her. And there was another surprise. She had a daughter, Cara.

He wondered where the daughter was now and if she was involved somehow. He pulled up the file. A psychology student. Also tall and beautiful—although nowhere near as stunning as her mother. Her file was thin. It did contain two other surprises that set Fourget rubbing his chin. The first was that Cara's father was Jason Kennedy. Having a daughter was something his boss had never mentioned once in the two years he had known him—probably not to anybody, since the gossip would have reached him if anyone else at the office knew. The second was that Cara Malone had also been in Washington with her parents, although she had been just fifteen at the time. The Malone women clearly started their lives of adventure and danger early.

He made a note of Cara's netID and home address and closed the files. It may or may not be important to know about Jay's secret daughter but Fourget liked to set up the future so that the dice fell his way as often as possible.

* * * *

The hire car rolled up outside her gran's house and called her to say it had arrived.

"I don't know, Cara," Dot said. "Your mum should be here by now. I don't like it that I can't call her."

Cara bent down and kissed her cheek. "Oh, the comms

are down all over still. She'll call when she can." She tried one more time to put the old woman's mind at rest. "Mum knows about the party. It's all arranged. She knows I don't get to see my friends in London very often. She's fine with it, honest."

Her grandmother sighed. "Maybe I should call Jay?"

Cara put on a smile. "Yes, you should. I'm sure he'll be fine." She could imagine her father's reaction when he heard she'd gone off on her own. He'd go through the roof. Well it would serve him right. Maybe he'd do something about it then instead of just sitting around in his office... doing whatever the hell he was doing. "I think he's a bit busy at the moment. Look, the car's arrived. I'd better get going."

"Does your mother know you go out dressed like that?"

"Like what?" She'd had to dress up a bit to match her cover story, which was a pain, but she'd kept it as low-key as possible, and wore nothing she couldn't climb a wall in.

Her grandma shook her head. "Never mind. You know, I can still remember the very first day I saw your mum. She was even younger than you are and she had on just a simple summer dress, but she looked like she'd just walked off the page of a fashion magazine. I was so pleased for Jay, and so worried that she'd break his heart. She was so... out of his league, I suppose."

Cara was acutely aware of the seconds ticking by, but she said, "She's not, you know. She still loves him. She's never loved anyone else."

"Then why aren't they...?" But they both knew the answer to that. "Oh, never mind. You have a lovely evening, and try not to get home too late."

Cara gave her a smile. "I'll try."

The hire car was a little, underpowered affair but there was no chance of driving fast with the roads the way they were anyway, so that didn't bother her. She gave it the address of Clarke Engineering and let it take her at its best speed. On the way, she called Dominic again. A transparent display of his face appeared on the inside of her windscreen.

"Any news?"

"News?"

"Dom, I'm trusting you to keep track of my mum's commplant signal. You're doing that, aren't you?"

"I thought—"

"Dom! I need to know where she is. I'm in a car heading for that place now. I don't want to get there and find she's moved on."

"Hang on." There was a thirty-second silence as he looked through her to the other elements open on his display. "No. She's still there. Hasn't left for a moment."

Cara absorbed the news. "What is that place, Dom? What do they do there?"

This time her friend was on the ball. "Light engineering. They fabricate machine parts for small robots and the like. They supply factories. You know the kind of thing—a shed full of industrial fabbers printing out bearings and cams. They're part of the HiQua group. You know that mega corp that makes all kind of shit?"

"HiQua? You're sure?"

"I'm looking at their corporate structure right now."

"Bugger."

"What's up?"

"It's the company my mother works for."

"What does that mean?"

Cara had no idea at all. It might mean the whole thing was completely innocent and she was getting as paranoid as her mother, chasing around in the night, seeing dangers everywhere.

"Why would a light engineering company have a commplant suppressor installed, Dom?"

"I dunno. They put them in at concert halls and such so that people don't start yakking in the middle of the show."

"Not helpful."

"Some places have them so that their staff don't make social calls or play online games during work hours."

"They don't do that where Mum works. I call her all the time."

Dominic shrugged.

"Do you have a floor plan?"

"I've got the usual satellite images."

"Yeah, I've got those. I need floor plans."

Dominic squirmed as if he was fighting the urge to run. "I suppose I could dig around for plans—maybe at the local planning department or something but that would be—"

"Illegal. Yeah. But this is important, Dom. Really, really important."

He hesitated more than she liked to see. "OK. I'll take a look, but if I get busted I'm saying you hypnotised me or something."

"You're an angel."

"Yeah."

She hung up and watched the streets roll by. She tried calling Jay but all she got was his answering service. She didn't leave a message. With a heavy sigh, she slumped down into her seat. She supposed she'd better start thinking about what to do when she got there.

* * * *

Farid Hamiye left Sandra tied up in one of Hong's storerooms and went off to the little kitchen to get himself a coffee. He was not a happy man.

He didn't like one single thing about this situation. He didn't like having a British secret service officer tied up in a storeroom. He didn't like the way Lee was so casually intent on having her killed. He didn't like that Dr Hong had gone into a funk, or that the technical staff were standing around in small groups muttering. He especially didn't like the way his prisoner's eyes followed him around, like some kind of predator waiting for a chance to jump him and tear his throat out.

It was all very well for Lee to tell him to hold the woman there for four days, but if anyone wanted to know where she was, it would be child's play to find out. He needed to move her as soon as possible. Which gave him another thought. If someone did come looking for the woman—and the chances were good—he didn't have a hope of protecting the place on his own.

So he made some calls to set things up as soon as Lee flew off in the helicopter. He'd much rather have got in a plane and flown away himself, but, if he could just keep this thing together for four more days, he'd have enough money that he would never need to work for men like Lee again.

There were two technicians talking quietly in Mandarin when he entered the kitchen. They shut up as soon as they saw him, and left the room. It seemed pretty clear to him that Hong's people were psyching themselves up to walk out on the job.

An odd thought struck him. *Why was the whole special projects team Chinese?* It had never occurred to him to wonder before, taking it as read that Lee and Hong would hire people they knew and trusted. Now, suddenly, it seemed sinister.

His phone chirruped and he took the call. "Mr Hamiye, we're approaching the factory."

"Good. There's a delivery dock on the west side of the building. Park there and wait. I'll be out in a moment. And be discreet."

"Of course."

He grabbed a chocolate bar and a can of something fizzy and headed for the side exit. A large black van was pulling in as he left the building. His own car was parked nearby. The van sat quietly, its engine off. He crossed to it and a man emerged.

He was a giant, tall enough and broad enough to make Hamiye look slight beside him. He wore combat pants and a black singlet under a lightweight bulletproof vest. His bare arms were massive trunks of knotted muscle, his neck a sinewy column on which sat a head that seemed carved from granite. A submachine gun hung on a clip at his hip. It looked like a toy beside his beefy hand. From his size-fourteen army boots to his close-cropped blond hair, everything about the man said do not fuck with me.

"You must be Langbroek," Hamiye said. He didn't offer a hand.

The man-mountain gave a nod. "You Hamiye?"

"Yes, I am. Let's see the rest of your team."

Langbroek slapped the side of the van and the door slid open. Four more giants in combat gear climbed out. One of them was a woman but she was hardly less heavily muscled than her male companions. They eyed Hamiye with steady scowls that seemed to have been chiselled onto their stone faces. *All part of the theatre,* Hamiye thought. The muscles, the clothes, the weapons, even the bandanna the woman wore, were all part of the show these guys put on to scare away the faint-hearted. Not that they weren't tough sons of bitches. Hormone cocktails, gene work and surgery were just the beginning for these guys. They probably also had carbon-fibre-reinforced bones, amped-up metabolisms and, just for good measure, enough amphetamines in their system to outrun a racehorse.

"This is the mission," he said, turning back to Langbroek. "This building is quarantined. No-one gets in and no-one gets out for the next four days. It's an easy job and I don't expect any trouble. The people inside are just scientists and technicians. There shouldn't be any visitors. There are only two entrances and all the windows are barred. I want this to be low profile but, if there's trouble, I need you to handle it, quickly and efficiently. Just keep the place locked down for four days. I'll be on this netID if you need a decision on anything." He touched Langbroek's arm and transferred the data. The man's bare skin was hot despite the freezing weather. "I'll be back at the end of four days and it's all over. Any questions?"

Langbroek took his time thinking about it. "When you say quarantine—"

"I don't mean there's any disease outbreak. It's nothing like that. The work going on in there is top secret. We're in the final phase of it and I don't want news leaking because some disgruntled worker decides to talk to the press or whatever."

Again Langbroek pondered. "Is it legal, what you're doing in there?"

"Does it matter?"

The giant pursed his lips and shook his head.

"If the cops come sniffing and they don't have a warrant,

refer them to me. If they do, call me and stand by. OK? I need you to help me organize a couple of things and then the place is all yours."

Hamiye led the giant through the building, past shocked and gaping technicians, to Dr Hong's office. There he explained, with two hundred kilos of scowling muscle at his elbow, that Hong and his team were not to leave the building for any reason. The old man blustered and threatened him with Lee, then with Waxtead, then with a refusal to work.

Hamiye let him sound off for a while then said, "Doctor, the only way you will ever leave this building alive is to complete the project. On schedule. Now, it's just four days and no-one was going to get any sleep in that time anyway, were they? So it's hardly a big deal. I'll send in some campbeds tomorrow. You can call Lee by all means. He will tell you to stop making a fuss and get on with the job. If you call Waxtead, I will have Mr Langbroek break your legs. Do you understand me?"

Hong regarded Langbroek with wide-eyed horror. He swallowed hard and nodded.

"Excellent. I'll leave you to explain it to the staff." He left and Langbroek followed him.

He found Sandra Malone with the tape around her right wrist almost cut through. She glared at him with animal ferocity as he walked in. Then her snarl faded as she noticed his massive companion. Hamiye crossed quickly to her, irritated that she had almost freed herself. He grabbed her right hand and examined it. She held a button, pulled from the cuff of her blouse. It looked like the other buttons but its edge had been filed sharp, no doubt just for this purpose. He studied it for a moment in amazement. She had not had time to plan for the unlikely contingency that someone would tie her to a chair before she left home that morning... which meant she was always ready for it. Probably all her shirts had sharpened buttons on them. What kind of woman was this? He stepped back, threw the button aside, and looked at her. She was studying him and Langbroek. He could see her eyes darting back and forth, planning her moves. If he cut her free and tried to take her out to the car, she would attack both of them. It was unnerving. It was as if the odds didn't matter to her or, if they did, she was confident of her chances. Somehow the bulk of Langbroek at his back didn't reassure him. The big man and the small room made him feel hemmed in, vulnerable. If this spitfire were let loose he would need more room to manoeuvre.

He drew his stunner. Her eyes widened in surprise the instant before he fired.

* * * *

Fourget studied the Clarke Engineering building from a distant rooftop. The lenses and electronics in his face mask amplified the dim light to the point where the night seemed like day; they magnified the image so that he could see the registration number of the black van parked by the loading dock; and their augmented reality software, working with the building plans, made it seem as if he could see through the outer walls to the rooms within. The full-body combat suit he wore was just a precaution but at least it kept him comfortably warm despite the bitter cold.

This was the third vantage point he'd used to study the building and he thought he understood the situation well enough. Every car in the parking lot belonged to a HiQua employee, except for the black van. Infra-red revealed that the number of people in the building squared with the number of cars and the number of employees, except for five extremely bright signatures that probably belonged to the van.

He knew very well what such bright IR signatures meant: he'd seen them often enough on combat missions. Hamsters—hormonally augmented mercenary soldiers— whose metabolisms ran far higher than normal so that they could manage their supersized bodies at a rate that would kill a normal human being. They were super-soldiers, strong and fast, with genetic modifications that gave them big advantages over anyone else they were likely to come up against. Tough sons of bitches, made unstable and mean by the shit they took to maintain their powerhouse physiques.

Someone was paying a lot to make sure that building stayed secure. Five hamsters were enough to hold off a small army. Fourget had however failed to find any sign of a captive inside the building. So what were they guarding? He itched to get over there and take a look. Jay had said the Malone woman had a lead on some illegal time-travel technology. Something at least that big was going down here, but his primary mission was to find Sandra Malone—and he did not want to risk getting tangled up with those hamsters. That would be suicide.

His mask optics had been recording everything he saw. He packaged it up and squirted it back to Jay on a secure channel along with a quick message saying he was moving on to locate "the target". Jay could send a team to investigate if he wanted to—a big, well-armed team. Meanwhile—

He froze. He'd seen movement in the property next to the Clarke Engineering building. A cat? An urban fox? He turned up his magnification and studied the area. He saw steamy breath rise from behind a pile of boxes. Someone was hiding, but was it from him or from the HiQua guards? The idea that one of the hamsters was stalking him made his stomach tense. Those guys had good IR vision, superhuman hearing. It wasn't impossible that they'd spotted him, despite the combat suit's insulation.

He didn't move, kept his gaze fixed on the breath that coiled up into the freezing air. One of the guards appeared and walked slowly along the length of the building, checking doors and windows and stopping occasionally to look around and sniff the air. As the giant moved around the corner, out of sight, the person hiding at the other side of the fence broke cover. Fourget's software analysed the person's height, shape, movements and began feeding data into his displays, but he didn't need the flickering dimensions and probabilities to know he was looking at a woman, a tall, slightly-built woman, long-limbed and supple. Had he found Sandra Malone? If so, she was more reckless and daring than even her file suggested. And her taste in clothing was bizarre. Her tight-fitting jeans sparkled in the dim street-light, he saw jewellery flash on her hands and ears, and her short jacket was pink. Not the outfit he'd have chosen for breaking into a heavily guarded building.

She ran to the fence, to a spot where a piece of carpet had been thrown over the razorwire, and scrambled up. She climbed like an amateur and made a terrible job of it. What the hell was she doing? Reaching the top, she looked left and right before vaulting over and Fourget got his first good look at her face. This was no thirty-five-year-old femme fatale from Jay's dangerous past. This was a young woman, pretty as all hell, and scared half to death. He recognized Cara Malone just moments before his facial recognition software popped up her name.

Merde!

He had jumped off the roof before he knew he was going to do it, dropping three stories to a landing cushioned by the suit's servo-assisted combat exoskeleton. Then he was off and running, heading for his car.

* * * *

Cara staggered away from the fence and almost fell. For a moment she stood still and listened, then hurried to the side of the building and the extra shadow of a doorway. Carefully, she tried the handle but it was locked. She had no idea what she was going to do. The windows were too high to see into and covered in bars. This was nothing like what she'd expected. Every light was on inside and the little parking lot was full. Worst of all, some kind of armed giant was patrolling the building. She'd never seen anything like him except in games. His arms were as thick as her whole body. He looked like he could pick her up with one hand and snap her like a toothpick.

God, Mum, what have you got yourself into?

She needed to get around to see more of the building, to see if there was another door, or an accessible window. But she daren't move. What if the guard was round the corner? And what if he came back while she was standing there, dithering?

She'd gone that far on an unrealistic expectation of how easy it would be to find her mother, but now the impossible reality of the task was sinking in. She needed to get out of there, fast. She needed to get well away and call her father again. She could tell him where her mother was now, and about the armed guard. He'd have to do something then, wouldn't he?

The racing of her heart and the sickening clenching of her stomach were horribly familiar. How long had she felt that way in Washington? How often had she told herself since then that it would never happen again, that she was safe, that lightning never strikes twice?

She was still standing in the doorway, still not moving. She took a deep breath, then another, preparing herself to cross the open yard and reach the fence. She stepped out of the doorway, looked right, then left.

"Hello, love. What's your name then?"

The giant was not three meters from her. He'd been watching her. His right hand held a gun, although it wasn't pointed at her. Cara's heart leaped in her chest as if it was desperate to get out through her throat. She tried to speak, to spin some yarn about looking for her lost dog. It was her cover story. But she couldn't speak. Slowly, the monstrous man raised his gun.

"I said, what's your name?"

"I—I—" She had to swallow, had to force some words out. "I lost my dog." It was a stupid story, she realized.

"You're coming with me," the guard said, flicking his head towards the front of the building.

She couldn't move. She certainly couldn't go with him. Desperation gave her strength. "Where's my mother?"

"Your mother?"

"My—" She stopped, seeing a pair of headlights coming in through the front gate.

A car was heading straight for them, moving fast. The giant turned towards it, his speed startling her. Though the car was almost upon them, the giant managed to get off a couple of shots and leap aside. But the shots went wide and the leap was too late. The car hit him a glancing blow that sent him spinning and tumbling across the yard. Cara stared in horror as the car kept coming, brakes screeching and body lurching as it spun through a half circle and came to a rocking halt beside her.

"Get in!" someone shouted from inside the car, reaching across to push the door open. She saw a black helmet with a glass front, and an arm in a black suit with black struts and hinges. It could have been a robot.

"*Merde!*" the robot man shouted. Then again, "Get in. There's another one."

He disappeared into the car then reappeared outside it having thrown open the driver's door and climbed out. He raced back the way the car had come, drawing a weapon as he ran. She looked ahead of him and saw another giant appear, running round the corner at incredible speed. It took Cara a moment to realize the new giant was a woman. The giantess drew her gun when she saw the robot man but he fired before she did, missing her but forcing her to duck and dodge.

Then he crashed into her. They rolled onto the floor and his arms moved in a flurry of blows, but the giantess did not seem especially bothered by it. She pushed him hard in the chest and he flew into the air, arms and legs flailing. Incredibly, he landed on his feet and instantly charged back at her.

The woman was on her feet too and drew a knife the size of Cara's arm. She slashed at the robot man with shocking speed. Cara cried out, certain the man would be sliced in half, but he somehow managed to block the giant's arm with his own and ran into her again, hitting her chest with his shoulder. As they connected, a flock of small birds seemed to take off from the man's back. The little birds scattered as the enormous woman grabbed the man and raised him over her head, her massive muscles bulging with the strain. It looked as if she would bring him down and break his back across her knee, but she wavered and staggered, shouting and cursing. She dropped the robot man, using her arms to protect her face as the little bird things swooped at her. There were tiny, bright flashes of intense light on her skin, and Cara realized the "birds" were little drones firing lasers at the woman's eyes.

Like a cat, the man was on his feet again and racing to the car. "Get the fuck into the car!" he yelled and, seeing that he was doing just that himself, Cara hurried to obey. The vehicle was moving before she'd had a chance to shut the door after her and it was clear her new friend meant to run down the woman. But it wasn't going to be so easy: the car had no speed and the woman had already caught and crushed two of the birds. No doubt hearing the engine revving, the woman whipped her head round to look at them. Ignoring the remaining laser-spitting birds, she flipped her huge knife, caught it by the blade, and threw it straight for Cara's head. It came like a rocket. Cara had no time even to blink. The car swerved and the knife smashed through the windscreen. She felt it whistle past her ear and thud into the back seat. An explosion of glass fragments rained over her face and upper body. She hadn't had time to scream. She looked back and saw the woman grabbing her gun up from the ground. She moved so fast. Everything was so fast.

Her companion swore again and again the car jerked sideways. Three more giants had appeared ahead of them. They all had machine guns. "Get down!" the driver yelled and aimed the car at the newcomers. She squirmed to the floor, huddling into a ball as the machine guns roared. The rest of the windscreen disintegrated, bullets tore up the seat she'd been sitting in. She looked up at the driver and saw his body jerk as round after round hit him in the chest and face. Then the car hit something hard and she saw one of the giants roll over the bonnet and over the roof.

She found her voice at last and screamed.

Chapter 12

Dinner Date

Jay settled the bill for the meal and Olivia said good night. He watched Sandra's old friend make her slightly unsteady way to the lifts and turned to Laura.

"I'll call you a taxi," he said.

She laughed. "How old-fashioned you are. Besides, I feel like another drink. Come on, let's find a nice bar."

She put her arm in his and led him out into the street. He wanted to protest. He wanted to go home and sleep. But he caught the reflection of the two of them in the hotel's window. It was a shock—it didn't look like him at all. It looked like someone from a vid, someone who walked around with attractive women on his arm, someone who enjoyed his life.

"I'm…" he began and wondered what he had meant to say. Something like, "I'm not used to being out with a woman." Luckily, he stopped himself. Instead, he said, "There's a place over there that looks OK."

They found a quiet spot and ordered. She had a glass of Rioja and he ordered a light beer.

"Always on call," she said.

"Right now, for sure. I don't really know any other way to be. I had a boss like that, Jacques Bauchet, lived the job twenty-four/seven." Yet, somehow, Jacques had managed to court and marry Marie. How had that happened?

"He set you a bad example, then. I would go crazy if I couldn't switch off at the end of the day."

"I know what you mean, I suppose, but…" How did he explain the fear that drove him, the idea that a major timesplash could happen on his watch, that the death and destruction he'd seen could happen again if he failed to prevent it?

She moved closer to him. "Well, tonight you can take a break. It will be good for you. Trust me: I'm a doctor."

He smiled. "I don't think a doctorate in physics counts."

"Sure it does! If nothing else, it means I'm cleverer than you and you should listen to what I tell you."

She was a little bit drunk, he realized. He supposed he must be too, although he didn't feel it. How much wine had they had with the meal? Olivia and Laura had been cheerful and talkative, renewing their old friendship. Jay had been gloomy, trying to hide his disappointment in the way the day had gone. His team was letting him down. Laura was letting him down. And so was Olivia. He needed them to find some brilliant explanation for what had happened, some way of tracking the perpetrators and preventing it from happening again. But all they had come up with was Olivia's pie-in-the-sky nonsense about travelling into the future.

For a second, he thought how good it would be to forget all about that, to just lose himself in the moment, to make a joke, laugh, take Laura's hand and tell her he was glad he'd stayed. But he couldn't. His heart felt like lead in his chest.

"What would happen if we went forwards in time?" he asked, killing the mood.

Laura sighed and drew back a little. It was a tiny gesture but eloquent. "As you've said, many times, it's impossible."

"Yet they're working on it at Aldermaston."

"The military works on all kinds of crazy projects all the time. Generals are easy to persuade and they have lots of money to speculate with when it comes to new super-weapons."

"But what would happen?"

She looked away, perhaps to hide her irritation. When she looked back, she wasn't smiling and playful any more. "We move into the present as each quantum-level event makes a choice about its current state. The future is simply the next set of states based on the next set of choices. Even so, we can't fully describe the present because there's a fundamental uncertainty about it, and we can't predict the future because there's a fundamental randomness in the progression from one state to another. To move ahead of the present, you'd either have to be able to outguess the Universe about where it's going or somehow force a set of choices on it. Even then, I can't see how any choices you force on the Universe could lead you to the actual future, just a more-or-less probable one."

"And if you got there, to this probable future?"

"I don't know, I suppose it would be like being in the present."

"But you could still generate anomalies, couldn't you?"

"Could you?" She was patently angry and bored now but he pressed on anyway.

"If I met my own son in the future—and I don't have a son, let's say—and immediately killed myself, that would be an anomaly, right? So what would happen?"

"This is all hypotheticals piled on hypotheticals."

"Would there be a timesplash? Would things start trying to fix themselves up?"

She lifted her hands, fingers splayed. "Maybe. Your guess is probably as good as mine. It's only a probable future, and not one that has actually happened. If you die in the future and never come back to have a son, then that future won't happen. Maybe it will just collapse out of existence. Who knows?" She started gathering her things. "I should probably be going. It's getting late."

"And if a future collapses, could that create some kind of disturbance in the past—in the present, I mean?"

She stood up. "We've probably both had too much to drink to have this conversation."

"Laura, would there be a backwash?"

She sighed and her shoulders dropped a little. "No, I don't think so. The timestream flows only one way. If you start in the future, it would always flow away from you."

"But we can jump back. It isn't true that the future can't influence the past."

"Jay, can we do this in the morning?"

"I'm sorry. I know I'm being... Please, just answer that one question."

"Very well. You're wrong. We cannot affect the past. Whatever we do to it is corrected. That's what the timesplash does. You know this. When the bricks are yanked back to the present, the past becomes exactly what it used to be." She repeated it for emphasis. "Exactly what it used to be. If last night's event had been some kind of time-travelling disruption from a future anomaly, it would all have been put right by now and none of us would remember any part of it.

For us, it would not have happened."

"But…"

"Good night, Jay. I'll see you tomorrow."

She walked away briskly, leaving Jay in a whirl of logical conundrums and emotional turmoil.

Surely if the future affected the past but the past was really the present, it wasn't the same as if you went back from the present to change a past that had already happened—even if, from the point of view of the future, what Jay thought of as the present was really the past. He shuddered with the mental effort of trying to make sense of it.

Tomorrow, he would make Laura set it all down in a report for him. If Laura were still speaking to him.

The first pang of regret hit him. *God, what an idiot you are,* he told himself. If Laura had been any clearer about wanting to start something with him, it could only have been by carrying a placard around saying, "Here I am, you dumb bastard: do something about it!" And yet, when it had come to the moment when he should have acted, he'd gone all obsessive workaholic on her and driven her off.

He drank down the last of his beer and stared into the empty glass. It wasn't his fault! He felt an urge to go after her and explain. It was just bad timing. In fact, now he thought about it, it was a pretty stupid time to suddenly come on to him. There was a crisis going on for God's sake. What was he supposed to do, drop all his responsibilities and take a roll in the hay? It was the worst possible time. What was the woman thinking? This was the moment to keep a clear head and sort things out, not…

And then it hit him and made him feel even worse.

Not a time to be reaching out to someone you liked, looking for comfort and companionship to help dispel your anxiety and fear.

He slammed his glass down hard and people glanced quickly round at him. "God! God! God!" he cursed softly between clenched teeth. Could he have been more stupid if he'd tried? Just because she seemed so relaxed and self-possessed didn't mean Laura wasn't as scared as everyone else about what had happened. Of course this would be the moment she would reach out. The whole world had been shaken to its foundations by a force no-one understood. There had been ghosts and apparitions. Only a complete fool wouldn't be holding out their hand for a bit of human comfort.

A fool like him, for example.

He snatched up his coat and got to his feet. He'd try to catch her. She might still be outside waiting for a taxi. If she wasn't, he'd call her and try to apologise for being such an unspeakable jerk.

But he'd only gone two paces before his phone rang. He saw Cara's name on the caller ID and took the call.

"Dad!" She was distraught, sobbing into the phone. "Dad, you've got to help. Everything's awful."

∗ ∗ ∗ ∗

Wind blasted in through the shattered windscreen, whipping Cara's hair around her face. The suited man who had saved her was slumped in the driver's seat. The car was driving itself at high speed along the almost empty motorway. Before he'd passed out—or died—the man had given it some kind of override command that made it take off like a bat out of Hell. It had ignored her demands that it stop.

Her commplant was synced with the car's systems so that

her father's face looked at her from the dash display, given there was no longer a windscreen. Beside her, the suited man's head rolled from side to side as the car swerved along the road. The metalglass visor was cracked, having taken a machine-gun round at close range. By some miracle, the round had not penetrated. Pale discs on the suit's black fabric showed where he had taken three more direct hits in the chest.

"It's all right," Jay said. "I think I know who that is." He said something to the car, quoted a badge number, gave a clearance code, and it slowed down and parked itself on the hard shoulder. Cara was panting from the exertion of trying to breathe against the gale that had been pummelling her.

"Can you get his helmet off?" Jay asked. "There should be a couple of studs just under his ears."

Reluctant to touch what might be a dead man, Cara felt under the rim of the helmet until she found the catches. She pressed them and pulled. There was a click as the neck seal opened and the helmet came away. She tossed it in the back and looked at the injured man. He was beautiful, younger than she had expected, with a strong, clean jaw and a broad, unfurrowed forehead. He looked as if he'd fallen asleep, peaceful and at ease. In his armour, his soft hair falling across his brow, he might have been a knight in a pre-Raphaelite painting.

"It's Fourget," Jay said. "One of my men. I sent him to look for Sandra. What the hell is going on, Cara? No, wait." He gave the car instructions to drive to the nearest hospital. As soon as it stared moving, he said, "All right. Let's hear it."

* * * *

Fourget opened his eyes then squeezed them shut against the bright hospital light. He tried to sit up and fell back down against the soft pillows, dizzy and nauseated. He heard someone move—quick, light steps across the room. He opened his eyes a crack, expecting a nurse, and saw Cara Malone, dishevelled and anxious.

He tried to ask how long he'd been out. He needed to reorient himself, assess the situation, but his throat was dry and the words were a croak.

"It's all right. You're safe."

He brought a hand up to his throat and it trailed tubes and wires. "How long…?" he asked and this time managed a dry whisper.

"Ah, that's good. We're awake at last." The new voice was a telepresence robot. It trundled up to the bed and tilted its "head" down to look at Fourget. The label under the face said Dr M Singh. "You took quite a battering, young man. Lucky for you you're even tougher than that remarkable suit you were wearing."

"Is he going to be all right?" Cara asked.

"And you are?"

"I'm his sister."

Fourget turned to look at Cara; even as someone who was trained in lies and deceit, he was surprised at how quickly and easily that had tripped off Cara's tongue.

The doctor gave a forced smile. "Ask a silly question," he said. "It's all right, I've already had the Men in Black read me the Riot Act. I'll just stick to the medicine from now on. Now then, let's take a look at you."

The robot unfolded a couple of arms and used a variety of scanners and other sensors to explore Fourget's body. As he watched the delicate appendages move around him, he saw that his chest was bandaged and remembered the impact of the bullets. Everything after that was a blur. To Cara, he said, "How did we…?" but his voice gave out again.

"There's water on the table there," the doctor said, "if you'd like to give your, er, brother a drink."

Cara fetched a bottle with a bent tube and helped him drink from it. The water was warm and tasted of chlorine but the relief was wonderful. He made her keep squirting it into his mouth until the bottle was empty.

"I want you to stay here for twenty-four hours just to be on the safe side, but it looks as if you got away with little more than a bit of bruising. Those ribs will be sore for a week or two, but nothing that a bit of rest and recuperation won't cure. I've given you a sedative to help you sleep and I'll pop by in the morning to check on you."

At the mention of the word "sedative" Fourget struggled to sit up. "No, I have things to do." He grabbed at the cannula on the back of his left hand and tried to pull it out. He couldn't fall asleep now. His mission was nowhere near complete. The room darkened as if the lights had been dimmed. He still had not found Sandra Malone. With a jolt, he snapped awake, realizing he was lying on the pillows again, the cannula still in place.

Blackness swarmed in on him.

Chapter 13

Forwards

Hamiye had tied Sandra hand and foot and gagged and blindfolded her before driving her through the city. Still, she'd had worse rides—at least she'd been warm. And sitting in the interior of her captor's luxury car was way cosier than some car boots she'd travelled in.

Her commplant was useless. Blocked, somehow. She reminded herself to search her clothing for a portable jammer when she got the chance. She had tried to keep track of the route, counting the turns and listening for telltale sounds, but long before they arrived, she had given up. The journey seemed to take hours. At last, they swung off the road, down a ramp, along a gravel drive. The car crunched off the gravel onto a smoother surface and stopped. As the whine of the engine died away, Hamiye pulled off her gag and her blindfold. She was inside a garage. He pulled a knife out of his pocket and flicked out the blade.

"OK, I'm going to cut your legs free," he told her in a conversational tone. "If you try anything stupid, I'll bury this knife in the closest body part I can find and then tie you up again. There is no way in the world I could take you to a doctor, so you'd just have to hope I didn't stab anything important. You understand the situation, don't you?"

She gave him a cold stare. "Do all women scare you this much, or is it just me?"

He grinned. "Trust me, it's you. I've seen all kinds of killers in my time, but there's something in your eyes that gives me the creeps."

He bent over and cut Sandra's bonds. She didn't break his jaw. She didn't crush his windpipe. She thought she could have. The knife was a deterrent, but she was also thinking about what he'd said. It was true that she'd killed people. But only out of direst necessity. Did that make her a killer? Was it something people could see in her? Did Cara see it? Or Jay?

She let him lead her out of the car. She noticed that he kept the knife handy, blade out.

"This is your house?" she asked. She'd expected to end up in another HiQua facility.

"Safest place to keep you for a few days." They walked in silence from the garage into the main building. It was a big house, one of those renovated farmhouses in the Home Counties, she guessed, rough-plastered and white-painted walls inside, with exposed beams and leaded windows.

"What, no horse brasses?" she asked.

He didn't reply but carried on in silence to the kitchen. It was of a piece with the rest, slate floor, a huge wooden table and an imitation Aga range that was really a state-of-the-art central-heating boiler. No doubt one of the distressed wooden cupboards hid the food printer and similar mod cons.

"Would you like a cup of tea?" he asked, showing her to a wooden chair at the table. She watched him fill the kettle and fetch teacups and saucers. After he had put leaf tea into the bone china pot, he stopped, as if he'd forgotten the next step in his little performance.

He turned to face her, grown suddenly grave. "Here's the thing," he said. "I've got a room I can lock you in. I can put a folding bed in there and get you a heater. You'd be OK. You heard what Lee said. I'm supposed to hold you for four days and then dispose of you, so it doesn't really matter what state you're in at the end."

Sandra watched him in silence, wondering where this was going.

"But I'm not going to do what Lee wants. Yes, I'm going to hold you, but after that, you're free to go. I'll be leaving the country then. So will Lee and Hong and anyone else who has anything to do with this."

Sandra waited for him to go on, but he didn't. "So? What are you suggesting? That I cooperate? That we play house in your little mock-gentry hideaway? Do you want me to be grateful?"

He studied her intently, his soft brown eyes looking for something which, in the end, he couldn't find. "There's another way to do this," he said. "I could send some people to pick up your daughter."

A wild rage burned away all thought, yet she fought the urge to jump up and tear his throat out with her teeth.

He must have seen the sudden tensing of her muscles, the snarl on her lips, because his eyes widened in alarm and his hand darted to his shoulder holster. A couple of heartbeats passed before he decided she wasn't going to attack him after all and relaxed. "You really are a very scary woman. All right, you get to spend the time locked up." He looked as if he regretted it.

"You know I've got friends who will come looking for me?"

He put a cup of tea down in front of her. "Oh, really? You think I should get a few of my hamsters to come and watch the house?"

"Is that what you call those muscle-bound apes guarding your lob site?"

A little frown crossed his brow. Then it cleared. "You saw the platform through the window, of course, and jumped to the wrong conclusion."

"I know a lob site when I see one."

"Do you really?" He sipped his tea and studied her. Then he put it on the table and drew his stunner and walked round behind her. She felt a tickle between her shoulder blades as she imagined the weapon's targeting laser dancing there and anticipated the fifty thousand volt jolt to follow. Instead, she felt the hard plastic of a handcuff on her left wrist. "I'm going to free your hands now so you can drink your tea," Hamiye said in his ridiculously correct English. "If you struggle, I will stun you." She said nothing, resigned to her captivity for the time being.

When he'd fastened the other end of the handcuffs to the bulky kitchen table, he put away his gun and went to sit opposite her with his tea. "That's better."

"If this is about money," she said, "it's not worth it. They'll track you down and put you away."

"Who? MI5? I don't think so."

Sandra couldn't decide if it was better for her to let him go on thinking she was MI5. Probably not since he seemed to have no respect for them and the first time they'd met he effectively told her his boss could shut down any investigation. The only time she'd been involved with Five was back in 2050 when Jay was working for them. At that time MI5 almost failed to save London from Sniper because they'd been infiltrated by the bad guys. If she were Hamiye, she wouldn't have any respect for them either.

She decided to try another tack. She picked up her tea and took a drink. It tasted like tar but she pulled an appreciative face. "You're just about what I expected from your file. Between the lines, I saw some Lebanese street kid who reckoned there was no future fighting stupid tribal wars and decided to get out. A bigger, tougher thug than all the rest, who fought and clawed his way to the top of one small dung-heap, then a bigger heap, and then a bigger one still, until he was in a position to bully and bribe his way out of the whole stinking mess and come here."

Hamiye smiled. "That's my glorious homeland you're talking about."

"Which you love dearly, of course. Which is why you shook it off your boots as soon as you could and started acquiring all the trappings of a civilized life—the rather-too-posh accent, the kind of home a car-dealership executive would die for, not to mention a car that makes other men feel small and shrivelled when they see it. How am I doing?"

"Not bad. Did you ever work as a profiler? You seem to think in stereotypes."

"But you were greedy, weren't you? You wanted all this yet you couldn't see a way of getting it if you stayed on the right side of the law. Which is why Mr Lee was such a godsend. He had all kinds of shady little things he needed doing and you no doubt showed yourself willing and able."

He was still smiling but the amusement had gone from his eyes.

"But here's the thing I don't get. Lee's current project is a nasty, vicious, mass murder. When he unleashes that timesplash he's planning, thousands will die. You know what happened to Beijing, Mexico City, Washington." She watched his eyes for a reaction and knew she was heading the right way. "I can see you're comfortable with a bit of threatening and bullying. I bet you've slapped a few people around for Lee, possibly even worse. But despite the life you've led, despite how keen you are to do what it takes to get right away from all that, here you are, helping plan an unimaginable atrocity. Just like the good old days, watching some damned imam urge some shit-scared kid to put on his suicide vest and walk into a Beirut coffee shop. The very opposite of everything you want."

He stood up angrily and crossed the room. She raised her voice. "Civilization isn't about Italian shoes and Royal Doulton tea sets. Those things are a by-product, a side effect. Civilization is about putting down the Lees of this world, not propping them up. It's about believing there are more valuable things than money and power."

"Who the hell do you think you are? A spy? A sneaking rat? Giving me lectures on civilization? You don't know a damned thing about me. Or Lee."

"I'm not a spy, you stubborn *arse*. But I know what you've got in that building in Enfield. I know what it does. If Lee has fed you some crap about how no-one's going to get hurt, you're a bigger fool than you look."

"It's not what you think. You have no idea what you're talking about."

"Oh yes? Which one of us has the degree in temporal engineering? Which one of us has built displacement rigs from the ground up? Which one of us has actually travelled in time—three times—and survived it?"

He pulled the stunner again. "Get up. You're going in your hole."

"While Lee and Hong kill half of London?"

"That's not going to happen."

"How the hell would you know? You're just the hired muscle."

"Because I've seen it. Hong sent a man forward two years ago and not a damned thing happened. It's different from a lob. Is that why the spooks are sniffing round HiQua, 'cause you think we're timesplashers? Terrorists? Jesus!"

Sandra's world seemed to stop. In the echoing silence of the kitchen, she looked into Hamiye's scowling face.

"Forward?" she asked.

* * * *

"You did what?"

Crystal wasn't exactly angry, Jay decided, more incredulous.

"I sent Fourget to find Sandra Malone."

"In the middle of a global crisis that has stretched my department to breaking point, you sent one of our top operatives to check up on your girlfriend?"

"I've already explained. She called me to say she might have a lead on a planned temporal crime." Which was something of an exaggeration, to say the least. "Then she disappeared." For a couple of hours. "I thought it prudent to send someone to investigate."

"And then your daughter got involved."

"Fourget hasn't been able to make a report yet. He's under sedation. Based on what Cara says, she went to find her mother and encountered a group of hamsters guarding the

131

facility where she thought her mother was being held. Fourget intervened and rescued her, sustaining some injuries in the process."

"And writing off a million-euro combat suit and a hire car in the process."

"Yes, Ma'am." Jay rarely called Crystal "Ma'am" but today seemed like a good opportunity. "We'll know more when Fourget wakes up."

Crystal stared at him for a long time. "At the very least, Jay, this looks like extremely poor prioritisation on your part. At worst, it looks like gross misconduct. As far as I can see, there is no evidence for an imminent temporal crime by..." she consulted a note. "...HiQua." She paused to study something. Her screen was virtual and Jay could not see what she was reading.

"What is it?"

"Just a note that's appeared on the HiQua file. The British Home Secretary has asked MI5 to explain its interest in HiQua and the presence of an agent of theirs—one Sandra Malone—in one of their Oxford offices." She looked up at Jay. "She doesn't really work for Five, does she, Jay?"

"That's what I've been trying to tell you. A HiQua security man spotted Sandra... Ms Malone... and has flipped out about her being a spy. But she's not. Sandra—I mean, Ms Malone—"

"For heaven's sake, just call her Sandra."

"Right. She went off after HiQua because... well... before she knew what this was all about, but she's stayed on their tail because now she thinks there's a temporal crime involved."

Crystal screwed up her face. "Does she work for Five?"

"No. She doesn't work for anybody. That is... she works for HiQua, or used to; I'm assuming she's fired now. The point is she tracked Hamiye to an engineering works in Enfield and then her commplant went offline. Cara... I mean..." He gave up any pretence at being professional. Since Crystal was no doubt going to sack him after all this, it could hardly matter now. "Cara then turned up at the same place and so did Fourget. There was a fight—involving five super-soldier mercs—and now Fourget is in hospital."

He drew a breath, calming himself for a final appeal. "Ma'am, something is clearly going on at that HiQua facility and Sandra Malone—a civilian—is almost certainly being held captive, or worse. I know the world went to shit two nights ago and we still don't have the slightest clue as to why, but if this company is planning a timesplash, the present state of confusion would make this a perfect time to do it—while we're all looking the other way."

Crystal shook her head and sat back. Jay could see her decision was made, even before she spoke. "It's a company, Jay. One of the biggest in the world. Connected at ministerial level all over Europe and elsewhere. Companies like that don't blow up capital cities. It's not good for business. Now, correct me if I'm wrong, but you don't have a single shred of evidence that anything is going on with HiQua except your girlfriend's hunch, the fact that she went offline for a while, and that HiQua vigorously defended themselves against intruders in the night at one of their engineering works." She hardened her stare. "It doesn't justify an investigation. It barely justifies a moment's consideration. Get Fourget back here and get on with the job you're supposed to be doing. That's all."

Her expression was a shield against any attempt by Jay to argue. He said, "Yes, Ma'am," and left her office. He found his way back to his own floor and sat behind his desk. He pulled up a software assistant and told it to keep trying Fourget's netID and to alert him the moment the lieutenant answered his phone. Then he put in a call to his counterpart in UK Military Intelligence. He wanted to talk to somebody at Aldermaston. Somebody from Project FORESIGHT.

* * * *

Fourget opened his eyes. Was it morning? He checked the time and groaned. Yes, it was. His tongue was sore and dry and his body felt weak and heavy. For a moment he stared at the wall of his hospital room, his mind blank. Then he struggled onto one elbow and looked around. In a chair, curled up awkwardly but fast asleep, was Cara Malone. Her sparkly jeans seemed even more incongruous in the sterile room than they had last night. She was clutching a hospital blanket but it was mostly lying across the floor. She seemed younger and prettier in repose.

His phone rang, a software agent trying to connect him to Jay. He ignored it.

He removed his cannula and took a drink of water. The pain in his chest was tolerable if he moved carefully. He took off his gown and got out of bed. Standing barefoot and naked, he studied his body for damage. Grazes and bruises. Nothing to worry about.

In a cupboard beside the bed, he found his bag with his clothes and shoes still inside. The girl must have brought it in from the car. He dressed as quickly as he could and walked to the door.

"You're leaving?"

He stopped, hand on the door handle.

"After all that, you're just going to sneak away without

even saying goodbye?"

He turned to face Cara, who was sitting up in the chair, looking hurt. "Thank you for... getting me here. I must go."

"Go?"

He nodded. "My mission is not complete." He grabbed the handle and pulled the door open. "Goodbye, Cara."

She was beside him, following him along the corridor. "Your mission? You mean to find my mum?"

Again, he nodded but kept on walking. He hoped she would tire soon and leave him to his work.

"No. I'm coming with you. You don't even know where to look."

"Do you?" She was silent. "No, I didn't think so." He lengthened his stride, the movement making him feel better all the time.

"I'm going with you," she said, keeping pace with him. She was about his height and had longer legs. He was never going to out-distance her.

"You should call your father and ask him what he thinks."

The young woman bridled. "I'm not a child. What would your father think, you pompous sod?"

He stopped. They were passing the hospital cafeteria and the smell, while not appealing, made him realize how hungry he was. Cara, hurrying along beside him, bumped into his shoulder, making him wince with pain.

"I'm sorry," she said, wincing in sympathy. "I didn't mean to." Then she noticed the café too. "Food! Yes. Let's sit down and have breakfast and we can talk it over, work out how to proceed, yeah?"

With a sigh, he went over to the counter and surveyed the fare. If the girl wanted to follow him, that was her privilege. Jay's agent called him again and again he ignored it. Avoiding the greasy fried food, he chose a couple of rolls, butter, cheese, and an apple. He made Cara pay.

"Why would a hospital sell the kind of food that probably put half its patients in here in the first place?" he asked Cara as they sat down. She blinked back at him as if surprised he could say so many words all at once. She had a bowl of muesli and a pot of yoghurt. *Vegetarian?* he wondered.

"My dad helped me get you here last night," she said. "I— I was in a panic. I didn't know what to do. For a while I thought you were dead. That suit you were wearing... it's incredible. And those people, with all their gross muscles and stuff, I thought they were going to kill us. Well, they would have if not for you. You were so brave. I just don't know how to thank you. I was too scared to do anything useful at all. When I saw the way that woman just picked you up and threw you..."

He let her speak. She had been shocked. It would do her good to talk it all out. Meanwhile, he buttered a roll and considered his options. One thing was certain. He would not be answering Jay's calls. His discreet little mission was probably common knowledge by now and Crystal would be roasting his boss's balls in a pot. If he took the call, Jay would tell him to stand down and he would have to. If he ignored the call—as he might if he were still unconscious—he could do what Jay really wanted him to do.

"So then all the penguins marched up to the senate building with their woolly hats on."

"*Pardon?*"

Cara was glaring at him, obviously aware that his mind had been elsewhere. *Eh bien.*

"When you speak to your father," he said, "you must tell him I am still in the hospital. Still unconscious would be better. Tell him I have a concussion."

"You tell him."

"No. It is better this way."

Cara frowned at him, lips pursed. She was very cute. He should try to persuade her to go home but he did not think that would be easy.

"Is my car in the car park?" he asked.

"Your car is junk. We had to leave it at the side of the M25 and come here by ambulance. It's a miracle it got us as far as it did. Don't worry, my dad spoke to the police about whatever weapons you might have had stashed in the boot."

Not good news. "Do you have a car?"

"I had a hire car that I left a couple of blocks from Clarke Engineering. I expect it has given up on me and taken itself back to the car hire place by now."

"I need you to get me a car."

"You... need me?"

"To get me a car."

"Well, of course. Where are we going?"

She was smiling sweetly at him, as if she had scored some great triumph. Yes, it was her mother who was missing, but who knew where the trail might lead, or what he might find at the end of it?

"Can you fight?" he asked. She frowned, puzzled. "Are you a good shot with a pistol?"

"Not bad," she said, but he did not believe her. He chewed on his roll and regarded her.

"You are no use to me."

Her face set. He thought he was about to see her cry, but he was wrong.

"You really do need me," she said. "You want EDF MI to think you're still here, unconscious. So you can't use them to get you transport and weapons. You're on your own. In fact, you can't even use your personal credit because they could find out and you'd get in trouble—or they'd make you stop and go back to Berlin. True?" He said nothing. "Well I've got resources you haven't. I've got money and places to go and people who can access data for me. How do you think I found out where they're holding Mum?"

"She's not there."

"What?"

"They moved her. I scanned the whole place yesterday before you turned up. She's not there."

"No. She must be. Why else would they need all those gerbils?"

It was a very good question, but not his concern. "Hamsters. Can you get me weapons?" She shook her head, deep in thought. "But you have money?" This time a nod. "*Bon*. You can help."

She snapped out of her reverie. "Really?"

"Your father will have me busted to private for involving you, but..." He gave a shrug. He needed support. It was an operational decision. Jay would have to live with it.

"Let me worry about my father. If he ever says anything, just remind him how well he did keeping me out of the Washington job."

Cara started a call to a car-hire company. "Make it something big and solid," he said, remembering the mercenaries from last night. She seemed to understand. In fact, she had demonstrated a whole lot more competence and determination than her angelic looks promised. A chip off the old block, perhaps. Jay did not impress at first sight, either. And then there was the mother, Sandra. He was looking forward to meeting that one.

* * * *

Dr Hong clicked his antique biro. His father had given him that pen when he received his doctorate from Zhejiang University. For a while, he had used it, writing notes by hand in expensive, paper notebooks, the way his father had once done. He was not an attractive man and the pen gave him an air of eccentricity which he believed compensated to some extent. Certainly, his first wife, Lihua, said she had only noticed him because of the pen, so it must have worked.

But Lihua was gone now. She had died of tuberculosis during the Adjustment. And Hong had stopped using his pen to write with. Now it was his good luck charm, and something for him to fidget with when he was nervous. His second wife, Mingxia, had noticed him because he was the head of her research lab, a famous and powerful scientist. He had loved Lihua with all his heart. Mingxia was very beautiful, she laughed a lot, but she was not a woman with much depth, and he had come lately to suspect that she worked for China's Central Military Commission.

"We're ready, Dr Hong."

"Good, good. Proceed."

He watched the pilot walk over to the chronosphere, lift the hatch and climb inside. He hardly knew the man. All the pilots were hand-picked and trained by Lee. This one was like the others, compact, young, self-assured. In his pressure suit he looked like a fighter pilot—or maybe just a fighter—and walked with a slight swagger. Given the risks involved, Hong supposed it must take a certain kind of reckless courage to climb into that sphere. *Rather you than me, young man.*

The pilot put on his helmet and the tekniks leaned inside

to fasten his harness. The pressure suit was just a precaution. The sphere had its own air supply and heating. He gave a thumbs-up sign and they closed the hatch. Hong checked the displays around him. All systems were nominal, in the sphere and in the lab. A countdown began while the tekniks went through the final checks with the meticulous care of a spaceship launch. All unnecessary. The systems were fine and essentially automatic once the hatch was closed. It wasn't at this end that things would go wrong.

The countdown hit ten seconds as the final green lights came on from the various systems specialists. Despite his confidence, Hong waited with his hand hovering over the big red button that would abort the launch. With his other hand, he clicked his biro.

A teknik read off the seconds as they passed. Pure drama. He didn't remember ever asking anyone to do that. It was a tradition that had arisen spontaneously. He could make them stop, but it was somehow settling in these final moments.

"Five. Four. Three."

The big antennae around the sphere glowed with St Elmo's Fire.

"Two. One."

The supercapacitor banks discharged with a bang followed instantly by a higher-pitched clap as the chronosphere disappeared and air collapsed into the void it had left.

It was up to the pilot now to judge just how long to explore at the other end: the sphere would return with or without him in two hours.

Hong checked the displays. Everything had been perfect at the moment of launch. If the roll of the quantum dice inherent in every time shot fell in Hong's favour, the sphere would go exactly as far as it should. But what the pilot would find when he reached the other end was literally impossible to guess. Hong clicked his pen and hoped for good luck.

* * * *

Sandra woke up slowly. All was silent. Piece by piece the memory of the previous night assembled itself. Gradually, she understood why her head was throbbing, why she was on a mattress in a small empty room, why her left wrist was handcuffed to a metal ring in the wall. That bastard Hamiye had stunned her again. She'd waited and watched him but he had given her no chances. So she'd taken a wild risk, thrown her drink in his face, heaved the big wooden table over onto its side, slid her cuff off the leg, hurled a chair his way and run for the door. He'd still managed to get off a shot and bring her down.

She tugged at the handcuffs, but the ring did not budge. From the little pile of powdered plaster and brick under it, she concluded it was bolted into an external wall and that Hamiye had put it there last night while she was unconscious. She checked her commplant. No signal. It was already mid-morning and she was hungry. She found a tin bucket standing near the bed and banged it against the wall, shouting to let her jailer know she was awake. She needed the bathroom too and was not happy to think why the bucket had been left there.

Hamiye took ages coming for her, giving Sandra plenty of time to sit on her mattress and fret. Cara would be going crazy with worry by now. The events of two years ago in Washington had left her daughter far more shaken up than she would ever admit. Sandra knew that Cara's fear of that insanity starting over again was always just below the surface.

She'd coped amazingly well and Sandra was proud of how strong and resilient her daughter had turned out, but Cara had been practically still a kid when it happened and there were scars despite everything that she and Jay had done to help.

Sandra herself had been just fifteen when she had been forced into a timesplash by her psycho boyfriend, Sniper. She'd seen a little girl murdered, a friend beaten to death, and all the other casual brutality and mayhem of a timesplash. It had completely unhinged her. She'd spent the next two years in a mental health institute before escaping and embarking on a crazy vendetta to kill Sniper.

Jay had saved her. Sweet, gentle Jay had shown her another version of existence, one in which people loved and cared for one another, where she was free to value herself as more than a beautiful body, a commodity for others to bargain with. She'd never told him how much she owed him. And maybe Cara too would have gone off the rails if Jay hadn't been around, and if he hadn't opened Sandra's eyes to the woman she had become. Worse, if she hadn't had that time with Jay all those years ago, if they'd just used each other's bodies without her seeing how beautiful his heart was, what kind of mother would she have been to Cara? It was a question that scared her so much she picked up the bucket and slammed it against the wall again.

At least Cara wasn't alone. She was with Dot and, by now, must be bending Jay's ear about mounting a rescue. Whatever happened, she knew Jay would do everything he could to keep Cara safe. Although, to be honest, his efforts at guarding her last time had been pretty hopeless.

When Hamiye arrived, he looked clean and smart, the opposite of how Sandra felt. He also looked worried, which gave her some small pleasure.

"What?" he asked with the air of a man who had more important things on his mind.

"Breakfast," she said, matching the belligerence of his tone. "Or do you plan to starve me to death?"

He looked, for a moment, as if he was contemplating it. "I'll get you something."

She listened as he locked the door after himself. Two heavy bolts, one top, one bottom. If it came to an escape that way, she'd probably be better off trying to kick a hole through the door itself than to break the bolts or the hinges. For that matter, the internal walls were probably just plasterboard, although the house was old enough for them to be made of cinderblock. For all her karate training, she had never gone in for smashing boards or blocks. That stuff was just for demonstrations, to please the crowds. Pointless. Sandra liked to focus on speed and accuracy and leave the power to her testosterone-fuelled teammates. On the other hand, kicking down a cinderblock wall would be a handy skill to have right now. She wondered if she could do it if she had to.

Hamiye appeared with a paper plate of scrambled eggs and a plastic spoon.

She took it without a word and began eating quickly. "I need the loo," she told him, mouth full.

"Bucket."

"Fuck off."

"Take it or leave it."

"If I have to use that thing, I'm going to stick your head in it."

He shrugged and left.

She listened for the bolts to slide home, then finished her

breakfast. She took the plastic spoon and twisted it until it snapped. The break was diagonal across the handle, leaving her with two short, pointed weapons.

* * * *

Hamiye kept telling himself that he just needed to keep the lid on this for a few more days and it would all be over. He didn't want to kill the woman but keeping her a prisoner was like holding a tiger by the tail. If he wasn't careful, she would kill him. The spirit in her was like a fire, it burned so bright. She was magnificent—and not just because of her beauty, although that would be reason enough to admire her. He wondered about the man who had fathered her child. What kind of man would it take to conquer such a heart? Was this the man she had threatened him with? The one who would come looking for her? He supposed she must be right. If Hamiye had a woman like that he would move Heaven and Earth to keep her.

And yet there she was, shackled to a wall, hating him with that scorching passion of hers.

He paced the room. It was always the same. All his life he had been coiled in an endless chain of bad decisions, unfortunate friends, desperate necessities. He sometimes looked back to his childhood on the streets of Beirut, running through the ruins, dodging the bullets, doing favours for one faction or another, and he thought about how far he had come from that dark, dangerous place. Sometimes he congratulated himself that he had dragged himself out of the mire of endless war, endless fear and oppression, patted himself on the back for making this life of ease and plenty. He was a butterfly, he told himself, and the chrysalis of his old self had been left behind in a Cairo hotel room the day he swapped every euro he owned for a chipful of travel documents and visas.

But the fear had not ended there. Nor had the torture and killing. Eastern Europe had been difficult. The money had been better but the things he'd had to do to get it were not so different. There, as much as in the Middle East, he had been on a relentless treadmill and he couldn't get off.

So Lee Shaozu had seemed like his deliverer. By the standards he was used to, Lee was a respectable man. His business interests were almost legitimate. The past three years had been the culmination of everything he had worked for since he was a child. Lee had brought him to England, had given him a job title he was not ashamed to speak aloud, and the bonuses and extra rewards associated with the Special Projects Division had bought him all the luxuries he had ever wanted.

And yet... Lee's ambitions had been beyond Hamiye's wildest dreams. When he heard them, he wanted to run and hide, but by then it was too late. He was bound to Lee by this dangerous knowledge. He must see it through to the end; with luck and good management, he would come safely through. And the money... The money this scheme of Lee's would pay made him dizzy. He could go to South America and live like a prince, or buy a new identity and stay in safe, civilized Europe, find a beautiful, sophisticated wife, raise a family, found a dynasty...

The buzzer sounded. Someone was at the front gate. He popped up a display and the gate camera showed him a black Mercedes. Lee's car. No-one got out. The car simply waited. Hamiye opened the gates and let the car in.

He went to the door and out onto the porch as the car

crunched across the gravel to a halt. The windows were tinted so that Hamiye could not see inside. The driver's door opened and Lee's driver got out and put on his cap. Another Chinese, Hamiye noted, also called Lee if he remembered correctly. It was such an affectation to have a driver in these days. It had once appeared to Hamiye as a mark of Lee's grand style. Lately it seemed a symptom of his megalomania.

The uniformed man marched up to where Hamiye stood. "Mr Hamiye, Mr Lee requests your presence at the Enfield facility immediately. I am to take you there at once."

Hamiye frowned at the man. "Is Mr Lee there, at the facility?"

The driver's face was completely expressionless. "Yes," he said.

"Is there a problem?"

"I do not know."

"Why didn't someone just call me? Why send you all the way out here?"

"It seems your phone is not working."

"What?" He checked and, even as he saw the "no signal" message, he realized what an idiot he'd been. The jammer he'd put on the Malone woman must be blanketing the whole area. Why the hell would that fool Langbroek have given him one so powerful? On the other hand, why had he been so stupid as to fail to check?

"I can't leave. I—" He had almost said he had a prisoner to guard, but he didn't know how much Lee's driver was in the great man's confidence. "I have things to do here."

"Mr Lee says to bring the woman."

"Bring her? What for? She's safe here."

The driver's expression did not change. "Mr Lee says to bring the woman."

Hamiye shut his mouth against any opinion of Mr Lee that might slip out. He took several angry breaths through his nose while the implacable driver waited patiently. "Fine," he said at last. "Wait here."

He stormed back into the house and went through to the large walk-in wardrobe that was Sandra's makeshift prison. He didn't want to stun her again—repeated use of a stunner could leave permanent nerve damage—but he drew the gun anyway and held it in his left hand, close to his body, as he threw back the bolts. She was sitting quietly on the mattress, watching him as he entered the room.

"I'm taking you somewhere else. There's no need to worry. Just cooperate and I won't have to shoot you again. All right?"

"Where are you taking me?"

"Does that really matter? Now stand up, I'm going to uncuff you from the wall and then cuff your hands together, like before." Her jaw clenched, but she stood up and waited for him. The handcuffs were an old-fashioned kind, with a key. Hamiye didn't like to overcomplicate things. He switched the gun to his right hand and stepped up close to her. He reached across and grabbed her shoulder, turning her to face the wall. He reasoned that he was perfectly safe until the moment both her hands were free. He pressed the barrel of the stunner against the small of her back. "Whatever you're thinking of doing won't work. So just relax and do as I say." He passed the key from his left hand to hers. "You know what to do," he told her. He took a small step back from her and his world exploded in pain.

Sandra turned on the spot, her right arm swinging across the front of him, at the same time knocking the stunner aside and raking across his stomach with some kind of sharp weapon. He completed his backwards step, looking down at himself. There was a small white object sticking out of his abdomen, blood oozing from a tear in his shirt. He had barely time to register that he was looking at the bowl of a plastic spoon before Sandra's foot connected with the side of his head and sent him spinning into the wall and then to the floor.

* * * *

Sandra could barely believe how well it had gone. She unlocked the handcuff and ran for the door. Hamiye was out cold. Her kick had been absolutely perfect. She wished she could do it that well when she was in front of her students. She pulled the comms jammer off her blouse and clipped it on the unconscious man as she ran from the room. It took her a while to find her way to the staircase and down to the front hallway. The door was standing open and she raced through, intending to keep on running until she got a comms signal and could make a call.

On the porch, she skidded to a halt. A long black car was standing in the drive and between her and the car was a man in a dark suit and a peaked cap.

"You must be Ms Malone," the man said, completely unruffled.

She ran, angling across the drive, hoping to get past him. He moved too, running to intercept her. Before he could, she stopped. He stopped too. They were just a few meters apart. If she were going to get clear, she would have to go through this strangely calm young man. The good news was that he hadn't drawn a gun.

"I don't want to hurt you," she said.

His straight face cracked a small smile. "You are most kind. I too have no desire to inflict pain or injury. If you would kindly wait in the car until Mr Hamiye joins us, we can be on our way with no harm to anyone."

Who the hell was this guy? "I'm afraid it's a bit late for Hamiye. He won't be joining us."

"Most unfortunate. Please, do not try to run."

Sandra had been shifting her position, hoping to get a clear line to the gate for a quick sprint, but the guy in the cap moved to block her.

"OK," Sandra said, losing patience. "Let's do this."

She moved closer, dropping into a balanced stance, fists balled, one arm bent close to her side ready to punch, the other up and angled across her chest, ready to block. Over many years of fending off unwanted attention, she'd found that simply assuming a fighting stance was enough to scare most men off. Some, however, needed a good kicking and this guy appeared to be one of them.

Then her heart sank as he too adopted a pose not too dissimilar from her own, only with his hands open and both raised in front of him. Her odd challenger was also some kind of martial-arts expert. From the stance, she guessed Kung Fu.

"What are you?" she asked. "The chauffeur?"

"Indeed."

"You don't have to do this. No-one will know I didn't just sneak past you. I'm sure they're not paying you enough to get your bones broken." He didn't reply, just watched her with careful eyes as they began to edge around one another, feinting, looking for openings. He shot out a punch. She blocked it and punched back, but he dodged away and resumed his catlike circling. He was fast and light on his feet. This was not going to be easy.

"What's your name?" she asked and saw surprise on his face. She struck, hard and fast, punching and kicking in a rapid, concentrated burst of violence. He blocked and counterpunched for all he was worth but he was in retreat. She cursed the slippery gravel of the drive, which made balance hard and took the force out of certain blows. But then she realized her opponent had the worst of it, wearing smooth-soled town shoes while she at least wore sneakers. The thought must have distracted her because the chauffeur ducked under a kick and leapt high into the air, swinging one of those very town shoes at her head. She blocked it awkwardly, was caught off-balance and had to retreat and re-establish her equilibrium before the follow-up came.

"Lee," the driver said, not pressing his attack, preferring also to centre himself and focus his mind.

"Any relation to the boss?"

"Sadly, no. Lee is a very common name."

The circling and feinting resumed. She was beginning to wonder how long this might go on. Lee was pretty good and in good shape too. She, on the other hand, had been stunned twice in the past twelve hours and had had little sleep the night before. If she let the dance go on too long, Lee would have the advantage. The key to winning was the gravel.

She let Lee fire a few punches at her, blocking and retreating, trying to look alarmed and panicky, letting him come in a bit harder, feel a bit more confident. Then he aimed a kick at her head, the very move she'd been hoping for. She caught his leg by the ankle and held it as she swung inside his defences and kicked down hard at his knee. His bones did not break but the foot still on the ground slid out from under him and she pulled hard on the captive ankle to make his fall fast and clumsy. As his back hit the ground, she was already down on one knee beside him. She hit him three times in the face, as hard as she could. Even as he went into choking paroxysms, he managed to twist his body and kick her in the back. The impact was more annoying than dangerous, yet it shifted her aim. Instead of hitting his face, her final blow struck him in the throat with deadly force.

She stood up and stepped back from him. He writhed on the floor, clutching at his throat. She must have crushed his windpipe. She could still feel the hideous softness of his neck against her knuckles. He might have just minutes to live. She had only meant to hurt him, to disable him. She had not meant... this.

She had no idea what to do for him unless she could perhaps find a tube—a hosepipe maybe, or something from the car—and force it down into his lungs. She cast about desperately, a part of her mind yelling that she had to run, to get out of there fast.

That's when she saw Hamiye, lurching across the porch towards her, stunner raised. The lower half of his shirt and the top of his casual slacks were soaked in blood.

She pointed at Lee. "We've got to—"

Hamiye roared with fury and fired.

* * * *

"Where are we going?"

Fourget looked up from the virtual display he'd been studying. "For a day in the country."

Cara had been giving the Frenchman a lot of leeway, not just because he was helping her find her mother, but also because he was really hot in a strong-silent-type kind of way. It was a type she had not known she liked until now. But he didn't seem to get the fact that they were a team and that teammates shared their information.

The car they were in was a big, off-road monster. It was driving itself while, in theory, Cara and Fourget relaxed in the back. But Fourget had spent the past hour studying—his commplant slaved to her own so that it did not access the net directly—while Cara slowly grew more agitated with her taciturn companion.

"You're some kind of agent, right?" she asked. He ignored her. "You probably work with other agents all the time, don't you? So you must at least be somewhat familiar with the idea of discussing things and coming to an agreement and all that teamwork kind of thing." He did not react. "Am I right?"

He looked up at her. "When I am on a mission, I give the orders, and my team follows them."

She gave up trying to reason with him. "Where are we going? Tell me now or I'll stop the car." The car was hired in her name. Her commands overrode his.

He looked at her again, this time with tight lips and hard eyes. "Do you have to be such a silly little girl all the time?"

She caught her breath and felt tears spring to her eyes. He might as well have slapped her, it hurt so much. "I just wanted…" Her self-justification stuck in her throat as a wave of anger overcame the shock. "How dare you speak to me like that? You coarse, inarticulate bully." And then she was awash with self pity. Tears poured down her cheeks. She looked away quickly to hide them. What the hell was wrong with her? Why was she going to pieces like this?

"I just want to find my mother. Even you must have a mother. How would you feel if some sick bastard had her tied up somewhere? Eh?" She was appalled at her own outburst but the anger was coming back and she couldn't shut up. "I suppose you'd just grunt and shrug and get on with the mission. You know, I thought you were a robot when I first saw you in that stupid suit and the helmet. Well, I was right. You're an emotionless machine without an ounce of sympathy. You just think I'm some kind of nuisance, but it's my mother we're looking for. My mother! I know you don't know many words, but surely you know that one?"

Some kind of primitive emotion was working its way to the surface of his chiselled features, but she could not bear to wait for whatever robot beeps and chirps he might utter. She raised a hand to cut him off and moved to sit as far away from him as she could, staring out of the window at the hedgerows streaming past. "If you say anything, I'll attack you with a can opener. Your programming only lets you speak ten words a day or something and I don't want you blowing a fuse. Not till we've found my mother. Just get on with whatever the hell you were doing that was so important you couldn't answer a simple bloody question from someone who needed a bit of human consideration."

The car turned into a drive and pulled up at a two-meter-high metal gate. Neither Cara nor Fourget moved for several seconds, then the Frenchman got out.

She watched as he inspected the gate for a moment. He touched it gingerly but nothing happened. Then he jumped, caught the top and vaulted himself over it, landing lightly at the other side. Cara saw him grimace and remembered his bruised ribs. He set off up the curving drive, moving from tree to shrub as he went, keeping low and moving fast. In a moment, he was out of sight. Cara got out of the car and followed him.

She found him at the side of the house, studying it from a bank of rhododendron bushes. It was a bright day but cold, with a thin icy wind blowing at them across the front of the building. It took her a moment to take in the scene. A large black Mercedes saloon parked in the drive. The big house, silent, with its front door standing open. Perhaps someone had come from the car and run inside in a hurry. Beyond the car, a round black object lay on the gravel. It looked like a peaked cap from some kind of uniform.

Fourget drew a gun Cara hadn't realized he was carrying and straightened up from his crouch. "Wait here," he said, keeping his eyes on the house. "Run those plates." He raised his gun in a two-handed grip, sighting along it. He kept the gun along his line of sight, she noticed. When he looked left or right he turned his body from the waist, so the gun always pointed at what he saw. He crossed the drive, then went up to the house and in through the open door.

Run those plates? Just like that. Fourget gives the orders and the team follows them! Unbelievable. And how am I supposed to "run those plates", mon General? Then she remembered telling him that she had resources and that it was actually true. She phoned Dominic. He answered with a big smile, pleased to see her, and began asking about her mother.

"Dom, not now," she said, cutting him off. "I need you to run some plates."

His face fell. "You need what?"

"Can you do it?"

"Run some plates? You mean find information about a vehicle registration?"

"If you can't do it, just say so."

He flapped his lips in silence for a moment, presumably trying to find a way to tell her how illegal it was and how much trouble he'd get into. Then he stopped, closed his eyes and said, "Yes. What's the number?"

She read off the registration of the Merc. "How long will it take?"

"I don't know. A few minutes maybe."

"Good. Call me back."

She hung up. She left her hideout behind the bush and walked over to the house, arriving just as Fourget re-emerged. He was staring at the ground and when she followed his gaze, she saw the trail of blood. It was just a few drops here and there, not even a trickle, but her stomach turned. "Oh God," she said. Fourget said nothing but walked out onto the drive. For several seconds, he stood still, looking back and forth across the gravel.

"Is it Mum's?" Cara asked. It was all she could think.

Fourget raised a hand for her to be silent and a bolt of anger shot through her. Before she could say anything he walked briskly away back towards the house, this time, to the other side. He disappeared around the corner and she ran after him. She found him kneeling beside a young Asian man in a black suit, touching his throat. The man's face looked dark and puffy. Fourget got up quickly and stood between Cara and the body.

"It's a bit bloody late to go all gallant on me. Who's he?"

"The driver of the car, I think." He motioned for her to go back to the front of the house and she started walking.

"Is he dead?"

"Oh yes." He looked at her, his expression grave. "You have seen a dead man before."

She could see them now if she closed her eyes. All of them were always with her. But she had grown skilled at not letting them haunt her. Except in her dreams.

They rounded the house and came to a halt in the drive. "So?" she asked. He raised an eyebrow. "So what's the story?

I saw you Holmesing the place. What happened? Where's Mum? And where are we anyway?"

All he said was, "We should get back to the car."

She felt a scream boiling in her chest. "Just fucking..." She took a deep breath. "I really need to know, so just... please... tell me."

Their eyes met and she thought he looked genuinely confused by her outburst.

"*Eh bien*," he said. "In the house, there is a room where a prisoner was held. Your mother, I think. In the room also, there was blood. Someone had been stabbed there with a plastic spoon. Farid Hamiye, we must suppose. It would make no sense for him to stab her with such an implement." He looked at her as if seeking agreement, but Cara's emotions were all over the place—pride in her ingenious mother, horror that there had been violence, fear for her mother, confusion about how the Asian man in the bushes fit in.

"If we assume that is true, and not that for example Hamiye stabbed Ms Malone *and* dealt with this chauffeur alone, or that while he was fighting with the chauffeur Ms Malone, injured, escaped her prison and came out here to surprise her captor, then the rest follows sensibly." Fourget glanced at Cara and hurried on. "I mean that the first scenario is the most, perhaps the only, likely one. The gravel of this drive is kept neat, you will see," he said, nodding towards an expanse of smoothly raked driveway. "But over here, the gravel is kicked up and disturbed. I think someone had a fight here. My guess is it was your mother—I know she is skilled in these arts, while Hamiye's file suggests he would prefer other methods—and the driver of this car," he flicked his head towards the black Merc. "I say this because whoever fought the man in the suit probably knew well how to kill a man with her bare hands."

"But if Mum won the fight…?"

"Where is she? I think she was taken away, perhaps by Hamiye. It was he who escaped, injured, and surprised the fighters. There is a trail of blood from inside the house to where the fight took place. Then there are drag-marks and blood leading from there to where I found the dead man. The driver was pulled there by Hamiye, who continued to drip blood as he went. Then there are other drag-marks from the fight that end up at the garage, where another car might have been waiting."

"But if Mum won the fight…?"

Fourget shrugged. "She may have been injured or she may have been unconscious. I do not know. But Hamiye took her away in a car, so she is most likely still alive—or why would he not have dumped her with the other body?"

It was cold comfort, but Cara clung to it. "So Mum stabbed Hamiye, ran for it, met some Asian guy, fought with him, killed him, but Hamiye came out after her and dragged the dead guy out of sight and put Mum in a car and drove away?" Fourget nodded. "So she's still alive but Hamiye might be bleeding to death?"

"Not bleeding to death. There would be far more blood." He gave a small wry smile. "Very annoyed though, I would think."

"So where has he taken her?"

She'd been so impressed with his deductions so far that she was genuinely surprised when he said he didn't know.

"But I know where we should look," he said.

Before she could ask him, her phone rang. She answered it, staring at Dominic's smiling face for a long moment before remembering why on Earth he'd be calling her. Fourget stepped up and touched her arm. He tapped his ear and Cara patched him into the call, sound only, his touch being all that was needed to establish a link between their two commplants.

"It's a black Mercedes, right?" Dominic asked. She nodded. "Good, then it belongs to Lee Shaozu, Senior Executive Manager, Special Projects Division, HiQua." He put on a shrewd expression. "That's your mother's company, right? No coincidence, eh?"

"Thank you, Dom, you're a—"

Fourget interrupted her. "We need to track Hamiye. Can your friend do that?"

"Did you hear that, Dom?"

"Hear what? Is someone with you? Who's there?"

"It's no-one. Dom, I need you to track a guy called Farid Hamiye. He's another HiQua employee. I think he's kidnapped my mum."

"Kidnapped? Look, Cara, this is all getting really heavy. Don't you think you should go to the police?"

"Let me talk to him," Fourget said.

"It's all right, I can handle—"

"Let me talk to him. We don't have time for this."

Tight-lipped, she gave him full access. Fourget's face appeared on the call. "Dominic, I am Lieutenant Pierre Fourget of EDF Military Intelligence." Dominic swallowed hard but said nothing. "I need your assistance in tracing that car. Serious crimes have already been committed and we need that information in a hurry. Cara says you are some kind of genius. She has faith in you. So if you can do it, do it quickly. If not, tell me right now."

Cara jumped in with a quick summary of where her mother had been and where she might be now.

Dominic looked terrified. "I—I don't know—"

Fourget cut him off. "My friend, a woman's life is at stake. Now give me your answer."

"Er, yes. Yes, I can do it, but—"

"Good. We'll await your call."

Fourget hung up. Cara scowled at him. "I never said he was a genius."

"But you do have faith in him. Let's get back to the car." They set off at a jog up the drive. Casually, he said, "He seems like a nice boy. You could have done worse."

Cara narrowed her eyes at him, hoping he was just teasing her and didn't really think Dom was her boyfriend. Perhaps she liked him better when he was silent.

* * * *

They were weaving through dense traffic by the time Dominic called back. Several times they had encountered police diversions, although they had seen nothing to explain them.

"Aren't you watching the feeds?" Dominic asked when Cara complained about it. "Big demonstrations all over the city. All over the country. That guy, whatshisname, is talking in Hyde Park about the whatsit, the tempocalypse. You know, end of the world stuff. All the God-botherers are out waving placards."

"Why? What do they want?"

"I dunno. They say the government should stop messing about with time, or something. Anyway, it's all pretty peaceful so far but I wouldn't want to be out driving around London today."

Cara didn't want to think about religious protests. After Washington, her views on organized religion were unprintable. "Did you find the car, Dom?"

"No, but I did the next best thing." He waited, as if expecting her to ask.

"Don't play games, Dom. Just tell me."

"We know the engineering works had a suppressor jamming your mother's comms signal, right? And it never appeared again, even when they took her away. So I reckoned she must have the suppressor on her, attached to her somehow."

"How does that help?" How would they *ever* find her?

Dom was grinning. "I just had to look for comms outages."

"But the country's got outages all over the place." The disappointment was threatening to choke her.

"Yes, but the one I was looking for was moving. All the rest were standing still."

Of course! She breathed in pure relief. The boy really was a genius. "But…"

"But how could I track nothing, even if it is moving?" She let him take a moment of triumph. "The national roadNet. It's a system of sensors that covers all the main roads and a lot of the minor ones too. They report to a central database using the comms network. They send signals just like a commplant does. Each time your mother's car passed a roadNet node, it went offline and the SCADA system—don't worry what that is—reported a fault. All I had to do was track the faults." He grinned. "And where do you suppose they lead?"

Cara shook her head.

"Right back to the engineering works!"

"Oh God, Dom, you're amazing! Thank you, thank you, thank you!" She hung up on his beaming face. "They've taken her back to Clarke Engineering," she told Fourget, remembering, even as she spoke, the giants that guarded it.

"Good," the Frenchman said and continued his brooding silence.

"Good? Why is that good?"

His blue eyes swivelled to look at her. "Because that's where we've been heading all this time."

* * * *

After a couple of false starts, Jay eventually found himself speaking to a Colonel Forrester at Aldermaston. He was a round-faced man in his thirties, with a cherub's mouth and eyes that would have liked to twinkle had not the occasion been so serious. "So you've been chatting to Olivia," he said. "I don't suppose I need remind you how highly classified her work is."

"You've seen my clearance, Colonel. I'm sure you wouldn't be taking this call if it wasn't sufficient."

"All the same, we try not to let this kind of information spread any farther than is necessary."

Jay was impatient to get down to business. "Colonel, would you rather I asked my boss to call your boss and smooth the way for this conversation?"

Forrester's little mouth turned down at the corners. "I'm just being cautious, Mr Kennedy. Setting the scene. I'm sure you understand."

"Call me Jay."

"Very well. Robert. Bob, if you like."

Whatever name might suit such a chubby face, Bob was definitely not it. "So, Bob, tell me about Project FORESIGHT."

Forrester shifted and pursed his lips, as if the mere mention of the name made him want to hide under his desk. "What do you want to know?"

"Is it possible to travel to the future?"

"Not at the moment, no."

"But you believe it can be done?"

"That's what Olivia and the others tell me. I'm an administrator, not a physicist."

"So you haven't done it yet?"

"No."

"Has anybody else?"

"Anybody else?"

"Olivia mentioned a Dr Hong. Has he done it?"

"Hong is reported to have died. All we really know is he went missing three years ago. It's possible that the Chinese have him under arrest—or that they executed him."

"Or that he's working for them somewhere in secret?"

"It's possible."

"So, have the Chinese managed to travel forwards in time?"

Forrester pursed his lips. "Your guess is as good as mine."

"Where do you get your information, Bob?"

"MI6, mostly."

Jay nodded. Six was supposed to share any time-travel-related intel with K Section, but Jay had never seen anything about Hong. He tried another approach. "Bob, if you ever get FORESIGHT working, what will the side effects be?"

"Side effects?"

"The consequences of creating temporal anomalies. Is there an equivalent of a timesplash?"

"We won't know until we've done some experiments. The future is *terra incognita* I'm afraid."

"But you've done risk assessments."

"Yes."

"And what did they turn up?" It was like pulling teeth.

Bob hesitated and Jay could see as clear as day that the man had something to hide.

"Look, Jay. FORESIGHT is long-term speculative stuff—like uploading minds into robots and star travel using Alcubierre warp drives. We might not have a result for years. Decades. The risk assessments we've done are little more than our tekniks sitting around in a meeting room brainstorming wild ideas."

"Do any of those wild ideas sound like what happened two nights ago?"

Forrester's face set hard. "I'm sorry, Mr Kennedy, but that's all I'm prepared to say on the subject without explicit orders from my superiors."

"Come on, man, we're on the same side here."

"Maybe. I'd rather someone else made that decision, to be honest."

Jay pressed him again but Forrester had shut up inside a shell that was particularly well plated across his arse. He did give Jay the name of a two-star general he could approach if he wanted to take his "information request" any farther.

They hung up and Jay swung back in his chair to stare at the ceiling. Forrester was hiding something—but, if his people hadn't actually got FORESIGHT to work, why would he need to be so secretive about its possible side effects?

And where the hell is Sandra?

The thought surprised him, popping into his head without any warning. But, on reflection, it shouldn't have been such a surprise. He knew Fourget was pretending to be unconscious—despite the call that morning from Cara, who was a surprisingly convincing liar. Which meant the Frenchman was in the wind and on the trail again. And Jay would have been very happy to collude in the feeble subterfuge except he knew that, whatever Fourget did or said, his headstrong daughter would stick to him like a limpet until she found her mum. Which meant Cara was still in danger too.

He stood up and paced about. He should go over there. To hell with this useless investigation. His family needed him. Commercial flights were just about back to normal. He could be in London in a couple of hours. He was wasting his time in Berlin, chasing half-arsed leads about future time travel. At the very least, he could catch up with Fourget and hog-tie Cara to get her out of the man's hair.

And yet... What if FORESIGHT, or something like it, really could work, and really could create the havoc and the weirdness the world had witnessed the other night? Was any other agency following this line of investigation? Would they all miss it if he let it drop? He had to face it: the event had been *something* like a backwash. It had also been nothing at all like one. How many people investigating this would see that, would know it from personal experience?

"Jay?"

He turned sharply to find Kadan Dudding standing in his office doorway.

The Chief Analyst pulled a comic face that clearly asked if it was a good time. "I can go away if you like. Only I've got a few things that might be adding up to something."

Jay waved him in and Dudding closed the door after himself.

"Whatcha got?" Jay was more than ready for some hard facts and a theory that didn't involve impossibilities like travelling to the future. He sat down and so did Dudding.

"We've been looking at timings. The sunspot data was extremely valuable there. In fact, I reached out to a few observatories and got some very interesting stuff." He paused for effect but probably saw the impatience on Jay's face and so hurried on. "There was an increase in sunspot activity—a massive one. While we were experiencing quakes down here, the Sun was experiencing the same kind of thing. So was the Moon. So was Mars."

"How do you know?"

"There are working seismometers up there still. In fact, the astronomical data was fantastic. It's all timestamped to the tiniest fraction of a second and there are observatories— on Earth and in space—looking at almost everything in the Solar System all the time—and at stars in our galaxy and at other galaxies. Huge amounts of extremely precise data." He seemed very happy about it but Jay was beginning to worry about where all this was leading.

Dudding leaned forwards in his excitement. "There was a scintillation in the rings of Saturn."

"A scintillation?"

"The best explanation is that a significant portion of the particles in the rings were displaced slightly and that new particles appeared." Again he paused, waiting for the penny to drop.

Slowly, Jay said, "You think the same thing that happened here happened to the Sun and to Saturn."

"And the Moon and Mars and, as far as I can tell, to every astronomical object within the Solar System, up to and including the inner fringes of the Oort Cloud."

"The Oort Cloud?"

"It's a huge cloud of comets and other junk that orbits the

Sun way out beyond all the planets, way beyond the Kuiper Belt. It extends to almost a light year away from the Sun."

Jay struggled with the implications. "You're saying that whatever affected us affected the whole Solar System, even out as far as this...?"

"Oort Cloud, yes. Unfortunately, we've only got a couple of days of observations. The speed of light limits how far we can look in that time, but so far every new piece of data that comes from the period of the event the other night is consistent with this thing happening everywhere. Trouble is, since the far end of the Oort cloud is as much as a light year away, we won't know for a full year if the effect went out that far. Same with the stars: Alpha Centauri is a very long way out."

"That's the closest star, yes?"

"Well, it's a binary but, yes, it's the closest—at four-point-two light years. That means—"

"Right. Four years before we know. All the same, it's... staggering."

Jay sat back to contemplate the incredible size of the phenomenon. He did a quick look-up and found that two light days came to fifty billion kilometres.

"Yes, it is," Dudding agreed. "But that's not the most interesting thing about all this. We've been trying to—"

"We?"

"A couple of astronomers I've been working with. They're sworn to secrecy. Don't worry. Anyway, we've been trying to calculate the rate of spread of the phenomenon and it seems to be instantaneous."

"Instantaneous?"

"It happened everywhere at once. It's got the astronomers very excited."

Even Jay could see the importance of this. "So it didn't come from Earth?" Because, if it had, the effect would spread, at an absolute maximum, at the speed of light. The backwash from a timesplash expanded at a very much slower speed than that.

"That's right. It might be happening everywhere in the Universe simultaneously, but even if it's local to our Solar System, it's still on a massive scale."

Jay found himself staring at Dudding and blinking. He had barely a thought in his head, just, *Not a timesplash. Not from Earth. Not future time travel.* He pulled himself up. "So it was some kind of natural phenomenon?"

Dudding pulled another comic face that said, What else could it be?

"What do your astronomer friends say?"

"They say it could only be a collision between branes. They think it's wonderful."

"Brains?"

"Branes. Short for membranes. Some variant of string theory that has multiple Universes floating about in a multidimensional soup, bumping into one another from time to time." He waved a hand past the top of his head. "Didn't understand a word of it. Cosmology's not really my thing."

Jay felt his body lift as if he'd been pumped full of air. If the event had been a natural phenomenon, it was none of his business, none of K Section's business. He could drop the whole damned investigation and focus on what Sandra had dug up, make it all official.

"Kadan, I want that in a report and in my inbox in half an hour. I'm going to see Crystal right now." He got up and Dudding scrambled to rise too. Jay was so elated, he grabbed the analyst's hand and shook it. "Excellent work. Brilliant."

He swung open his office door and left Dudding open mouthed in his wake. He almost ran to Crystal's office. He burst out laughing. Time travel to the future indeed!

* * * *

"Time travel to the future?" Sandra asked, incredulous. "In that?"

The black sphere sat on its platform at the dead centre of the six pillars. It was scarred and dented, as if people had been hitting it with sticks and throwing rocks at it.

"Come closer," Dr Hong said, and set off towards it. One of the giant super-soldiers held her arm firmly and urged her to follow. At the best of times, she'd have thought twice about tackling such a brute. Today she didn't bother with the second thought. She felt weak and her muscles ached. That last stunner attack by Hamiye had really shaken her up. With her hands cuffed behind her back again, she felt wrung out and helpless. So she walked tamely along after the morose old physicist, hoping for a miracle.

Close up, the damage to the sphere looked even worse. Some of the gouges in its skin were so deep they had cut through the paint to expose bare metal. And that added to her scepticism. If you were going to make a vehicle to travel in time, you'd make it light, as light as possible. Every gram of mass cost energy. Sure, they had plenty of F2 generators in the building but a metal sphere that size couldn't be lobbed very far even if they could draw on the entire National Grid.

Hong put his hand on a green button on the rim of the sphere and a section opened and lifted up. They moved to the front to look inside. There wasn't much room in there. A large black padded seat with restraints; instruments embedded in the door that was now above their heads; and thick, cream-coloured padding on the walls—that was it. From the difference in internal versus external volumes, there was plenty of space in there for electronics or other machinery.

"Cosy," she said. Then she noticed the large brown stain on the floor and other, smaller smears on the walls and door. Her stomach knotted. Someone had bled in there. Possibly, they'd died.

"What's this all about?" she asked.

"They need another pilot," the giant said. The idea seemed to please him.

Hong spoke up. "It's very simple. We don't need you to do anything much, just push a couple of buttons. We could reprogram it to be fully automatic if we had the time."

Sandra could hardly believe what she was hearing. "You think you're going to put me in that thing after it killed your last volunteer?"

Hong hurried to correct her. "No, no, the chronosphere did not kill him. That was... something else. The sphere is perfectly safe."

Meaning someone had definitely died in there. "Of course, and that's ketchup on the floor, I suppose?"

"No that's blood all right," the giant said. "Damnedest thing. Tell her what happened, Doc." Not waiting for Hong, he leaned into the inside of the sphere, pulling Sandra along with him. He poked a sausage-sized finger into a small tear in the seat. "What do you think did that?"

The tear was a couple of centimetres long and quite neat. She noticed another and then another. There was one in the wall padding too. It looked as if someone had repeatedly stabbed the chair and wall with a small, sharp knife.

"Arrows," the big man said, grinning. "When it came back,

the pilot was like a pincushion. Shot full of arrows."

Sandra turned to Hong. "I don't understand." When was the last time they used bows and arrows in England? The Middle Ages? And why would the arrows come back with the sphere anyway? They should have stayed in the past where they belonged.

Hong was agitated. "There was a miscalculation. The sphere overshot, went far into the future. It should not have happened. A careless error. Everybody is rushing so much. There is no time to make proper checks. It has already been fixed. It won't happen again. There will be no danger."

And there was that talk about the future again. Sandra looked at the sphere, at the tall gantries around it, at the blood on the cream padding. Finally, she looked at Hong. "The future isn't made yet," she said.

The old man shrugged. "Should that stop us from making it ourselves?"

"But—But there's nothing there yet. To go forwards would be to create the Universe. The energies…"

Hong shook his head. "We make only a narrow strip. A path to travel along. The energy is there waiting. We need these reactors only for an initial shove, if you like, to shake the sphere loose of our spacetime. The Universe is straining at the leash. It wants to be born, to grow. Time wants to flow. All you need to do is give it a nudge and it will do the rest. The trick is to rein it in, to control the immense power you unleash. To go a million years into the future is trivial. To go one day is almost impossible."

Sandra felt her heart beat faster. Despite herself the idea was exhilarating. To travel into the future! Then she remembered her predicament. "Send one of your tekniks. Send pretty boy here." She nodded towards the giant still holding her by the arm. "Go yourself for all I care. You're not getting me in that thing."

"The tekniks are too valuable to risk." She turned at the sound of Hamiye's rich, cultured voice. "Mr Langbroek's men…" he glanced at the mercenary "… have already made their position clear. I'm afraid it has to be you, Sandra."

"How's your stomach?" she asked. She could see a neat bandage beneath the tear in his bloodstained shirt. "I hope it doesn't get infected or anything."

Hamiye didn't rise to the bait. "Such a fuss," he said, walking past her to look inside the sphere. "You'll only be going two weeks into the future. You won't have to do anything, just pop out for a minute, confirm the date, hop back in, and bring it home. Honestly, even a child could do it." He turned suddenly to face her. "Your daughter for example."

Her jaw set but she said, as calmly as she could. "You don't have my daughter. You don't even know where she is."

Hamiye smiled. "Tell her, Dr Hong."

To his credit, the old man looked ashamed of himself. "You tell her," he snapped.

"One of Dr Hong's clever young assistants found her for me. You won't believe this but, at the moment, Cara's in a rental car, driving here. I think stupidity must run in your family. She's just been to my house, by the way. I hope all that blood didn't upset her."

Relying on Langbroek's unshakeable grip to support her, Sandra leapt into the air and fired a fast, high kick at Hamiye's head. It would have connected easily, Hamiye was so unprepared for the attack, but, with a quick jerk of his arm, Langbroek threw her aim off and the kick went wild. Too late, Hamiye cringed away from her. She let her momentum carry her round the giant's body, closing the gap between herself and his massive chest, then threw all her strength into smashing her free elbow into his nose, hoping it might hurt him enough to make him let go. But Langbroek pulled back his head as if they'd rehearsed the move all morning and the blow missed. With a strength that almost dislocated her shoulder, he pulled her back to his side.

Hong had stepped away from them and was looking horrified. Hamiye stood there scowling. When she looked up at Langbroek, she found him grinning down at her.

"So," Hamiye said, regaining his composure. "What's it to be?"

She wished she could stab him with that spoon again. "If I do this, you leave Cara out of it?"

"Scouts honour."

"Honour?" She almost spat the word.

She saw a hint of bitterness in his pursed lips. "Believe me or not," he said. "You don't really have a choice. You do this for us and Cara won't be hurt. Langbroek?"

The hamster shrugged. "It's your dime. The kid's off limits. But if she comes back with that special forces jerkoff, the bastard's hide is mine."

"So long as the girl's safe, you can do what you like to anybody else." He turned to Sandra. "Satisfied?"

She looked into his eyes. The fact was she had almost nothing to bargain with and she would have to take the risk. All the same, she thought she could see something trustworthy in Hamiye's face, ridiculous as that seemed. She turned to Hong.

"All right. Show me how to drive this thing."

* * * *

172

Crystal heard Jay out in silence and then called for Laura and Kadan to join them. "How's your man?" she asked as they waited.

"Fourget?" Jay worded his answer carefully. "I had a call from the hospital this morning to say he is still unconscious and has a concussion." He didn't mention that the call had come from his daughter.

"Sounds serious."

"Oh, I'm sure he'll be all right. Knowing Pierre, he'll be on his feet and chasing after bad guys before we know it." *Quite literally*, Jay thought.

"And your investigations into future time travel?"

"Hit a wall. The Brits are being cagey about their findings but everyone seems to agree it hasn't happened yet and probably never will."

"And your, er... Sandra Malone?"

Jay wished Laura and Kadan would get a move on. "She's still missing. And I still believe there's something fishy going on at HiQua. In fact, once you've spoken to my people, I'm taking a team over to the UK to get to the bottom of it." He didn't need Crystal's permission to set his section's operational priorities. He just needed her to agree that the event of two nights ago was not their problem.

"Assuming I agree."

"Yes, of course."

Laura and Kadan came in carrying coffees and took seats. Laura didn't meet Jay's eyes and he took that as a bad sign. Jay had his chief analyst go over the astronomical findings once more.

"Laura?" Crystal asked when he'd finished.

The physicist asked the analyst a few questions, mostly about the quality of the evidence and the teams that had worked on producing it.

"Well?" Crystal asked, cutting the discussion short.

"It sounds convincing," Laura said. "It's definitely not a timesplash—unless it happened in interstellar space an unimaginably long time ago and was unimaginably huge, and we're just feeling it now. We'd be able to test for that by finding asymmetries on a galactic scale."

Crystal wasn't interested in technical asides. "So you agree it's a natural phenomenon?"

"I agree it's too big to have anything to do with us. Disruption across the whole Solar System is well beyond human capabilities. Whether there's some natural explanation for this or if it's our first encounter with extraterrestrial intelligences, I couldn't say."

"Extra—?" Crystal bit her tongue. "But you agree this is outside the remit of K Section?"

Jay waited for Laura to give her seal of approval but, instead, she hesitated. "There's still an unknown."

"An unknown?" Jay asked, his irritation showing.

Laura glanced at him, obviously surprised by his tone. "There's still the future time-travel angle. Olivia—" She looked at Crystal. "Dr Olivia Bradley, our consultant from Aldermaston, has shown me the Hong formulae. We'd be wrong to dismiss all this as blue-skies research."

Jay couldn't keep the impatience out of his tone. "Is there anything at all in these Hong formulae that suggest you can shake a whole star system to its foundations with them?"

"Well… no, but nor is there anything in the gigarange formulae for *backwards* time travel that would lead you to expect a backwash."

Jay found it hard to sit still. "Look, I was the only one taking this forward time-travel stuff halfway seriously ten minutes ago, and now you're telling us it exists and it can rattle the whole Solar System. No, that's not it, is it? You're saying that because we don't know what it can do, we can assume it's the most powerful force we've ever encountered, that it can shake the Universe and raise the dead and do it all simultaneously everywhere?"

He was glaring at Laura, waiting for her response. Then he realized that everyone in the room was watching him.

Crystal looked away first. "Thank you, Laura, Kadan. That'll be all for now. Jay, if I could just have another minute or two."

The others got up and left the room. Jay kept his eyes on Crystal's desk until the door closed behind them. Crystal leaned back in her chair and regarded him. "Not like you to be snappish, Jay."

"No. Sorry."

"I'm seeing it a lot, lately. People in the corridors of power are having kittens. The rumour is that it's a Chinese secret weapon."

"Against who? God?"

"Others are just starting to add up the cost. I don't think they have enough zeroes in their spreadsheets for what it will take to repair all the damage. They're working on a fifty-trillion-euro bailout for the insurance companies. Either that or they'll all go bust. It drives civil servants a bit crazy when they have to explain that kind of thing to their political masters. We're looking at yet another recession—and in an election year too."

"It's nothing to do with any of that," Jay said. "I just probably need to get some sleep. It's been a long forty-eight hours."

Crystal went on studying him. "You've got plenty of

vacation time to take."

"No! I mean, I have things to do. Maybe later. In a week or two." He needed the section's resources in London. HiQua was using hamsters. He needed something more than an optimistic outlook and a stunner.

"Is it your daughter?"

"What do you know about Cara?"

She held up her hands, palms out. "Nothing specific. Don't worry."

Jay wondered if that was concern in her eyes and, if it was, whether it was for him or her department.

She sighed and sat upright. A decision had been made. "All right, Jay. This is what we'll do. You're going to take a team to London and join Fourget in extricating Sandra Malone and your daughter from whatever mess they're in. I'm putting Captain Harnois in charge here until you get back." She paused to let him speak but he said nothing. "When you get back, I will review the details of your little adventure and come to a decision about whether it was justified as a legitimate K Section operation. If it was not, I will expect your resignation."

Jay had no idea if Sandra's hunch about HiQua's involvement in clandestine time travel was justified or not. All he knew was that she was in trouble, that Cara was probably heading into trouble, and that he had to go. "Thank you," he said, and he meant it. The director had been incredibly generous.

"I recruited you, Jay," she said. "I put a whole section in your hands because I trusted your expertise and your judgement. If what you're doing now is all for a love you lost eighteen years ago, I'm going to be seriously disappointed."

"Yes, Ma'am."

* * * *

"I just confirm the date and come right back?" Sandra clipped the harness around her. On the inside, the sphere was cramped but comfortable. She didn't wear any jumpgear or even a protective helmet, yet she had the strong feeling she was about to be fired out of a cannon—inside the cannonball.

Hong nodded. He was overseeing every step of the mission himself, checking and double-checking. The mistake that had killed his last pilot had left everyone on edge. Behind him were two of the muscle-bound giants, pointing their machine guns at her. Behind them stood Hamiye and Lee. The big man himself had come clattering in by helicopter just thirty minutes earlier and hung like a threat over everyone's head.

"You never told me why you didn't have a backup pilot, Lee." She'd been meaning to ask.

Lee cast an angry glance at Hong. To Sandra, he said, "The whole project is designed from the ground up to use a human pilot because of the uncertainties involved with the possibility of overshoot and the unexpected conditions we might encounter at the other end. In theory, we could – and should, given how things have turned out – reprogram your trip to be automatic. However, I'm told we just don't have the time to change everything. Some might consider that a stupid blunder by our chief scientist."

Hong looked away but said nothing.

"In fact, I had two backup pilots, Ms Malone. The first one was injured when a building fell on him the other night. The second one refused to step up. I had him shot. That's why we're so pleased you chose to volunteer."

Sandra noticed Hamiye glance quickly at his boss. So the head of security hadn't known about the second standby pilot's execution. "What's your story, Lee? I mean, I've known some managers I'd classify as borderline psychotic. Some not so borderline, come to think of it. But I don't think I've ever met one who has his employees shot."

Lee's smirk fell away. "And for a software tester, you seem quite an enthusiastic killer yourself."

"That was Hamiye's fault." She could still feel the chauffeur's windpipe collapse beneath her fist. Snarling, she said, "You know, for a business exec, you certainly have a casual attitude to murder."

The man's smirk was back. "I find it's very good for morale."

"A graduate of the Genghis Khan School of Management." Which made her think of horsemen shooting arrows, and then of her own possible fate. She turned to Hong. "Just how far into the future did your last pilot go?"

"About two hundred years." He unplugged a piece of monitoring equipment and stepped away from the sphere. "We're ready to launch," he announced. Before he left the sphere and went to his control desk, he added, "It was just one possible future."

The tekniks shut the hatch and a dim light came on inside. She heard the seals engage with a hiss. Her mouth felt dry as she gripped the arm rests, tensing herself against God-knew-what. *I have got to stop all this time travelling,* she told herself. It had helped to taunt Lee. It helped to be flippant. Yet here in the silence of the sphere, she felt the fear gnawing at her.

Fear and despair. She had expected Jay to rescue her. He'd let her down. Crazy as it was, she realized she had been waiting for him to come crashing in with a tank, or a squad of

Marines, or something, tripping over his own feet probably, but being there, making it all right.

Alone, on the verge of this impossible trip to a future world that would only exist because she was going there, a world where no-one could follow her and any horror might await her, she felt numbing fear building like an explosion inside her.

"Pilot, please set the controls to external and indicate readiness," a voice said through a speaker in the door. She reached forwards and hit a big, square yellow button with the word "EXTERNAL" on it. The button lit up; they would now be able to control the launch from outside. The "Ready" indicator was inside a little red plastic casing. She had to lift the casing to reveal the small, silver switch. The switch had two settings, "Locked" and "Ready". It was in the locked position. If she threw the switch to "Ready", they could proceed with the launch. If not, the sphere would not respond. It meant the pilot had the final say in whether the sphere launched or not. It meant Sandra did.

She flipped up the cap, put a finger on the switch and closed her eyes. "What the hell?" she said, and flicked it.

"Ten seconds to launch," the teknik said. "Eight. Seven..."

And her mind threw her back to the cage in Ommen, twenty years earlier, the crowd screaming and the splashmusik thundering and Klaatu's robotic voice counting down to her first ever lob. She had never known fear like that in her life and, surprisingly, the memory of it calmed her somewhat.

"Five. Four. Three..."

She gripped the arm rests, pressed herself back into the padded seat, and screwed up her eyes, saying, "Shit, shit, shit..." Outside, the teknik finished the countdown.

* * * *

Jay was making calls, organising his trip to the UK, when the message arrived from Bob Forrester. It was a heavily encrypted package of documents with a brief note in clear.

"Jay," the note said. "Re that matter we discussed. Maybe this isn't the time to be hiding behind procedure. Bob."

Despite his curiosity, Jay set the package aside unread. Right now, he had more important things to do. He called Harnois and explained the situation.

"I'm taking one of Fourget's teams. You can stand the other down. In fact, get everybody back to normal operations. Let people take some personal time if they need it. They've probably got to sort out all kinds of domestic problems and we've had them on double shifts since the event." Jay himself had a crack in his apartment wall and a broken window that still needed fixing, but they would have to wait until he got back from London. "If Fourget calls in, tell him he can stop pretending. He'll know what I mean."

He fought the urge to give the captain a long list of directives and advice. Harnois was a safe pair of hands in which to leave the section. All he added was, "If you have problems, take them to Crystal. She's not as bad as she pretends to be."

He called Cara.

"Dad! What is it?"

Jay took a deep breath. "It's all right. Just tell me where you and Fourget are and what you're up to."

She looked flustered. "I don't know what you mean. We're at the hospital. Pierre is—"

Fourget joined the call. "*Bonjour*, Jay. We're in a car,

headed for Clarke Engineering. We believe that is where your... er... Sandra is being held."

"You're taking my little girl to an enemy stronghold, guarded by super-soldiers?"

Fourget grinned. "Before you say any more, I am supposed to remind you of your own trip to Washington DC."

Damn the girl! Yes, it was true she had forced him to take her on a ridiculously dangerous mission, once, but that didn't mean she could brag about it. Besides, blackmailing and browbeating every man she met to get her way was not the life-lesson she should have taken away from that. He bit down on the lecture that was forming in his mind and tried to focus.

"Lieutenant, I'm coming to London on the next available military flight. I'm bringing Alpha Team with me. Your mission is now official and I'm taking personal charge of it. I want you to meet me at North Weald airfield at seventeen hundred and if you don't have my daughter with you—in a sack if necessary—I will have you cleaning lavatories for the rest of your military career. Do you understand your orders?"

Fourget seemed more than happy with the new situation. "Yes, sir. Have a good trip."

His image disappeared, leaving Cara's to goggle at him in outrage. "I've never heard such a load of macho bullshit in my whole life. If you think for one minute I'm trailing along after soldier boy here while Mum is in that place, alone, you must be out of your mind."

"Darling, relax. The cavalry is coming. Let me look after it."

But Cara wasn't having any. "Do you know she killed one of them and stabbed another one? Do you suppose they're going to be very gentle with her after that?"

Jay's heartbeat stuttered. What the hell was Sandra mixed up in? "Would you put Fourget back on, please?"

The young lieutenant's face reappeared. "Sir?"

"Your assessment, please?"

"They're holding Sandra at the engineering works. They moved her briefly to Hamiye's home. I don't understand why. They have had plenty of chances to kill her; I don't know why they haven't. Perhaps they think she is protected somehow, or they want information from her and she's holding out. Even when she stabbed Hamiye he didn't kill her—just took her back to Clarke Engineering."

"So we have time?"

"Impossible to say."

Jay brooded on that for a moment. Was this some kind of rerun of Washington? Had someone grabbed her to help them build a displacement rig? If so, Sandra would stall them, knowing Jay would come looking for her. There would be time. There had to be.

"What about the dead man? Do you have an ID?"

Fourget sent an image of a smartly dressed Asian man, lying on the ground. Jay flicked it across to the facial recognition software, which immediately came back with its best guess. Meanwhile, Fourget was saying, "We think it's the chauffeur of a HiQua executive called Lee Shaozu. We found Lee's car at Hamiye's place. Chauffeur and bodyguard, I'd guess, from the evidence that he managed to put up a good fight against Cara's mother."

Jay looked at the file for Lee Peizhi, occupation driver, employer HiQua Corporate Services, UK. "How old would you say he was, Pierre?"

The Frenchman shrugged. "Early twenties?"

"His employment record says he's forty-two."

"Fake papers?"

"Either that or he is blessed with excellent genes."

Wherever Lee Shaozu got his driver from didn't matter. The man was hired muscle. His death was unlikely to lead to retribution against Sandra. "OK. Your orders stand. I'll meet you—and Cara—at North Weald as arranged."

He cut the call before Cara could renew her objections. Fourget could deal with them for now. No doubt he'd need to deal with them too, in time. But first things first.

"Jay?"

He looked up to find Laura Thalman standing in the doorway.

"You're heading off to rescue your damsel in distress," she said.

"Laura, about last night..."

Laura dismissed whatever he was about to say with a gesture. "*Es macht nichts.*"

He got up and went to her, closing the door behind her. "Oh but it does matter. In another life, in another world, you and I..." He'd seen it, just a glimpse. But in that other world, Sandra had been dead. And he realized that she would have to be dead. Else, in this world, the only woman he would ever be happy with was Sandra.

Laura gave him a sad smile. "Maybe, maybe not. I just wanted to say I should not have been so forward. It was inappropriate."

"No, no. I should never have—" He stopped himself. There was nothing he could say along those lines that would make anything any better. He smiled back at her. "If you can forgive me for being so fucking inept, maybe we could go back to being good friends again."

She laughed. "Of course. Only promise me this, that one day you will tell me all about Sandra Malone and what she means to you."

"If I ever understand it, I promise you, I will explain."

The door opened and a young soldier poked his head inside. "Sir, Alpha Team's ready to depart when you are."

"I'll be down in two minutes." As the soldier hurried off, Jay went to pick up the bag he'd prepared for the trip. "Sorry about snapping your head off in the meeting," he said, returning to Laura. "This situation has been bringing out the jerk in me. And I'm sorry your future-time-travel theory didn't work out."

"It would have been sensational," she said.

He rolled his eyes. "God preserve me from the dreams of mad scientists."

* * * *

Sandra's teeth clacked together as the sphere crashed and rattled along what felt like the whitewater rapids of the timestream. Her knuckles were livid as she gripped the arm rests. Her body fought the rapid accelerations that battered the sphere from all directions. She couldn't see out but the sensation of plunging headlong down a steep slope clutched at her chest as her every instinct told her there was a crash coming.

A bad one.

She yelled along with the wild, pounding forces that beset the sphere and shook it like a snow globe in the hands of a deranged toddler. Roaring against the madness was a small relief. She blessed Hong for installing a safety harness.

The mayhem stopped as suddenly as it had begun, leaving

her shouting into the silence. For several seconds, Sandra continued to hang on to the seat, legs braced and head back against the rest, breathing fast. Only when she was certain the violence would not start again did she dare unfasten her harness and pull the door release.

The hatch swung up and out. The sphere should still have been in the engineering works, exactly where it had started, but what she saw outside bore little resemblance to the place she had just left. She climbed out and looked around.

She was in a devastated ruin. Every surface was blackened and burned. There were walls still, but most of the roof had gone. Rain had come in and soaked everything. Of the six gantries around her, only one still stood; the others had collapsed like wilted flowers. Of the many focus fusion generators, only scattered debris remained. An explosion, she realized, and wondered at the profligacy of destroying millions of euros worth of equipment. A fire had raged through the building, the fire Lee had told Hamiye to set, perhaps. At the far end of the building, a burned-out helicopter was embedded in one ruined wall.

She stepped away from the sphere, her feet crunching on cinders. She was in the future. Two weeks in the future, if Hong had got it right this time. She looked at her hands as if they might appear different. They didn't. She looked at the sphere and, for all the insane battering it had taken, it too looked the same. She remembered to set a timer in her commplant. The sphere would return to the past in two hours, with or without her. She checked for a net connection but could not get one. Which made checking the date and time a bit of a problem.

It was also strange. She had assumed the jamming of her commplant had been done by a transmitter in the factory, then by the one that Hamiye had attached to her and she had passed on to him. But the factory was a wreck. So the jammer was either in the sphere or…

She took off her jacket and patted it down. She felt nothing. So she examined it carefully, turning it slowly, lifting pocket flaps and lapels until she found the device, a small disc of cloth, no doubt with the circuits woven into it, stuck to the back of her lapel, powered by, what? The biological decay of the fabric itself? And how had Hamiye managed to sneak a second jammer onto her? It didn't really matter. She pulled it off and dropped it into a puddle. Instantly she had net access again.

Her first thought was to call Cara, to check she was all right, but she hesitated. What if Cara wasn't all right? This was only a potential future. The real future might be nothing like this. If Cara were safe here, it would mean nothing. If she were not, it would also mean nothing. But, if she knew Cara was hurt or in danger or dead in this future, how would she cope with the knowledge? It wasn't just a possible future, Hong had told her, it was a probable one. If Sandra called Cara and she was OK, it would give her no peace when she went back to her own time. If she called and got no answer, it would be unbearable.

She made the call.

"Mum?" Cara was white with shock.

The background looked like Dot's house. Bugger. If future Sandra was right there with her, seeing another Sandra on a commplant display at the same time was going to freak Cara out. Even so, she was suddenly so overcome with relief, she could barely speak. "Cara! Oh darling, I'm so glad you're there. I—"

"Mum?" Now Cara looked scared. Something was not

right. Her daughter turned and called to someone else. "It's *Mum.*" Pause. "No, it's really her. I know my own mother." Pause. Angrily, "Yes it is. I don't care. Come and talk to her if you don't believe me." She spoke directly to Sandra again. "Oh God, Mum, where are you? We all thought you were dead. How did you—?"

"Sandra?" It was Jay, breaking into the call. He stared at her open mouthed. He looked worn, ragged. His voice was hoarse. "You've come forward, haven't you? From the past?"

Something in his face sent a chill through her. "How did you know?"

He didn't speak for a long time.

"From the past?" Cara asked in a small voice. "You mean from before…?"

"Before what?" But Sandra had already guessed.

"Don't go back," Jay said. His voice was urgent, desperate. "You can stay. Don't go back. There are no consequences. No extra consequences."

The damp chill of the burned-out factory seemed to force its way into her bones. She'd be going back to *die*? What kind of death? Did knowing it was coming mean she might prevent it? *Should* she stay? No, *no*, because—"I'd disappear from my own time," she said. "What about Cara? My Cara from back then?"

"I'm your Cara!"

Sandra stared at her daughter's horrified expression, her mind blank.

"If you go back you will die," Jay said, his eyes imploring. "She'll lose you. We'll all lose you. But if you stay…"

Sandra's head was spinning. She couldn't just abandon Cara in the past. And yet Cara was right there. "What about

Lee and Hamiye and HiQua?" she said, stalling. "Did you stop them?"

Jay hesitated. "There was more to it than we knew. It was complicated."

"You mean they got away?" It was so unexpected that indignation briefly overcame the distress she was feeling. "A corrupt businessman and a few hired thugs? What kind of outfit do you run in Berlin?"

And you let me die?

"How?" she asked.

"What?"

"How did I die? Please tell me I at least took that bastard Lee with me."

"No!" Cara shouted over Jay's reply. "We're not talking about that. None of that matters any more. You're here and you can stay here. Can't she, Dad? And it's just like you went missing for a couple of weeks. That's all. Please, Mum."

"She's right, Sandra."

Yes, she's right, but somewhere here there's a grave with my body in it. And somewhere else, there's another Cara who still believes her mother will come home to her. She felt a sob catch in her throat.

Jay looked like he might cry too. "I know what you're thinking," he said. "That you'll go back and make things work out differently. The indomitable will of Sandra Malone against the force of Time itself. But what if it doesn't work? What if you die in every probable future? Will you just consider that? Will you just think about what an incredible second chance you've been given, that we've all been given?"

"What's the date?" she asked. Jay was right. She knew he was right. She checked her commplant without waiting for his answer. Hong had done it. Two weeks exactly.

"Sandra, please."

She looked at Cara. There were tears running down her daughter's face. "Cara, darling…" Her throat closed and wouldn't let her go on. She clenched her jaw against it, forced herself to speak. "I can't imagine how hard it's been for you." Her daughter wailed, already seeing where this was going. Her pain tore something inside Sandra. "But for me, there's another Cara, waiting for me, searching for me I'm sure, trusting me to come home. Do you want me to leave her there and just disappear?" She drew an arm across her face to clear away the tears. "I'm guessing I didn't get to say goodbye to you, to tell you how much I… Oh God!" It felt as if there were a rock filling up her chest, crushing her heart. She struggled for breath before she could go on. "So let me tell you now. I love you with all my heart and soul. And that's why… That's why I can't abandon that other Cara. The one who's still waiting for me. I wish… I wish I could stay for you but I have to go back. I have to change this. Make it right."

Cara had collapsed into a huddled ball of misery. Maybe she wasn't listening any more, but Sandra said, "Cara, my darling baby girl, it's because I love you so much that I have to go back for you."

She was spent, wrung out and exhausted. Jay stared at her as if she were dying again right in front of him. "I love you too, Jay."

"Wait!" he cried, but there was nothing else for her to say. She cut the call as Jay said, "Hong had a—"

She stumbled as she took the few steps back to the sphere and fell against its wall, clinging to its rough exterior. She gave way to the howling grief that filled her, lost in a storm of racking sobs. Her legs gave way and she fell to the filthy wet ground, burying her face and crying for her poor, shattered family.

* * * *

Later, she pulled herself up and stood beside the sphere, shivering from the cold, numbed by her encounter with Cara and Jay. She climbed back into the padded seat and struggled to fasten the harness with frozen fingers. When she finally managed and the hatch was closed, she found the button marked "Return". She stared at it, mesmerised by the thought of how easy it would be to press it, how one finger could do it, change her life, change her daughter's life, here and back there. One touch, one tiny movement, to make the future fork one way or the other.

As if she had no control over it, her arm reached out and her finger pressed the button. She felt a thud as a circuit closed and power surged through the sphere. The return trip was a kind of lob, Dr Hong had told her. The sphere generated its own displacement field and threw itself back along the path it had previously made, but it didn't go into the past—not her own past—it fetched up at the advancing wavefront that was the present and could go no farther.

It took just a few seconds to make the journey back, just enough time to wonder what became of the future she had just seen. Would it vanish without her, somehow crumble back to the shapeless void it had once been? Or would it still be there when the present caught up with it, seamlessly integrated into her own world, with Cara and Jay grieving still, and herself dead and gone? She had never wondered about the future. She'd simply accepted what she'd learned at uni: that the future could never be visited because it did not exist until the march of time built it from the pattern of the present. But she did now. She had been there, touched it and felt it. Jay had said she could stay there and he sounded as if he knew.

The opening hatch took her by surprise. A group of tekniks came to look inside with Hong, Hamiye and Lee behind them. Something about her appearance made them all stare at her. She didn't feel like speaking, or getting out. Eventually, Lee broke the spell.

"Well?" he demanded.

She looked at him, despising him for what he'd just put her through. Then turned to Hong. "The date was correct."

"Get her out of there," Hamiye said and two of the super-soldiers appeared. She let them unfasten her and lift her out by her arms. They led her away from the sphere, towards the storerooms and offices.

"Wait," Lee called after them and the giants stopped and turned her. "What the hell did you see out there?"

She gave him a long, hate-filled look and then smiled. "I saw you—all of you—scattered across the ground, everyone dead. It was a massacre. I can't wait for it to happen."

There were gasps and exclamations from the tekniks and stony silence from the others. Lee turned to his people and snapped at them in Chinese. Everyone fell quiet. "Take her away," he said, glowering as she grinned back at him.

* * * *

It was mid-afternoon by the time the big C-130T troop transport lumbered to a halt on the runway at North Weald airbase. The rear ramp lowered itself and as it hit the ground six men appeared, pushing trolleys stacked with equipment.

They were laughing and joking, in good spirits, casting expert eyes around the airfield, casually taking in the situation, no doubt seeing Fourget with his convoy of three Range Rovers waiting nearby. One of them snapped out a few orders. The banter quietened but did not stop as the men lined up their trolleys and pushed them over towards Fourget.

"Is that all of them?" Cara asked. "Six men?"

Fourget could understand her disappointment. If you didn't know how good Alpha Team was, you could be forgiven for thinking a single squad wasn't much. He saw Jay Kennedy and Gerhard Stoeffel, Alpha Team Commander, walking down the ramp. "I count nine," he said.

She looked at him out of the corner of her eyes and said, "Ten."

He shook his head. The girl had plenty of spirit. The only reason they were there now was that he had discharged two rounds into their car's dashboard, killing its electronics, to prevent her taking them straight to where her mother was being held. Summoning a car from the local EDF MI pool had wasted two hours and he'd had to tie her up to stop her running off—which had raised a number of eyebrows in the quiet suburb in which it had all taken place. Spirit alone would not be much use against a team of monstrously augmented mercs.

The bindings and the gag had been off since they arrived at North Weald but he had the strong feeling that if the girl ever managed to get a gun in her hands, his life expectancy might be very short indeed.

He cast his eyes over the heaps of equipment Alpha Team had brought with them and caught the eye of Sergeant Connolly as they approached. "Are you planning to start a war, Jock?"

The big Scot grinned back at him. "Someone said there were hamsters about, sir. Nasty buggers, hamsters. Take a lot of exterminating."

Fourget smiled back at him and nodded towards the cars. The sergeant barked out a few words and the team began loading.

"Aren't you going to introduce us to your lady friend, sir?" one of the men called.

"Looks like you're dressed for a party, darlin'," said another. "Need a date? I'll be free in a bit and happy to show you the town."

Fourget glanced at Cara to find the familiar scowl firmly in place.

"Gentlemen." Jay's voice, as he arrived, made everyone stop and turn to him. "May I introduce my daughter, Cara Malone?"

Her would-be date grimaced and looked sick. "Sir, I was just—" he began but Jay cut him off.

"Best not say anything else, Peel." He turned to Cara. "Standard punishment for chatting up the Section Head's daughter is to spend a day in her company. Sound about right, Pierre?"

"It sounds cruel and unusual, sir."

"OK, Gerhard, finish off. Cara, come with me. Fourget, you too."

He walked away from the cars to stand alone on the airstrip, Fourget followed him and, after some hesitation, so did Cara.

"What was all that?" she demanded when she arrived. She was angry but Fourget thought she also looked hurt. "Why are you trying to humiliate me?"

Beneath his cool exterior, Jay also seemed ready to

explode. "Do you want us to save Sandra or not?" he said.

"Of course I do. What's that got—?"

"You're a distraction. That's what."

"Just because your disgusting Neanderthals can't keep their minds out of their—"

"Don't be ridiculous." From the shock on Cara's face, Fourget suspected her father rarely, if ever, spoke to her that way. "You're a civilian and this is a military operation. People could die. And I'm not going to burden any one of my men with the job of trying to keep an eye on a reckless, headstrong child when he should be focusing on staying alive."

"Child? Most of those guys are barely older than I am."

"You're not listening. So pay attention to this. Go back home to your gran's. I have someone waiting to drive you. Stay there. I'll bring your mother to you when this is over."

"You can't just order me around."

"You don't think I have the authority? I can have the base military police arrest you right now and put you in a cell for as long as I please. If you leave the base, I can have MI5 or the Met pick you up and hold you."

She glared into her father's face. "You wouldn't dare!" But Fourget could hear the uncertainty in her voice.

Jay stood his ground. "Try me."

"I'll never speak to you again."

Fourget heard a sharp intake of breath from his boss and, for a moment, thought Jay might back down, but after a while, the tall Englishman raised a hand towards the gate and made a beckoning gesture. A pair of headlights came on and a car drove up to them—an Air Force limo with a uniformed woman inside. The three of them watched it in silence as it crossed the tarmac and pulled up. The airman got out and opened one of the rear doors.

Cara gave her father a final, withering glare. There were tears glittering in her eyes. Then she turned quickly and hurried into the waiting car. Jay watched it pull away with a face of stone.

* * * *

"What the hell are you people doing?" Sandra asked.

"Getting rich," Hamiye said. "You could too, if you were sensible."

"What?"

"Lee wants you to do the next trip. The final one. Only you need to do more than just find out the date and come home."

"Tell him to do it himself."

"Lee doesn't take personal risks."

"You do it then. You're his bitch."

She saw his mouth tighten in anger and then relax. "I don't take personal risks either."

"Really? Gosh, I hope no-one's found the dead guy in your garden yet, then."

He'd been sitting astride a wooden chair, now he stood up and hurled it aside. "Why are you so bloody provocative all the time? Can't you just talk like a normal person? You're tied to a chair, I have armed guards outside and my boss has already told me I should kill you. Yet you still spend every breath trying to wind me up. Are you completely fucking insane?"

She watched him carefully. She'd love to explain it to him, to say, "Because I'm not your fucking victim and I never will be, because I've been held and threatened by people a lot scarier than you, Sunshine, and because keeping you wound up is the only entertainment I've got in this craphole." But she didn't because her whole strategy of keeping him angry was to stress him out and encourage him to make stupid decisions. It was better that he did think her completely insane. Besides, when she looked into Hamiye's eyes, she didn't see a zealot or a psychopath looking back, she saw only a man who was in deeper than he wanted to be. It didn't mean he wasn't dangerous, but it gave her some hope that, if he did fall apart, he would as likely turn on his own people as on her.

So she said, "All right, let's hear your offer." It caught him off guard. "Come on, you obviously came in here to buy my cooperation with some irresistible prize, so let's hear it."

"Ten million euros."

She pulled back in surprise. That really was a very good offer. For a moment, she let herself think what it would mean to have that much money. It was a pleasant daydream.

He smiled. "Well?" he said.

"No."

"No?" He seemed genuinely surprised. "Twenty, then."

She laughed. The situation had gone from grisly to ridiculous. "Listen, Farid, if I was going to be bought, you could have had me for ten."

"So why the hell won't you take it? All you have to do is sit in the damned sphere and go forwards one day. Get us some information and come back. An hour's work, tops, for twenty *million* euros. There's a small risk, of course, but isn't it worth it?"

"I'm not scared of your hit-and-miss time machine—at least not as much as you are. I just don't want your money."

He looked away. "Money is money."

"You don't believe that any more than I do. Who's getting

hurt, Farid? Who is Lee going to screw over to make you all so rich you can spend twenty million on a bribe?"

"No-one. Listen, it's a kind of insider-trading scam. You go one day into the future and you bring back the prices of various stocks and derivatives, the outcomes of sporting events, and so on. We've done it before. Hong's first shot was two years ago. The pilot went two years into the future for information and Lee used our backer's money to buy various financial instruments and place several bets. It was just a trial run but it made a ton of money—even though only sixty percent of the deals paid off. That's why we needed to get the distance travelled as short as possible. Two years is too uncertain, but one day is ideal. That's what Hong's team has been working on all this time. And now we're ready. The trip you made was a proof of concept for some new tech he's been building, and he's ready now to do one day. Lee's got the money ready. The traders and the bookmakers are all primed and ready. All we need is a pilot to go get the information."

"Is that what you think? That the only people you're hurting are some pension funds and bookies?"

Hamiye seemed genuinely confused. "Well, who else?"

She wasn't certain about it, even now, but she wanted to try it out on Hamiye anyway. "Let me guess when your first shot matured. Was it, say, two days ago?"

Hamiye's face took on a hunted look. "So what?"

"Bit of a coincidence, don't you think?"

He was pacing around the room again. "Yes, it was. A complete coincidence. Hong's machine didn't have anything to do with what happened the other night. How could it? He sent that pilot off two years ago. If there was going to be a backwash from the time travel, it would have happened then.

197

I'm not a scientist but I've done my reading. If you make a timesplash, the backwash follows you back right away. It's there within minutes, or hours, not years."

"It worries you, though, doesn't it? What Hong did was no ordinary lob. This has never been done before. What if it is connected? You go forwards two years and create some kind of latent apocalypse. Two years later, you catch up with it and there it is waiting to shake the whole planet. Do you know how many thousands of people died? Do you know how many trillions were wiped off the global economy? How many times do you think that could happen before we don't have a civilization any more? Is that worth what you're being paid? I know it's not worth twenty million lousy euros—or any amount of money—because money's going to be worthless." A thought struck her. "The last poor sucker you sent came back stuck full of arrows, remember. Maybe what you're doing led to that. Maybe we caught a glimpse of what's in store if we keep on taking trips into the future."

Hamiye set his face against the idea. "Rubbish. Hong says it's a coincidence and he's the one who should know, right?"

"Whatever helps you sleep at night."

His jaw worked. "All right," he said, as if it were the conclusion of an internal argument. "So what? We're only going to do it one more time. And only for one lousy day. Even if a two-year shot did cause the event, a one-day shot would be, what, seven hundred times smaller? You'd never even notice it."

Sandra agreed he had a point. "We don't know how it works. Maybe it's not how far you go or what you do in the future; maybe it's what you do to the future. Maybe all this gambling changes how things should be and the Universe has to make some kind of correction. I don't know, but I do know you shouldn't be messing with this stuff. No-one should be."

"For a teknik, you certainly talk like a Luddite. No-one is 'messing around' with this stuff. Dr Hong is the world's leading expert on it."

"And yet you want me to fly the thing because the world's leading expert and his team are all too scared to risk their lives in it."

Hamiye stared at her for a long time as if he didn't know what his next move was. Finally, he said, "We can pick up your daughter any time we like, you know."

Sandra felt a cold hand squeeze her heart. Her first reaction was to lash out at Hamiye. But she knew that by now Jay would be searching for her, that Cara was bound to be with him, that her daughter was safe, whatever Hamiye said. She took a slow breath and let herself relax. She noticed the hunted look in her captor's eyes and took a punt.

"You don't want to be that guy, do you?" He wouldn't meet her eyes. "You don't like what's going on here any more than I do, but you feel sucked up in it, somehow. You keep getting in deeper and you feel like it's out of control." She was encouraged by his sharp look, his quick frown. He was asking himself how she knew that—even though it was written all over his face. "Sure, you want the money, because that sets you free from this whole mess. Am I right? But you didn't know, when you hooked up with Lee, where this was all going. And now people are dying—the pilot, the driver, maybe me next. The police will connect you with it for sure. You'll get your money—if Lee doesn't double-cross you, if this half-tested technology ever works—but you'll be on the run. You'll spend the rest of your life in half-civilized sink-holes with no extradition treaties. That wasn't the future you had planned, was it?"

She could see she was reaching him, saying out loud the thoughts he'd been pushing down into dark corners. He managed a weakly defiant, "What the hell do you know?"

"And then there's the event from the other night. You can tell yourself it was just coincidence as much as you like but we both know coincidences like that don't happen. I've been through timesplashes and backwashes and I know when time-related shit is happening. That event wasn't anything I'd seen before, but there was enough acausal craziness in the mix that it was obvious someone was screwing with time. Thousands dead, Farid. Tens of thousands. And if it happens again, maybe it will be worse. I don't know if your conscience can handle all that death and misery but, even if it can, once they connect you to what's happened, there won't be a sewer on this planet deep enough for you to hide in—extradition treaty or not."

He had his back to her; his shoulders were drooping. In a hollow voice, he asked, "And your solution to all this is what?"

"Get me out of here. I know someone you can talk to who will give you a fair hearing. Help them mop up Lee and his crew. Show you're not a monster like them."

She stopped talking and waited. Seconds ticked by as he stood there. She didn't know what else she could say. Anything else might undo any effect she'd had. She leaned forwards against her restraints, waiting for his reaction.

At last, he said, "You're right about one thing." He turned to face her and she searched his grim expression for some sign of hope. "I'm in too deep. The only way out of this for me now is to see it through and pray you're wrong about the event."

Damn! She'd laid it on too thick, or he wasn't as decent as she'd thought. Bitterly, she said, "Pray? That's your plan?"

He sneered, at himself, it seemed. "I'm not what you'd call a devout Muslim, but I still have my faith." He straightened his shoulders and pulled himself upright. "So you don't want our money and threatening your daughter doesn't seem to persuade you. That leaves us with just one option. Either you pilot the sphere and bring back the information we need, or you will be shot."

He stepped quickly to the door and left without waiting for her response, slamming it behind him.

"Oh well," she said to the empty room. "If you put it like that…"

* * * *

Hamiye went straight from Sandra's room to search for Lee. He found his boss in Hong's office, walking in on what seemed to be a heated argument.

"They will not be happy if we bungle another shot," Hong was saying.

Lee advanced on the scientist, snarling. "Bungle another shot and *I* will not be happy. We do not have time for any more tinkering. You're supposed to be a genius. Can't you grasp that simple fact? We must do it tonight and get out of this place. Tomorrow, we—" He stopped dead, noticing Hamiye in the doorway.

"Who won't be happy?" Hamiye asked, looking from Lee to Hong.

Lee looked as if he might start snarling again but he composed himself and said, "Our backers. Will the woman do it?"

But Hamiye didn't want to change the subject. "Backers? I thought only Waxtead knew about this."

"There are others. It's none of your concern. What about the woman?"

Hamiye wanted to push him on it but decided not to. All right so Lee was a slimy, lying weasel, but that's the kind of person you did business with if you wanted to be in on the deal. His own cut was agreed and if there were a thousand secret backers he didn't know about, what difference would it make, especially at this stage of the game? He didn't like it, but what could he do except make waves?

"She'll probably do it," he said, distracted.

"Probably? Did you offer her money? Did you threaten her daughter?"

"Yes, yes. She thinks Hong's equipment knocked the world out of joint the other day. She doesn't want our money. She thinks we're mass murderers." His tone was surly. It occurred to him that if Lee had lied about the backers, he might be lying about the side effects of the machine too. "As for her daughter, she seemed to know I was bluffing. She's probably got her hidden away safe somewhere." Lee was looking at him as if he could not believe what he was hearing. "So I told her I'd shoot her if she didn't do it."

"Very well," Lee said, as if the matter was settled. "She will do it."

But Hamiye didn't see it that way. "I don't think we should let her. She's... Well, you need to get to know her. She's determined and cunning. She beat your driver in a stand-up fight. Killed him with her bare hands. She's got this passion inside her. It's... scary."

Lee was studying his security chief with an appraising eye. "Maybe you'd like to set up home with her? You seem very impressed with the woman."

Hamiye bit down on an angry retort. "I'm just trying to explain that you can't trust her. Whatever you threaten her with, she'll find some way of getting out from under it. I am very impressed. I admit it. I admire the woman. And I respect her the way I'd respect a caged lioness. That's why I think it's too dangerous to put her in that sphere again."

"We have no choice."

"One of the tekniks could do it. Double his pay-off. Quadruple it."

Lee pulled a sour face. "Tell him, Hong."

"We have no tekniks to spare," the old scientist said. "It's what we were talking about when you came in. Some members of my team have run away, left the facility. Your soldiers caught two of them and killed them. We have almost no-one left. It's impossible to do another shot right away."

"We're doing the shot," Lee said, wearily.

"What do you mean, ran away?" Hamiye didn't understand. "Why would they run away? They're being paid, aren't they?"

Hong didn't reply. He looked anxiously at Lee, passing the responsibility for an answer to him.

"It doesn't matter," Lee said. "None of the tekniks speak English. None that are left, anyway. They can't do the job at the other end. So that leaves us three and the woman. I'm not doing it. Hong's not doing it. So that leaves you. Now what do you say?"

Hamiye shut his mouth. There was no way he was going in that thing, not after what happened to the last pilot. "What about bringing someone else in? I could find you someone. I know people. People who won't ask questions. I could make a few calls."

"No." Lee barked the word. His eyes were hard and his lips tight. "We will not bring anyone else in. That is final. The woman will do it. She has done it before. No-one wants to die, not even your pretty lioness."

Hamiye could see there was no more to be said. He dropped his gaze from Lee's and nodded. "She'll do it," he said.

"Good," Lee said. "See to it. And tell your gorillas not to kill any more of Dr Hong's team!"

* * * *

Alpha Team set up its base in an empty hanger at the RAF base. A complete virtual model of the interior of Clarke Engineering had been run up from the plans. Gerhard Stoeffel and his men had their commplants synced to the simulation so they could wander around inside and outside the building in hi-def augmented reality and plan their assault. Jay left them to it.

Fourget was deep in conversation with their base liaison, an RAF captain and head of base security. "Hello, I'm BaseSec," she'd said when she introduced herself. Jay had already forgotten her name. He sat alone in a quiet corner with a three-bar electric heater shining a dull red glow on him but making almost no difference at all to the frigid air of the chill, echoing hangar. "I'll rustle up a few space heaters," BaseSec had said, smiling encouragingly. "Soon have the place warm as toast." But Jay had turned down the offer. He didn't expect to be staying long.

He started making calls, catching up on what the analysts were digging up for him back in Berlin. It wasn't much. HiQua seemed to be a completely legitimate company. Its present CEO, Sir Roger Waxtead, looked like a bit of an idiot. He'd inherited his major shareholding and his current position from his astute and ruthless father and was in the process of eroding the company's value little by little as his incompetence slowly revealed itself. But HiQua was a massive, multinational conglomerate and would take years, probably decades, to run into the ground. Nothing in Waxtead's background suggested anything criminal or even particularly reckless about him. "Although there are increasing signs of a willingness to take risks to improve the company's performance," as the analyst said. A case in point being a series of major stock-market gambles in the recent past, which had surprised everyone by coming good just two days earlier. Jay set the coincidence aside and moved on.

The Special Projects Division of HiQua Research International Ltd. appeared to have been set up when Lee Shaozu first joined the company. Until then secret projects had been conducted within the various specialist divisions of the subsidiary. Jay's analysts were unable to come up with any evidence of particular projects the division had spun off into the company. No patents had been applied for. "If they're doing long-term, blue-skies research," the analyst said with a shrug, "that's not really too surprising. The budget is pretty big—enormous, actually—and, apart from the top management, admin functions, a handful of technicians, and security, I can't find anybody on the payroll. Which is a bit weird, isn't it?"

"Anything else weird?"

"Only one thing. They have a top legal firm on retainer. Costs them a fortune."

"Patent lawyers?"

"No, that's the weird thing. Immigration specialists. Do

you want me to find out what services they've been providing?"

Jay said yes. "I want to know what they're working on in the Enfield facility. Reach out to the local security agencies. Pull rank if you have to. Remind them that EDF MI is the overarching security agency for the whole European Union." He recognized his own frustration talking and shut up. Interagency turf wars were the bane of his life. He wrapped up. "Find a disgruntled ex-employee. Someone must know something. Only don't let anyone go near that engineering works."

He moved on. Lee Shaozu turned out to be a man of mystery. Like Farid, his past was murky and probably fake. Which added to Jay's unease. Why would a respectable company like HiQua set up a shadowy research division and put shady characters like Lee Shaozu and Farid Hamiye at the top of it? Was Waxtead pursuing some kind of crazy high-tech long-shot? Something not quite legal, maybe? And, if so, who was the brains behind it? Not Lee for sure: his qualifications and experience—which were also probably fake—pegged him as a manager, not a scientist or engineer. Jay added instructions to find out who was chief scientist in the Special Projects division, again with the caveat that no-one go anywhere near Enfield.

Kadan Dudding, unlike the rest of his team, who were now focused on the current mission, had allowed himself the privilege of continuing to study the global event.

"I told you HiQua and their Special Projects Division were our top priority." Jay couldn't hide his irritation.

Dudding pulled one of his eloquent faces. This one seemed to say, "Yeah, but…"

"I took another look at the timings—"

"Simultaneous, you said."

"Yeah, not the spread this time. I was looking at the apparitions."

Jay felt his body and mind go still. He saw Cara on the staircase of his apartment block, fading to nothing as he reached for her. "Go on."

Dudding seemed to sense his intensified focus. He swallowed and straightened up in his seat. "There seems to be a two-year horizon on events leading to every encounter."

"Meaning?"

"Meaning no dead person who came back died more than two years ago. No building that appeared was built more than two years ago. People turned up in places that they couldn't have been for reasons invariably less than two years old. There're a few exceptions but every one of those I've looked into had a pretty unreliable source in my view. The vast bulk of the reports are completely consistent."

"So?"

"So it's not a splash, that's a guarantee. But it is a spacetime event. Something hit us—something hit everything. The only thing that's as big as everything is, well, another everything. And the horizon means that it's a two-year-old everything, max."

Jay didn't like the implications of this. He didn't like them at all. "You told me it was a natural phenomenon. Now you're telling me it's some kind of parallel-universe thing that started with an event two years in the past?"

Dudding's face made a What can I do about it? Them's the facts! expression that Jay found particularly irritating. "I'm not saying someone went back two years and did something. It might still have nothing to do with time travel at all. My physicist friends tell me that in an infinite universe of branes we might have bumped into one that just happens to be similar."

Jay treated that idea with the contempt it deserved. "Get with the mission, Kadan. I don't want you wasting any more time on this stuff."

"I thought—"

"We've got a team ready to go into a heavily guarded facility over here. People whose lives are on the line. I don't want to hear crap about branes and apparitions. I want something I can use to keep those men safe and increase our chances of success. Do you hear me?"

Dudding looked stricken. "Yes, sir. Understood."

Jay hung up on him, knowing he was unreasonably angry. He was twitchy and distracted. Gerhard would come and tell him when his team had worked out a solid assault plan. Then they'd brief him and they could all get on with it. In the meantime, all Jay could do was wait. He remembered the material that he'd received from Aldermaston and popped up a reader. He pulled out a document called, "Project FORESIGHT: Worst Case Scenarios—Report of a facilitated brainstorming session held at the Army Staff College, Camberley, 15 May 2067." He began flicking through it, barely paying attention, letting the obscure physics jargon and technical language wash over him until a section heading leapt out at him. He blinked in surprise and read it again to be sure. "The Possibility that Future Time Travel Might Create New Branes Displaced in Time."

He stared at the words as long seconds ticked past, knowing what they meant but finding himself unable to move past them to act on this shocking revelation. With a shudder, he shook himself free of their spell. He made a phone call. "Laura," he said, when she picked up. "I need you here in

London, right now. Requisition whatever is the fastest means of getting here. I want you with me when we get into that facility."

* * * *

Cara sat quietly in the car as it wound through the London streets to her grandmother's house. The young airman tried to start a conversation a few times but finally got the message and gave up. Cara didn't want to talk. She wanted to think.

Her mum was being held by bad guys for reasons she couldn't begin to fathom but which were probably something to do with time travel—a technology that she could only see as a curse on her family and on the whole planet. Her father had brought some tough-looking guys to go and get her out of it, and she had every faith in him doing just that. For all the stupid reasons he had for staying away from Sandra, Cara knew that the bond between Jay and her mother was like one of those classic love stories of star-crossed lovers. He would do anything to save her. Anything.

It was a notion that had often comforted her, but now it scared her. Fourget and the other soldiers were hard as nails and they had tech that made them superhuman, but those monstrous creatures guarding her mother were even tougher. She'd seen one pick up Fourget and toss him around like a child's doll. She knew Jay would send his men in to their certain deaths if he thought it would help free her mum. And she wanted that! She wanted him to do anything and everything that might get her mother back. Even if it meant Jay himself died in the attempt.

She found herself crying, feeling wretched at the admission she'd just made. Jay was her father. She shouldn't want him to die, even to save her mother. Yet she did. Her mother had to come back. She had to, no matter what the cost.

And there was the nub of her fear. She had seen death and injury. She'd seen people suffer in hideous ways. And yet she would condemn all those soldiers to pain and death to satisfy her own selfish need. Even her own father. What kind of monster was she?

On an intellectual level, she understood. At least, she thought she did. She'd been almost sixteen before she even met her father. He'd been an abstraction. She'd only really known him for a bit over two years. And her relationship with her mother had always been abnormally close. She'd hidden Cara from Jay, from the whole world, avoiding friendships, keeping a low profile, creating a bubble of isolation around Cara in which the two of them developed a too-tight, co-dependent relationship.

And now the nightmare was happening again—although Cara still had no idea what was going on. That man who had pretended to be from the electric company was part of it. Why wouldn't they leave her alone? Why hadn't she and her mother just run? That was the plan, wasn't it? But instead her mum had gone chasing after them and now they'd got her and Jay was going to…

She put her head in her hands and screwed her eyes tight shut. Nothing made sense and she wanted to scream.

The airman said, "Are you all right?"

Cara had forgotten she was there. She looked up, finding a focus for her anger. "Why don't you fuck off? You're my jailer, not my friend. So just sod off."

The young woman stared at her for a moment. Her lips twitched in contempt and she looked away. Cara could plainly see what the woman thought of her. Some bigwig's spoiled brat, wasting everybody's time. Well, she wasn't going to explain herself. It was humiliating enough to be there under guard, being sent home like a child so the grown-ups could get on with the serious business of setting her mother free. A wave of anger against Jay surged through her but, infuriatingly, she couldn't sustain it. She knew he was doing what he thought was best for her. She knew her mother would wholeheartedly approve of what he'd done. Sandra had been furious with him for taking her to Washington to help rescue her, even though Cara had explained over and over that it wasn't Jay's fault, that she'd made him do it. She seemed to think that Jay should have behaved like a brute and had her locked up or something. Well, he seemed to have taken her accusations of weakness and irresponsibility to heart. Cara had never seen her father be so rigid and authoritarian.

"Is this the place?" the airman asked.

Cara realized they were in Gran's street, coming to a halt outside her house. She didn't bother to answer, just reached for the door handle. But her companion reached it first and climbed out of the car ahead of her. For a while the airman stood blocking the car doorway with her hand on her sidearm. It was the first time Cara had noticed that the woman was armed.

"All clear," the airman said and stepped back to let Cara out.

The idea that the woman wasn't her jailer but her bodyguard made Cara suddenly anxious and she scanned the empty street as she emerged from the car. She caught the woman's eye and said, "Thank you," properly. At the same moment, Jay's mother opened her front door and stepped out onto the porch. Cara hurried up the path to meet her and hustle her back into the house. Behind her the car door closed and its engine whined as it pulled away.

"Gran, listen, I've got to go out again. Right now." She shut the door and began taking off her shoes. "I just need to change and make some calls. I'll explain everything later, honest."

The older woman looked at her with a steady gaze that made Cara aware of how shifty her own manner was. "You don't need to explain anything. Your father called and told me all about it."

That was a surprise. "Did he tell you Mum's life is in danger?"

"Yes, for once he told me the truth. And he told me you'd be in danger too if you went after her. He also told me you nearly died last night."

Damn it. It wasn't fair setting Gran on her like this. "He's exaggerating. He wasn't even there. Look, Gran, it's my mum, and I have to go. You understand, don't you?"

"You don't trust Jay to bring her home?"

"It's not as simple as that."

"You know he loves her more than anything in the world?"

"I know he'll do everything he can—"

"And you don't think that'll be enough."

Cara threw out her arms, helpless to explain. "I don't know, Gran. I just don't know. And the thing is, what if it isn't?"

The sympathy in her grandmother's eyes brought a sob to her throat. Or was it helplessness that welled up in her? She pushed down on all of it. She wasn't helpless. Summoning anger at her own weakness, she looked her gran in the eye and said, "I'm sorry, Gran, but I'm going and there's nothing you can say that will stop me." The old woman looked hurt. Cara had only ever seen her on family visits—Christmasses and summer holidays, happy times—she'd never seen her hurt. "Look," she said, hardening herself. "You know I have to do this." She stepped up to her gran and took her by the shoulders. "I promise I'll come back." She kissed her on the cheek and ran off up the stairs before there was time for any more argument.

She tore off her stupid dancing gear and tossed it in the bin. It was completely ruined. She replaced it with dark jeans and a warm jumper over a long-sleeved T-shirt, put on thick socks and walking boots and grabbed a fleecy jacket and a woolly hat. Her running-away bag contained all kinds of useful odds and ends, like a torch, a pocketknife, a cigarette lighter, and other things she might need in a situation she couldn't have predicted. She grabbed what she thought might be useful and went downstairs.

Her grandmother was still in the hallway only now she was wearing a coat and shoes and carrying a twelve-bore shotgun. She held it up when Cara appeared. "Your grandfather got hold of it during the Adjustment. Things were a bit wild back then. I've got shells in my handbag."

Cara wondered if her gran meant to try to stop her with it. "What are you doing, Gran?"

The old woman smiled and swung the long-barrelled gun up onto her shoulder. "I'm coming with you, dear."

* * * *

Fourget ran his men through the planned assault on Clarke Engineering. Jay watched, then had them do it again. The big, hulking avatars that stood in for the HiQua mercenaries made his scalp itch. He glanced at the readouts on the simulation as the rehearsal ended. Probability of success: sixty-five percent. Casualties: friendlies, three, hostiles, five, non-combatants, six. Fourget watched him in silence as he studied the figures.

"This is unacceptable," he said so only Fourget could hear him.

"The simulator gets it wrong."

That was only partly true. The real-life parameters of an engagement like this were so complex that no machine could hope to get it right. Intangibles such as team morale and quality of training were hard to estimate and could throw the calculations off by a huge factor. Also, the simulation was built to be conservative. Three dead was probably the worst of all likely outcomes.

Even so.

"A good plan violently executed now..." Fourget said.

Is better than a perfect plan executed next week. Who said that? General Patton? Jay didn't like the way "executed" kept cropping up in the quote. All he knew about Patton was that he wore a shiny hat and carried a pearl-handled revolver.

But a general, however eccentric, would have been welcome just then. Jay very much wanted to pass the responsibility for this decision to someone else, someone for whom rescuing Sandra was not so damned important. His own judgement was tainted. Even if he told himself there was far more at stake than Sandra's life, that there could be a FORESIGHT machine in that factory that could destroy the world, he should still disqualify himself. People could die— his own people, civilians... He had no right to put them at such risk when he couldn't even know whether his reasoning was compromised by his need to save Sandra.

"OK. Pack up here and prepare to move. We go in as soon as Laura arrives." For better or worse, the decision was made. Now he'd just have to live with the consequences.

Fourget said nothing but clearly approved. He moved off to organize his team. Jay put his hands in his pockets and wandered out onto the taxiway. Night had fallen already. He raised his head to stare into the ruddy bellies of the clouds above London. Cloud cover was total and the weather report said there would be rain before the morning. Cold, winter rain. He saw a light in the sky to the south and watched it as it drew closer. It came in fast and he soon heard the whup-whup of helicopter blades. As he watched, Fourget came to join him. They stood together in silence as the aircraft bore down on them, slowed to a crawl and began its descent.

"What the hell is that?" Jay asked. The bizarre craft had a body and a rotor just like a normal helicopter but also had two stubby wings with forward-pointing propellers and a broad tail fin where the tail rotor ought to be.

"Eurocopter ADS955 rotorcraft," Fourget said. "Fastest chopper in the fleet. When I heard Dr Thalman needed a ride, I set this up for her. We're keeping it to use on the mission."

"You can get six hundred kilometres an hour out of those things," said BaseSec, who had also joined them. "I see your team has all the latest toys to play with."

"I'm sure the RAF has a few nice toys of its own, Captain," said Jay, but only to be polite.

The strange helicopter was already down and its rotors were slowing. A ground crew airman with a couple of bots in tow made his way to the craft and opened a side door. One of the bots pushed a short ladder into place.

The sight of Laura Thalman's elegantly-shod foot reaching

down towards the top step snapped Jay out of his reverie. "All right, Pierre, which car do you want me in?"

"Number three, sir."

"Right. I'll be there with Laura if you need me. Carry on."

Jay hurried across to the chopper and met Laura. She had a small overnight bag with her, which he took as he steered her towards the assigned Range Rover. He dropped the bag behind the seats and joined her inside.

"You read the report?" he asked, taking the seat opposite her.

She looked as if she might object to his peremptory plunge into business matters after barely saying hello, but she said, "Wild stuff. I know which part got you so excited."

"The creation of free-floating universes. Explain it to me."

She opened her mouth and closed it again. Perhaps she thought the back of a car on a British air force base late in the evening was a strange setting for a physics lecture. Perhaps she also saw the intense focus in Jay's face and decided not to comment.

"I know you don't know much physics, so I'll keep it simple. The best theory we have of how everything works is called MT-theory. Most other theories we had before the Adjustment took a severe battering when we discovered that a bunch of kids were travelling backwards in time. We had to rewrite everything we knew about time—and that meant rewriting physics. There was a candidate back then for a unified theory of everything called M-theory. With a bit of modification—well a lot, really—it managed to accommodate the new models of time. It became the MT-theory we all use now."

"Can you skip to the part where time travel somehow shakes the whole solar system?"

"No," she said, and carried on. "One of the more exotic corollaries of MT-theory is that there should be multiple Universes, existing as four-dimensional membranes in a higher-dimensional medium. These so-called branes are completely independent of one another but they can occasionally bump into each other."

"And that's bad?" He was pretty sure now he owed Kadan an apology.

"Maybe. The new physics in MT-theory suggests they should repel one another so that collisions are extremely rare."

"Repel? As in negative energy?"

She studied him for a moment. To Jay it seemed she was trying to decide whether he knew more than he was saying, or was just a complete moron.

"If they do collide, it could be the end of one or both universes. It could trigger a new Big Bang. Some believe that's how the first one happened."

Jay's mouth felt dry. It was starting to get scary. "You still haven't explained—"

"Then do be quiet and let me."

The noise around them increased as Alpha Team arrived and began stuffing materiel into the vehicles. Car doors opened and slammed shut. Men shouted.

Laura went on. "The idea in the FORESIGHT report is that, if you push forwards through time, forcing a path into the future ahead of the present, you're effectively creating a branch sticking out from our universe. There are reasons why this branch is stable for a while, but it is probably quite transient and therefore does not permanently affect the direction our own future will take."

"Probably?"

"This is all new to me too, Jay. Anyway, it doesn't matter. The important thing is, when you stop the time travelling and go back to letting time flow at its normal rate—"

"When you arrive in the future?"

"That's right. The future you get to is a very strange place. Informationally, it should be complete, but—"

"What?"

"There's a way of seeing the multiverse as a hologram, deducible from the information on its most distant surface."

"That didn't help."

She screwed up her eyes with the effort of trying to find a way to make it clear. "No, no. I see that. OK. Don't worry about it. Look, when you get to the future, everyone there— every particle and field there, in fact—will feel as if they have a complete and full history. But the reality is that your arrival has seeded a whole new universe that expands outwards from the moment and place that you arrive. Like a growing bubble."

"So you arrive in a possible future and a new universe starts growing around you but, to everyone in the new universe, it seems as if they've always been there."

"Exactly!" She gave him a big smile that felt like a gold star on his workbook. "But now we've got this new universe growing right next door to our own, expanding at the speed of light."

Jay groaned. "Why does the speed of light always have to come into it?"

Fourget opened the car door and looked in. He was dressed in a combat suit minus the helmet. "Ready?" he asked. Jay nodded and Fourget disappeared again. A few seconds later all three cars started up and left the airfield in convoy.

Laura looked nervous. "You're taking me with you on the mission?"

"Don't worry, you get to stay well away from the action. I just might need you to come in afterwards and look at some equipment."

"To see if it could send someone into the future?"

"That's right. Now tell me about the speed of light thing."

She took a long breath. "Don't think of it as the speed of light as such. Think of it as the maximum rate at which events can happen."

"The speed of time."

"If you like. Time really has two components. There's a kind of time field—which you can think of as part of the geometry of spacetime—and there's the time stream which is a kind of entropic—"

Jay held up a hand to stop her. He struggled for a moment to frame a question that might get her back to what he needed to know. "Tell me why it matters how fast the future universe expands."

"It matters because that tells us how long it will take before we bump into it." He must have looked as astonished as he felt because she hurried on. "It's not really likely that two universes would ever collide. As I said, they ought to repel one another. If they collide at all it could be that the smaller one will just bounce off, like a ping-pong ball hitting a tower block. Of course, the farther you go into the future, the bigger the new universe will be by the time it hits you. If it's going to hit you. Which it probably won't. If you go a hundred years into the future, say, the new universe will expand from that point and it will take a hundred years before its brane nudges our own. It will only be two hundred light years across by then. Very, very small compared to our own universe."

Jay could see the light at last. "What if you went forwards two years?"

"Then, two years later, there's a possibility of bumping into the future universe you started. It's always the same. If you go forward X years, then the potential collision is X years away."

"But isn't our own universe expanding too? Shouldn't it be half the time? You know, you go forward two years, it starts expanding, but we're expanding too so we meet after one year?"

"You'd think so, but there's the relative motions of the two universes to take account of too." She shook her head. "Look, my analogy is very three-dimensional but the reality is eleven-dimensional. It isn't really like two bubbles bumping surfaces, more like they overlap, occupying the same spacetime. I don't know the maths well enough to really understand it but that's how it works out. You go forwards two years; two years later, you bump into the new universe."

"I think that's what happened."

"What?"

"I think, two years ago, someone went forwards in time. The universe they created bumped into ours two nights ago." He found himself squirming in discomfort as he tried to explain his mental image of what had happened. "It's probably all this multidimensional crap I don't understand but it's like the two universes merged for a brief while." He spread the fingers of both hands and pushed one set through the other. "Not like the ping-pong ball bounced off the outside, but like it went through the inside. It would explain everything—especially the weird juxtaposition of things that are…" he held up one hand, fingers spread "… with things that might have been." He held up the other, then interlocked them again.

Laura's eyes glazed. He supposed she was pondering the mechanism. Eventually, she shook her head again. "I don't know. I can't say if it could happen like that or not. It would take better minds than mine to work it out."

"But it's not impossible?"

She turned down the corner of her mouth. "I can't rule it out. That's all I can say."

"Then we have to stop these people, just in case the next lob they do starts a new Big Bang. Don't you agree?" Laura was looking sceptical. He wondered how he could convince her. It would be important to have her support if he needed to go back to Crystal for more resources.

"I do agree," she said, slowly. "However small the chance that you're right, the danger is so astronomically high it has to be investigated."

"But?"

"But what makes you think we'll find a FORESIGHT machine in this factory you're taking me to? If it exists, it could be absolutely anywhere."

Jay began to answer but stopped himself when he realized how stupid it would sound. The time machine had to be at Clarke Engineering because that's where Sandra was, and he knew, with a completely irrational conviction, that Sandra had sniffed and stumbled and smashed her way to the very heart of the mystery.

It was a gift she had.

Or a curse.

* * * *

Night had fallen but the little engineering works was awash with the glaring white light that shone perpetually within its walls. Hamiye prowled around, restless and unhappy. Lee and Hong were at the console again, arguing. The sphere sat with its hatch open, the centre of everything, the metal gantries looming over it like curious adults peering down at a baby about to say its first word.

And what if that word was "Apocalypse"? What if the woman was right?

Everything had been so certain just yesterday. Now there were mysterious backers, a desperate rush to complete the project before MI5 or the SAS turned up, the tekniks fleeing, and the time shot depending on the goodwill of one crazy woman.

He should do it himself. He knew he should. Using Sandra was insanity. But so was risking his life. And the way Hong was gesticulating and complaining to Lee only convinced Hamiye more that the next trip the sphere took would be a one-way ride for its passenger.

"There's a car approaching," Langbroek said through Hamiye's commplant.

"No-one comes in."

He crossed the broad factory floor and wound his way among the offices to reception. There he looked out through the glass doors along the drive to the main gate. All he could make out were headlights and two of the hamsters, guns ready. As he watched, a man approached from the car and stood at the gate, speaking to Langbroek.

"Says he works for Lee," the mercenary said over the comm. "Cocky little bastard."

"Stand by." He called Lee and asked if he was expecting a visitor.

"Let them in," Lee said at once.

"Who are they?"

"Don't worry about that. Just let them in."

He began remonstrating but realized Lee had hung up. Through clenched teeth, he called Langbroek and told him to admit the car. "Ask them for ID," he added.

"Already did. The little shit told me to fuck off. All in Mandarin. No speakee Engrish, so he says."

Hamiye wanted to tell Langbroek to take his visitor by the ankle and shake him until he started cooperating but instead he said, "Let him in anyway. How many in the car?"

"Four."

Four? Was Lee bringing in reinforcements? "When they're inside, have somebody search their car."

"Looking for what?"

"Anything that shouldn't be there."

The gate swung open and the man walked back to the car, legs flickering past the headlights. Then the lights bobbed into motion and the car drove up to the entrance. Three Chinese men got out and two of them dragged a European out of the back. He was gagged and his hands were tied behind him. Hamiye's breath caught as he recognized the prisoner as the CEO of HiQua, Roger Waxtead. Had Lee lost his mind? Waxtead was in on it. He controlled all the money. Even if he'd been nothing to do with it, Waxtead was the kind of high-profile figure you don't just kidnap on a whim. People would miss him, important people who could bring down a world of grief on Lee's head. They were probably already looking for him.

Hamiye stepped in front of the leader of the little group as they came through the door, forcing them to stop. The man only came up to Hamiye's shoulder but there was not the least sign of intimidation in his hard brown eyes. Instead there was an air of calm, professional appraisal as he studied Hamiye. The scrutiny lasted a couple of seconds, then he settled back to wait for Hamiye's next move. The security chief had a strong sense of having been weighed in the balance and found wanting.

"Follow me," he said and turned to lead the group to Lee.

Hamiye found Lee still standing over Hong and his tekniks as they laboured to get the rig ready for the coming time shot. Hong was grumbling as he worked, endlessly clicking his stupid pen. Hamiye caught a little of Hong's complaints as he crossed the factory floor. "We have enough data already," the scientist was saying. "We don't need to do this. You'll get us all caught." He stopped abruptly when he noticed Hamiye and the newcomers.

"Did you arrange this?" Hamiye demanded as they drew near, flicking his head towards Waxtead.

Lee ignored him. He had a quick exchange in Mandarin with the head kidnapper. One of the men holding Waxtead pulled their captive's gag loose.

"What the hell do you think you're doing, Lee?" Waxtead wanted to know. The man was trying to stand on his authority but Hamiye could see how shaken and scared he was.

Again, Lee spoke in Mandarin and this time the guy who had removed the gag hit Waxtead in the stomach. The billionaire convulsed, gasping for air.

"Please understand," Lee said. "Once you signed over the funds for tonight's trading and wagers, you ceased to have any value to me."

"To you?"

Lee's henchman hit him again. This time Waxtead threw

up on the floor. Lee looked away from him with an expression of distaste. Hamiye noticed Hong watching, wide-eyed with alarm.

"I need you to listen to me," Lee said. "There is a strong possibility that the police or the secret service will be here soon. There was an altercation last night. Someone snooping around. One of them was wearing a state-of-the-art combat suit. With any luck, he died from his wounds."

"What's that got to do with—?"

Again, they hit Waxtead in the guts.

Lee shook his head in mock sadness. "You are a very slow learner, Waxtead. Speak again and I will have them break one of your legs." He turned to look at Hamiye but continued to address his remarks to Waxtead. "Thanks to the incompetence of one of my trusted lieutenants, we seem to have drawn the attention of a government agency. So, you see, we might need a high-value hostage to bargain with if things don't go well." He turned back to Waxtead and gave him a thin smile. "And that's you, Sir Roger. Hopefully, all will be well and we can leave this place without interference, but I like to plan for all contingencies. Farid, here, will see to your needs while you are our guest." He dismissed them all with a wave. "Lock him up with the woman."

* * * *

Hamiye and the three Chinese took Waxtead to the storeroom where Sandra was being held. Hamiye unlocked the door and stood back as the leader of the Chinese group pushed forwards and opened the door, giving commands over his shoulder. Sandra Malone barrelled into him, butting him in the solar plexus with her head then cracking him under the chin with the back of her skull as the unfortunate man doubled over and she straightened up. He staggered back into the hall and fell heavily onto his backside. Sandra, head up now, froze as she took in the five men outside her door.

"Fuck," she said.

Recovering from their shock, both the men holding Waxtead let him go and drew guns. Their leader jumped to his feet and assumed a fighting stance. Hamiye couldn't help but smile at the man's obvious discomfiture. It cheered him up immensely.

Sandra took a step back. Her hands were tied but she seemed willing to take on her opponent with only her feet. Hamiye had a strong urge to stand back and watch the fight, but, seeing that it would upset his Chinese co-workers even more, he stepped between them, facing Sandra, and held up his hands.

"No, no," he said. "Don't hurt him any more. You've had your fun, so let's all just settle down, shall we?" Behind him, a barrage of what sounded like fluent Mandarin cursing brought another smile to his face. He let it drop and turned to face the angry Chinese. "Could we put away our guns, please, gentlemen?"

The injured man wiped at the blood that was running down his chin. He stepped up to Hamiye and said quite a lot to him in a low, threatening voice. Then his companions put away their guns. He reached out, caught hold of Waxtead and threw him at Hamiye. With a final burst of angry invective, he and the others stalked off down the corridor.

Hamiye turned to Sandra as soon as they were gone, remembering that he had his back to her. He held Waxtead between them and grinned at her. "How do you like my new friends?"

Watching him out the corner of her eyes, she walked over to a chair and sat down. "You guys make the Keystone Cops look like a tough, well-disciplined outfit. What you got there? Dinner?"

Hamiye shoved Waxtead into the room. "Sandra Malone, meet Sir Roger Waxtead. It seems he's our hostage in case your friends turn up."

"Waxtead? As in…?"

"The very same."

Sandra pushed up her lower lip in mock appreciation. "Wow, you guys just get stupider and stupider."

Since this was almost exactly Hamiye's opinion, it did a lot to wipe the grin off his face.

"I'll give you a million euros if you'll help me escape." Waxtead's first words were directed at Hamiye but Sandra was the one who laughed.

"You've got to do better than that, Rog. You're in the hands of master criminals here. They've already offered me twenty million to help them."

"What?" The billionaire seemed shocked. Then an even more astonishing idea seemed to strike him. "You turned it down?"

Hamiye didn't like to be reminded. "Waxtead, save your breath. No-one's getting out of here until the shot's over and we all leave."

"The shot? But that's not for another week."

He noticed Sandra glance sharply at Waxtead, no doubt realizing that he wasn't just a hostage—or hadn't been. "You've been out of the loop, I suppose. We shoot tonight and we're out of here. The trades happen on the South

American and Asian exchanges, and we pick up our money in the morning."

The fear was back in Waxtead's eyes. "So why am I here? Why am I being treated like this?"

Hamiye felt sorry for the big idiot. "You heard Lee. He doesn't need you any more now he has control of the money. I suppose you should be grateful he still wants you as a hostage, otherwise you'd be dead already."

"And what about when he doesn't need *you* any more?" Sandra asked.

That very thought had been on Hamiye's mind for some time now. He said to Sandra, "I'll come for you when the device is ready. It shouldn't be long. Look…" He hesitated, not certain that what he was about to say was true, but he said it anyway. "After the shot, I'll do what I can to make sure you two walk away from all this. I… just can't promise much." He made for the door.

"Farid?" Sandra's tone lacked its usual hostility. "Those Chinese guys just now. The way they held themselves, the way they handled their weapons: they were well trained. They didn't look like rent-a-thugs. They looked like police, or armed forces. You didn't bring them in, did you?" He looked back at her without speaking, turning over the implications of what she'd said. "You need to find out who they are, Farid."

He gave her a small nod and left.

* * * *

Jay and Laura struggled to make small talk as their car followed the others through the night.

"What's your plan?" she said, after a long silence.

"My plan?"

"For when we get there."

"Pierre and the guys have worked out a way to storm the place if we need to, but first we'll reconnoitre, assess the situation. We've got satellite coverage for the rest of the night."

"And you?"

"Me?"

"Are you part of the plan?"

"If Fourget needs me. Otherwise, I'll go in after the main assault. When it's all quiet, I'll call you and you can join us to assess the equipment."

"Why don't you just get the local police to surround the place and hold a siege until they surrender? Then nobody would get hurt."

The idea of a long siege and protracted negotiations gave Jay a visceral feeling of revulsion. "No, it has to be quick. They could do another lob at any moment—do you still call it a lob if it's into the future?" Laura shrugged. "Then there's the prisoner to think of."

"Your Sandra."

Jay chose to ignore the comment. "And I don't want them destroying any of the evidence. If we ended up with a three-day siege, they could disassemble their rig, wipe their files, and we might be hard pressed to prove they've done anything illegal except a bit of kidnapping."

"Kidnapping's not insignificant."

"No but one of their underlings might try to take the rap, with the bosses denying they knew Sandra was even in the building. I don't want the people in charge slipping through the net."

"Even if it means they might be killed in a raid?"

Jay had put this question to himself many times over the

years. "These are not innocent victims, Laura. If they really did cause the event we saw the other night, they've got the blood of thousands on their hands."

"Perhaps they didn't realize what would happen?"

"Perhaps they didn't care." It irritated him that she should try to defend them. "They must have known. Hell, if I can work it out, whoever they've got in the role of evil genius can work it out too."

They fell silent again. Jay brooded on the likelihood of the brilliant Dr Hong disappearing from China three years ago and then someone else suddenly working out how to build a FORESIGHT machine in London. He popped up a display with Hong's image—a blurry 2D shot of him at a conference from ten years back. It would not surprise Jay to find that face looking at him from the inside of a cell if tonight's raid went well. Or a mortuary slab if it did not.

Laura interrupted his thoughts. "Is Sandra the reason you became such an intense and isolated person, Jay?"

"No, I blame that on not having been breastfed for long enough as an infant."

"Seriously. She broke your heart, didn't she?"

Yes! She smashed it to pieces then trampled on the pieces until they were dust.

"We're nearly there. I just need to make a couple more calls."

She flopped back in her seat. "Fine. Make calls."

* * * *

Hamiye went outside to talk to Langbroek as soon as he had the opportunity. The night was getting colder all the time and a thin rime of frost covered everything, sparkling in the streetlights. He turned up his collar and clutched his jacket tight at the front. His breath was a stream of grey smoke as he crossed the courtyard to where Langbroek and the woman stood waiting for him. They were still bare-armed and oblivious to the bitter thin wind stinging his cheeks and making his fingers ache. The woman wandered off as he approached.

"All quiet?" he asked Langbroek.

"I'd let you know if it wasn't."

"You search the car?"

"Sure."

"And?"

"Three travel bags in the boot. All popular Chinese brands. Same for the clothes inside."

"Anything else?"

"Nope. Looks like the new guys are planning a trip after they finish here."

"Aren't we all?"

"And it looks like they're Chinese."

"Yes, it does, rather."

Hamiye thought about this new intelligence as the gigantic mercenary watched him. Actual Chinese, probably military, or maybe just well-trained Chinese mercenaries, called in by Lee to kidnap Waxtead. Why would Lee do that? Why wouldn't he ask Hamiye to arrange it? How did Lee even know people like that? There were plenty of questions and no answers at all.

"We're finishing here tonight," he told Langbroek. It elicited a small frown.

"You told me four days."

"After the run-in with the odd couple last night, we've moved up the schedule. You'll still get paid for the full contract, only it would be better to get out of here as soon as we can. Just in case."

Langbroek nodded. "Can't argue with that."

"It'll be just a couple of hours now, I think, so be ready to move out."

"Sure."

"I'm going back inside." He could feel his muscles tensing already. He'd be shivering soon. "Keep a sharp eye out. Don't relax. If they come, they'll come fast and hard."

Langbroek seemed completely unperturbed by the idea. "Yeah. Don't worry about it. My team's the best, right?"

"That's what it said on the box."

Langbroek grinned at him and Hamiye hurried back into the factory.

Five pumped-up super-soldiers, three Chinese military, and himself against... what? An SAS squad? Backed up with MI5 agents? If so, it sounded far too much like a fair fight for his taste. The factory would not be easy to defend with so few people. All-in-all, it would be better if they just got the time shot over with and got out of there as soon as they could.

Before he went in through the glass door, he took a last look out across the drive and the parking lot to the dimly-lit road beyond. He was glad they had Sandra inside—even Waxtead. It would be a piece of cake to hide someone out in the shadows and lob mortar shells at the building, or to fly in out of the black sky in a military helicopter and fire a couple of missiles into it. At least the hostages prevented that kind of attack—or they did if anyone knew they were there. And the guy in the super-suit turning up meant that someone did.

He shivered and went inside. No point in dwelling on it. If it came to a shoot-out they were stuffed any way you looked at it. Their only hope was to get out before the shooting started.

Even as he thought it, an unearthly screech rang out nearby. Then a window smashed.

* * * *

The presence of Waxtead in her cell gave Sandra renewed hope. She showed him the plastic tie that bound her wrists behind her and explained what he had to do.

"Are you kidding? I'll rip your hands off."

"No you won't. These things break quite easily if you apply enough pressure. It's just hard to do yourself when your hands are behind your back." Waxtead was wide-eyed and skittish, jumping at every sound and unable to sit down for more than a few seconds. It was hard to keep his attention. It looked like the spring had broken in his brain and was unravelling at speed. "Listen. I'm going to kneel down and you're going to put your heel right over the ratchet—the little box on the outside of the tie. When I say so, you need to kick down hard and fast with all your weight. Got it?"

He wrinkled his nose as if the idea smelled bad. "They'll kill us if we try to escape."

"They'll kill us anyway. They're going to make me run their time scam soon. It could be any minute. After that they don't need this place any more. They disperse, disappear down whatever escape routes they have planned, and they torch this place. With us in it. Do you want to be burned alive?"

He shook his head but it was in denial. "I'm a valuable

hostage. That's what Lee said. Damn that shifty, lying little bastard!"

"Rog, focus. Get my hands free and I'll free yours. Then we stand some small chance of surviving this."

She knelt on the ground, facing away from him, bracing her arms against her body, ready to resist the weight of a hundred-kilo man.

"It's crazy," Waxtead said but he positioned himself behind her and she felt the hard heel of his shoe against her wrists.

"Remember, jump. Push down as hard and fast as you can. Imagine it's Lee's face you're stomping on."

"Oh God," he said and jumped.

There was a second when he was in the air and Sandra clenched her shoulder muscles and abdomen. Then pain shot up through both arms. The unbearable slicing weight of him lasted just a fraction of a second before the plastic tie snapped and her wrists were free. Behind her Waxtead stumbled. He fell against her and trampled on her calf before he got his balance back, stammering apologies. She climbed to her feet quickly to avoid being trampled again, and examined her wrists. They were both cut and bleeding but it didn't look too bad. The chafed and sore skin all around the cuts was testament to her earlier efforts to snap the tie on her own. Her shoulders hurt after being so long in one, awkward position, but she slowly, carefully eased them back into action.

Waxtead was staring at her bloodied wrists and she could see he was ready to turn down her offer of setting him free. She grabbed him by the arm and turned him, refusing to put up with any nonsense and, with a swift blow from her elbow, snapped the tie. The billionaire yelled in pain but a quick inspection showed there was not even a cut. He cradled his arms, obviously feeling very sorry for himself.

"What now?" he asked, but Sandra was already onto it.

She needed to get out of that room and there was only one way. She stood on a chair and rested her palms against the ceiling. She pushed and it gave slightly. Plasterboard. Like most office space, the rooms in the factory had an artificially low ceiling, allowing room above for air conditioning ducts and wiring. Given the height of the rest of the building, she suspected the gap above her was plenty to crawl around in. She checked for where the plasterboard pieces were nailed and joined, faint indentations that could easily be made out from that angle, and picked a spot well away from the wooden beams that must criss-cross above her. Drawing back one arm, she clenched her fist and punched upwards, fast and hard. Her hand went straight through the fragile board, leaving a small dark hole when she withdrew it, wincing as her already-damaged wrist scraped along the board. The noise had been loud but not too loud, she hoped. She grabbed a piece of the edge and pulled, a handful of plasterboard came away.

She climbed down and pulled Waxtead towards the chair. "OK," she said. "Get up there and make us a hole big enough to climb through. Try not to make any more noise."

"What? Me?"

"Well, one of us has to guard the door, in case someone comes in. Which job do you think you'd be better at?"

"You're that MI5 agent Lee told me about."

"It took you this long to work that out?" She pulled him closer to the chair. "Come on. We don't have much time." She urged him up onto the chair and he stood there looking like he might fall off at any moment.

"Why don't you just scream rape or something and then jump the guard when he comes rushing in?" he asked, as if that too had just occurred to him.

"Why don't you scream rape, you prat?" She had to wonder how people as stupid as Waxtead could actually survive in the real world. By inheriting money, of course. But even so... "Look, I don't want to fight anybody. And we don't know who's out there. It could be one of your Chinese friends, or it could be one of those augmented monsters. Inviting someone in to beat the crap out of me is not my idea of a great escape plan. Now, will you please get on with it before Hamiye decides to be friendly and send us some food."

Reluctantly, Waxtead reached up and pulled at the plasterboard. A big chunk came loose and it seemed to encourage him. He set to work, spluttering as dust fell into his open mouth.

"And I'm not MI5. I'm not anything. I'm a single parent, I live in Oxford and I test software for a living. For your stupid company, by the way." The thought of HiQua started anger bubbling inside her. "What the hell are you doing with these people anyway? You're a fucking billionaire. You've got more money than God. Do you really need more? Or is it killing innocent people that gives you a kick?"

He looked at her, wide eyed. "Killing...? Then it's true about the tempocalypse?"

"The what? No. That's just crap. I'm talking about whatever it is Dr Hong's device does when it sends things into the future. That's what caused the quakes and stuff the other night, not some idiotic fantasy with a stupid name. I'm talking about the real Apocalypse that you and your friends have been cooking up. The one that's going to kill more people if we don't get out of here and stop it."

"But Lee said—"

"Lee? What, the same guy who wants to kill us? The one who used you to fund his get-rich-quick scheme? That Lee?" She realized that Waxtead was standing on his chair looking stricken instead of breaking up the ceiling and told him to get on with it. He went back to work, absent-mindedly extending the hole one handful at a time.

"So what do you need the money for? Are you running short of yachts or something?"

"It's the company. Ever since I took over, it's been sinking. I don't know what to do about it. Everything I try just makes things worse." He sounded bitter and not a little sorry for himself. "Lee came to me with a proposition. Said he could guarantee me safe investments and a billion euros on the bottom line. I thought he was mad but he introduced me to Hong and they talked me through the technology. I was getting desperate and I thought, Why not? There isn't a businessman on Earth who wouldn't take a peek into the future if he had the chance. It sounds like cheating, I suppose, but really it's just exploiting a technological edge. It's what entrepreneurs have always done. And it's not risk free. I put up five million for that first trial and only about half of the trades went as expected. We only made twenty million but it could have been much worse. Hong said we were very lucky. Of course, that was a two-year shot. If we can get it down to one day, there should be almost no risk at all."

"Except to everybody in the world."

The excitement that had been building in him as he told his tale drained away again. "You don't know it was us that caused it."

"Don't be a moron."

"It was too widespread to be a backwash. It wasn't localised."

"You keep telling yourself that."

Angrily, he ripped at the ceiling and a big chunk came loose. The hole was big enough. She looked up and the void seemed endless. "OK, Rog," she said. "Time to go."

* * * *

Fourget and his men set up in the parking lot of a building two hundred meters from the target. The building had a high roof from which they could observe the engineering works and a rear yard in which they could unpack and assemble their equipment without being seen. The owner was there along with a couple of Metropolitan Police officers who were EDF MI's liaison for the evening. There was also a team of MI5 agents who would operate under Fourget's command. Or so the agreement was. Fourget's experience of working with local security services had never been good. As Gerhard briefed them on the plan, Fourget watched their faces, wondering what their hidden agenda would turn out to be this time.

Before everyone went to suit up and move out to their assigned positions, Jay came in briefly to give them a pep talk. He didn't introduce himself, or even say hello, but jumped straight in.

"We believe there's a device in that building that is a direct threat to this nation, to Europe, and to the whole world. It isn't confirmed yet, but we also believe there is a civilian hostage being held there. We have no idea yet what kind of forces are guarding the building but there are at least five hamsters and you can expect them to be entrenched and well armed. It won't be easy but I have every confidence that, if called on to do so, you can subdue the guards, secure the device, and save the hostage."

Jay paused and seemed reluctant to go on. When he started speaking again, it was in a different, less confident tone. "I want to add that the hostage is a personal friend of mine. That shouldn't make any difference. You would do your best, within the parameters of the mission, to rescue any civilian and bring her out safely. I just want you to know that, if you get her out in one piece, you will have my personal, undying gratitude." And, with a "Thank you, Lieutenant," he left. Fourget saw a couple of the MI5 people exchanging glances. He would rather Jay had said nothing, but there it was. And could he blame the man for being human and yielding to his fear for Sandra Malone's safety? He doubted that he would have done it himself. On the other hand, having met the daughter, he was prepared to believe that the mother was something special too.

He had asked Jay about Cara and Jay had confirmed she had been delivered to her grandmother's door safely. It gave him some relief, which he did not bother to analyse. It also left him anxious.

"What if she just hails a cab and comes back here?" he had asked.

"Then I stick her in another car and send her home again." Jay had eyed him with a quizzical look. "Any particular reason for your concern, Lieutenant?"

"No," Fourget had replied. "You should perhaps have that car standing by."

Women had not figured large in Fourget's life. He had been a soldier since he left school and spent most of his leave with his parents in Provence. There had been one-night stands—sometimes with women in his various units—and a relationship with a girl from his home town. She had been his first lover and, if he had never moved away, they might have gone on together for many years, but his world had broadened while hers had narrowed, and, in the end, neither could find anything to say to the other.

A number of tables had been arranged in a semi-circle in the room next-door and they now held piles of boxes and wiring. Large, physical displays had been unrolled and mounted above them, showing camera feeds and other telemetry from Alpha Team and the MI5 contingent. There were also maps of the target with overlays indicating plans, troop positions and other intel. Fourget went through there to join Gerhard, who sat at the centre of it all, soaking it up.

"Report," he said.

"All quiet, sir. Observers moving into position. We'll be getting live updates any second. The satellite feed still isn't ready. We'll be relying on ground-level observations until it gets into position."

"What delayed it?" A satellite's orbit was well known and it didn't get caught in traffic.

"Bit of an admin cock-up, sir. Too many agencies having to sign off on re-prioritising its mission. We should have gone for a high-level drone."

But that wasn't really an option: the mercs might have portable radar equipment and a drone would give them away.

"How long?"

"For the satellite?" Gerhard glanced at a countdown on one of the displays. "Seven minutes."

"We'll wait."

They both watched the displays for a while.

"Gerhard?" Fourget said, breaking the silence. "Do you think I don't talk enough?"

"Talk enough?"

"You know. Am I too reserved, do you think?"

"Why do you ask?"

"Someone was complaining about it. They seemed to find it... annoying."

The captain grinned. "Put it this way, sir. In the past minute you've said more than I've heard you say in the past week. So if she's trying to get you to change your ways, it seems to be working."

"I didn't say it was a she."

The grin widened. "It's always a she."

Fourget pulled a sour face. There. That's what talking too much got you. "Just watch the displays."

* * * *

Sandra led Waxtead over the ceiling of the office units. The space was high enough for them to walk upright—a second story of offices could have been installed up there—and enough light leaked up from below through light fittings and joints that they could see easily. They had to walk on a wooden framework of rafters across which various ducts and bundles of cables ran. She kept having to tell Waxtead to keep the noise down. The man was so clumsy—at any moment he could misstep and go crashing through the ceiling.

"We shouldn't be doing this," he said. "This is crazy."

She turned and hissed at him, "Will you shut up?"

"I don't know why I'm up here. They're not going to kill me. That's just you saying that."

"If you don't shut up, I'll kill you myself."

"Do you even know where we're going?" He looked around and spread his hands. "There's no way out of here—no windows, no skylights, just brick walls and a solid roof."

She grabbed him by the collar and pushed his head in the direction they'd been heading. "There, you moron. An inspection hatch." The rectangular hatch was quite clear in the ceiling ahead of them. "Do you think they'd just seal this off with no way to get at it?" She let him go. "Come on. Or stay here. Frankly, I've stopped caring."

She made for the hatch and lifted it. It was a simple wooden rectangle sitting in a wooden frame, no catches, no hinges, and, she thanked the gods, no bolt on the underside. It simply lifted into the roof space, revealing an empty corridor below. She glanced back to check that Waxtead was making his way towards her. She poked her head through the hatch. The corridor was clear as far as she could see, so she lowered herself through and dropped to the ground. The outer wall she wanted was just one office over on her left. She found a door on that side of the corridor and tried it. It was unlocked and unoccupied. Back in the corridor, Waxtead's legs had appeared from the hatch and were flailing about helplessly. Cursing him silently, she hurried over and grabbed his ankles, steadying him and guiding him down, even taking some of his weight as he worked his body through the hatch.

When she had him safely down, he glared at her as if all of this were her fault. She bit down on what she'd have liked to say and led him into the office, closing the door behind them.

"We're going out through that window," she said, pointing to the only window in the room, just so that he wasn't under any misapprehension.

242

"But it's got bars. How can we…?"

She grabbed a metal ornament from the desk. It was a small Eiffel Tower. "The bars are inside a metal frame. There are eight screws holding the frame in place and they all go into the window frame—which is probably just pine. It's cheap and nasty security and that's lucky for us. We dig the screws loose, then we pull the bars out all in one piece. Got it?" She took him to the window and showed him how easy it was to dig into the wood and lever chunks of it up. It would not take long. She found a pen-knife in a desk drawer and joined him.

"You think I'm a complete waste of space, don't you?" he asked as they worked.

She rolled her eyes. "I'm sure you've got loads of really valuable skills," she said.

"No, I don't think I do." The self-pity in his tone made her want to scream. "The only qualification I've got is a degree in business administration from Cambridge and I probably wouldn't have that if Daddy hadn't built them a new robotics institute. You'd certainly never guess, the way I've stuffed up HiQua."

She glanced his way. He was still digging at his first screw while she already had three loose.

"How do you get to be like you?" he asked.

"Just lucky I guess."

"No, seriously. You're beautiful and strong and you can do all this stuff. Is it all just MI5 training, or what?"

"I've told you, I'm not MI5."

"Yeah, well, you would say that wouldn't you?"

"Suit yourself."

"So what makes you turn out like you, and me turn out a complete failure?"

"You should ask Dr Trev," she said, naming a popular TV psychologist.

"I had all the advantages, you know. Nannies, private tutors, Eton, you name it."

Sandra's patience snapped. "All right, you're a useless piece of shit. It was no-one's fault, you're just inherently pathetic. Happy now? Good. So, if you'd just focus on getting these screws loose, we can get you to a nice private club where long-legged hostesses can massage your flagging ego. You'll be right as rain with a bottle of fifty-year-old single malt inside you."

He threw his Eiffel Tower down and scowled at her for a moment before stalking off to the far end of the room and sitting down to sulk. Luckily the carpet tiles absorbed most of the noise of the statuette hitting the floor. Sandra thought seriously about beating the crap out of him—even if it did get her caught again—then went back to work, attacking the wooden frame with renewed vigour.

Two minutes later, she was ready to try pulling the bars loose.

She went over to Waxtead and dragged him back to the window. "Grab the bars here. Use both hands. When I count to three, pull as hard as you can." He nodded with sullen ill-will. Sandra took hold of the bars too and counted down. The corner they were pulling came away from the window frame with a hideous screech as the wood sheared and tore. There was no way Hamiye's people had not heard that. How long would it take them to find her? She could only assume they were on their way right now. "Again," she said, not bothering to keep her voice low. They heaved at the bars and, this time, the whole assemblage came out, smashing the window as it did.

She handed the bars to Waxtead, who promptly dropped them, then stepped back from the window and kicked out the rest of the glass with a series of rapid, high kicks.

"Not MI5, my arse," Waxtead said.

Sandra picked up a rug from near the door and laid it over the jagged shards in the window sill. "Anyone could do that," she told him. "All it takes is to train like your life depends on it for twenty years or more. OK, out you go."

She waited long, agonising seconds for Waxtead to climb out through the window, then hurried through after him. They were at the side of the building—the opposite side to where she had spied on the time sphere and its rig when she had first sneaked into the factory. It was dark and there was a high fence to climb to get into the adjacent industrial unit. Waxtead would never manage it but fifty meters farther along was what looked like a truck, parked next to the fence. If she could get Waxtead up onto the roof of the cab, they could maybe jump over from there.

She grabbed him and started running. She could hear shouting from inside the building. They must have found the empty cell and now the hunt was on. The truck was close to the front of the building, which was a risk, but she had to take it. She pulled Waxtead harder, forcing him into a sprint.

They were still twenty meters from the truck when two people came running round from the front of the building—Hamiye and one of the hamsters she guessed from their profiles. They spotted the fugitives and skidded to a halt, both raising their weapons. Surrender seemed like the only sane option, but Sandra hadn't got that far by taking the sane option. She stopped too and cast about for some kind of shelter, heart racing, fists clenching. If she could—

Waxtead's arms wrapped around her from behind in a

bear hug. "It's me," he yelled. "Don't shoot. I've got her. Don't shoot."

Too surprised to react for a second, she hung there, facing the two guns. "You fucking tosser. What the hell do you think you're doing?"

"Choosing sides," he said.

"Christ, you're stupid," she said and slammed her head back into his face.

He cried out in shock and pain, letting her go as he reached for his shattered teeth. She grabbed his inert bulk and used his weight to swing herself round and behind him just as two shots exploded and bullets thudded into Waxtead's torso. She left him to fall and threw herself at the fence in a reckless leap, vaulting up and over it as gunshots barked from out of the darkness. Bullets zipped past her.

* * * *

"Gunshots!" It was Jock's voice over the comm. "Two shots fired. More. Stand by."

"Where is he?" Fourget asked and Gerhard lit up Jock's avatar on the tactical display. He was on the far side of the building, setting up an observation post two hundred meters beyond the perimeter fence. "Where's that damned satellite?"

"Thirty seconds out. Jock, what can you see?"

"Not a damned thing. We're trying to find a line of sight."

Gerhard touched another avatar. "Davidi, relocate to grid fifty-seven. I want eyes on that shooter."

"I can hear footsteps, Captain," Jock said in a whisper. "Sounds like a bloody rhino heading straight towards us." His head cam revealed only an empty car park with shrubbery about ten meters away. Fourget could hear the footsteps too now. There was a crash as the shrubbery exploded and a gigantic figure emerged onto the tarmac. Jock's head cam jerked towards it, just as the giant turned to stare in the EDF soldiers' direction. The picture broke up as Jock and his buddy moved. Fourget heard him say, "Stop or I'll shoot. Lay down your—" But the giant sprang into action, moving with incredible speed, he raised his weapon—a massive machine gun few ordinary men would be able to wield—and fired in Jock's direction. The image streaked up the display as Jock went down. The Scot's companion's head cam still showed the merc, now swinging his weapon towards him. There was the familiar burp of the man's standard-issue Heckler & Koch UMP9c as it spat bullets at fifteen rounds a second at the hamster. Even as the super-soldier blasted back with his massive weapon, Fourget could see dust rise from bullet impacts on the giant's armored vest.

Davidi was on the comm asking for orders. Gerhard sent him and others to help Jock, but Fourget could see it was too late. The display of Jock's vital signs showed him fading fast. His head cam gave them an unmoving shot of the sky. Jock's companion was in better shape but unconscious and undoubtedly wounded. As Fourget stared in shock at the image from Jock's head cam, the mercenary walked into view, towering into the sky above the dying man. He knelt down and peered into Jock's face, reached out a hand and turned his head from side to side. He looked puzzled, as if trying to work out who he'd just killed. Graphics flashed quickly across the man's face as facial recognition software measured and coded the image.

"Piers Langbroek," Gerhard said, reading from another display. "British national. Wanted by Interpol and several African states for murder and other crimes."

Fourget studied the hyper-masculinised face. "Tell me about the gun," he said and Gerhard set the software to identify it. When Fourget had encountered Langbroek and his team, his combat suit had protected him from their gunfire as it should. But they'd been carrying submachine guns. The weapon in Langbroek's hand looked more like a.50 calibre field gun.

A page of specifications came up on the display. The machine gun was an L21 heavy machine gun. The kind of gun that would normally be mounted on the back of an armored vehicle. He checked the ammo for it and found a range of nasty options, including a variety of armour-piercing rounds, some designed specifically to penetrate advanced body armour.

"Tell Davidi and the others to proceed with extreme caution," he told Gerhard. "Tell them that gun will shoot straight through their combat suits."

Gerhard relayed the message and Fourget, scanning the displays, noticed that the satellite image was up at last, showing an infrared display of the target area. He located the bright spot of the merc standing over Jock. His own men were invisible, shielded by their suits. Another person, a normal person judging from the heat signature, was moving about nearby. Around the target building, there were four more mercs plus three more normals. Inside the building another half-dozen people moved around. There was also someone lying on the ground outside, in the area where Jock had first heard shooting. The figure did not move. Someone was dead or injured.

He called Jay. "Sir? You'd better get in here."

Fourget could think of only one person it could be.

* * * *

"Looks like the bitch did us a favour," Langbroek said. Hamiye crossed the parking lot looking around himself all the time. The merc stood up as he approached. "If we hadn't been out here chasing her, I'd never have surprised these two."

"Are they dead?" Neither man was moving. There were scars on the combat suits where bullets had torn through, but the suits had already repaired themselves and he was spared the sight of the smashed and bloody bodies inside.

"Come on," Langbroek said, heading back to the bushes. "There'll be more of them on the way."

Hamiye dragged his gaze away from the men on the ground and followed the giant. Neither spoke again until they were inside the factory building.

Lee was standing inside the reception, waiting for them. Two of his Chinese henchmen were with him.

"I hope Hong's ready," Hamiye said. "We've got to do it right now or not at all. There are government agents outside and it won't be long before they're all over us."

He'd expected Lee to go off in a rage but the Head of Special Projects seemed oddly composed. "How long can you hold them for?"

Hamiye glanced at Langbroek. "So long as they don't decide to blow up the factory," the merc said, "we can keep them busy all night."

"Bring Waxtead inside," Hamiye told him. "Tie him to a chair. I want them to think we still have a hostage. Then they won't start lobbing missiles in here. Mr Lee, I'll need those new guys on the team too. We'll need every gun." For some reason, he wanted Lee to fight him about it but his boss just nodded and said something in Mandarin to the men beside him. "What about a pilot?"

Lee regarded him steadily. "You let the woman go. You are the pilot."

"Someone has to coordinate our defence."

"Mr Langbroek can do that quite well without your help, Farid."

There was no alternative, of course, and Hamiye had known it from the moment he'd seen the dead special forces men outside. The time shot had to be done now. The only suitable pilot was himself. As much as he didn't want it, that was how it had to be. He nodded. Lee turned away and left.

He took a deep, steadying breath and turned to the hamster. "How do you read it?"

Langbroek sucked his lips. "We surprised them while they were setting up their obbo. They were fully suited so I reckon they were just doing a quick recon before swinging through the windows on ropes. Probably led by a special ops team— SAS, maybe—with an MI5 anti-terror squad as backup and maybe the Met out there somewhere to mop up. I bet there's a chopper coming in to drop guys on the roof too. Their plans are shit now. No surprise any more. They'll either negotiate or they'll try rushing us. Negotiate for sure. When the woman contacts them, they'll know our hostage is Waxtead."

Hamiye could only agree. It was the only scenario that made sense. So it would be a siege. They had plenty of time.

"OK. You're in charge. Good luck."

"Where are you going?"

Hamiye gave him a weak smile. "To see what tomorrow brings."

* * * *

Jay watched the satellite image as one of the bright blobs moved towards the cooler shape of the person on the ground, merged with it, and went back inside the building. He hadn't spoken since Fourget explained the situation. The idea that it was Sandra lying there chewed at him like a live animal in his chest.

"We need to establish a perimeter," he said. His voice, even in his own ears was hollow and emotionless.

"Done," the lieutenant said.

"And notify the Met liaison."

Gerhard grunted. "That will make them happy. They've been in my ear all night asking for updates. They want to know why the spooks are involved at all when this is clearly a police job."

"At least someone will be happy."

"We're going to negotiate, then?"

Jay could hear the reluctance in Fourget's voice. He tried to ignore it. With Jock dead and a man injured, with Sandra… The need to strike back was like a physical force in the room. He had to control it, for everybody's sake. For Sandra's sake, in case she was still alive. Their plan had been risky enough when they had a full squad and surprise was on their side. Now it would be a bloodbath.

"Sir?" It was Gerhard. "I've been watching what they did with the person they just brought inside. Watch." He replayed a few seconds of the satellite imagery, zooming in tight on the shooting victim. Jay saw the bright blob of the mercenary move down a corridor, into a small room, then deposit the person it was carrying. But the dead or unconscious person did not lie on the ground. It continued to have a small profile, as if it were standing or sitting. The bright blob moved from one side of the person to the other, as if working on it. Then it left the room. The victim remained where it was.

"They've tied whoever it is to a chair," Gerhard said. "I'll tell the Met we have a siege situation with one hostage."

"She's still alive," Fourget said, amazed.

"If it's her," said Jay, but he too felt the elation. It changed nothing, of course: the planned attack could not proceed. They had to surround the factory and try to talk to the people inside. But the hostage was alive.

Sandra was alive.

But injured. Perhaps dying. He pulled in a deep breath through his nose. His skin crawled. He felt as if every muscle trembled. This was worse than ever. Sandra was dying in there and his duty was to set up a siege that might last hours, or days. He reached out, took Fourget by the arm and led him out of Gerhard's hearing.

"I'm going in, Pierre. Just me. I have to get her out."

"It will take more than one," the Frenchman said. "She is injured and cannot walk. When do we leave?"

Jay felt a rush of gratitude towards his taciturn friend but couldn't accept. "Thank you, but someone needs to run things. You have to stay."

"Pfftt! To organize a siege?" He waved the idea aside with contempt. "Gerhard can do it."

Jay had to agree. The captain's skills were wasted on such a task. The police could handle it perfectly well—up to the point where the mercs decided to break out. But there was no time for finessing the decision.

"I'm going to suit up. Meet me by the cars in five minutes."

He hurried through to where Laura was still waiting in another room.

"How's it going?" she asked.

He threw open the case in which his own combat suit was kept. He took it behind a chest-height cubicle screen for privacy. "Badly," he said. "I don't understand why but they were running patrols in the nearby buildings. They surprised Jock while he was setting up. He's dead. The man with him was wounded. We're bringing them back here now. The plan's no good any more. We're going to have to talk them out."

"Dead?" Her voice was small and weak. After a moment she said, "Wasn't he wearing one of those things?"

He glanced her way and realized she was referring to the combat suit he was wriggling into. "They can't protect you against everything," he said.

"You're going in, aren't you?" Her eyes went wide with revelation. "You're going after Sandra. *Ach du Lieber.* Isn't that, like, really stupid?"

"Sandra might not think so. She's hurt. Probably dying. I can't wait for the people in there to decide what it's worth to hand her over."

"But you wouldn't do it if it was anybody else, would you? Well, Cara, I suppose."

A denial sprang to his lips but he suddenly felt he owed Laura more than that. He stopped wrestling with the suit for a moment and looked at her. "No, probably not. Don't ask me why it is. Our relationship is… complicated. But if I could swap places with her right now, so she was here, safe and free, I would do it in a heartbeat." And he knew that was true. So true that the knowledge was stamped into the fabric of his being. So much a part of him that pulling it out and putting it on display like that was as surprising and strange as if he'd pulled out his heart and could study it beating in his hands.

He shook off his amazement and finished dressing. "I've got to go."

Laura simply nodded. "I wish…" she said, but didn't finish the thought.

He grabbed up the helmet and ran for the door, his mind already on tactics, access points, tools and weapons.

* * * *

Sandra didn't stop running until she was absolutely certain she'd lost her pursuers. She'd taken a direction away from the main road into the quiet streets nearby. She wanted to be able to hear Hamiye and the hamster if they got close. She wanted to hear vehicles if any came prowling the streets, hunting for her. But all she heard was the rasp of her own breathing, the pounding of her own heart.

At one point she thought she'd heard heavy-calibre gunfire, way behind her. She hoped it was Hamiye, shooting at shadows.

She went to earth in a scruffy, half-derelict suburb, crawling through a damaged front door, peering out through a broken window. Her wrists hurt, her mouth was dry, her stomach was tight with hunger, and she was woozy with sleep deprivation.

She had glimpsed the bizarre flying-saucer shape of Southgate tube station, so she knew where she was. It had been shuttered and barred like so much infrastructure in the outer London suburbs. One day, the Lord Mayor of London promised, they would revive and refurbish the whole underground network and breathe life back into these areas the Adjustment had left to die. But various city governments had been promising that for over thirty years and the right time never seemed to come. Europe continued to stagger from recession to recession as the shock of the Adjustment continued to reverberate through the world's economies. The economic pundits said that, if the rebels won the civil war in the U.S., and the American economy came back from the dead, perhaps things would grow more stable and prosperous. Until then, they reckoned, the world was like a three-legged stool with a leg missing.

She looked at the shabby buildings around her and wondered what it must have been like to live in a world of riches and plenty, as people had done at the beginning of the twenty-first century, burning through the world's resources without a thought for what would happen in the future. It must have been such a good time, that bonfire of the vanities.

Confident at last that she'd lost her pursuers, she sat down on the kibble-strewn floor of the abandoned house, rested her back against the cold, damp plaster, and called Cara. The signal was strong and all the usual net services were available, but Cara's netID was out of service. She called Dot and got the same message.

What the hell...?

How could Cara and her grandmother be offline? She supposed a lingering fault in the comms network could have cut them off. It was possible. But, given the situation, other, darker possibilities seemed a lot more likely.

She called Jay. A recorded message told her he was unable to take her call.

She called his office and a pleasant young woman in an EDF uniform gave her the same message.

"Look, I need to talk to him, it's an emergency."

"Would you like to speak to somebody else, perhaps?"

"Yes! Who did he leave in charge? I want to talk to them."

"Who shall I say is calling?"

She gave her name and waited.

"Ms Malone, I'm Captain Harnois. I work with Mr Kennedy. Are you all right? Are you safe?" It was pretty clear her name had triggered an alert from the K Section computers.

"So he is out looking for me?"

"I'm afraid I can't—" He stopped, seeming irritated with himself. "Yes, he is. Where are you, Ms Malone?"

"I'm not sure. Southgate, London. I'm within a couple of kilometres of Clarke Engineering. That's where he's gone, isn't it? You need to tell him not to go storming in there. I'm out. I'm OK. The only hostage they've got is Roger Waxtead, and he's probably dead. I was there when they shot him." She remembered the way his body shook as the two bullets thudded into him. "Look, I'm not far away. I'm going back to see if I can stop Jay."

"No. I think you should—" but she cut him off.

"You need to find my daughter. She's staying with Jay's mother, Dorothy Kennedy. Something's wrong. Please hurry."

She hung up and ran back out into the street. It was so typical of him to turn up to save the day after she'd already got herself out of there. Now he'd probably get himself killed. Which would serve him right. She set off at a run back the way she'd come. If Jay and his storm troopers went marching into that factory, the hamsters would tear them to pieces. It would be a massacre.

And the growing conviction that Cara was caught up in this too drove Sandra to forget her exhaustion, her thirst and hunger, and run faster.

* * * *

Laura Thalman was prowling around the command console, unable to settle, knowing Jay was out there, when the call from Captain Harnois came through. Gerhard put down a sandwich he was about to start eating beside a steaming mug of coffee and eyed them regretfully.

"No, no," Gerhard told Harnois. "We have stood down the attack. We're waiting for the police to arrive."

She could see Harnois's face in the display, brows knitted, but could not hear his reply.

"Something's wrong," Gerhard said. "I can't raise him." A brief pause. "Fourget's offline too." He glanced nervously around his displays. "Look, give me a moment to find out what's going on and I'll get back to you."

Harnois's image disappeared. Laura chewed her lip as she watched Gerhard frantically querying his men and flicking between the various camera feeds.

"Captain," she said, when she couldn't stand it any longer. "I know where he's gone. And Fourget too."

The young officer swivelled his seat to face her. "You do?"

She nodded and would have said more but a perimeter alarm sounded on Gerhard's console. In an instant he was on it, flicking through the camera viewpoints again, asking for information. He stopped with a sharp intake of breath. Laura saw in the display the image of a man lying on the ground. One of the MI5 agents.

There was a scuffle in the corridor outside the room and they both turned to face the door. Gerhard reached for his pistol. Laura's heart was racing. She wasn't supposed to be in danger here. There wasn't supposed to be any fighting. There was a thump and a whoosh of breath. Gerhard was on his feet, moving to stand between Laura and the door. A man came staggering backwards into the room and fell down hard on his backside. Gerhard raised his weapon and took aim at the doorway. Laura stepped back. She'd seen pictures of augmented mercenaries, had been revolted by the things they did to their own bodies, but she'd never expected to come face to face with one.

Into the room stepped the exact opposite of what she was expecting. Tall and long-limbed, the woman was dirty and dishevelled, her blouse spattered with blood and her long, thick hair matted, yet she moved with confident economy, and she was undoubtedly the most beautiful woman Laura had ever seen.

"Not another step," Gerhard said. "Peel, on your feet, man."

"She took me by surprise, sir," the fallen soldier said.

"It's so unfair when the enemy does that," the woman said. "Are you in charge here?"

"Name," the captain said.

"I'm Sandra Malone. Where's Jay Kennedy?"

Laura's mouth fell open. "You're Jay's Sandra?"

Sandra glanced her way and frowned but kept her attention on Gerhard. "He's gone off to the engineering works to rescue me, hasn't he?"

Gerhard pursed his mouth into the beginning of a question but didn't ask it. He turned to Laura.

"Yes, he has," Laura said, to Sandra. To Gerhard, she added, "He's probably taken Fourget."

Gerhard slowly lowered his gun. "What the hell is this?

There's an MI5 agent down out there. Did you do that?"

"I didn't have time to waste on persuading your men to let me in. It was quicker this way. They'll be all right." She turned to the soldier with the injured pride and the bruised coccyx. "Won't you?"

"He thinks you're injured," Laura said. "They shot someone."

"That was Waxtead."

"Waxtead?" Gerhard asked.

"Yeah, owner of HiQua, billionaire, co-conspirator with these bozos. Look, I haven't got time to bring you up to speed. You need to get onto Jay right now and call him back. It's suicide to go in there without a small army behind him."

Gerhard hesitated.

"She's right. Hurry," Laura said.

The captain shook himself, holstered his gun, and went back to his console. He'd obviously accepted the situation, however reluctantly.

"I can't raise him on the comm," he said, "but maybe I can locate him and Fourget from their suit telemetry and send someone to intercept them."

Laura and Sandra went to look over his shoulder at the displays. Absent-mindedly, Sandra picked up Gerhard's sandwich and began chewing on it. He glanced sharply as it moved past his ear but he said nothing.

"There," he said, pointing. Two avatars were blinking beside the factory fence. "Alpha five, alpha six," he said into the comm. "Rendezvous with alpha one and two at grid forty-two. Standby for further instructions. Oh shit." As they watched, the two avatars crossed the fence line and separated on the other side, moving rapidly apart. "They've gone in. It's too late. Hey!"

Laura had been fixated on the two avatars circling the factory. Now she looked round to see Sandra Malone striding away.

"They're going to need help," the tall beauty said.

"Peel," Gerhard snapped and the soldier moved to intercept her.

She stopped and turned back to Gerhard. "Jay's a friend of yours, right?"

Gerhard was cagey. "He's my commanding officer."

"What about the other one, Fourget? Are you going to sit there and let him die?"

With a suddenness that made Laura jump, Sandra whirled around and kicked Peel's legs out from under him. As the man hit the floor, she grabbed his sidearm and sprang away towards the door. "Surprise!" she said. She didn't point the weapon at anybody but the threat was there.

Gerhard stood with his hand on his own weapon for a moment, then relaxed. "Get off the floor, Peel, and get this woman a holster and some spare clips." He sounded angry, mostly with the hapless Peel. To Sandra, he said, "Do you have any kind of plan at all?"

She thought for a second. "I'm going to shoot as many bad guys as I can and hope that it helps Jay get out of there. It would be good if you could do the same."

Gerhard snapped again. "Peel, are you still here?"

The soldier ran off. Laura could understand him standing there in a daze. She felt completely overwhelmed by what was happening. She'd been with EDF MI for four years and she'd been aware of many missions, some of which ended badly, but she'd never been there in the field, never had to face the fear or deal with the shocking pace of changing circumstances. She'd never seen people making life-and-death decisions more quickly and casually than she would decide on which dessert to buy in the canteen.

Gerhard faced his displays again. "I need your commplant codes. I can watch you from here. Help you."

Sandra nodded, presumably sending them. "And your troops?"

Gerhard hesitated. He looked sideways at Laura and in a flash of insight she saw what the captain was seeing—a representative of the senior management. Her heart fluttered as she realized it was her turn to step up, that she could do something now to change the course of events, that what she said next, even her silence, might affect the lives of everybody on the mission.

"You should do what you think is right, Captain," she said. "I will back you up, whatever you choose to do."

Gerhard and Sandra stared at her hard, perhaps trying to judge the strength of her resolve. She saw a small smile touch the woman's lips.

Peel returned with a shoulder holster with gun and spare ammunition, and a lightweight armored vest. He brought them to Sandra, who gave him his gun back. As she reached to take the holster from him, he held it back and said, "I want a rematch."

She grinned at him. "In your dreams, tough-guy."

He grinned back and let her take the weapon. Sandra slipped on the vest and the holster as if she did it every day of her life. Laura watched, trying to reconcile the strength and courage of this Amazon with Jay Kennedy's quiet, gentle manner. There didn't seem to be any match and yet Jay was out there already, creeping through the night, ready to die to save her, behaving in a way she would never have expected. It made her feel disoriented, as if anyone she knew might suddenly change in an instant.

Sandra exchanged a few brief words with Gerhard, they ran a comms check, then she was gone. No goodbye. No ceremony. She just turned to the door and left. Laura could hear her footsteps in the corridor as she broke into a run.

Gerhard spent a minute more organising his men for an attack. Laura didn't quite follow the details but it looked like a direct assault through the main entrance with Alpha Team in the lead and the MI5 guys supporting from behind. He called up the helicopter too and then went to find the police liaison to explain what he was doing. Before he left the room, Laura called to him and he stopped, looking vaguely surprised, as if he'd forgotten she was there.

"You won't blow up the factory, will you?" she said. He seemed confused. "Only, Jay was keen for me to inspect the device they're using in there."

She could see from the frustration on his face that blowing up the factory was definitely something he had in mind. "I'll try not to," he said. "Not without the boss's say-so. OK?"

She nodded and he hurried off. Alone, Laura drifted over to the tactical displays and found the map with Jay's avatar. But, though she watched Jay, her thoughts were on Sandra. She could see why a man would fall head-over-heels in love with a woman like Sandra Malone. Hell, she was half in love with her herself and she'd only known her for five minutes. One thing Laura knew for certain now, she could forget about Jay Kennedy. Even if he and Sandra never got together, there was no way Laura could ever compete. It wasn't the woman's incredible beauty, or her obvious competence and commanding presence. It was seeing her strap on a gun and run, single-handed, into a building filled with armed killers to save him. With the bar set that high, there really wasn't anyone else who stood a chance.

* * * *

Jay pulled up sharp at the corner of the building. There was a hamster twenty meters away, walking towards him. A woman. If he could get in a headshot, or even hit a leg, he might bring her down. But he wasn't confident enough in his marksmanship to risk it. He promised himself he'd spend more time on the ranges if he got home alive and not let his skills slip as he had done lately. Meanwhile, he had about thirty seconds to decide what to do before the giant reached his location.

He stepped back from the wall and looked around. There were places he might hide but that wasn't what he'd gone there to do. The roof was flat but high. Even with the servos in his suit's exoskeleton, he doubted he could jump high enough. He should know, of course. He should know exactly how high he could jump. Know it by instinct from long hours of practice. But he was an administrator these days, damn it. A manager. He had no reason to be training for combat. That was for the professional soldiers, like Fourget and his teams.

So what are you doing out here, stupid? he asked himself.

He could hear the mercenary's footsteps as she sauntered closer. If he popped out from the corner, aimed and fired, she might be close enough now for a hit. But hamsters were fast. Scarily fast. Their nervous system augmentations gave them reflexes like cats and, in combat, they'd be hopped up on adrenaline, testosterone and artificial stimulants.

Shut up, you're just scaring yourself.

He took a deep breath and listened to the footsteps. How close would she come? Would she look around the corner?

Of course she would. He pictured the massive machine gun she was carrying. She had it in a right-handed grip, finger on the trigger, holding it at an angle across her body with her left hand around the long barrel, ready to swing it round and up in an instant. He swapped his handgun into his left hand and flicked the switch to automatic. Another footfall. Another.

He stepped out from the corner, right in front of her. Tall as he was, she towered over him. His right hand went out to grab the barrel of her machine gun even as she swung it forwards into his grip. He gasped as she pushed harder, forcing his arm back. He stepped into her, blocking the rise of the gun barrel with his right shoulder. Her right hand let go of the gun and shot up to his throat. If the suit hadn't absorbed most of the force, it would have torn his head off. Even so, it lifted him off the ground. The strength of the woman was staggering. But he had enough presence of mind still to squeeze the trigger on his gun, the one that was pressed against her right leg.

With a cry of pain, she used her grip on his neck to throw him aside. Helpless, he flew across the yard and rolled on the concrete. She was down on one knee when he could see her again, swearing like a trooper and regaining her grip on the big machine gun. Fast. So fast. He took aim at her head and fired, just as she fired back at him.

A bullet bounced off the side of his helmet like a hammer blow and he dropped his gun, momentarily stunned. He came to himself in an instant but he knew there was no leeway in this fight. He scrabbled to pick up his weapon and to see what the merc was doing, all the while cringing against the bullets that might be flying towards him right at that moment. Then the panic drained out of him. The super-soldier was lying on the ground, not moving. Her face, what was left of it, was a bloody pulp.

He grabbed his gun and reloaded as he ran for the relative shelter of the building. His heart was thudding so hard he had to take a couple of seconds with his back against the wall to let himself calm down. He was shaking so much he could barely hold his gun, let alone shoot it. He kept thinking how lucky he'd been. How incredibly, stupidly lucky. But two seconds was all he could spare. He pushed off and ran.

* * * *

Hamiye was with Lee and Hong. They were explaining again what they needed from the future even though Hamiye knew full well.

"And what if the cops are waiting? They're out there right now. Why should they go away?"

"Show him, Hong."

The scientist gestured for Hamiye to look at his displays. "Here," he said, pointing to a button in the sensor field. "You push that when you get back. Five-minute delay then the incendiary devices explode."

He looked at Lee. "You're not waiting for me? How am I supposed to get away?"

"I'm leaving you a driver and a fast car."

"I've got a fast car."

"Not like this one."

"The cops will track it however fast it is. I was supposed to leave in the chopper with you." Hamiye could feel his anger building. Lee was shafting him, he was sure. The escape was in a helicopter gunship, a stealthed machine that would take them to a boat waiting offshore, a machine that could fight its way out of any potential problems.

"Plans change," Lee said.

"Not the plan that involves me getting away."

Lee did not seem to be taking his concerns seriously. He spent a moment asking Hong whether the device was ready for the shot. Hong seemed to think it was—with his usual concerns and caveats. Finally, he returned to the topic. "Would you feel happier leaving with the mercenaries?"

They were going to fight their way out in their armored van if they had to. They had a route planned and surprises arranged for any pursuers. Even so, the cops would have RPGs and choppers too. Their escape was not guaranteed.

"You only have to wait two hours at the most," Hamiye said. "If I don't get out, you don't get the information you need."

"That's why I've arranged a car for you. Relax, Farid. Your escape vehicle is well armored, very fast, fitted with all kinds of weapons, and my driver is one of the best. It will get you away. To be honest, it was my own contingency escape plan, in case there were problems with the helicopter. Now it is yours."

Again, Hamiye wondered how on earth Lee could acquire hardware like that except through himself. "I want to see it."

"There is no time."

"Even so."

Then they heard gunfire from outside. An automatic, then one of the heavy machine guns the hamsters used, then the automatic again. The silence that followed told Hamiye that the merc was down. His heart rate kicked up a notch. The thing they all dreaded was happening. Against all reason, the cops were storming the building.

"Into the sphere now," Lee said, drawing a gun.

"No. This is crazy. They're coming in now. They'll be

waiting for me when I get back."

"Only if they get this far. Now get in the sphere."

Hong started urging Lee in Mandarin. It seemed he too wanted Hamiye in the sphere.

"No, I said. If the attack has started, we've got to go, now."

Lee pointed the gun at Hamiye's chest. "We have to go. You have to get into the sphere."

Hamiye looked his boss in the eye and his stomach tightened. There was no doubt in his mind that Lee would shoot him if he didn't do as he was told. He considered attacking him. Hamiye had the advantage of size and reach and he doubted that Lee had seen much hand-to-hand combat. But there was a pace-and-a-half of space between them. Plenty of time for Lee to pull the trigger before Hamiye could lay a finger on him.

"If they're here when I get back," he said, still looking Lee in the eye. "I will surrender and tell them everything."

"We'll hold them off. Don't worry. The gunship will be here in a moment. Any of their people outside the building will die soon after."

"Who the hell are you, Lee? If you're a bloody HiQua executive, I'm a primary school teacher."

The line of Lee's mouth hardened. "Into the sphere now. Speak again and I will shoot you."

Hamiye dared not risk it. He turned and walked over to the sphere.

"Inside," Lee said.

Hamiye looked at the soft, padded interior. His choices seemed to be to die there, or risk dying in the future—either tomorrow or in two hours' time. He took the small chance of survival the future offered and climbed in. Lee closed the hatch as Hamiye fastened the harness around himself. He hit the big yellow button with "EXTERNAL" printed on it and it lit up. He flipped up the red plastic lid over the little silver switch and flicked it from "Locked" to "Ready". Now Hong could fire him off into the future. He gripped the arms of the seat and waited.

* * * *

Fourget heard the shooting and cursed silently. They'd discovered Jay and the chances of him surviving were almost zero—as were the chances of Jay reaching their target. He kept moving along the wall of the building. He might be Sandra Malone's only chance now.

The window with the missing bars was just where Jay had said it would be—near where they'd shot their hostage. Fourget holstered his gun and pulled himself up and through with little effort. He found himself in a small office and made straight for the door, drawing his gun once more. The corridor outside was quiet although there was shouting and the sound of running elsewhere in the building. He switched to augmented reality and green arrows painted themselves on the floor of the corridor. As quietly as he could, he followed them.

At the first corner, he stopped and hooked a finger around the edge of the wall. The camera at the fingertip of his suit fed an image into his commplant which displayed itself on the inside of his mask. Five meters away, two Asians in business suits were standing outside the room he was trying to reach. As he watched, one of them left. The other stood in the doorway, guarding it, cradling a snub-nosed machine gun that hung from a lariat around his neck.

It would have been easy for Fourget to step into the corridor, raise his gun and shoot the guard. Even if the man had time to aim his weapon and fire, the combat suit could handle the impact of a few small-bore bullets. But Fourget needed to stay silent. The whole building was on alert and more shooting would draw their attention to him. His first encounter with the hamsters had put him in hospital. He would not be so lucky again.

He watched the guard and waited. Every now and then, the man would look up and then down the corridor. Each time, his head was turned away for three seconds. That was how long Fourget would have to reach him if he sprinted down the corridor. But his best estimate of how long it would take to cover the five meters between them was six seconds, giving the guard three full seconds to raise his gun and shoot. It was almost impossible, but Fourget would have to take the chance. There was nothing else he could do. He readied himself, steadied his breathing, crouched slightly to launch himself into the attack.

The sound of gunfire deep inside the building startled him, then brought a grin to his face. *So Jay is still alive after all.* The shots also startled the guard, who stepped away from the door to face in their direction, weapon ready. His back was to Fourget. With a lunge that strained his suit's servos to the max, he leaped into motion, powering down the corridor at more-than-human speed, barrelling into the guard, who barely had time to look over his shoulder before Fourget was on him. The impact knocked the guard off his feet and, as they hit the ground, Fourget delivered a single, power-assisted punch to the back of the man's head that cracked his skull against the floor and left him unconscious, if not dead.

Fourget lay across his victim's back while he took a couple

of deep breaths and thanked the gods for his survival. Then he was on his feet and dragging the limp body back to the room in which the injured hostage might still be alive. The door was locked. He pushed it open with a shove of his free hand, threw the guard inside and followed him, closing the door behind him.

On a chair in the middle of the room was a man he did not recognize. Not Sandra! Not Cara's mother bleeding out before his eyes. There were two bullet holes in the stranger's chest and he was dead. Fourget tried to access the man's commplant but there was no signal. Someone was running a jammer. He reached out and touched the body, creating a direct bridge between them. Across the residual electrical field from the corpse came the information he requested. Sir Roger Waxtead, CEO, HiQua.

Fourget's relief at finding that the hostage was not Sandra Malone was offset by two things. One was confusion about what this Waxtead guy was doing there, in fact, the whole question of what the hell was going on. He'd been completely convinced that they would find Sandra in that room. The other thing that marred his relief was the burning urge to kick himself—and Jay—for getting into this mess for no good reason at all.

Another burst of gunfire reminded him that Jay was still fighting for his life elsewhere in the building.

He crossed back to the door and eased it open. The corridor was clear. Silently, he slipped out and headed towards the noise.

* * * *

Hamiye waited an age but nothing happened. He knew

something must have gone wrong and called Hong over the intercom. No reply. Fearing some kind of malfunction that would shoot him into a distant, dangerous future, he popped the hatch of the sphere.

Immediately, he heard gunfire. He slapped the release on the harness and peered out over the edge. He could see Hong hiding under the console, hands over his head, as if that would save him from a bullet. He craned his neck to see farther and there was Lee with two of his Chinese security men. They'd taken cover behind the capacitor cabinets and were firing across the room at someone who only rarely got the chance to fire back. He risked poking his head right out to get a proper look. They had a tall, slender man in a grey combat suit pinned down behind a steel cupboard that was already dotted with dozens of bullet impacts.

The scene didn't make sense. The guy in the suit was only facing small-arms fire. He could come out from behind his cover and stroll out of the room without any risk of being seriously injured. Also, he must know that one or more of the hamsters could appear at any moment and take him down. It took Hamiye a couple of seconds to realize the man in the suit was stalling them, keeping them busy while something else was happening.

He swung himself out of the sphere on the side away from the shooting and made his way towards the intruder around the back of the room.

"Langbroek," he whispered into his comm as he closed on the suited man. "What's the status out there?"

"No movement, boss. I'm in the main corridor, heading your way. One of my team is down."

Damn! How did one guy bring down a hamster—even in a combat suit? "Send someone to check on our prisoner. I think there's more than one of them in here."

"Sure." There was a pause, presumably while he gave the order. "I'm outside the main door now."

"OK. The target is on your left, crouching low, range four meters. Do not kill him. I know he shot your friend, but do not kill him. I want to know what's going on." He waited until Langbroek acknowledged the order. "Thank you. On my mark. Mark."

The hamster burst into the room, big gun aimed at the intruder. At the same time, Hamiye came out of cover shouting, "Drop your weapon. Get down on the floor. Arms straight out." He saw the man's helmet swing round, saw him look first at him, then at the giant. Given the circumstances, he took a very long time to respond. Slowly, he stood up, holding his handgun between two fingers. He looked around at all of them, Lee and his two sidekicks, Hamiye, and, finally, the merc. Then he tossed his gun aside and, again slowly, lowered himself until he was lying down, as instructed, with his arms out. *Still stalling,* Hamiye thought. *Something's going on that this guy thinks is worth risking his life for.*

Hamiye walked up to him. Lee joined him above their prisoner. "Take off your helmet." Slowly, the suited man complied. Hamiye still had plastic ties in his pocket from dealing with Sandra Malone. He knelt down and tied the prostrate man's hands behind his back. "OK, you can get up now." He glanced at Langbroek. "Help him up." The giant reached down and grabbed the man by his wrists and hauled him upright with such force it would have dislocated both shoulders without the suit's servos taking the strain.

Hamiye found himself facing a man in his mid-thirties, broad-shouldered but slim, with eyes that held no fear, only wariness and determination.

"You're Farid Hamiye," the prisoner said. He turned to face Lee. "You are Lee Shaozu. And the older gentleman crawling out from under that table is Dr Hong Minzhe. And that…" he looked over at the sphere "… must be your FORESIGHT machine. Although I suppose you call it something else."

Hamiye couldn't help smiling at the man's audacity. Even now he was stalling, trying to sidetrack them so they wouldn't ask the obvious questions.

"How do you know about the machine?" Lee demanded, pushing his gun in the prisoner's face.

Hamiye reached out a hand and gently pressed Lee's gun down. "Never mind that. Tell us what's going on. You're obviously not here alone. How many of you are there and where are the others?"

"One's just been to see Waxtead," Langbroek said. "My guy reports one of your Chinks is down. No sign of any intruders."

"Who are you?" Lee asked, irritating Hamiye by putting his gun back in the man's face and asking stupid, irrelevant questions that only wasted time.

Before the man could answer, Hamiye said, "Langbroek, tell your guy to head towards us. That's where any intruders are heading. Mr Lee, if you would send your men to guard that door…" He pointed across the room towards the front of the building. "They might be able to surprise them as they try to get in here."

Lee gave the order then turned back to the prisoner. "I still want to know who you are."

The man regarded Lee's gun for a moment and sighed. "You know, you should really put your gun down. I've always made it a rule not to talk to people who point guns at me."

"Talk or die," Hamiye said, losing interest. He needed to find the other intruders. "He's all yours, Mr Lee."

"Jason Kennedy," the prisoner said. Another attempt to forestall Hamiye's departure. "I'm—"

Hamiye saw the surprise on Lee's face. "I know who you are, Mr Kennedy," Lee said. Hamiye didn't remember ever seeing his boss surprised before. "You are the head of K Section, European Defence Force, Military Intelligence." His face hardened as he turned to Hamiye. "That means the woman wasn't MI5 at all, you idiot. She was EDF MI."

Hamiye had reached the same conclusion. But how was he to have known? Besides, if not for him, Lee would never have known there was a spy in their midst, whatever agency the damned creature was from.

"Get back into the sphere, Farid," Lee said. "The mission must not be delayed."

"What? There are other agents in here. In this very building. Getting in that sphere would be suicide until we've rounded them all up and eliminated them."

"The woman doesn't work for me," Jay said. "She doesn't work for Five, either. She's a civilian. You should let her go."

Lee placed the barrel of his gun against Jay's temple. Hamiye saw the Englishman stiffen. He was going to die bravely, at least. "Goodbye Mr Kennedy. I wish I could take you with me. There are people who would love to have a long talk with you. But I'm no longer in a position to take prisoners."

Machine-gun fire exploded nearby. Hamiye flinched and looked round in time to see a section of ceiling give way and another man in a combat suit fall from above in a shower of plaster. He held a snub-nosed machine gun in one hand and an automatic pistol in the other and both muzzles were flaring as he fell, spraying scores of bullets around him. Hamiye turned to run as the man landed with a crash in a cloud of white dust. Bullets whipped through the air and he managed just one stride before pain stabbed up through his left leg and he found himself falling.

He hit the ground hard but tried in desperation to see the man who had shot him, as if knowing what the gunman was doing might help save him. He saw Lee's two Chinese henchmen come running back into the room, guns up. He saw Lee, still alive, holding the man Kennedy like a shield. He saw the shooter's handgun was no longer firing, out of ammo, then the machine gun stopped too. The agent threw it away and took off, running straight at the two Chinese, ramming a new clip into his handgun as he went. Then the thunder of a heavy machine gun boomed nearby and the EDF MI agent went down, armour-piercing bullets knocking him off his feet as blood splashed from his lower back and legs.

Sudden silence echoed around the factory, ringing in Hamiye's ears. His leg was on fire, pain burning along every nerve. Yet it seemed distant, like the drum drum of his heartbeat. The echoing, rushing silence whirled around him; he felt sick. For a moment he was confused about the giant legs striding past him, the prisoner shouting, "Nooooooo!" until blackness flooded in to claim him.

* * * *

Jay stared at Fourget's body, unable to believe what had happened. The man who'd hidden behind him, Lee, let go of him and stepped forwards to stare at Jay's fallen friend.

"I—I have never seen such courage," Lee said. His voice

was shaky and hushed. "I wish I had men like that." Jay glanced at him. There was something in his tone, as if he spoke to Jay as a fellow soldier, an equal. He saw blood dripping from Lee's fingers. Wounded in the arm, then. At least that was something.

He looked about. The mercenary had gone over to poke Fourget with his machine gun. There was no sign of life. The other man, Farid Hamiye, was on the floor, blood oozing from a leg wound. Everyone seemed stunned by what Fourget had done. He looked over at the two Chinese men in suits. They were too calm and disciplined to be hired thugs. Soldiers, perhaps. And Lee was their commanding officer. So not soldiers, but spies. Chinese agents on a deep-cover mission that had lasted at least three years to his knowledge. And Hong… He looked across the room to find the elderly scientist back under his table.

"You're here to conduct experiments in future time travel," he said aloud.

"The dangers were unknown," Lee said, not looking at him. "Influential people refused to let us work within our own borders. After Beijing, a timesplash in Chinese territory would be unthinkable."

"And this whole elaborate set-up with HiQua, what was that all about?"

Lee turned to face him. A sad smile played on his lips. "Money. Deniability. But mostly money. There is a very important general, you see, who was only persuaded to support the project in return for a very large consideration. We've done enough to prove the technology, but to go back with empty hands would be unacceptable. It complicates the mission."

Jay looked away, anger rising like gall. "You know you are

responsible for the catastrophe that happened the other night?"

"That is not certain. Dr Hong thinks it is unlikely."

They both watched the old man climb shakily from his hiding place. Jay's tone was beyond scornful. "Dr Hong might prefer to lie to himself than to face the truth about his work. He doesn't strike me as a particularly brave person."

Lee seemed to snap out of the reflective state his near-death experience had caused. "Your people are attacking at last. I have a helicopter gunship outside watching them. Tell them to pull back, or it will blow them to pieces."

"You've got a jammer running. Shall I stand on the roof with a megaphone?"

Lee called to Hong and the scientist reached into his console and worked the controls with trembling hands. His team's comms chatter was suddenly audible through Jay's commplant. He sighed.

"Here's the thing, Lee. I'm willing to let you and your agents go. I'll even let the hamsters go. We can always track them down later. But I want him." He pointed at Langbroek. "And I want Hong and your equipment. I also want the civilian woman you've been holding."

"No fucking way, Kennedy," Langbroek said. "I ain't going with you and the fucking Chink can't make me."

Jay pursed his lips. "Then we have a problem, I'm afraid." Silently, he said into his comm, "Gerhard?"

"Jay! Where have you been? Are you all right? You won't believe—"

"Gerhard, shut up and listen. There's a helicopter—"

"Yes, we're tracking it."

"It's just received orders to shoot the men you've sent here."

"Ah. OK."

Lee had been speaking but Jay had missed it. "Sorry? What was that?"

The Chinese agent snarled. To Hong, he shouted, "Get that damned jammer back on." To Jay he said, "I said to tell them to pull back! It won't help to warn them. They'll be just as dead. You missed your chance to save their lives. Langbroek!" The gigantic mercenary was right behind Jay, as he discovered with a start when he turned. "Keep an eye on him. I'm keeping him in case any more of his people get in here." He turned to his Chinese agents and snapped orders at them in Mandarin. Langbroek did not move. "What's wrong? Why aren't you doing anything?"

The hamster looked down at him and said, "It's time I took my team and got out of here. You just need to settle my account."

"What? You can't go yet. We need to…" Lee stopped as he noticed Hamiye, still lying where he'd fallen. There was no-one left to pilot the sphere. The mission was over. His shoulders sagged. His eyes closed. The energy seemed to drain out of him. "You're right. We should all leave while we can. I don't suppose you or one of your men would like to pilot the sphere? There'd be a very big bonus."

"We already earned a big bonus when that one killed Alice."

"Alice? Oh, the woman."

"And another one for this." He turned slightly to reveal a patch of torn and mangled flesh on his leg just below the hip. Jay winced, even though Langbroek seemed able to completely disregard the wound. "And the agreement with Hamiye was we get paid the full four days. It's all there."

"You've done an invoice?" Jay asked, amazed. "Just now,

while we were talking?"

From outside came the sound of heavy machine-gun fire. The kind that might come from a helicopter gunship strafing the surrounding roads and parking lots. Jay clenched his jaw and prepared to snap the tie that held his wrists together.

"The transfer is complete," Lee said. "Try to make as much fuss as you can when you leave."

Langbroek gave him a withering look. "Yeah, right. Nice doing business with you." He took one step towards the door and the back of his head exploded.

Blood and brains spattered Jay and Lee, who both stood frozen in shock as the giant crumpled and fell. In the doorway ahead of them stood Sandra Malone, legs apart, gun raised in a two-handed grip, smoke curling up from its barrel.

* * * *

Sandra swung her gun to point at Lee. At the edge of her vision she saw the two Chinese agents take aim at her.

"Tell your men to drop their weapons, Lee, or you're next." Jay was staring at her, open mouthed. Hamiye was on the floor, dead or dying. *One too many bad choices*, she thought. Across the room, one of Jay's soldiers lay face down, not moving. Lee said something and the two agents lowered their guns but did not drop them. "Jay, get over here."

As Jay finally got his brain in gear, she noticed Hong, over by the console. Something about the old man unsettled her, like a memory of something bad. She kept her eye on Lee and told Jay to hurry up. He had his hands tied behind his back, which infuriated her. He was wearing a combat suit for God's sake. Why didn't he just—?

She heard his voice. Not in the room, but in her mind.

What had he said? It was in the future, in this room, something important. Something…

Wait, she heard him say. *Hong had a—*

She dropped to one knee and swung her gun up towards the old scientist. Hong stood there pointing a handgun at her. *A gun. Hong had a gun.* She fired and her shot took the old man in the shoulder, spun him around. His gun clattered to the floor. *A closed time loop*, she thought. Had she just created a closed time loop, with her and Jay and Cara trapped in it forever? Or had she just escaped from one?

That was the least of her troubles.

She heard the snick of a machine-gun bolt being drawn. Even as she understood what it meant, that Lee and his men had seized the opportunity her brief distraction had given them, she threw herself sideways, out of the doorway, across the floor. Bullets ripped up the floor and the wall behind her. The noise and violence of it took her breath away. Chips of wood and concrete blasted at her, stinging her hands and face. She could hardly believe she was alive—and her luck wouldn't last for long. The machine-gun barrels would swing her way, track her scrabbling progress across the floor. Bullets would tear her body apart.

She heard a roar, a bellow of rage, audible above even the screaming machine guns, and saw Jay tearing his arms free of the cable tie around his wrists with the power-assisted exoskeleton and charging the gunmen, recklessly, wonderfully, hurling himself into them, dozens of rounds thwacking into his armour but not yet his unprotected face. He crashed into them, knocking the two agents down, silencing their guns, if only briefly.

Sandra was on her feet by then and running for cover, the only cover she could reach.

The sphere.

Lee, shouting furiously at his agents, turned to track Sandra, firing at her repeatedly but missing with every shot. He was shooting left-handed, she realized. His right hand hung, useless, by his side, still dripping blood. She felt blessed by the gods. She dived into a roll that took her behind the squared-off base the sphere rested on. She lay on her belly, facing Lee, both arms straight ahead, sighting along the barrel of her gun.

Wide-eyed, Lee ran.

"Jay, over here," she shouted and aimed at the struggling threesome on the ground. It wouldn't take the two Chinese agents long to get a gun, even a knife, into Jay's face. "Run, you idiot."

His head came up and looked at her, his face a mask of indignation. "Idiot? That's bloody rich." With a swipe of one arm, he knocked one of his opponents back so hard Sandra heard the man's head bounce off the floor. Jay was on his feet and running. "You're the one who came storming in here with nothing but a sunny smile and a can-do attitude." Behind him, the agent who wasn't stunned brought up his gun and took aim at Jay's head.

"Head down, Beanpole, before they shoot it off."

He ducked his head between his shoulders and ran faster. Bullets raked across his back before Sandra had a chance to fire at the shooter. The agent must have been wearing armour beneath his business suit because, of the three shots that hit him, only the one that hit his hand made him squeal and stop firing.

Jay came crashing to the ground beside her, panting and grey-faced. He propped his back against the base of the sphere and let his head fall back, eyes screwed shut and lips pursed. For the moment, no-one was shooting. In the quiet, the boom-boom of the helicopter guns could be heard outside. Jay's people were still taking a pounding.

"Are you hurt?" Sandra asked, although it was obvious Jay was in pain.

"Feels like I was trampled by buffalo."

"Those suits are incredible."

"Smart materials," he said, easing himself into a more comfortable position.

"Your guys are on their way. I spoke to Gerhard. Why don't they shoot down that chopper?"

"Waiting."

"For what? Christmas?"

One of the Chinese agents had fallen back to the cover of the doorway. The other was behind the dented cabinet that Jay had once used. Between them, they had Jay and Sandra pinned down. There was no sign of Lee.

Outside, the helicopter noise seemed to grow louder. There was a whoosh and a massive explosion.

"That," said Jay. "That's what they're waiting for. I'd say our own chopper just arr—Shit!"

Everything shook as the flaming wreckage of a helicopter gunship smashed into the far side of the building and exploded. Windows burst and flame rolled across the factory. The fireball was gone in a moment but several blazes had taken hold where the searing heat had blasted walls and furniture.

"We should go," Sandra said.

"I insist that you stay." Lee's voice was just a couple of meters behind them. Close enough that even he might not miss. Sandra dropped her gun and turned around, slowly.

"You didn't see him coming?" she asked Jay who was

sitting there facing him.

"I had my eyes closed."

"You what?"

"Shut up," said Lee. He looked angry but not out of control. "Get up."

Sandra couldn't understand why he had not killed them yet. She saw the two agents come out of hiding and advance on the sphere.

"The chopper was your escape, right?" Jay said. "So now you need hostages. Is that it?"

Lee backed them towards the control console. As they moved past the front of the sphere, Sandra nudged Jay and glanced towards the open hatch. He gave her a quick frown, clearly not understanding. She could have thumped him.

"You are not getting out of this alive," she told Lee, stopping.

"Keep moving."

She looked around and saw Hong climbing to his feet, leaning on the console for support.

"I see Hong's recovered," she said.

And, in the instant his eyes involuntarily flicked across to the wounded scientist, she kicked out at Lee, her boot connecting squarely with his jaw. Whirling around she grabbed Jay and pushed him towards the hatch shouting, "Get inside!" And, as the two agents brought up their guns and opened fire, she dived in after him.

It was a compartment designed to hold only one person and both Jay and Sandra were tall. By the time they were inside and the hatch was down, bullets rattling across the tough exterior, there was barely room to move.

"Hang on," said Jay. He was more-or-less in the pilot's seat with Sandra scrunched up on top of him. "Won't they just hit the button and send us off into the far future or something?" No doubt it had not escaped his notice that the generators were running and the capacitor banks were charged.

"It's all right," she said. "You have to go through a process in here to enable external control of the time shot. Unless we do that, they can't send us anywhere."

"That process wouldn't involve hitting a yellow button with 'EXTERNAL' printed on it, would it?" Sandra felt her heart sink. "And maybe flicking a little switch from 'Locked' to 'Ready'?"

"Oh, fuck. Turn it off. Right now. Turn it off."

Jay heaved under her. "I'm trying but I can't get my arm free."

Gritting her teeth against the pain, she tried to turn herself towards the controls, but it was impossible. "Look, I'm going to move over this way, then you—"

But it was too late. With a jolt, they broke loose of the present and rattled away into the future.

* * * *

When Gerhard led his team into the grounds of Clarke Engineering, they found three men standing there waiting for them. All were wounded and all were unarmed.

"I am Lee Shaozu," said the well-dressed man with blood dripping from his fingers. "These are my colleagues. We are cultural attachés working for the Chinese Embassy. We have diplomatic immunity. I wish to contact the Ambassador."

Gerhard studied them with a jaundiced eye. "Chinese spies, eh? Where are the mercs? Or are they cultural attachés too?"

Lee shrugged. "If you mean the terrorists who have been holding us hostage, my government will be making an official protest at how long it has taken you to set us free. As you can see, we require medical attention."

"Stick it up your arse, Lee."

Gerhard had not been having a good evening. The helicopter gunship had wounded two of the MI5 men—it would have been worse if not for Jay's warning—and had proved to be so well stuffed with electronic counter measures that none of their hand-held surface-to-air missiles could get a lock on it. So they'd hunkered down and waited for their own gunship to arrive while the one above them circled around ploughing up the neighbourhood. All the while, he could hear sporadic gunfire coming from the factory, see the muzzle-flashes in its windows, and could do nothing for Jay and Fourget except pray that the shooting didn't stop.

He sent people to search for the hamsters. The satellite had lost track of them ages back, probably because they were now wearing hooded, insulated ponchos to hide their infrared signal. Another bloody cock-up.

To make matters worse, the Metropolitan Police had sent what looked like a whole armored division to "provide tactical support". In other words to try to take over, probably because the Mayor or the Home Office didn't like the way things were going. Well, Gerhard didn't like the way things were going either. He looked at the burning wreckage of the enemy helicopter and thanked the Lord that at least the RAF guys knew what they were doing and had managed to bring it down within the factory perimeter. If it had gone down on the motorway, or among houses... He shuddered. Things were bad enough without having to explain that to a court-martial.

"Cuff these bastards and get them in a van," he told his men. "They're my prisoners, so you don't hand them over to MI5 or to the Met, OK?"

A sudden squealing of wheels made everybody turn and grab for their weapons. The mercenaries were making their run. The armored van burst from the back of the building, rapidly gaining speed. Machine-gun fire roared from ports in the vehicle's sides. "Leave it," he shouted into the comm. "The Met can have them." Another decision he'd pay for later, but he was damned if he'd put what was left of his team at risk chasing down a few mercs. Besides, there was more to do here.

"Peel, Davidi, you're with me. Let's get in there and see who we can find before the whole place burns down."

"You shouldn't go in there, Captain," Lee called out as he was being led away. "I believe the terrorists you just allowed to escape planted incendiary devices throughout the building. Any minute now it will be an inferno."

Rage boiled up inside Gerhard. He stomped over to Lee and grabbed him by the collar. "Thank you for volunteering to help us search, Mr Lee." He dragged him along as he led his men into the factory. Lee, his hands cuffed behind him, stumbled but could not fall in Gerhard's servo-assisted grip.

They went in through the front door and marched straight through to the back.

"There's one in a room down there," said Lee, nodding in the direction of a side corridor as they passed. He was very eager to cooperate, Gerhard noted, now that his life might depend on them getting out quickly.

"One of ours?" the captain asked, pausing.

"No," said Lee and they pressed on.

The factory was filling with smoke from a dozen small

fires burning at the far end of the room. There was a body nearby on the floor, a big man in civilian clothes, Arab features. Not Gerhard's concern.

"Over there," said Lee and Gerhard had to squint to make out the shape of a man in a combat suit face down on the ground. His heart stilled as he realized it was Fourget. He stared for a second or two, fighting down the urge to pound Lee into a pulp. Then he said, "Davidi, get Lieutenant Fourget out of here."

He turned Lee to face him, gripped him by the throat and lifted him onto his toes. The Chinese spy looked frightened but defiant. "Anybody else?" Gerhard asked softly. Lee met his gaze although he struggled to breathe.

"Dr Hong is over there, shot by your agent Sandra Malone. Also around the place are a few of his tekniks, killed by the terrorists, I believe."

"Where are Jay Kennedy and Sandra Malone? Think carefully before you answer."

"They went away," Lee croaked. "They escaped from the terrorists and went back through time." He nodded to the platform where the sphere had stood.

Gerhard studied the banks of F2 generators, the cabinets of capacitors. He knew a displacement rig when he saw one. Maybe the murdering bastard was telling the truth. "How long till the incendiaries blow?"

"Less than a minute."

Now *that* he could believe. "All right. Everybody out. The building's about to blow." He jogged for the exit, dragging Lee behind him, not caring if his prisoner occasionally crashed into door frames or desks. He was barely through the outer doors when the incendiaries went off. Hot clouds of flame blossomed in the corridors and erupted through the opening behind him. His combat suit protected him but Lee must have suffered badly the way he screamed. Gerhard dropped him a few meters from the burning building and marched on to where two of his men were tending Fourget.

"Is he alive?"

"Just," said Davidi. "We need to get him to a hospital right now."

Gerhard called the helicopter on the comm and explained the situation. It was still in the vicinity, with an ETA of thirty seconds.

"That one," he said, turning to point at Lee, who lay on the ground, moaning, smoke still rising from his singed clothing, "can wait for the ambulance to arrive."

He stared at the burning building. Anyone still inside was dead now. Any evidence of what really happened would be lost. So much for Dr Thalman inspecting the device. He shouted into the comm over the roar of flames, "How long till the fire engines get here?" The answer was not encouraging. "Tell them I want this fire out within one hour." Even he could see it was hopeless. "One hour," he insisted. "They need to use whatever technology will do the job." He'd seen film of bushfires being water-bombed and there was a new thing that created a sudden vacuum. "Two lives depend on it. Make sure they understand. Two lives." Returning from a timesplash to materialize in the heart of that inferno was the stuff of nightmares.

"Sir?" It was one of the surviving MI5 officers. "The Met just called. Seems they picked up two women trying to run the blockade."

"Two women? Nobody got out of here that we don't know about."

"No, sir. They were trying to get in from outside. They

claim to be relatives of Mr Kennedy. The police have them in custody and they're waiting for instructions."

"Custody? Two of the Section Head's relatives in custody?"

"Yes, sir. The older one was armed with an unregistered shotgun and the younger one… she seems to have bitten one of the arresting officers."

Chapter 14

The Future

Darkness.

Jay blinked but the darkness remained.

"Cognitive subsystems online." The voice was melodious but not human. "Sensorium booting. Selecting environment."

He saw a sketch of a landscape, wireframe hills, trees that appeared in outline and were filled with monochrome texture as he watched.

"Wake-up in three, two, one…"

He was on a hillside, standing still with his arms by his side. It was a sunny day. A light breeze touched his cheek. With a start, he realized there was someone beside him.

Sandra.

She turned to look at him at the same moment he saw her.

"What the hell…?" she said.

He was so glad to see her he could have shouted. The last thing he remembered was being in the sphere. They were being thrown around, smashing into things, into each other. He had tried to hold her to him, to protect her, but the buffeting was too violent, the sudden shocks too extreme. He tried to manoeuvre her into the seat so he could strap her in.

Then he felt his arm break.

He looked down at himself, raised his arm. It was fine. No pain. No pain anywhere, in fact. Which was impossible.

And there was another impossible thing. Both he and Sandra were wearing lightweight, blue coveralls. "Sandra...?" She was staring at something behind him. "I think I'm having a dream."

"We've got company," she said, ignoring him.

He turned and saw a woman approaching across the grass. She too wore a simple jumpsuit. He stared. She seemed familiar. She was a woman of about his own age, tall, attractive, with a slim, athletic build, rather like Sandra's.

"Cara?" Sandra said. It was as if the woman suddenly came into focus. Of course it was Cara. And yet...

The woman's—Cara's—face lit up. She ran towards them, arms out. "Mum! Dad! It's so good to see you again. It's been so long."

She rushed up to them and embraced them both. Cara! But she was in her mid-to-late thirties. Had they gone forwards a whole twenty years?

Sandra was the first to step back from the embrace. "What's going on?" she said. There was a wildness to her eyes that gave away her distress. "Where are we? What happened to the sphere?"

Jay realized that the sphere was nowhere to be seen. If they'd landed twenty years in the future, why wasn't it there? In fact, where was London? And how come their bodies were healed and their clothes had changed? He realized that even the cuts and scratches that had been on Sandra's face before they got into the sphere had gone. Her skin was as smooth and healthy as it had ever been. Perhaps even more so.

"How long have we been here?" he asked.

Cara looked from one to the other of them, still beaming. "I'll explain everything. Don't worry. Oh God, it's good to see you. I've missed you so much." She laughed. "And I'd forgotten how *young* you both were! Come on. Let's go inside and I'll tell you all about it. This place is just a kind of reception area. Somewhere nice to wake up."

She linked her arms into theirs and led them towards an archway in a shady spot between two trees. It was a rustic wooden arch with wild roses climbing up and over it, flowering in great profusion. Jay had been looking right there a moment earlier and he had not seen it. He felt a tiny curl of fear in his stomach. He didn't understand what was happening and he didn't like it. But the sunny day, the gentle breeze, and Cara's arm in his were all reassuring. Cara would not lead them into danger. Cara loved them. Above all, she loved her mother.

They passed through the arch—Jay caught the scent of roses as they went—and found themselves on the edge of a large cobbled piazza. He stopped dead. Medieval buildings rose around the piazza on three sides. On the fourth side, there was a wide expanse of water with more buildings beyond. A river? No, the Lagoon. He was in Venice. Not the Venice of 2068, half-drowned by rising sea levels and pretty much abandoned as it crumbled into the sea, but the Venice of a hundred years earlier. Still intact. Still beautiful.

"A virtual reality," Sandra said. She reached behind her and touched a stone wall. Jay saw that the arch they had passed through was now a doorway in the same wall.

"Let's get a coffee and talk," Cara said, tugging them towards a group of tables outside a little café.

"How are you doing this?" Sandra asked. "I've used VR. It's not like this. Even Cara's—your—best immersive games are not a patch on this. I can smell the sea. I can feel the fabric of my clothes pull as I walk. You can't tell me it got this good in just twenty years."

"Twenty ye—? Oh, I see. Because of my age. No, no." They reached a table and Cara ushered them under a sun umbrella and into seats. "Look, let's sit down and I'll tell you all about it. Isn't it lovely here?"

It certainly was. Jay looked out across the sparkling water. He'd never visited Venice—what would be the point in his day?—but he'd seen it in vids and read about it in novels. It was just as he had imagined it would be. He touched the surface of the table beside him, noticed the textures, touched one hand with the other, felt the warmth and softness of his own skin. The illusion was so good, it may as well have been reality.

A small servitor appeared and Cara ordered cappuccinos and cannoli for each of them. She spoke in Italian and the little robot answered in the same language.

"When did you learn Italian?" Jay asked. Cara had never shown an interest in learning other languages.

"I didn't. It's just…" Her eyes went from Jay to Sandra and back. "I should start at the beginning."

"Where are we?" Sandra asked. "I mean, our real bodies. Where are they?"

Jay could see that Cara didn't have good news by the way she bit her bottom lip. It was one of her tells. Sandra must have seen it too because she tried to lighten the mood, saying, "Well I know we're not dead because, if this were Heaven, you'd be six again, not a woman my own age."

The servitor reappeared and distributed the coffee and cannoli. Jay could smell the coffee and chocolate. He wondered if the VR was good enough that he could drink it.

"This is one of my favourite cafés," Cara said. She picked up her pastry and bit into it, closing her eyes in enjoyment. Jay saw crumbs fall and white icing sugar stick to Cara's fingertips.

He felt Sandra stiffen and he looked across at her. She was growing tense and angry. To head off an explosion, he said, "Maybe you could start explaining things, Cara."

His grown-up daughter swallowed her mouthful, looked at Sandra and grinned. "Sorry, Mum. You really should try them. They're to die for." Perhaps Sandra's expression was more eloquent than he had been. Cara put down the confection, brushed the icing sugar from her fingers and sat back in her chair.

"OK," she said. "The first thing you should know is that you're not twenty years in the future, you're more like two thousand."

Jay felt the news like a slap. "What? No, that's impossible." He turned to Sandra. "Is that possible?"

Sandra kept her eyes on Cara. "How come you're here then?" Which Jay realized was a very good question.

Cara bit her lower lip again. "The thing is, I died in 2137." Jay did the sums. She would have been eighty-seven or eighty-eight by then. So what was he talking to? A recording? A simulation? "I was an old woman, but I'd spent much of the latter part of my career researching ways to upload human minds into computers. I became one of the first post-humans." The pride in her voice was unmistakable.

Jay was too stunned to ask a sensible question but Sandra said, "So, you're a copy of Cara's mind, running on a computer."

Cara smiled. "If you like. As far as I'm concerned, I'm Cara. I never stopped being me. I simply transferred myself from one kind of existence to something superior."

"Superior?" Jay couldn't see how living inside a box was in any way superior.

"I'm immortal, Dad. I have…" she gazed out at the Lagoon "… all of this, and so much more, an infinity of worlds and places and times. I can even be corporeal if I want to—put on an artificial body and walk the Earth like a mortal soul."

"God-like," Jay said, not because he thought that's how she was, but because that's how her tone suggested she saw herself.

She seized on the idea eagerly. "Yes! That's it exactly. We moved beyond being merely human, and, since then, we've moved so much farther."

"You were expecting us, weren't you?" Sandra asked. Jay was still processing the astonishing revelations, trying to imagine the world his daughter now lived in, but Sandra remained focused on their own situation.

"You told me, when you got back… That is, you will tell me, when you get back to your own time. I gave you… I will give you a set of coordinates in a spatio-temporal system that has not been invented in your time, so that you can give them to me, so that I will be waiting for you."

"Sounds like a paradox," Sandra said.

"Yet it worked. You turned up just where and when I expected you to. I even knew to expect you to be—" She stopped abruptly. "I'm sorry, but this is going to be a bit of a shock. When we found the sphere, you were both dead." She held up her hands to prevent them interrupting her. "But don't worry, we got to you in time to get a good clean read from both your brains. We didn't lose a thing."

"Holy crap!" Jay said.

"So we're stuck here?" said Sandra.

"We're programs? In a computer?"

"But you said we went back." Sandra sounded almost pleading.

Cara must have picked up on what that implied because her tone grew a little impatient. "Yes. Don't worry. You're not going to end up like me."

"I didn't mean…" Sandra began, but, of course, that's exactly what she meant.

"So we're dead," Jay said, trying to understand it. "And you copied our brains. And now we're programs in a computer?"

"Not a computer like you're used to, but yes. That's about it."

"So how do we get back?" Sandra was growing insistent.

"What's wrong?" Jay asked. Her concern was making him feel it too. What had she seen about their situation that was worse than he had understood?

She addressed herself to Cara. "No offence, but we've got a daughter, a real daughter, waiting for us in 2068. I want to know how we get back to her."

Cara looked hurt, stung by what Jay saw as Sandra's callous disregard for her feelings. "What your mum means is—"

Cara cut him off before he had to think up something consoling. "It's all right, Dad. I understand." She turned to Sandra and reached out to take her hand. Sandra let her, which surprised Jay. "I do understand, Mum. I know you, don't forget. I know how fiercely you love. And I know that, for you, Cara is and always will be the version of me who shares your timeline." A tear ran down her cheek, perhaps the most surprising thing Jay had seen yet. "That fierce love was always the bedrock of my life. The memory of it still is. If I didn't know how much you would want to go back to her—to me—I'd be begging you to stay here." She reached out and took Jay's hand too, smiling at him. "Both of you. You'll never know how much I've missed you."

Jay felt tears pooling in his own eyes. Even Sandra seemed to soften. "I'm glad you understand. You were always such a bright kid. So tell me, if we're dead, how do you get us home?"

"Oh, that's easy. We're rebuilding your bodies. We've got them in a repair shop right now. They'll be as good as new in a couple of weeks."

* * * *

After a short tour of Venice, Cara took them to another world. They sat in a natural amphitheatre on a soft, red carpet of some mossy plant. The sky was black—almost no atmosphere, Cara explained—and in it a gigantic blue gas giant hung, subtly striated, partially obscured by a grey, pock-marked minor moon. "This is a moon too," Cara said, looking around at the bright mountains that surrounded them, steep, their sharp peaks all skirted in red. "It's a real system. Beautiful, isn't it?"

There were other people on the slopes with them—in fact, a large crowd had gathered.

"Are any of these people real?" Jay asked. He'd wondered the same thing about the people they'd seen in Venice. "I mean, real like you, not real like…"

Cara seemed happy to ignore his *faux pas*. "I don't know. Most of them are sims, put here to create the right atmosphere—some of our realities just don't feel right without other people and there aren't enough of us, or at any rate enough of us wanting to see this play right at this second, to make up an audience. But there might be a few post-humans among them. I could make them show up, if you like."

At the focus of the curving slope, a flat area that was clearly meant to be a stage, its set a building, a shabby little hut, materialized out of the air. The crowd became silent. A group of women walked onto the stage and formed into a chorus. An old man came on and stood alone, declaiming to the audience, "O Argos, ancient land, and streams of Inachus, whence on a day king Agamemnon sailed to the realm of Troy, carrying his warriors aboard a thousand ships."

So they were going to see a play. A Greek drama, Jay supposed, though he did not recognize it. He looked at Sandra and she looked back at him. Despite the fact they were sitting—albeit virtually—on a moon in a distant star system, two thousand years in the future, watching a performance of a play that was well over four thousand years old, in the company of their immortal daughter, Sandra didn't seem happy. He pulled a "What's up?" face which she dismissed with an irritable shake of the head and turned back to watch the play.

Ten minutes later, Sandra leaned in to Cara and said, "I've had enough. Can we go now?"

Cara was on her feet in a moment. "Of course," she said. "Come on."

They walked up the slope to the rear of the amphitheatre. Jay was not surprised to see that there was a clear path for them, even though the crowd behind them seemed randomly spread. Cara led them to a cave mouth in the rocks. They walked in and were immediately somewhere else. A concourse in a futuristic city of delicate glass towers and flying cars.

"Couldn't you just click your fingers or something and teleport us between places?" Sandra asked.

Cara seemed taken aback. "I thought this way would be easier for you to cope with. I didn't mean to be patronising or anything."

"You could stop treating us like idiots then and tell us what's going on here."

"Sandra!" Jay saw the hurt flicker across Cara's face. "Why are you being so...?"

"It's all right, Dad. It's just, Mum... being Mum." She turned to Sandra. "I only wanted to show you what an amazing place this is, let you know how happy I am here. There's so much more I could show you but... well... you'd find it hard to take in without certain augmentations. This is just the tip of the iceberg: we can travel to any place or time in the known universe—or even the imagined universe. We can literally invent any world we want to, just by thinking it up. Would you like to be mermaids, ride a spaceship at near the speed of light, visit Odin in Asgard? It's no trouble at all."

Sandra looked unhappy and Cara was becoming tight-lipped and irritated.

"I'd rather meet your friends," Sandra said. "I'd rather talk to you, to hear what it's been like these past two thousand years, to hear about your hopes and dreams for the future. If I wanted a tour guide, I could probably ask one of these sims to do it, couldn't I?" She pressed her lips together, as if angry with herself, as if trying to stop herself from going on. She clearly lost the struggle because she said, "All this sight-seeing just makes me suspicious. It makes me wonder what you're hiding from us, why you're trying so hard to distract us."

"Distract you? God, I'd forgotten how completely paranoid you are. I'm showing you something wonderful, here, something so astonishing…" She had raised her voice and seemed suddenly to realize it. She took a calming breath and said, "I should have known. All this freedom, complete and unfettered freedom, is wasted on someone who spent her entire life jumping at shadows and making her own daughter afraid of the neighbours, her teachers, the other schoolkids!"

Jay was shocked all over again. "Cara, that's not fair." And it wasn't, though it was probably all true.

Cara turned quickly and walked three brisk paces away from them. Sandra stared after her. Her mouth opened but she did not speak. Nobody spoke for several seconds. Then Cara turned back to them.

"Maybe we should all take a break," she said. "I've got you a room…" she snapped her fingers, watching Sandra, and the building beside them morphed into a glittering hotel "… here for the night." She raised a hand as if to forestall their objections. "I have no idea if you two are having sex at the moment. I was always confused by the way you both carried on. I often thought you were secretly having it off behind my back." Jay began to protest but she stopped him with the same hand. "So you're in the Presidential Suite. It's got so many bedrooms you'll need a map. I'll pick you up after breakfast…" again, she looked pointedly at Sandra "… And I'll take you to visit a friend of mine. Goodnight."

With a click of her fingers, she was gone.

* * * *

The Presidential Suite was about as splendid as a set of rooms could be. Decorated in a style that was part Versailles, part botanical gardens, it had enough room to house a large, extended family and came complete with two servitors to fetch and carry. Sandra didn't even look around but stomped over to the nearest sofa—its gigantic proportions dwarfed by the broad expanse of the room it was in—and threw herself down to brood. Jay was left alone to fend off the attentions of the manager, another bot, hell-bent on demonstrating every one of the room's ten thousand luxurious features, and shoo it out of the door.

He took a chair opposite Sandra and studied her while he worked on what to say. He'd been upset by the sudden antagonism between Sandra and their daughter. He felt it was all Sandra's fault but the important thing was to broker some kind of peace between them.

"Are you going to sit and stare at me all night?" Sandra asked.

"I'm thinking."

"Try not to break anything."

He sighed. "What's got you into such a bad mood?"

"Why don't you go take a shower or something instead of wearing out your two good brain cells trying to understand things?"

Jay refused to rise to the taunt. "Virtual body," he said. "No showering necessary."

"Heaven." Her tone said it was anything but.

"Look, Sandra, I—"

"It's not Cara," she said, looking at him for the first time.

Jay knew immediately what she meant. "It's Cara who grew into an eighty-seven-year-old woman and then lived for two thousand years in Wonderland."

"Maybe. It's still not my Cara."

"Is that what this is all about? Why you picked a fight with her?"

"I'll be glad to get home."

Jay didn't feel the same way at all. He was in the future—a future, anyway—and he had a million questions he wanted to ask. He wanted to make the most of it. He struggled to find a way to say that without driving Sandra into a rage.

"If we can go home," she said.

"What do you mean? Why shouldn't we go home? They've got the sphere. They're going to fix up our bodies. Cara said—"

Sandra became animated. "Who's 'they', Jay? Cara kept mentioning them, but she hasn't told us a damned thing about this society. Who runs it? How's it organized? Why are they being so kind and generous? They're fixing up our bodies. What does that cost? Who's paying? What do they even use for money here? What has value? Computer cycles? Information? Novelty?" She leaned forwards. "And where is here, anyway? Are we in London still? We're in a computer, she said, but where is it? Its servers? Its power source? In a bunker? In orbit? We don't know anything about these people except that they've kept themselves hidden while Cara keeps us distracted."

Jay had to admit he hadn't considered any of that. He opened his mouth to start speculating about how a post-human society of immortal uploads might work, but Sandra cut him off.

"You think I'm paranoid. Cara thinks I'm paranoid. Did you hear what she said? That I isolated her and made her life miserable? Do you think that's what I did? Do you think I'm some kind of crazy woman who can't see what's real any more?"

Tears sprang from her eyes. The sight of them made Jay's heart pound. Before he knew it, he was out of his chair and beside Sandra on the sofa. He took her by the shoulders, turned her to him. Her eyes were wide and distraught, seeking something in his face, some sign of betrayal, perhaps, or of understanding.

"Everything you've done has been for Cara. I know that. And she knows it too. And it's not paranoia if they really are out to get you. And, God knows, the world won't seem to leave you alone. Washington vindicated you. So did this little business with the FORESIGHT machine. If anything, you've never been quite paranoid enough. But you've kept her safe and look, she lives to a ripe old age—at least in one probable future."

The need faded from her eyes. A small smile played on her lips. "So you think I didn't do enough then?"

He smiled back at her. "Did you dig a moat around your house? Did you wrap her in cotton wool, with barbed wire on the outside? No, I didn't think so."

For a moment, her smile lingered, then it fell away. "I didn't give her the father I should have. I kept her a secret from the one person in the world who would have helped me protect her." The tears were falling again. Jay's heart was a solid lump in his throat.

He heard himself saying, "You remember, after Washington, you gave me a chance to be with you and Cara?" She nodded, watching him intently. "And I told you you'd hurt me too much and I couldn't forgive you?"

"I know. I understand. You don't have to explain."

"It was true. You'd taken so much from me by excluding me from Cara's life. I couldn't see past the hurt. All I wanted to do was get away somewhere and wallow in my misery."

She turned away, on the verge of flight. "I'm sorry, Jay. I was a child when Cara was born. I was so screwed up."

He took hold of her again and turned her back to face him. "I know. I see it now. I've had more than two years to think about it and, even with just two good brain cells, I finally got there. It was wrong of me to turn my back on you. Wrong of me to walk away from the only woman I've ever loved. Could ever love. What I'm saying is…" God, what the hell *was* he saying? His heart was pounding like splashmusik, he was light-headed with the utter giddifying momentousness of what he was saying. A small frown crossed her brow as she waited for him to find the words.

"What I'm saying is, I love you. I want you. Will you marry me?"

She convulsed in what might have been a laugh, or a sob. He blinked at her in astonishment at what he'd said. Yet, now it was out there, he knew it was exactly what he wanted.

With a quick shrug, she shook off his hands and stood up. She took a few paces across the room and stopped, her arms wrapped around herself, her gaze fixed on the far wall. He closed his eyes, misery sweeping through him. "God, I'm such an idiot," he said aloud.

"You think?" She turned back to face him. She looked more sad than angry.

"It was a stupid thing to say. Here. Now. I'm sorry."

"Sorry? You had two-and-a-half years of perfect moments, and you pick today." She closed her eyes, head down, opened them and lifted her chin. "I'm going to bed. I'll see you in the morning."

"I meant it," he said to her retreating back. "Every word." Yet he didn't try to call her back, or prevent her leaving. The inappropriateness of the situation bore down on him like a great weight. Why hadn't he just kept his mouth shut, waited for a better time and place? Had he expected her to throw herself into his arms, let him carry her off to the bedroom? No, not her, he realized, a simulation of her. Then what? Two programs locked in rapture. The ultimate cybersex. The whole idea was impossible. A joke.

He groaned and flopped back into the sofa's embrace. A part of his mind was saying "Stupid, stupid, stupid, stupid, stupid…" But another part was exultant. He knew now what he wanted. Knew it with his whole heart. It was monumental. It dwarfed everything, his work, his life, even being here in the future. He wanted to marry Sandra. He wanted to be with her, for the rest of his life. Every moment he wasn't with her from now on would be wasted. In a sense, he'd always known it. It had been his destiny since that night in his flat in London when he was nineteen and she'd cried on his shoulder. Maybe before that, even. Maybe from that night at the splashparty in Ommen when he'd seen her up on the stage, so young and beautiful, so scared, and he'd tried to save her.

All right. He was an idiot and he didn't deserve her, but he was going to marry her. All he needed now was for Sandra to agree.

Chapter 15

Apocalypse

Sandra woke to sunshine pouring through the hotel windows. She'd lain awake for hours in the night, thinking about Jay and his ridiculous proposal, about the fight in London they'd escaped from to end up in that disturbing unreality, about her virtual daughter and what the millennia had made of her, about her own virtual self and her real body lying in a real hospital somewhere. In the end, the transition from fretful night to bright morning had come in the blink of an eye. She knew from many, many such nights that she should be feeling exhausted and hungover, but she didn't. She felt great. It made her wonder if post-humans needed sleep at all.

She had slept in her clothes on top of the bed. She thought about washing her underwear in the bathroom. How long was it now that she'd been wearing the same clothes? With an irritated shudder, she remembered these weren't the same clothes. They weren't even real clothes. Everything here was an illusion.

She found Jay sitting on the sofa as if he hadn't moved at all since the last time she'd seen him. He turned and smiled. He looked cheerful. She'd expected sulks, or recriminations, or grovelling apologies, but not cheerfulness.

"OK," he said, not to her. "Room service, we'll have that breakfast now, thank you."

On a table across the room, an assortment of foods and crockery appeared. The smell of bacon and coffee filled the room. He bounced out of the sofa and crossed to it. "How about something to eat? I've ordered everything I could think of, eggs, bacon, bread, cold meats, cheese, croissants, coffee, tea, fruit juice, cereal, but you can get anything else in an instant if you want it. Do you fancy kippers, or devilled kidneys, or pancakes, or something?" He was helping himself to scrambled eggs and hash browns, toasted muffins and coffee.

"How come you're so perky?" she said. She tried to sound gruff, but she was secretly pleased. The day could have started out much worse. He was waiting to take her order so she said, "I'll have some of that coffee," and he grabbed up the pot to pour it.

"I've been playing with the facilities here," he told her, handing her the cup. He took his plate to another table to eat. "I hope you don't mind room service. I thought eating in a restaurant full of sims might not go down too well."

"Good thought." She joined him at the table. "I've been thinking—"

"If it's about what I said last night—"

"Can I speak?"

He closed his mouth around a forkful of eggs and signalled with his eyebrows for her to go on.

"We're both dead. You realize that, don't you?"

He blinked at her. "Pardon?"

"Cara said it. We died in the sphere. Then, thanks to some process I can't even imagine, they copied our minds out of our dead brains and set them running in their virtual world. That's us. Copies of dead people."

He screwed up his face with the effort of taking it in. "I don't feel like a dead person. I feel like I always feel. Like me. Only more…"

"Perky?"

"Something like that."

"Yeah, well. We're just very good copies. And, of course, we think we're the originals but we're not. And, here's the thing. When they put us back into our bodies—those dead bodies that they're 'fixing' somehow—we'll be copied again. Then we'll be copies of copies, in bodies that might well be copies of the originals."

"Like clones, or something?"

"If we're lucky, they'll at least be flesh and blood. For all we know, they're going to put us into robots."

He pulled back in surprise. "Jesus. I never thought of that. Surely they'd—"

"Tell us? Maybe that's what the meeting's about this morning. You know, with Cara's friend?"

"Ah, yes. When I spoke to room service they passed on a message to say he'd be arriving at nine."

Sandra checked the time on her commplant. It was eight-thirty. It gave her a jolt of irritation that they'd faithfully simulated her neural implants too.

"And here's some more paranoia for you," she went on. "Since our minds are just programs running in the bloody Matrix, there's no reason why they couldn't be watching everything we do. For all we know our conversation is being broadcast across the galaxy to a trillion novelty-hungry post-humans who get their kicks eavesdropping on mugs like us."

"Surely not. Cara would—"

"And not just watching us and listening to us, but also hearing our thoughts, too. Why not?" She thought Jay looked a little alarmed by that. And could it be he was blushing slightly? There were plenty of times she'd have loved to know what was going on in that head of his, but maybe today was not one of them. "I tell you, this whole thing creeps me out. We need to speak to someone in authority and get assurances that we're not the latest reality interactive."

"It's probably not as bad as all that." Jay sounded more hopeful than convinced. "They've probably got all kinds of privacy laws, like any society would."

"Maybe, but would they cover humans as well as post-humans? What kind of privacy do we allow monkeys when we put them in zoos?" The whole night's worrying was pouring out now and she felt the same tension that had kept her awake so long. "And what if it's worse than that?"

"Worse? What could be worse?"

She shook her head in dismay. "You and Cara think I'm paranoid—"

"We don't!"

"—but you're just so naïve and trusting. Since we're bits of software running inside Multivac, what's to stop them modifying our code, tweaking our subsystems, controlling every thought we have even? Our endocrine systems are simulated too, obviously, so are our neurotransmitters. Maybe your outburst last night was them screwing with your oxytocin levels?"

"Sandra!" He looked hurt and she regretted it immediately.

"I'm not saying it was. I'm just saying, how can we trust anything we see, or hear, or think, or feel? If I wasn't paranoid before I came here, I'm sure I'll be a twitching, gibbering wreck before I leave. How do I know you're even you and not some sim? It would explain your bloody cheerfulness in the face of all this."

He grew defensive. "I'm cheerful because… well…" He cast about for a distraction. So transparent. "What did you mean last night when you said we might not be able to go home?"

She shook her head and walked away. She could see right through him. Always could. He was happy this morning because he'd asked her to marry him and, even though he'd had no answer, it had resolved things for him. Jay was a man who liked things to be clear. Problems made him unhappy, especially the intractable problem of what his own feelings might be. And yet, obvious as he was, he always managed to surprise her. She always underestimated the depth of his feeling, the goodness of his heart. It was her own failure, she knew: her own inability to truly understand him, or to trust anyone. She needed to work on that.

So she said, "The sphere was meant to return to our own time after two hours. If they've still got it, maybe it isn't working. Also, Hong said something about following the sphere's own path back, but that the path decays eventually. We might be trapped here."

Jay was silent for a long time, then he said, "Two thousands years. Who knows what adv—"

A knock at the door stopped him. They both checked the time. It was nine. They exchanged suspicious looks. Surely a whole half hour had not passed.

"Ready?" Jay asked her. She nodded and he went to open the door.

Cara came in looking youthful and breezy in a bright summer frock of the kind she had favoured as a teenager. The man with her was tall and handsome, dressed in a style that emphasised his deep chest and athletic build, yet also proclaimed him as a man of substance and importance. His brows were smooth and his eyes dark and penetrating. Cara introduced him as Ashley Raines. Sandra thought the name sounded like he should be a writer of serious fiction. Indeed, there was something of the deep, brooding intellectual about him and she could easily imagine he'd copied the look from the black-and-white author photo in a 1930s novel.

She wondered if he and Cara were lovers but even in the small actions of offering and declining coffee, taking seats, making introductions, Cara treated the man with far too much admiration and respect for there to have been any real intimacy between them.

"The good news is," Raines told them, "you can go home in about two hours."

"Two hours?" Sandra was surprised but not unpleasantly. *The sooner the better.* "I thought Cara said a fortnight."

Raines smiled. It was a beautiful smile, but condescending. "It's both, actually. We have the concept here of r-time and e-time. Real and experiential. Where your bodies are, in Base Reality, about two weeks will have passed. Here, time is running at a fifteenth of the speed. So, for you, just one day will have seemed to pass."

Sandra looked at Cara, who seemed to see nothing odd about what he'd just said. "Why?" she asked. Cara let Raines answer.

"We thought you'd be keen to get back home. Of course, we had to offset that against letting Cara spend some time with you. We thought a day might be a reasonable compromise."

"We're a little concerned," said Jay, "that the sphere might be damaged. It should have returned automatically after two

311

hours. Also that a fortnight here might be too long for it to be able to retrace its route."

"Don't you worry," said Raines, and Sandra imagined him patting Jay on the head. "We know an awful lot more about time travel now than you did back then. Out technical people had no problem disabling the auto-return timer and they have made modifications that will allow it to find its way back despite the path degradation." He sighed. "One small caveat, I'm afraid. I asked them to make sure any new technology they added destroys itself as soon as you get back. Nothing explosive. Don't worry. It will simply decay once it has completed its job."

"That's probably for the best," Jay said. "We'll have enough trouble trying to contain our own tech when we get back."

Raines smiled politely. Sandra hated the feeling that he saw them as children, or primitives.

"Speaking of technology," he said, "I'd like to ask you both a favour." There was a twinkle in his eye as if he had an exciting game he was about to let them join. "There's a little something you can do for me and my people. And for Cara, of course. Did Cara tell you about the Apocalypse?"

Sandra glanced at Cara as Jay exploded with, "What?" Cara was looking calmly at Raines. He already knew she hadn't mentioned it and Sandra thought she had not been meant to mention it. This conversation—every conversation since they'd woken up—had been carefully planned.

"Your people?" she asked, not rising to his bait.

He was unfazed. He smiled his irritating smile. "My people. Cara's people. All the people."

But why should he be fazed? It was quite possible that a part of his mind was running fifteen times faster than hers.

Perhaps thousands of times faster. Even so, she didn't want to let him steer the conversation wherever he liked.

"What about the humans?" she asked.

His expression became sombre. "That's why I mentioned the Apocalypse, and why your help is so important." It was quite possible that anything she said would lead back to the Apocalypse and Raines's script.

"What apocalypse?" Jay asked and Sandra could have kicked him for it.

"Just after I died," Cara said, as smoothly as if she and Raines had rehearsed it, "back in 2140, tensions between Europe and China grew worse. Through Arab and African proxies, they'd been skirmishing for decades but, finally, full-scale war broke out."

Raines took up the tale. "It grew very nasty very quickly. Nuclear weapons were used and..." He paused. "Were they mining asteroids in the Earth and Lunar orbits in your day?"

"The first asteroids were on their way," Jay said.

"Well, both parties—and their allies in North and South America—began nudging their asteroids onto collision courses with enemy cities that had survived the bombing. It was the ultimate slow-motion train wreck. People had plenty of time to evacuate, to dig in, to hide, but it did them no good at all. The climate disruption after the asteroid bombardment lasted twenty years. Black skies, acid oceans: a frozen world punctuated by violent volcanoes and radioactive wastelands. In that time, no crops grew and the few survivors starved."

"It was the end of the world," Cara said, awe in her voice. "The human race was wiped out. So was almost everything else."

"Oh my God." Jay obviously believed them. His eyes were

wide and pained. His mouth fell open as he struggled to take it all in. Even though Sandra didn't want to believe anything they told her, she felt her heart grow still at the mere possibility that it had really happened.

"Yet you survived," she said, trying to rally her scepticism.

"There were quite a few of us by then," Raines said. "We mostly lived in orbiting computing facilities. We remained neutral throughout the war. Even so, we lost several installations on the ground and in space." He fixed his gaze on Sandra. "Humans were not a trusting species, nor were they trustworthy. Our neutrality was resented by many who thought we should be on their side. But, yes, we survived. And we managed to pick up thousands of survivors and uplift them into our society."

"We saved what we could of human culture," Cara said, "preserving it. It wasn't all lost."

"Just the people," said Sandra—unfairly, if they were to be believed. "So what is it you want from us? This favour you mentioned."

Raines's expression was sad but grateful as he opened his mouth to speak. But Jay jumped in, holding up his hands to stop the proceedings.

"Hang on, hang on," he said. "Can I just take a couple of minutes to deal with this? I mean, the end of the world!" He looked to Sandra for support, his eyes pleading.

"It was a long time ago, Dad," Cara said. "Thousands of years. Everything's fine now."

"No. Not fine," Jay insisted. "It's just fifty years away for us."

"Jay." Sandra reached out and took his hand. He really looked very upset. "It's just one possible future. Even if you found all the probable futures from where we started, there'd still be an infinite number of them."

Raines studied her with his calculating eyes. "Since you came here, this is now a very real future. Its physical existence has been set in stone. A whole Universe, independent of the one you left."

"That's where you can help us, Mum. We need you to close the loop."

Sandra looked at her keenly. This was the pitch, at last, and it involved creating a temporal anomaly. A closed time loop.

"I don't think I should be tied into another one," she said.

"Another one?" Jay and Cara said together.

"Long story. Why would you want us to screw with the future like that?"

"Because you already have done," Raines said. "In our own timeline. You provide a key piece of science to Dr Kurt Brandt's team at the University of Zürich. It helps them develop the first scanning process for copying an entire human neural system. In 2121, Dr Brandt successfully copies the very first human mind into a computer. A company is established to do it on a commercial basis and, by 2130 is processing over five thousand uploads a year. Without the key research finding you pass on, we estimate that Brandt would not have made that breakthrough until after the Apocalypse starts. You can see what that would mean."

"No uploads," Jay said. "Everyone would die and there'd be no-one left at all."

"Quite."

"What makes you think I gave Brandt the tip-off that led to all this?"

"Because Dr Brandt is with us still. She uploaded her own mind. And she told us about your visit to her in Zürich at the end of 2068. Would you like to meet her?"

"Her?" asked Jay. "You said Kurt."

Raines gave a wistful smile. "Gender tends to be a matter of preference or even mood among us. So does sexual orientation, skin colour, body shape, even species. Post-humanity is free in ways you can hardly imagine." Abruptly, he was deadly serious again. "Will you do it?"

He was looking at Sandra. Waiting for her answer. She tried to work out what her cooperation might or might not mean for the timelines. If she went back and did as he asked, was she necessarily on the same timeline as this future? Might her Universe still not drift away from this path as the countless possibilities of every moment became fixed choices? It seemed almost certain it would. And yet, in this future, she had done it, *must* have done it. Was she already locked into this loop forever?

"Sandra?" It was Jay. She realized she was still holding his hand and let it go. "Sandra, if you don't do it, Cara couldn't be here. She will die in 2137. Really die."

As if she hadn't seen that immediately! As if that hadn't been the blackmail behind Raines's request all along, the reason they'd been allowed to see Cara and spend some time with her. As if it wasn't the only reason she'd give a damn whether a bunch of copied minds inside a machine lived or died.

"Yes," she said. "Fine. I'll do it."

Cara leapt up and threw her arms around Sandra's neck. "I knew you'd help us. Thank you, Mum. Oh, this is so important." She carried on squeezing her and Sandra put her own arms around Cara, hugging her back. The feel of this grown-up woman, the scent of her, were so much like her own Cara that, just for a moment, she let herself believe.

* * * *

They left the hotel room, stepping straight into what seemed to be a hospital. It had few of the usual signs—doctors, beds, nurses' stations—but there was something about the cleanliness of the place, its air of sterility, that gave Jay the impression. They were following Raines, who seemed to be in charge.

"This is where it all happens," he said as they rounded a corner.

Jay stopped dead. On a set of four reclining chairs, were four people: Sandra, Cara, Raines and himself. They all seemed to be asleep. Sleeping Jay and Sandra were dressed in blue coveralls just like the ones they were wearing.

"Very creepy," said Sandra. "Do you people suppose we don't have enough nightmares as it is?"

Jay stepped forwards and touched his sleeping doppelgänger. His hand slipped inside the body and he pulled it out quickly with a shudder. "They're not real," he said.

"No," Raines corrected him. "We're not real. This building and everything in it is completely real. We've synced with Base Reality and real time. We are all now virtual projections matched to the dimensions of an actual place—a building on the surface of the Earth, in fact. You can push your hand through the walls and floors too if you like."

"We're all ghosts," Cara said. She seemed quite cheerful about it.

Jay remembered what Sandra had said about them being dead. It had seemed like an abstract philosophical point at the time. But not now. He could see his old body—or a replacement—breathing in its recliner, restored to health, cleaned up and without blemishes. It made him feel insubstantial, insignificant. A disembodied spirit haunting a world he barely knew. Unable to touch anything. Unable to prove his existence. That curl of panic wound inside him again. He felt a strong urge to get back inside his body.

"Shall we get on with it?" Sandra asked. Her tone was cool but maybe she was feeling the same sense of insecurity.

"Of course," said Raines and everything went dark.

Jay felt a sudden disorientation, as if he'd fallen over. He put his arms out to balance himself and opened his eyes wide. It was light again. He was on his back. He could see the ceiling and the tops of the walls. He raised his head, dizziness sweeping over him. He was in the same room. The real room. Only now he was lying in one of the recliners. He heard Sandra say, "Bastard," and looked across at where she was sitting up in another recliner. Raines and Cara were there too, getting out of their own seats.

"I'm sorry," said Raines, addressing Sandra. "I should have warned you. I just assumed you'd understand."

"So," Jay said, looking at his hands, swinging his legs off the recliner, placing his feet on the floor. "So we're real now?"

"Yes," said Raines, patiently. "You're real now."

Jay stood up and looked around in amazement. There was no sign of the four phantoms who had been standing there a moment earlier. "So you copied our minds out of our virtual bodies and copied them into these real bodies, just like that?"

Cara came over to him. He thought her smile had a hint of embarrassment in it. "It isn't quite like that, Dad. You never were in a virtual body. You were always just running inside the computer. Now you're running inside your own brain."

"A rather inferior machine in many ways," Raines said.

"Nothing personal, Jay. The human brain just isn't much of a computing device. Not compared to what we run on these days."

"So you're real too now?" Jay asked Cara. He reached out and touched her arm. His fingers stopped at the surface as they should and he felt softness and warmth. It made her smile. He smiled back.

"Real, yes," said Sandra, "but not human, I'm guessing."

Raines burst out laughing. "Heaven forbid! No, we're inside android bodies. Very good simulacra. We keep a few handy for people who want, or need, to visit the real world for any reason. How did you spot it?"

Sandra did not share his jollity. "Before we all switched, yours and Cara's bodies weren't breathing. Mine and Jay's were. You haven't downloaded your minds into these bodies either, have you?"

"Now, why would we do such a limiting and risky thing as that?" He seemed completely unfazed by Sandra's distinctly accusing tone. "We're driving the androids through a wireless link. Come on, we should be going."

As before, he led the way. He took them out of the room and into a space that had other rooms leading off it. It also had a glass double door through which Jay could see a yard and several vehicles. Raines took them through it and they were outdoors. It was cold and dull and the sky was slate grey. It struck Jay that the artificial world they'd left behind had been a far warmer, sunnier place. They walked a few more paces and the sphere came into view. It had been cleaned up and polished. Its hatch stood open and he could see there were now two padded seats inside, not just one.

There were other buildings nearby in what seemed to be an enclosed compound. Outside a high fence was a cleared area beyond which were trees and scrubland. Inside, the buildings were all single-story rectangles with thick, grey concrete walls. The walls were raked back and gave the impression of military bunkers. The glass door they'd come out of was set deep in the wall and a couple of heavy metal blast doors lay against the outer wall, ready to be slid across the entrance.

"You seem to be expecting trouble," Sandra said. She too was looking back at the bunkers.

Raines laughed again. "I'm afraid it's the only accommodation we can get down here on the surface. Only heavily fortified military installations survived the Apocalypse and the ravages of time. Ugly place, isn't it? Fortunately, we very rarely come down here."

"We made the sphere more comfortable for your return trip, Mum," said Cara. Jay couldn't help thinking she was changing the subject. It annoyed him that Sandra's suspicions were rubbing off on him. "It'll be a smooth ride home, anyway, but you might as well enjoy it. We took out a lot of the equipment that was not needed for the return trip— which is basically a lob into the past, initiated by the sphere itself—and replaced bulky stuff with smaller, modern equivalents. It gives you a lot more space inside."

"I hope there's plenty of air," Sandra said. "Two thousand years is a long lob."

"Oh, don't worry about that. We know a lot more about time travel than you did. You'll only be travelling for about three minutes. Progress, eh?"

"OK," said Rains. "Let's get you inside. There are only two controls now: a button marked 'Start' and a handle to open the hatch."

"Oh good," said Sandra. "Nice and simple." Jay winced at

the sarcasm but the others didn't seem to notice.

"I suppose this is goodbye, then." Cara looked sad but was wearing her brave face, one he'd seen on any number of goodbyes over the past couple of years.

To Jay's surprise, Sandra embraced her daughter and held her tight. "Goodbye, darling," she said. "It's good to see you're so happy here."

They pulled apart but were still linked, arm to arm. "It's been wonderful to see you again, Mum. Those things I said, yesterday… Well, you know I love you, don't you?"

"I know. I love you too."

They embraced again, then stepped apart. Cara turned to Jay. He looked into the eyes of his beautiful daughter, a woman now, older by far than himself. "Bye-bye, Cara," He stepped forwards to hug her. He knew it was a robot really, remotely controlled by an ancient mind whose mode of existence he could barely fathom. Yet he knew it was Cara too and, for him, that mattered more than the mere circumstances of technology and the strange cosmology that had allowed them to be there together. He held her in silence and felt tears run down his cheeks. "Look after yourself," he said, finding it hard to speak at all.

They parted and Cara went to stand beside Raines. "The information you need to give to Dr Brandt is in the pocket of your jumpsuit, Sandra," he said. "Good luck." She nodded to him and they both turned towards the sphere.

In that instant, explosions erupted all around them.

* * * *

Jay grabbed Sandra and pulled her towards the sphere, the only shelter they could reach. Concussions from the blasts buffeted them as they dived for cover. They hit the ground in the sphere's shade and scrabbled to turn and see what was happening. Machine guns were firing in long, angry belches. Jay saw Cara and Raines standing were they'd left them. They didn't move but stood unnaturally still, like mannequins. A line of little puffs of smoke crossed Cara's chest as a machine gun found her. She didn't twitch or scream but slowly toppled backwards.

Jay's heart thudded. He surged into motion. He had to reach her. But Sandra fought him back to the ground.

"It's not Cara," she shouted in his face. "It's not her. She's not even here. No-one's dead. Just disconnected."

It took a moment to sink in but she was right, of course. Cara and Raines had cut the link as soon as the fighting started. The thing on the floor was not Cara. It was an empty husk. Even so, his heart wouldn't slow and his breathing was laboured. "Jesus Christ," he said. "I thought…"

As the shock subsided, he began to take in what was going on. A hole had been blown in the boundary fence. Several explosions had gone off among the buildings inside the compound. Mortar shells, he guessed. People had appeared in ragtag armour and were storming the compound. They were the ones firing the machine guns, but nobody was firing at Jay and Sandra. Instead, they were shooting at various automated weapons that had popped up out of the ground, little turrets that swivelled back and forth at terrifying speed, spitting laser fire at the attackers with deadly accuracy.

"People!" Sandra exclaimed. "Jay, they're people. We've got to help them."

The logic of that wasn't quite clear to him. "They just shot Cara."

"They shot a machine. Come on."

There was a turret not ten meters from them. Sandra was on her feet and racing towards it before Jay could stop her. All he could do was follow. They had gone barely two paces before the laser projector swung their way in a blur of speed. Jay braced himself. People were being cut down by these things all over the compound and now it was Jay's turn.

But the laser didn't fire. It swung away and continued picking off the attackers. Jay stumbled and almost fell, so ready had he been to die that to be still alive and moving came as a surprise. Sandra reached the turret first. The weapon was flicking back and forth with incredible speed. Its inner workings were exposed and Jay could see the complex system of pistons and gimbals that jerked it around. Sandra was watching it too. She raised a hand as if she were about to reach inside. He saw the cable at the back of the weapon and realized what she was about to do.

"No," he said, putting a hand on her shoulder. "Let me." If she timed it badly, the jerking mechanism could crush her hand.

She shook her head. "I'm faster than you."

"Says who?"

But, even as he spoke, her hand flashed into the machine and re-emerged clutching a bundle of wires. The gun kept moving but it was no longer firing. She turned to look at him and raised an eyebrow.

"You got lucky," he said.

An explosion went off nearby and they pressed themselves against the ground. More explosions followed.

"They're using RPGs," Jay said. The trails of the little missiles criss-crossed the compound. Some of them exploded in mid-air as the laser turrets shot them down, but enough hit their marks that in a few minutes, all the nearby turrets were gone.

Jay and Sandra stayed where they were as the attackers slowly appeared from cover, then quickly formed into groups and dispersed back through the hole in the fence. Only half-a-dozen of them remained and they came straight over to Jay and Sandra. Jay stood up to meet them, moving to put himself between the ragged soldiers and Sandra. Their leader was a rangy man in his mid-forties who walked with a limp. His pale grey eyes had very clearly seen more than their share of pain and grief. A woman walked beside him, gun ready, expression equally grim. Two others moved out to flank Jay and Sandra while another two went to the fallen androids.

"My name's Shah," the leader said. "Local commander. You're coming with us." He had a country accent—Cambridgeshire, maybe—that seemed at odds with his haggard appearance.

"No, we're not." Sandra's voice was firm. She stepped out from behind Jay and he, at least, could see she meant it. The two soldiers exchanged glances.

"We thought all the people were dead," Jay said. "They said you all died in the Apocalypse."

"The what?" the man said with a sneer. "I suppose you could call it that. Who are you and where are you from?"

"We don't belong here," Jay said. "We were just leaving."

"In that?" He jerked his thumb towards the sphere.

"That's right. Whatever grievance you have against the post-humans, it's none of our business. We'd just like to be left to go on our way."

"Time travellers?" the woman asked. She too had a country burr. Neither Jay nor Sandra replied. "People saw you arrive, down on the edge of the dead zone, in among the ruins. Said it just popped out of thin air, like magic. Then the machines came and picked you up. So we followed 'em out here. You were dead and beat up when they took you out, scanners clamped all round your heads. Seems like they went to a lot of trouble to patch you up again. What makes you so important to the mechs?"

A pair of Shah's people kneeling beside the fallen androids were working on them with saws and hatchets. As Jay considered how to answer the woman's question, one of the soldiers heaved Cara's severed head free of its body. Jay started forwards, shocked. "What the hell are you doing?" he cried. Shah pushed his gun into Jay's chest. Sandra caught Jay by the shoulder and pulled him back.

"It's just tech," she said.

"Good tech too," said Shah's companion. Over by the bodies, the soldier with Cara's head stuffed it into a bag and went to work on Raines. "They'll get a satellite over us soon and fry this whole area with microwaves: you can't let tech like that go to waste."

"They want us to do something for them," Sandra said, answering Shah's earlier question. "In the past."

Jay had already realized that the appearance of human soldiers, obviously some kind of resistance army, meant that Cara and Raines had lied to them. Now other inconsistencies were becoming apparent—like the fact that all the weapons here seemed hardly any different from those of his own time.

"What year is this?" he asked.

Shah looked from one to the other of them. "You don't know?"

"We came here by accident."

"It's 2242," he said. "What did they want you to do?"

"Not even two hundred years," Jay said. Why would Cara

have misled them so much?

Sandra fished in her pocket and pulled out a data button. "There's a name and address on here plus information on how to upload human brains to machines. At least that's what they told us. Could be anything, really." She held it out. "Take it."

Shah reached out and took it, his dirty hands and cracked nails in sharp contrast to Sandra's manicure. "We got anything that can read one of these?" he asked the soldier at his side.

"Sure," she said. "HQ's got all kind of ancient tech."

Shah put it in the pocket of his combat jacket. "You were planning to help them?"

"Maybe," said Sandra.

"When you from?"

"2068."

Shah's mouth twitched into what might have been a brief smile. "2069 was the year the first uploads were made. By 2100, they had control of all the big corporations. Ran the world, more or less. We took a long time to realize we'd become their slaves and had to fight them. We started blowing up their data centres and brain farms. Did pretty well for a while but in 2109 they moved into space lock, stock, and barrel, and started their campaign to cripple us so bad we couldn't touch them. Dropped rocks on us. Used the big space-based solar arrays to microwave whole cities."

Looking into Shah's hard eyes, Jay didn't doubt for a moment that the commander was telling the truth. The post-humans had tried to use humanity and, when they'd grown to be too much trouble, had decided to eliminate their progenitors. "Like deciding to wipe out orangutans and gorillas so you can use their forests for growing palm oil and grazing cattle." He hadn't realized he'd spoken aloud until he saw Sandra looking at him. "To them we're just lower primates, I suppose."

"Except they needed us to go back and give Dr Brandt the secret of how to take that next step up the evolutionary ladder."

"Could we really have done that in the past?"

Sandra threw up her hands. "I don't know. I had one lecture on the physics of closed time loops when I did my degree. Some say they can't exist, some say they'd be more like a spiral than a loop, with quantum uncertainty making every passage through the loop slightly different from the previous one. Maybe this is our ten millionth time through and it's finally come unravelled."

Jay shuddered. He didn't like to think about temporal weirdness. It made his brain itch. Even so, he had to ask. "So what happens now? You gave him the data. We can't give it to Dr Brandt now. Does that mean this universe can't exist, or what?"

She looked pained. "I don't know. Obviously it still exists. Maybe the fact that we did it on our last pass through the loop means this universe is OK. When we get back and don't do it, that'll just mean a new probable future starts unfolding. Maybe one in which the post-humans don't go to war with the humans. This universe is an island anyway. I can't see why it wouldn't just keep going."

Shah was studying them. "If you don't go back, there's zero chance you'll tell the machines anything."

Jay's heartbeat quickened. Not good. "Listen," he said. "I'm pretty useless at this time paradox stuff but even I understand that it doesn't matter what we do any more. Not now you've got the data. This universe will keep on going its own miserable way. The loop's broken. We can't help or hinder you any more."

"Yeah, well, you would say that wouldn't you? Seems to me our own egg-heads should get a look at you, ask you a few questions."

Not good. Not good. They had to get into the sphere and go back before the path that led them there deteriorated and left them stranded. He knew Sandra was thinking the same thing and, for her, to think was to act. The thought of stopping her flashed through his mind but he knew she was right. They had to do something right now or lose the chance of ever going home. He turned to the soldier covering them from his left, threw his arms wide open and walked towards her, saying, "Surely you can see the sense in letting us go back?"

There was a scuffle from Shah's direction. Jay turned to find Sandra holding the commander in some complicated kind of arm lock with her left hand while her right hand held a pistol to his temple.

"Everybody stay calm," she said, loudly enough for them all to hear. "I'm not going to hurt him. We're just going to leave. Everybody lower your weapons. Jay, get over here." He walked the few paces to Sandra, painfully aware that half the weapons that had snapped up when Sandra made her move were aimed at him. To the woman who was with Shah, she said, "Give him your gun." The soldier hesitated. Sandra bored the barrel of her pistol into Shah's temple and glared at her. "Do it!"

Reluctantly, the woman handed Jay her weapon, a lightweight submachine gun.

He took it from her and waved her towards the group dismantling the androids. "Everybody over there," he said.

He waved the gun at the other nearby soldiers and told them to join the others by the androids.

He heard Sandra hissing in Shah's ear, "Do you really want to interrogate us so much you'd die for it? You've got everything from us that's worth having. We're not going to help the machines when we get back. So tell your fucking soldiers to lower their weapons."

Jay couldn't watch because he was busy trying to cover five angry soldiers any one of whom might decide to be a hero at any moment, but the silence from Shah told him the man was still seething.

"Shah," he shouted. "We're either going home, right now, or we're going to die here. You and maybe half your crew can die with us, or you can let us go. We've got nothing to lose and you've got nothing to gain by keeping us." Just to add a bit more pressure, he added, "That microwave satellite will be overhead any minute now."

Shah's silence continued. The guns were still pointing at him and Sandra. He could see the uncertainty in people's eyes. It had cost them a lot to capture Jay and Sandra. Friends and comrades had died. Lots of them. But now they were faced with more deaths, their own deaths, and the captives probably dying anyway. It had gone from expensive victory to expensive failure in a few seconds and nobody wanted to die in a losing battle. Beyond the immediate group of soldiers, he could see that others outside the fence had noticed that something was wrong and were drifting back. Finally, the commander spoke.

"Everybody stand down. Lower your weapons. I'm letting them go."

One or two of his men seemed very reluctant. Sandra kept hold of Shah and they backed towards the sphere. Despite the commander's order, Jay felt horribly vulnerable and exposed. The situation could turn into a bloodbath at any moment. The few meters to the sphere seemed to take a lifetime to traverse. He prayed that Sandra would not trip, and that nobody sneezed.

"I'm sorry, Shah," he heard Sandra say. "I promise you, we'll do nothing to help them. I don't think that will help you, but it might avoid this whole miserable future for my own timeline."

"Yeah? Thanks." His tone implied it was not enough.

"It's the best deal you can get," Jay said, angry at Shah's refusal to believe her. "We didn't write the laws of physics."

"Sounds to me like you've already helped them before. Lots of times."

"Yeah, well…" Jay had to admit that might have been true. So maybe Shah's distrust was justified. "They tricked us."

"Jay, get in." Sandra's command snapped him out of his unhappy musings. They were standing beside the sphere. He climbed inside, doing his best to keep his gun pointed at Shah's soldiers. Sandra released Shah and the resistance fighter stepped away from her. Jay kept him covered while Sandra climbed aboard and took her seat.

"There may be something in the data I gave you that you can use against them," Sandra told him. He stared back at her, grim-faced as ever. "Jay, you ready?"

He grabbed the handle on the hatch. "You?"

She nodded and he dragged the hatch closed. As soon as he began, Shah threw himself to the ground and shouted, "Shoot them!"

But the hatch was down before Shah's soldiers could respond. It hissed shut as a fusillade rattled against the sphere's tough outer shell. Jay whacked the "Start" button and fell into his seat.

Chapter 16

Home

"Bloody hell," he said. The sound of gunfire stopped. Jay's stomach lurched as he became instantly weightless.

"We've lobbed," Sandra said. She was lying back in her seat, strapped in, eyes closed. She looked across at him and put out a hand to help him float back into his seat. "That was pretty ballsy of you to take the initiative like that."

"Like what?" He squirmed into position and wrangled the straps round himself.

"Creating a distraction so I could nobble Shah. I was going to try some more talking, but you were probably right."

He winced. "Actually, I thought you were going to go for Shah anyway so I'd better give you a bit of a hand."

Sandra's expression flipped to astonished. "You thought I was…?" And then to angry. "What kind of crazy, reckless lunatic do you think I am? You really thought I'd risk both our lives before we'd exhausted every chance of negotiating?"

"Shit. No, no, I just thought…" Jay stammered and blustered his way through a long series of denials, aghast that he could have got it so wrong. Then a smile began to spread across Sandra's face. He stopped trying to excuse himself.

"You rat! I was right. You really were going to attack him."

"Had you going for a while there, spy boy."

Jay relaxed and found himself smiling too. "How long am I going to be cooped up in here with you?"

"A hundred and eighty-year lob? Couple of minutes."

"So they probably haven't got wonderful new insights into time travel, then?"

"Probably not."

"Do you...?" He almost didn't have the courage to ask. "Do you think that was really Cara we met?"

Sandra was silent for a moment. "I think so. Only... She wasn't the Cara I know."

"Maybe being a disembodied super-intellect changes a girl."

"If it was her, she was colluding with them in a genocide against the whole of humanity."

"That's teenagers for you."

He glanced at her face. She wasn't smiling. The hard set of her lips made him regret his feeble attempt at humour. After a while, she said, "Probable futures. But each future is only a product of its own past. If Cara really lived to be eighty-seven, we have no idea what kind of life she led and how that might have shaped her."

She would die nearly seventy years in the future. In seventy years, almost anything could happen. Seventy years ago in his own time, cars were petrol driven, the U.S. was the world's superpower, and the net had barely been invented. Jay wondered about the next seventy. "She never said what happened to us."

"Let's hope we grew old and died."

"You *really* don't want to be uploaded to a computer, do you?"

"I've just been uploaded—and then downloaded again. That's plenty for me. Who's to say we're not still running back there in 2242?"

Another shocking thought. "But we're here." Yet he saw immediately what she meant. Once they had a copy running in their computers, there would be no reason to delete it just because they wanted to install a copy in a human head. Maybe their continuing existence in 2242 was Cara's price for cooperating.

"Maybe I should hunt down Raines's grandparents and make sure they don't have children," he said.

"Way ahead of you."

They hit the ground with a jarring thump. Jay lay in his seat feeling as if he had a pile of sand on top of him. "I hate gravity," he said.

"At least we didn't die this time."

"We haven't opened the hatch yet. What do you think's out there? Will we be back in Clarke Engineering?"

Sandra shook her head, slowly. "I don't think so. We should be in the same location we started from. It's a lob, remember, not a yankback. Trouble is, we don't know where that was. They moved the sphere."

"If Shah was telling the truth."

"And we'll be a fortnight on from the night of the gunfight."

"If Raines was telling the truth."

He unclipped his harness then took hold of the hatch handle with one hand and raised his gun with the other. He checked to see if Sandra was ready. She was holding her pistol in a two-handed grip aiming at the hatch. He pushed the release and threw open the door.

Sandra was out and on one knee sweeping the area by the

time the hatch was fully open. He joined her outside, moving quickly to the back of the sphere to check all angles. They were alone in a large sports field. A light snow was falling, turning to slush on contact with the soggy ground. He checked his commplant. He had net access and all the usual services. The clock said it was eight twenty, AM. The date was fifteen days on from when they had left.

"We're in a little village called Haslingfield," said Sandra "A few kilometres south-west of Cambridge."

There were trees on three sides of the enormous, rectangular field. On the fourth side was a small pavilion and, beyond it, a few red-brick houses. Standing in the middle of a wet field with snow falling from an iron-grey sky, Jay regarded the houses with longing. He dialled the local police. He needed someone to guard the sphere until he could organize a truck to take it to the nearest military base. The police sergeant who took the call goggled at Jay's EDF MI credentials. He seemed so impressed that Jay also asked him to arrange a car to take them down to London.

"They'll be here in about ten minutes," he said when he'd hung up.

"Did you tell them to bring warm clothes?"

From the sphere, a flash and a dull "Whump!" made them raise their guns and turn. Jay dropped to one knee in the wet mud and immediately regretted it. No-one was around but a fire was burning inside the sphere. So, Raines had not lied about the self-destructing new parts. He grabbed the hatch and closed it as quickly as he could. The sphere was airtight and the flames would not burn for long.

"I was hoping we could keep that going, maybe throw in a couple of logs," Sandra said. "These overalls weren't designed for an English winter."

"Sorry. I need the fire to go out to preserve whatever I can. The Chinese have built at least one FORESIGHT machine and we'll need every little clue we can find to catch up."

"Seems like the kind of technology no-one should have."

He regarded the bullet-scarred sphere. "Yeah, real end of the world stuff. Worse than timesplashing." He could imagine Crystal's face when he told her there was a new universe out there waiting to bump into their own in about a hundred and eighty years. Which reminded him... "I need to phone the office."

"I'll call Cara. She's probably driven your mother to drink by now."

* * * *

Sandra and Jay spent the night at his mother's house and Jay left for Berlin early the next morning. Sandra was to follow on in the afternoon for what Jay called her "debrief". She wasn't looking forward to it. She had killed people, wounded others. If they wanted to, the authorities could make a lot of trouble for her. Jay's parting words were, "Don't worry. It'll all be sorted by the time you get there."

She checked the time. What on earth was Cara doing that was taking so long?

"Oh, I knew, of course, that he wasn't with the Met," Dot was saying. "He never really had us fooled with that one, but you go along with these things. I always suspected it was some secret work for the government or something like that. His father used to say he was probably a drug smuggler or an assassin, but I think he was joking, really. He'd be gobsmacked to hear that our Jay is such an important man in military intelligence."

Distractedly, Sandra said, "Yeah, they were probably a bit short staffed, had to take what they could get."

"Oh, you. You're as bad as his father. I'm sure Jay earned every promotion he got."

Sandra smiled. "You're right. He's not as daft as he looks. And what about you, Annie Oakley? Charging the terrorist stronghold with a shotgun? I can see where Jay gets it from."

"It was either that or let Cara go on her own."

"Yeah, thanks."

"She'd have given her life to save you, you know?"

"What's she doing up there, anyway?" She checked her commplant again. "I've only got a couple more hours before I have to catch my plane."

"Jay says you're not one of his mob."

"No. Not really secret squirrel material. I'm more the keep my head down, mind my own business type."

"And if you'll believe that, you'll believe anything."

Sandra looked up to find Cara standing in the doorway. "So that's why you took so long." Her daughter was looking unusually lovely and stylish in a very smart outfit that contrived to emphasise her natural attractiveness. She looked oddly mature. Not unlike the virtual Cara she might one day become.

"This is for Fourget's benefit, I suppose?" Sandra said. The plan was to visit Fourget in hospital on their way to the airport and now Sandra understood why Cara so solicitous of the young lieutenant.

Cara blushed. "No, I just wanted to look nice to see you off."

It was a tiny white lie, born of embarrassment, but it sent a cold chill through Sandra. *Is this how it began?* she asked herself, remembering how a future, disembodied version of her daughter had deceived her with no apparent compunction, lied to trick her parents into helping with the post-humans' war against humankind. She wished she could see it the way Jay did, see those futures she'd experienced as almost infinitely improbable.

"If you look back from the present," he'd said last night, "the chances of us ending up precisely here are infinitely small. It will be the same for any future you look back from. We can't assume any one of them is the particular future we're heading towards. It's chaotic—in the mathematical sense—the tiniest variations in starting conditions lead to vastly different outcomes."

She'd teased him, said, "For someone who doesn't know a Mandelbrot set from a tea set, you sure know how to bullshit about probabilities." Yet she believed he was right, and it was comforting, but it was an intellectual kind of comfort, not the visceral kind she needed.

Much better was the story she told herself, that, if Cara was alive in that post-human future, Raines had made some kind of puppet based on her, a heartless *thing* with Cara's memories and personality that could be directed by him to do his bidding. It wasn't Cara, not *her* Cara.

* * * *

In the taxi on the way to the hospital with Cara, Sandra said, "Jay has asked me to marry him."

Cara screeched, "What? Oh my God! You're getting married! That's amazing!" She leapt on Sandra and hugged her. She burbled excitedly about being the maid of honour, she asked about plans, the ceremony, the honeymoon, where they'd live. It was some time before Sandra managed to get a word in.

"I didn't say yes."

Cara pulled back and looked at her mother as if to check whether she was joking.

"I didn't say no, either. He picked such a stupid time to ask."

"But you're going to say yes, right? I mean, it's what you want?"

"Is it? I thought it was but…" But when she thought about the reality of it, it seemed like such a complicated decision. When she thought about how her life would be affected, and Cara's, the changes, the rearrangements…

Cara was frowning, trying to puzzle it out. "So you talked? You sorted out all that stuff about him resenting you for hiding me away and all that?"

It sounded so banal when she put it like that. "No, we didn't really talk. He just… changed his attitude. Didn't you notice how cheerful he was last night? I've never seen him like that."

"I thought he was just happy to be home again."

"How would you feel about it if we did get married?" It seemed a stupid question in the light of the exclamations and hugs, but she had to ask it anyway.

"I'd feel happy for you, of course. For both of you. No-one can understand why you didn't get together years ago."

"By no-one, you mean Olivia, I suppose."

"And Gran." She gave Sandra a stern frown. "You'll end up an old spinster at this rate."

Sandra was not really in the mood for playing but she said, "You just want me out of the way while you go chasing after your soldier boy." Her own words suddenly hit her. "Of all the types I was dreading you'd bring home, a soldier was not one of them."

"He's not just a soldier, he's special forces, and he works for Dad. Anyway, you've got it all wrong. He saved my life. And Dad says he saved his life too. And he says he's one of the bravest men he knows. I should at least go and see how he's doing, shouldn't I? I mean, he got shot going in to help Dad rescue you."

"I didn't need rescuing! What am I, some kind of storybook princess? And, don't forget, after their half-arsed rescue attempt, *I* was the one who had to go back into the place I'd just escaped from to save *their* stupid necks."

Cara was grinning. "I always thought these special-forces operations ran like well-oiled machines. That's how it looks in the vids, anyway. I didn't realize they were just a bunch of blokes with big guns making it up as they went along."

"Says the girl who was about to charge in there with nothing but her tooled-up granny to protect her."

Cara should have looked abashed but she just kept on grinning. "Who'd have thought Gran was such a fierce warrior-woman?"

Sandra couldn't help smiling too at the thought of Dot in a breastplate and horned helmet. After a moment the smile fell away. "It could all have ended so much worse than it did."

Cara reached out and took her mother's hand. "I knew you'd both come back. That police liaison woman they sent told us we shouldn't get our hopes up. But I knew there was no way you'd let some time machine beat you."

Sandra laughed. The idea that survival was a mere matter of willpower was the most ridiculous thing she'd heard all day. She saw the oddly cantilevered bulk of the New Europa

Hospital appear above the roofs of the older shops and office buildings, its bizarre architecture an ugly combination of post-Adjustment whimsy and solid functionalism.

"We're there," she said and smiled again as Cara started tidying her hair in a virtual mirror. Her phone rang and she checked it as the taxi turned into the main entrance. It was an encrypted call from a Dr Crystal in Berlin. Reluctantly, she took the call.

* * * *

Jay ran the gauntlet of his staff, each one, it seemed, hell-bent on congratulating him personally and at length on the success of his mission in London. The fact was that the mission had been an equivocal success at best. The only truly good thing was that Sandra had come through it alive. But Jock was dead and three of Alpha Team were injured, as well as Fourget, who was having a lung and a spleen grown and some serious reconstruction of his legs. Two MI5 agents were also dead and four more injured. Even the Metropolitan Police line had been strafed by Lee's helicopter gunship and they had another half-dozen injured officers to add to the cost of Jay's operation.

And for what? They'd caught a trio of Chinese spies—who were already being offered for trade—and a lot of burned-out equipment now sitting in a shed at Aldermaston while project FORESIGHT scientists shook their heads sadly over it and blamed Jay's team for not being careful enough.

Eventually, he made it to Crystal's office, two minutes late.

"How are you, Jay?" She poured him a coffee from a jug on the sideboard and waved him into one of the comfy chairs. *Not a good sign*, he thought.

"Look, I'm sorry I—"

She held up a hand to stop him. "Bit of a mess, wasn't it?" she said. "In fact, a bit of a bloody balls-up." Her tone was sweetness itself. She sipped her own coffee while he waited. "I'd like your resignation, Jay."

He'd half expected it. It wasn't such a shock. Even so, a heavy weight seemed to settle on him. It was finally over.

"Of course," he said. He moved to stand up. "Is that it?"

"Don't be such a martyr, Jay. Come back at me. Defend your actions."

He didn't feel like playing games. "I really don't see the point."

Crystal smiled at him over the rim of her cup. "All right then. Let me defend you." Jay could not begin to understand what strange fancy motivated the woman, but he nodded for her to proceed and sat back in his chair.

"While the rest of the world struggled to understand what on earth had hit us that night—including myself and every other agency boss in the civilized world—you had your team digging into the evidence and playing some remarkable hunches. While everyone around you thought your friend Ms Malone was just some crazy person who saw temporal terrorists everywhere she turned, you had unwavering confidence in her judgement. And it was you, Jay, who finally put the pieces together and led an attack on the true culprits—Chinese agents operating right under our noses, no less!"

"I still don't get that, actually. Why were they doing this from a factory in London instead of a bunker out in the Gobi desert or somewhere, safely under Chinese control?"

Crystal shrugged. "International espionage isn't what it used to be. The operation was only semi-official and completely unfunded. The general Lee reported to saw it as a bit of an earner too. Lee had to raise the money himself—not just for the experiments, but to stake the general's ambitious speculations—and keep it all out of Chinese territory. You know what they've been like since the Beijing timesplash. He found the delightful Mr Waxtead, and the rest is history."

"So," said Jay. "You think I was insightful and decisive and saved the world from destruction?"

Crystal pursed her lips. "Well, that last one is yet to be seen. We'll see what happens in 2242, won't we?" There had been no destructive event corresponding to the two-week time shot Sandra had been forced to take, it seemed. The natural repulsion between branes, as Laura had told him, meant it wasn't a hundred percent certain that a collision would occur even for branes that were very close. No-one yet knew the actual probability but the European Union would be funding plenty of PhDs in that area over the next few years.

"But you did bring to light a secret UK government project to do what the Chinese had been doing. That was a good thing. Heads are already rolling in the corridors of power."

"Great. So I'm a bit of a hero, really. Why do you want my resignation?"

She rolled her eyes mightily. "Jay, be serious! You went off half-cocked and almost got everybody killed when, really, you should have just handed it over to the police and let them have their siege."

And there it was. When it came to the crunch, he had chosen saving Sandra over doing his job. And so he had to resign. It was fair and he had no regrets. He put down his cup and stood up.

"I'll get that letter to you within the hour."

She smiled up at him. "Thank you. Now sit down again and listen."

* * * *

Laura Thalman was standing by the lifts with luggage at her feet when Jay caught up with her.

"Off to Aldermaston?" he asked.

"Crystal wants me to do an audit of the project." She hesitated before she said, "She told me you'd be leaving us." The lift arrived and the doors opened. "I'll get the next," she said but Jay stepped forwards and moved one of her bags across the door.

"I'll go down with you."

They ordered Laura's luggage into the empty lift and joined it there.

"We'll all miss you," she said.

"And I'll miss this place too."

There was a silence. On an impulse, Jay said, "I've asked Sandra to marry me."

The lift arrived at the lobby and they busied themselves herding Laura's luggage out of the lift. There was a taxi already waiting for her outside.

"I met her, you know. Did she tell you?" Jay shook his head. Laura smiled. "I liked her. She was…" She struggled to find the word and gave up. "Anyway, congratulations. Have you fixed a date?"

"She hasn't said yes, yet."

Laura raised an eyebrow but didn't comment. There was another silence.

"I should be going," she said. They came together for an

air kiss and Laura, looking troubled, asked, "What will you do now, Jay?"

He gave her a reassuring smile. "I'll think of something. Early retirement, maybe."

Laura laughed. "You'd go crazy without some bad guys to hunt."

She ushered her luggage out through the main entrance and into the taxi. Jay watched until she was gone.

* * * *

Sandra's debrief was held in a small meeting room several floors above Jay's office. She didn't see him before or after it. She was interviewed by two women in their forties, smartly dressed, pleasant and polite. They asked her to give "her version" of events and then asked a few questions to fill in some more detail of who was where at what time. It was relaxed but formal and the interviewers gave very little information back to her.

"All right," she said, when they reached the point where they were going over the same ground again. "We've done this. Maybe I could ask a couple of questions now?"

"What would you like to know?" one asked.

"The Chinese driver I killed. What's going to happen about that?"

The two interviewers exchanged glances and one of them shrugged. "He was a spy for a foreign government. How he met his death is not something the UK authorities wish to pursue. The Chinese government has made no representations on the matter."

"So it's all being swept under the carpet?"

The interviewer smiled. "If you like."

"And what about the eight-hundred-pound gorilla I shot, and Dr Hong?"

"The Chinese agent in charge of the operation—"

"Lee."

"—set off a number of incendiary devices, destroying the factory and all evidence that could possibly implicate anyone in any of the various deaths."

"So I'm off the hook?"

"You were never on it. In fact, it seems your actions uncovered serious illegal activity on European soil by agents of a foreign government. You also appear to have directly saved the lives of at least two of our own operatives." She smiled, sadly. "However, don't expect to receive any medals. I'm sure you understand."

"OK. We're finished here, Ms Malone. The agent outside will escort you out of the building."

She found Jay standing in the foyer, staring out through the main door.

His face lit up when he saw her. "Come on," he said. "Lunch is on me."

They walked out into the street and turned right. It was cold and grey but there was no sign of rain. The air had the ozone smell of electric vehicles. Although many parts of Berlin's business district were pedestrian-only, this was not one of them. The rattle and whine of Europe's busiest city made talking difficult. As they walked, Jay hooked his arm for Sandra to take. It was a gesture that would have been quaintly old-fashioned even fifty years earlier, but somehow it didn't seem odd. She took his arm and pulled herself in close.

He'd made a booking at a smart little place just a couple of blocks from the office and, although they were half-an-hour early for the reservation, a bot showed them to a table set aside in a quiet corner.

"Hungry?" he asked.

"Very."

She scanned the menu, which had been asking for her attention in her peripheral vision. "You should try the *Hecht*," he said. Her commplant automatically translated it as "pike".

"It's amazing."

"OK then."

He ordered and sat back to look at her, smiling. "I can't remember the last time we had a meal together. Just the two of us."

Sandra could. It had been nearly nineteen years ago, in London, just before she'd gone to voluntarily commit herself for psychiatric help at the Porringer Institute. She supposed Jay could remember too. He was always so clumsy at bringing conversations round to whatever he wanted to say.

"Jay," she said. "I'm scared."

"Scared?" He looked alarmed. He actually glanced around the restaurant.

"I mean, I'm worried, I suppose. Have you noticed anything about yourself since we got back from the future?"

"Like what?"

"Like your body isn't quite the way it used to be?"

"Ah, that."

"Well?"

"Well, yes. Scars are missing. That bullet I took in the leg in 1902? No trace of it But, look, they rebuilt us. For all I know, they regrew us from scratch. You'd expect the scars to be gone if that's what happened."

"And your hair."

"My hair?"

"You were starting to thin out at the front."

"No I wasn't."

"Yes, you were, but it's all back again. You look ten years younger."

"Actually, I feel it too. Not younger, just fitter, better somehow."

She nodded. "Me too. I've barely had a chance to train or even work out since all this started. I've been tied up, stunned, sleep-deprived, exhausted, kicked and punched, blown up even, yet I feel fantastic, as if I was at match fitness for a club fight. I haven't felt this good in years."

His eyes widened at a sudden thought. "You don't think...? I mean, these are real bodies, aren't they, not androids like Cara and Raines?" She looked at him as if to say, come on, now, you know better than that. "Ah, right. We both had to go through terahertz scanners to get into the office. If our bodies were artificial, it would have shown up."

"And we'd be in a basement lab somewhere being dissected instead of sitting here chatting."

"True. So, what are you worried about?"

She frowned at him. "Doesn't it bother you that we might not be ourselves any more? I don't just mean our bodies. What about our minds? What if they gave us back more than we started with?"

"Pardon?"

She leaned forwards across the table. "What if we suddenly get on a train and go see Dr Brandt, tell him everything he needs to know to start building post-humans?"

Jay's mouth opened and stayed open as he searched for an argument. "We don't have the data button. We gave it to the resistance guys, remember?"

Sandra dismissed the objection. "That could have been a decoy. Perhaps the data is written into our brains, ready to be triggered someday. Jay, we might be like living time bombs primed to destroy humanity's future."

Jay reached out and took her hand. "You're going to drive yourself nuts thinking things like that." The robot arrived with their meal but Jay held onto her hand and sent it away. "I'm pretty sure Raines was as surprised as we were when Shah and co. jumped us. There's no way he engineered all that. If you remember, we were all set to help them out until the humans turned up. He had no reason to stage such an elaborate con. Cara was his play, not Shah, and, as far as he knew, it had worked. We were his stooges. So please, please, don't worry about that."

The concern in his eyes was painful to see. At the same time, he had managed to say just what she needed to hear. She felt a sob in her chest and then another. All at once she was crying, her head down and tears dripping onto the white tablecloth.

"Excuse me, sir," the waitbot said, holding up the plates, hopefully. Jay told it to go away. He held both her hands in his.

"Sandra?" he asked, gently.

It was a little while before she could look up at him. She pulled a hand free and wiped her eyes.

"I don't know how much more I can take, Jay. Sometimes it feels like I've built a massive dyke against the sea but it's cracked and crumbling and the next storm might just smash it all to pieces." He kept looking at her with the same concern, trying to understand. She turned her head away in frustration. "I didn't ask for any of this, Jay. I didn't want it. Time travel and psychopaths, and revolutions, and Chinese spies, and people copying my brain into computers, it's just… more than anyone should be asked to cope with. And now…" She stopped herself, not sure whether she should say more.

"And now I've gone and asked you to marry me?"

It wasn't what she was going to say but he had a point. It was another stress she could do without. Then, to her horror, he reached into his pocket and pulled out a small box. "Well, my oxytocin levels are all my own today and my feelings haven't changed at all." He stood up and moved to stand beside her. "I've had enough too," he said. "Blame it on the fact that I've been shot at once too often, scared out of my wits once too often, or that I've nearly lost you once too often, but I've decided the only way I'll ever be happy for the rest of my life is if you're right there at my side. Always.

"You're probably thinking my brain is scrambled from transcription errors or something, but, I tell you, this is the one and only thing in the whole Universe—in any Universe—that makes any sense to me any more." He went down on one knee beside her and, even though she'd seen it coming, Sandra still caught her breath. Jay opened his little box and held it out so she could see the diamond ring inside. "Sandra Malone, will you marry me?"

Her heart was pounding. She looked down into his brave, expectant face and her head swam. The sheer weight of what was riding on her answer made her tremble under it. "Has Crystal spoken to you yet?" she asked in a voice weak with dread. She saw a frown cross his brow.

"She gave me the sack, if that's what you mean."

"And what else?"

The frown deepened. He looked around the restaurant. "I can't talk about that here."

She stood up. "Then let's go outside."

* * * *

They walked up the street a little farther and then Jay took them down a side street and into a small park. It was some kind of memorial garden, Sandra realized. A bronze statue of a man in a frock coat and large sideburns presided over a couple of wooden benches, a few rose beds and a very neat lawn. They sat together on a bench and a handful of hopeful pigeons gathered on the lawn nearby.

"I met Fourget this morning," Sandra said. "What's he like?"

Jay shrugged. "Brave. Loyal. Doesn't talk much. I dunno. Solid, I suppose. You went to the hospital?"

"Cara took me to see him. She's got a major crush on him. I've never seen her so besotted."

Jay became prickly, pulled in his chin and looked stern. "He's far too old for her."

"That's what I told her. She said ten years is nothing these days and, besides, all the boys her own age are milksops."

"What? She actually said 'milksops'?"

"She has a way with words."

"I should have a word with Fourget."

"You're not his boss any more."

"Is he encouraging this… infatuation?"

"Mostly he's just lying there looking confused."

Jay went into a sullen silence. Sandra watched his display of protective paternalism with mild amusement. Personally, she was sure the young lieutenant would come off worse if he ever was bold enough to take Cara on.

"How's he doing?" Jay asked after a moment's brooding.

"It'll be a while but they think he'll make a full recovery."

"He's a good man. He saved my life. Tried to help me save yours. Look, what's all this about Crystal? How do you know she said anything to me?"

Sandra took a deep breath. *All right. Here we go.*

"She called me this morning."

"Called you?"

"Please don't do that?"

"Do what?"

"Repeat everything I say."

"Repeat everything y—?" He almost visibly clamped his jaw shut.

"Now tell me what Crystal said—after she sacked you."

Again, he looked around. "She wants me to go to Philadelphia, to join the new European Union Embassy there."

While Jay and Sandra had been in the future, government forces in America had finally surrendered to the Revolutionary Army after the decisive Battle of Atlanta. The Republic had been restored and the old Constitution reaffirmed. The new government had established itself in Philadelphia and countries around the world had rushed to recognize it. The world's economy had bounced into optimistic territory in anticipation of the renewal of a vibrant and dynamic new market and corporations from all over Europe, China, South America and India were rushing into the vacuum left by the fallen theocracy. Embassies were planned to help coordinate all this diplomatic and economic activity. And more besides.

"She wants me to establish a spy network—help out European corporations, keep an eye on what the Chinese are doing, help reduce the influence of the South American Alliance, that kind of thing." He was watching Sandra carefully. "But you already knew that, didn't you? Crystal already told you."

"She wants me to go over there with you. She seems to

think we make a good team."

Jay was clearly unhappy. "Why didn't she tell me?" He gave it a moment's more thought and asked, "Did you agree to go?"

She tried to keep her expression neutral. "You first. What did you tell her?" Again, her heart was thumping as she waited for his answer.

He hesitated, perhaps realizing how much hung on his next words. He chewed his lower lip but took a long breath and steadied himself. "I told her I've finished with spying. I told her I've finished with time travel too, and getting shot at, and dying for the cause." He looked Sandra in the eye. "I politely told her to take her job offer and stuff it. I told her I'm getting married and my new wife didn't like all that crap either." He studied her reaction intently. "And you? What did you say?"

Sandra felt as if she were inflating, she felt her smile grow as if it were painted on an expanding balloon. "Me too," she said. "Oh, God, me too!"

They surged to their feet and into each other's arms. They kissed for the first time in nineteen years. It was a joining too long delayed by fear and anger but now it didn't matter. Sandra floated on air. The world melted and whirled around her. She was adrift on wild, powerful currents, and that didn't matter either because Jay was holding her and he was a rock, rooted deep in the earth. He always had been. He always would be.

The kiss ran its course and came to a lingering end. Jay stepped back from her, his eyes wide and glistening, his hands on her shoulders. Then he took another step back and reached into his pocket. He pulled out the box with the ring and again went down on one knee.

"Will you stop doing that?" she said. "Of course I'll marry you."

* * * *

Jay didn't go back to the office. He took Sandra to his apartment and they made love for the rest of the day. They grabbed snacks, ate junk food, drank the couple of bottles of wine Jay had in his fridge, and, in the evening, ordered pizza. At about seven, they pulled on some clothes and phoned Jay's mother and Cara. In a four-way hook-up he and Sandra broke the good news. Thirty seconds into the call, everybody was smiling and crying, especially Dot, who said, "I wish your father was alive to see this day. I think he'd decided you were gay." Cara wanted to know if "Pierre" would be his best man.

"Not the Frenchman I had in mind," he said, thinking of Jacques Bauchet and another call he needed to make.

When Jay broke the news that he'd been sacked, the mood turned to concern. Neither his mother nor Cara could understand how he and Sandra could be so blasé about having no income.

"I've got a fair bit put by," Jay said. "They've been grossly overpaying me for nearly two decades now."

Sandra grabbed him and kissed him and said, "Besides, we're in love. All we need is a bed and a supply of pizza."

Cara screwed up her face in disgust. "Mum! Stop being gross!"

Sandra laughed. "Sorry, darling. Do you really want to be maid of honour?"

"I don't know. It all seems a bit Medieval, don't you think?"

Afterwards, Jay and Sandra lay in each other's arms. A

gusty wind blew rain against the bedroom window. The crack in the living room wall had not been fixed yet and the house was cooler than it should have been. Jay closed his eyes and thanked the gods that this day had come.

Sandra was doodling figures on his chest. "So, what are we going to do for a living, Beanpole?"

"Well, my little strumpet, it may surprise you to know that I have given that some thought."

She lifted her head from his shoulder so she could see his face. He wriggled onto his side to make it easier for her.

"I think we should go to America."

"What? But you said—"

"Not to the Embassy. To California. It's beautiful there." He glanced at the window. "And warm. Just think. A whole nation rebuilding itself almost from scratch. Talk about a land of opportunity! You saw what it was like. After two-and-a-half years of civil war, they must need everything, utilities, transport, houses, schools, law and order. We could be part of something tremendous, something really worth doing."

She grinned at him. "Jay Kennedy, Nation Builder."

He grinned back. "Cara could finish her studies over there. Her courses are all on the net anyway: it doesn't matter where she is. Don't you think she'd love it out there? Don't you think it would be good for her?"

With mock seriousness, Sandra asked, "Can she bring Fourget?"

"No reason why not. He's out of a job too for his little part in my heroic rescue mission."

"No." Sandra seemed quite shocked.

He raised an eyebrow. When had doing the right thing ever met with congratulations and a pay-rise in his world?

Sandra made an acknowledging moue. She fell silent for a long time.

"So," she said at last, looking at him with happy eyes. "America it is. Let's go and be pioneers in the wild and woolly West."

"In our wild and woolly vests!" he cried. Too happy not to be silly.

She put a hand on his chest and pushed him onto his back, looking serious. "After the wedding."

"Of course." He didn't mention the false identities he'd been building for them ever since Washington. After the wedding, they could visit a woman he knew in Amsterdam and have their commplants reprogrammed. After that, a New World awaited them.

"I love you, Sandra," he said, something else that had remained undone for nearly twenty years.

"Prove it," she said and climbed on top of him.

Thank You

Thank you for reading *Foresight,* book 3 of the Timesplash series. I really hope you enjoyed it as much as I enjoyed writing it. If so, I'd be grateful if you'd leave a review on one of the book retail sites, your blog, or pasted to a wall on the nearest underpass. The rest of this series is available from your favourite online book store. To stay informed of when new books of mine are about to appear, please visit my website and sign up for my newsletter.

About the Author

I am a science fiction writer living in Queensland, Australia. A former research scientist, IT consultant and award-winning software designer. I now live and write in a quiet corner of the Australian bush with my wife, Christine, and a Tonkinese cat called Minsky.

Other Books By Graham Storrs

Timesplash, my début novel, was a Kindle best-seller. The series, *Timesplash* and its sequels, *True Path* and *Foresight*, was originally published by Pan Macmillan Australia. Both *True Path* and *Foresight* were shortlisted for Australia's première science fiction awards, The Aurealis Awards, as Best Science Fiction Novel.

In addition, I have been writing three series of novels set in my Placid Point universe: the Rik Sylver series, the Canta Libre trilogy, and the Deep Fracture trilogy, set eighty, three hundred, and ten thousand years in the future respectively. They are adventure stories, space opera, first contact novels, tales of the first transhumans, and so much more.

I also have a few stand-alone novels out there. *Heaven is a Place on Earth* is a thriller set in a near future dominated by augmented and virtual reality technologies, with all the opportunities for deception they bring. *Cargo Cult* is a sci-fi comedy in which the most ridiculous things that could plausibly happen, keep happening. *Time and Tyde* is a dark comedy set in the present day, about a man stalked by an amoral jerk from the future, or perhaps a man driven insane by a present-day stalker. Either way, it doesn't turn out well. And *Mindrider* – an urban sci-fi thriller about an alien invasion nobody wants and which even the aliens seem unable to prevent.

You can find links to fuller descriptions of all my novels on my website (grahamstorrs.com). Or just type my name into your favourite online book store and they should all appear.

Contact the Author

I am always happy to hear from readers, so don't be shy. And if you enjoyed this book, don't forget to post your review.

Follow me on Twitter: @graywave

or on Facebook:
facebook.com/GrahamStorrsAuthor

For details of all my novels and short stories, visit
grahamstorrs.com